THE PENGUIN CONTEMPORARY AMERICAN FICTION SERIES

ON GLORY'S COURSE

James Purdy is the author of several novels, plays, and collections of poetry and stories. Among the more notable are *Mourners Below*, *Malcolm*, *The Nephew*, and *63: Dream Palace and Other Stories*, all published by Penguin Books. Born in rural Ohio, Mr. Purdy teaches at New York University and lives in Brooklyn, New York.

Also by James Purdy

Novels

63: DREAM PALACE
MALCOLM
THE NEPHEW
CABOT WRIGHT BEGINS
EUSTACE CHISHOLM AND THE WORKS
JEREMY'S VERSION
I AM ELIJAH THRUSH
THE HOUSE OF THE SOLITARY MAGGOT
IN A SHALLOW GRAVE
NARROW ROOMS
MOURNERS BELOW

Poetry

AN OYSTER IS A WEALTHY BEAST
THE RUNNING SUN
SUNSHINE IS AN ONLY CHILD
LESSONS AND COMPLAINTS

Stories and Plays

COLOR OF DARKNESS
CHILDREN IS ALL
A DAY AFTER THE FAIR
PROUD FLESH

ON
GLORY'S
COURSE

James Purdy

PENGUIN BOOKS

PENGUIN BOOKS
Viking Penguin Inc., 40 West 23rd Street,
New York, New York 10010, U.S.A.
Penguin Books Ltd, Harmondsworth,
Middlesex, England
Penguin Books Australia Ltd, Ringwood,
Victoria, Australia
Penguin Books Canada Limited, 2801 John Street,
Markham, Ontario, Canada L3R 1B4
Penguin Books (N.Z.) Ltd, 182–190 Wairau Road,
Auckland 10, New Zealand

First published in the United States of America by
The Viking Press 1984
Published in Penguin Books 1985

LIBRARY OF CONGRESS CATALOGING IN PUBLICATIONS DATA
Purdy, James.
On glory's course.
(The Penguin contemporary American fiction series)
Reprint. Originally published: New York: Viking
Press, 1984.
I. Title.   II. Series.
PS3531.U426O49   1985   813'.54   84-20562
ISBN 0 14 00.7629 8

Printed in the United States of America by
R. R. Donnelly & Sons Company, Harrisonburg, Virginia
Set in Linotron Caslon 540

ON ~
GLORY'S
COURSE

*R*everend Lilley was never to become a popular minister of the gospel in the town of Fonthill (population 13,854 in 1930, when this story takes place), for the precise reason that the congregation always felt the preacher was singling a particular person out for condemnation in the sermon. There was the sermon on great wealth and absence of civic responsibility, which had hit home with the oil millionaire E. Finby Doland—he never darkened the door of the First Presbyterian Church again; the warnings against repeated divorce and remarriage, which struck out at the grass widows, few of whom ever returned. One of his most famous sermons was "Sins of the Flesh," with its text from First Corinthians 6:18, "Flee fornication," which castigated those who engage in sexual pleasure outside of matrimony. Halfway through this particular address, Adele Bevington, a handsome unmarried woman of about fifty, had electrified the congregation by rising and crying out in her rich contralto: "Prove it, why don't you, Reverend! That God begrudges his wretched children a few moments of respite!" She had stalked out without waiting for the preacher's rejoinder.

The preacher, still a young man, barely thirty (he had come direct from Edinburgh, Scotland, summoned by the elders of the church, who desperately needed a new pastor), was so astonished by this outburst he sat or rather fell down in his pulpit chair, letting out a sound like a sob or perhaps a loud hiccough, which incited the leader of the choir to rise, and the service was concluded with the lusty singing of the anthem, followed by the resounding notes of the recessional march from the new organ, the donor of which was another of the numerous millionaires Fonthill was famous for.

Some thirty years ago, went the story, Adele Bevington had become involved in a love affair with a prominent married businessman in Chicago, a close friend of her father's, had become pregnant by him, and had given birth to a boy in a distant city (without doubt Chicago), and much against her will had had to give up her son to a young married couple she never set eyes on, then or afterward. She had never seen her boy again once those first few wonderful weeks of holding him to her breast came to an end. His forcible removal from her had left her ineradicably obsessed with her loss. And though her seducer and her father alike had advised her to leave Fonthill forever, her anger at having been deprived of her boy and her resentment against the town itself caused her to remain, as if to engage in a lifelong contest with a deadly enemy.

"If Adele had only allowed herself to forget the past," Elaine Cottrell, the widowed mother of two strong-willed boys, Ned and Alec, aged fifteen and nearly twenty respectively, remarked after the service. "I declare, the scandal of her youth would never have been revived, or broken out into what seems a forest fire in her mature years."

Certainly Adele's scene, practically in front of the altar at the First Presbyterian Church, made tongues wag, and those who were too young to have heard of her disgrace of a generation ago now discussed it as if it were a recent event.

Talk had it that Adele received a rather munificent monthly stipend from some unknown source, and her portfolio of stocks and bonds was also said to receive frequent additions, perhaps from the same mysterious source. She lived in a white frame house of ten or fifteen rooms, which dated from before the great oil boom and which, in her father's day, had been situated in almost open country. But as the town had grown, the house now faced the main street itself and a garish movie theater called the Royal.

"Adele's behavior was so uncalled for!" Elaine Cottrell told her younger son as they walked home from the service. (Her older boy, Alec, seldom attended church now, but Elaine insisted that Ned always accompany her.) "Why cannot the poor thing let the past bury itself! After all, it was so long ago."

Ned eyed his mother with a sidelong glance. Elaine pretended Ned was too young to know about illegitimacy and unwed mothers, and therefore only spoke of Miss Bevington's "mistake of so long ago," which he was free to interpret in any way he pleased.

Adele Bevington had an almost obsessive interest in Elaine Cottrell and her sons and their way of life. She looked at the two boys sometimes, on her occasional visits to their house, in a manner that frightened the mother. What was that expression in Miss Bevington's eyes: longing, disappointment, anger, hopelessness, the vision of death? Perhaps her face showed all of these expressions in succession, like the faces of actors in the fast-moving reels of the movies at the Royal.

After her disgrace of this Sunday, Adele took to sitting in her huge front parlor with its eighteen-foot ceiling and watching the young couples as they would enter and leave the photoplay house.

For a while after the scandal, Adele saw almost nobody. For two months indeed she did not go out, but had her necessities brought in by one of the men who worked for the butcher down the street. The young men who ran errands for her were, like most people, total strangers to her story and therefore also uncertain of her true age. Her face was free of lines, and though her hair had gone snow-white, it had a beauty and luxuriance that made even her severest critics think she had merely adopted the platinum color and marcelled style of the period. Her features had the kind of cold, perfect, ageless handsomeness one sees in statues, or in a Burne-Jones painting.

Reverend Lilley paid a call on Adele a few days after the outburst before his congregation. He pointed out to her that she had been a member of the church since her baptism, and that, before her, her grandfather and great-grandfather had been members and elders. (She thanked God he did not mention the year of her birth, but was infuriated just the same that he knew exactly how old she was.) Languishing and solitary as she was, her one thought from morning to night (this was later confirmed by her diary, found after her death) was to find, if not her long-lost boy, then a substitute love to efface from her soul her excruciating loss.

More to get rid of him than anything else, Adele promised Reverend Lilley she would return to church "one day," and she half apologized for her conduct, ascribing it to nerves. (Later she was furious with herself for not defiantly defending her sin in front of him in her own home.)

Reverend Lilley's visit brought many slumbering memories back to Adele. It revived, for one thing, the thought of another preacher from an even more hidebound church, the Disciples of Christ, whose Reverend Farquar had succeeded in having her dismissed from her post as chief librarian of the heavily endowed town library. She had been summoned before the trustees of the library some years after her disgrace, and was accused of being unfit to recommend reading material to the young, or indeed the mature, readers of the library.

Any other woman, Adele often told herself, would have left town, especially after the death of her father (her mother had died some years before her disgrace) and the unexpectedly sudden deaths of her sister and brother shortly thereafter. "Any other woman but me! Yes, another woman would have gone to Chicago, or on to San Francisco. But I remained because I wanted to be near my unknown son. For I was convinced he had to be somewhere in the vicinity of Fonthill, and no matter how skillfully they had hidden his whereabouts and the identity of his foster parents, I felt at last I would discover where he lived."

Wherever her son was (some people doubted if he was even alive), his "sequestered state," in Adele's phrase, had been so very cleverly, even tantalizingly, carried through that he might indeed have been in Greenland or Africa. . . . And so her life, in her own eyes, was a vigil, first for her lost boy, and—failing that—for some new love to assuage the loss of her old love. For she felt as she stared out of her window that her boy would one day appear when she least expected him. One day, she was convinced, he would open the door, throw his arms about her, and they would take up their interrupted lives together.

Perhaps the most persistent whisper of scandal about Adele was what people in the town called the "matter of the diamonds," and indeed without the diamonds even the oldest residents might have forgotten her far-off disgrace. The diamonds, yes, the diamonds! For, mysteriously, less than a year after she gave birth to her son and, under orders from her father and her paramour, yielded the boy up, the anonymous gifts of the precious stones began to arrive: necklaces, bracelets, brooches. Every few months, a new gift of the precious gems was put in her hands. She summoned a well-known expert from New York finally to appraise them. He was struck dumb by their perfection. Indeed he offered to buy them from her at a price that was so high she felt faint. "You are certainly not trying to make fun of me," she told him. She refused to sell them.

The subject of the diamonds was a popular one in Fonthill, and frequently came up at Elaine Cottrell's boardinghouse. A few very "particular" people took their evening meal at Elaine's, and had there been no newspaper with local news in the town, almost every event would have been reported and commented on at the Cottrell supper table. And the scandal at the First Presbyterian Church was impetus enough to chronicle Adele's life all over again.

After her dismissal from the library, instead of retiring still farther from public notice, Miss Bevington became one of the first women to secure a position as reporter and feature writer for the local daily newspaper, *The Courier*. She not only wrote brilliantly, but she was so popular with the reporters, printers, and the management, including the owner of the paper, that she was treated as an equal—no, better than that—as a kind of muse for the men of the written word. She delighted them even more by smoking large black cigars with them when they worked late into the morning hours. Perhaps it was her smoking with the staff of the paper that made her even more notorious than did her possession of a fortune in diamonds bestowed on her for her sin.

Elaine Cottrell always gave a great Christmas party, and Adele would appear briefly, but without wearing any of her diamonds except for a small brooch, which was half hidden by her Spanish-lace collar.

Only in a town like Fonthill and in a time like 1930 would such jewels have been safe; for one thing, many people did not believe they were real. Elaine Cottrell, of course, was aware of the social difference between her and Adele Bevington, and the brevity of Adele's visits to the widow's house was not lost on her. For Miss Bevington, whatever had been the effect of her fall, belonged to a past grandeur, long before the crash of the last decade, and had once known great wealth. But even her family, who had lost most of their fortune when the oil boom burst, even they could not have bequeathed her such a fortune in diamonds. The jewels, everybody was in agreement, came from her seducer and paramour, George Etheredge, who, like Adele's father, possessed one of the most notable fortunes in this part of the country. And one story, which circulated endlessly, had it that every Christmas, even long after Etheredge's death, the diamond bracelets, earrings, lavalieres, and brooches continued to arrive.

"She kept them," Elaine Cottrell would end the chronicle, "and can you blame her?" Still, people in Fonthill did. They were, they felt, proof she was not sorry she had been a lost soul. They were payment for sin. She had never made any claim on her seducer, which confirmed her own role as the seducer rather than the seduced. Nonetheless George Etheredge must have felt her unspoken claim on him. His only act of contrition and pity had been the lavish gift of the jewels. And Adele had kept them, not for their value (she had never had any real knowledge of property or business matters, despite her braininess), but because they stood for the loss of her boy, more incalculable than the price of the diamonds.

And so, as the gossip at Elaine Cottrell's boardinghouse had it, long after George Etheredge's death as a relatively young man, or at least for a few years after his demise, the gifts of the diamonds had continued, usually at Christmas. And these gifts from her departed lover chilled her spirit. But she kept them. And had she not wished to keep them, to whom would she have returned them?

Often, at Christmastide, so the story went, she would put on one of her remaining party dresses, a sumptuous blue silk, and then slowly, like an actress preparing for some grueling long performance, one by one, put on all her jewels. The process took some hours.

Once, absorbed more in the spectacle of the jewels' splendor than in admiring herself so fantastically bedecked, she hardly heard the front door bell, but finally listening to its peremptory summons, and again, like an actress going before the footlights, she advanced to the door still in her glory, and opened it upon Ned Cottrell. Yes, there he stood, the younger of Elaine's boys, bearing her Christmas gifts.

Ned was still at the age, enviable indeed, when he accepted the outlandish as natural, and he did not see anything too extraordinary in Adele's coming to the door dressed like a queen, or indeed an empress. And it was, after all, Christmas and he presumed a Christmas party was in progress inside.

"Oh, Ned, Ned Cottrell!" Adele cried. "You have surprised me!" She blushed like a young girl and, as if by contagion from her, he colored also.

Being ushered in, he looked about the spacious front parlor, expecting company, perhaps, as gossip had it, illegal drinking. There was nobody. There was no tree. He did feel then a bit uneasy, but he was very fond of Adele, who, according to Elaine, spoiled him in season and out.

"But you're ablaze, Miss Bevington!" He finally let the words out.

She laughed uproariously and he joined in.

Nobody had ever seen her in all her jewels before, and indeed she had never allowed herself to be seen in all of them up till now. "Ablaze." She repeated his word and laughed again. It was lucky, she decided, that only little Ned was seeing her now.

She asked him to sit down while she looked at the fancy wrapping on the gifts he had brought her from Elaine.

"I will wait until it is Christmas Day," she said at last. She rose and presented him with her gifts for himself, his mother, and his brother.

But Ned went on looking at her jewels, smiling, nodding, while she shook her head at his being in on her secret.

"You could even put them on your Christmas tree," Ned said toward the end of his visit, and they burst into laughter again.

"That is exactly where they belong, I'm afraid," Adele agreed when she had got back her breath from the laughter, and had wiped her eyes with a silk handkerchief, for so much laughing always brought her to tears. "I am too old to wear such a display, I'm afraid. But, Ned, I don't have a tree! Not this year. Not for many a year!"

"You're right to wear them," he said thoughtfully. "You look . . . beautiful . . . in them, more than any old tree could."

She saw that he meant what he said. "You're a flatterer, like Alec," she said softly.

"Oh, no," Ned demurred. "You are beautiful. Everybody says so."

"Who? Neddy! Who?"

"Mother, Alec, Rita Fitzsimmons, the piano teacher."

"Oh, they only say it to be kind," she whispered.

"And Dr. Radwell said so!" Ned added to the testimonials, and then saw from the change on her countenance he should not have spoken the doctor's name. People claimed she had once been his mistress.

"About this time of year, you know," she began, ignoring his mention of Dr. Radwell, "when the old year is going out and loved ones gather together, it is very hard on those of us who no longer have families. . . . I hope you never have to bear it, Ned." She stopped herself from saying more, and then went on in a gayer tone: "I guess putting on these ornaments"—she touched her necklace—"is my only way of telling myself it's Christmas, Neddy!"

He felt then she was really going to weep, and he dug his heels into the thick carpet.

"But your gifts . . . Here we are talking about dull diamonds when you've brought me all this largesse! . . . Oh, Neddy, you shouldn't have . . . You really . . ."

"But of course we should have!" Ned repeated the words Elaine had told him to say. "We are all so fond of you . . . and you're coming to Christmas dinner."

What is this old woman's power of fascinating young men? Ned recalled that phrase from a conversation he had overheard his mother having with Rita Fitzsimmons, the piano teacher, and the two women had discussed the "curious phenomenon" of her attraction. Dr. Radwell himself, so immune to most human frailties, had been all too susceptible to Adele. *How old is she?* The two women's voices came back to the boy now. *Her untouched features, that alabaster face, cold like her diamonds, the deep-set sky-blue eyes, the long tapering fingers with the sparkling rings on almost every finger, and every one crying out "Not wedding rings!" Her lavishly furnished rooms, her many books, two thousand, it is claimed, her*

Victrola records, her—everything. And the young men who come and go like worker bees, obeying her every injunction and whim, sometimes coming only to call, and then staying till all hours. What is her secret?

This afternoon Ned had seen her mystery, he decided. But he would not tell anybody. She had shown her splendor only for him, after all.

But of course his brother Alec would worm it out of him, he supposed. Alec would get it out of him if he had to beat it out of him. He always did. Still he would not tell all.

As he was pondering all these things he heard Adele say: "Do you suppose your mother would object to your having just a tiny, tiny taste of some Napoleon brandy?"

Immediately she had spoken, however, she felt she had done a wrong thing, but she had never seen such enthusiasm on a face.

"Adele poured us two glasses," Ned told his brother later, who secretly relished anything that would contribute to his younger brother's downfall (he little suspected at the moment how far Ned would fall).

Ned coughed and sputtered as he tasted the Napoleon.

"Whiff it first like this, darling," Adele instructed him. "Mm," she muttered, while her nostrils dilated over the ancient crystal snifter.

He thought he saw her for a brief instant then as her seducer George Etheredge might have seen her long before, practically a generation ago.

Ned's lips parted, his tongue began to prepare the question he had so long wanted to ask her, for the taste of the brandy, the sight of the jewels, were breaking down any particle of reticence.

"You have a boy . . . somewhere."

She heard it. She did not order him out, she did not fume and rant or indeed curse, as she was said to have done in times past when somebody mentioned her shame and obloquy. And she drained all the brandy from her glass. She almost bowed to him, showing she welcomed the question from such unspoiled lips.

"I believe so, Ned . . . I would give the world to see him. . . . You must be like him, though so much younger. . . . I would cut my own heart out, I believe, to catch just a glimpse of him."

Ned was too moved to say more. He was almost deliriously happy she had shared such a famous secret with him.

"The jewels," she began, and looked down on the blazing stones, "the jewels you have caught me wearing, my dear . . ." She struggled with the words, or the tears, or her broken voice, and took another sip of her second brandy. "They're from my boy's father," she finished.

"Your boy's father?" Ned wondered, for the brandy had hit him, too, but with a greater force.

"They were sent to me," she explained as she touched the necklace, "to let me know he remembers." (She felt at that moment George Etheredge was still alive, still sent her diamonds.) "But if only the jewels were to turn into my boy . . . Don't you see? If he were to be sent home to me . . . Why, oh why did I give him away? You tell me! Why did they make me do so?"

In her anguish she began to open one of the gifts he had brought her.

"Oh, don't open your presents now, Adele," he had cried as her hand undid one of Elaine's fancy red ribbons secured with holly.

"Good God!" she cried out. "You are right!" She laughed now. "Why, it's not Christmas yet, is it? Brandy is so strong when it is old." She looked gratefully at him.

Rising, she went over to where he sat. He stood up immediately.

"Ned, Ned," Adele whispered. "You boys always bring me such happiness." She kissed him slowly on the forehead. Adele was a tall woman, but he was already, though not fully grown, quite a head and half taller than she.

"You are in possession of my secret, Neddy. . . . I never even told your brother Alec. . . . But of course he must know in any case. Everybody knows I am a harlot!" She finished this last remark with a laugh.

He hugged her when she said this, so that the words were barely heard.

"There would be no Christmas at all for me without you boys and your mother."

That Christmas visit of Ned's came just before the boy's own bad news. If life is full of portents and warnings and circumjacent road signs, it was not for nothing that young Ned had been so close to Adele just before his own moral fall.

He had heard talk once from the loafers at the courthouse that she had once been a "bad woman." So perhaps that was why he would come to her later with his own trouble.

Elaine Cottrell stretched out her small income after the death of her husband in a hunting accident (some people suggested it was a suicide) by boarding two or three ladies who were doctors' assistants, and more than a few young men employed by the telephone and oil companies. Elaine was known as a great cook, and she presided over the evening meal like a priestess at some hallowed ceremony. If she did not pray at the beginning of the repast, she gave every evidence she was about to. And no one must be late! Tardiness by so much as a minute was considered unconscionable. But if the boarders were excused for an occasional lapse in punctuality, her boys were never pardoned, and this was especially true in the case of Ned. Because he was the younger, he was given to understand that under no circumstances must he be unpunctual. Once, when he had arrived ten minutes behindhand, his mother had cried out from the kitchen, where she was ladling up the hot soup, "What would your father say if he knew of your lack of respect for this table?"

Ned and Alec exchanged looks with one another at their mother's appeal to their vanished dad, while the boarders lapsed into silence and stared at Ned in particular.

"I don't believe he would have cared a straw." Ned's voice, beginning to change, came out strong, if slightly cracked on the final word.

"What did I hear you say?" Elaine had rushed out from the kitchen to face her younger son.

"I said, Mother," he replied coolly, "I don't think he would care one straw!" He put down his napkin and placed it in the silver ring, for he presumed she would request him to leave the table. Instead, though more wrathful than ever, she cried, "Pick up your napkin and stay for your supper. I will take care of you afterwards."

Ned's disrespectful rejoinder to his mother had sobered everybody, but it had brought to Elaine's mind perhaps the lamentable truth that the younger boy, unlike Alec, had almost no memory of his dad at all.

But Ned's homecoming after his Christmas visit to Adele Bevington was to have still more serious consequences. For one thing he was a *half hour* late. For another, he was tipsy, if not drunk, and in that epoch only lawbreakers drank away from home.

Elaine rushed in from the kitchen to inspect the latecomer. Everyone expected her to order Ned to his room, but she took one look at him, and saw clearly what the boarders and even his older brother had missed, that he was not himself. (Perhaps they seldom looked carefully at Ned, and seldom included him in the conversation of the supper table.)

His mother did not serve him his soup tonight, but brought him his plate of beef stew, dumplings, and glazed carrots.

Ned stared immodestly at his mother, she felt, indeed brazenly. He winked at her. She was unwilling to believe what she saw. Then everybody turned their attention to Ned, and all saw what Elaine had seen at first glance.

"Come over to me, dear." Elaine finally spoke to him with a kind of crafty sweetness and forbearance.

Ned rose laggardly, dropping his napkin, and zigzagged toward his mother, who sat at the head of the table.

"Let me smell your breath."

The boy had turned his face away from her even before she spoke, but she took hold of his chin and brought his mouth down close to her face.

"There is liquor on his breath!" the mother cried. She had not meant to address the table with her discovery, but there it was, the public announcement.

Ned looked now toward the boarders and his brother, and grinned hopelessly, as much as to say that somehow somebody, without rhyme or reason, had poured a shot of hard liquor down his throat without his will or consent or, perhaps, remembrance.

"Oh, Ned, Ned" came the words from Elaine.

Seeing clearly his rather advanced state of drunkenness, she spoke in a lower voice to her older boy. "Help your brother up to his room, Alec, if you will be so kind."

Later that night after all the boarders had retired and the dishes were done, she and Alec went to Ned's room, and sat down beside his bed, in chairs drawn up only a few inches apart, and watched him sleeping.

"The idea of Adele Bevington, for Adele it must have been, giving a boy hardly fifteen that much to drink!" Elaine repeated this outcry again and again. "I am beginning to understand her reputation. I am indeed." She added this last statement in a half-whisper.

"Oh, but at Christmastime." Alec defended Adele all at once with a good deal of spunk. And he was glad, besides, that Ned had disgraced himself.

In a way, Ned's coming home drunk prepared both his mother and his brother for the real downfall that was about to overtake him. One could not say, that is, they were totally unprepared for what was to be made manifest. All last summer Ned had been working at the rather notorious Riverbend Amusement Park, first as the boy who replaced the rings on the merry-go-round, later on as the attendant for the pony rides, and finally as the ticket-taker and "host" at the Acadia Nights Dance Hall, which was re-nowned for an occasional murder, several rapes, and a long succession of pregnancies for unwary young girls.

Only bad times and finally the Depression had forced Elaine to permit her boy to work in such questionable resorts, but she had seen the change in him almost at once. He had lost some of his natural reserve, and he moved his head in a jaunty, insolent way, and sometimes sneered at some remark made by one of the boarders. In short, he had become something of a know-it-all, in Elaine's phrase, compared with the childish sweet air he had had prior to working in the amusement park. ("Know-it-all" had also been a phrase she had taunted the boys' father with in their occasional quarrels.)

Yes, Ned's coming home "dead drunk" at the age of fifteen had prepared her, she later would make the refrain, for the cataclysmic event that was to follow; and Adele's contribution to the boy's delinquency would be forgiven, if not forgotten, for they would need Adele's advice and support in the crisis that was about to fall upon them.

Young Ned's coming home drunk impressed on Elaine, too, the fact that her boys would not be boys much longer, that they would soon be grown men, and with that eventuality, they would leave home, leave her, and leave her to what? Her marriage, dissolved by her husband's early death, already seemed a fairly insubstantial part of her life. She sometimes thought she had always had two sons and had run an evening boardinghouse for the "quality." Marius Cottrell, shot accidentally, so it was claimed, by his hunting guide in Lake Winnipeg, Canada, came to be sometimes less real to her than John Barrymore or Gary Cooper, and her eight years of married life sometimes appeared to occupy fewer dimensions than a picture show. Only the sight of his mangled head in the morgue, where she had been summoned by the coroner on a hot July day, stamped in her mind his reality and her loss.

Elaine's only refuge when in "deep trouble" was to go to the studio of Rita Fitzsimmons. Rita belonged to a slightly inferior social class in the community, as Adele sometimes mentioned to Alec and Ned, and this judgment was passed on to Elaine. For whatever Adele's mistake of so many years ago had been, Adele's father, grandfather, and great-grandfather had been men of such considerable financial and political power (her grandfather had been a state senator) that, no matter how she had sullied her family's name in the first years of the century, she felt herself of the local aristocracy, and insisted on being treated with a certain deference, if not awe, by people in general. She was ruined but still seated on high. Rita Fitzsimmons, on the other hand, had never been acknowledged by Adele by so much as a nod on the street, though she lived only a block or two from Miss Bevington. But whereas Adele lived in a "mansion," Miss Fitzsimmons resided in a somewhat dilapidated apartment house, constructed during the oil boom. And Elaine, listening to Rita's complaints about Adele's cool treatment of her, remonstrated often bitterly to Rita that Adele recognized *her* only because she was so interested in the future of her two boys and because her husband, Marius, had come of an esteemed old family, though Elaine quickly pointed out her own people went back considerably before the Revolution.

In those far-off days a woman who smoked could feel the pleasure of committing the forbidden, even of being a sinner; cigarette smoking was almost a kind of sexual act, often or frequently committed alone or with a close woman friend. Elaine and Rita smoked like harlots waiting for a customer.

The walls of Rita's piano studio were covered with cut-outs from the Sunday newspapers, but although there was a portrait of Mozart as a child, and Beethoven at about the age of thirty, the rest of the faces looking down from the yellowing wallpaper were those of the reigning movie stars and matinee idols. Apart from the photoplay, Rita's main relief from the tedium of piano teaching was her once-a-year trip to New York City, from which excursion she would return filled with enthusiasm for all that was the rage in the great metropolis, filled almost to bursting with the splendors she had taken in, splendors barely heard of by her pupils and their parents. Afterward, returning to the dreariness and halting pace of Fonthill, she, like Elaine, was chilled by the haunting realization her youth and hope for true opportunity were ebbing low.

Afraid of the future, dissatisfied by the present, Rita and Elaine smoked and gossiped. The subject of Adele always came up. Adele had always been a kind of mute reproach to Rita, and now that the older woman had shown her cards by getting poor Ned drunk, the piano teacher could give vent to her own anger at having so long been ignored socially by the "queen of diamonds," as Rita invariably called her. But vilify Adele as Rita did, in the end she added little to Elaine's knowledge of her sons' mentor beyond what almost everybody knew: that she had given birth to an illegitimate son.

"I am not completely guiltless in this affair." Elaine finally brought to a summary their discussion. "I am afraid indeed I encouraged Alec to go there in the first place. He in turn, tiring, I gather, of seeing the old woman so much, suggested Ned take his place as her . . . errand boy."

And Elaine remembered even now at the moment of her greatest indignation that she had always been secretly pleased Adele had taken notice of her boys and had shown a genuine interest in their amounting to something. Pleased but jealous. She was actually jealous when anybody showed undue interest in her sons. And there were times when she mused bitterly over her lot as a widow, only to come out suddenly, as if from a wilderness, into a green and sun-drenched clearing where she felt a kind of ecstatic gladness that they had no father, that she could be their all-in-all.

"Adele! Adele!" It was Rita's voice of pretended alarmed outrage that brought Elaine back from her musings on the subject of her irreplaceability in the minds of her boys. Like the scented cigarettes they puffed, the name of Miss Bevington brought to the women mysteries, sinful intermissions, cloaked glamour, and always, thoughts of illegitimacy. They continued to tell the stories of her wealthy seducer, too highly placed to admit his love for her and sanction their sin with marriage. And where was this boy who had been born to Adele in a Chicago lying-in establishment? Why did no one know anything of his whereabouts? Had her seducer taken him, or was the boy bestowed upon another family of great wealth and position so that he could never recognize his mother?

Alec Cottrell had gradually been weaning himself away from Adele Bevington's sphere of influence. Since he had reached the age of nineteen, he had wanted to leave home and follow his inclination to be a singer in Chicago, but even before he had made up his mind to "run off" he had gone regularly to Adele's salon, as she jocularly termed it, and poured himself out to her. He bewailed his having no father, criticized his mother for her possessiveness, for having made him, against his will and ability, the mainstay of the family, and vented his intense anger and resentment against his younger brother, who always got all the plums and rewards, and was always favored and excused. "Just because he's the youngest!" Alec would utter this refrain with such vehemence that Adele was frightened.

During Alec's two or three years of constantly paying court to Adele ("Why does he have to lose his heart to an old woman, if he must get involved at his age?" Elaine would cry out one evening in Rita's company), he had been considerably strengthened by Adele's sympathy and attentive ear, had been grateful to her for lending him books, which had broadened his narrow country outlook. For Adele, in her youth, had traveled to Europe several times with her grandmother, had picked up French and

German tolerably well, and had read the entire work of Balzac, Flaubert, and Anatole France. She also possessed even more "forbidden" books, books at that time forbidden to be sent through the open mail: Petronius's *Satyricon*, Ovid's *Art of Love*, and even Krafft-Ebing's *Psychopathia Sexualis*, which she had borrowed from Dr. Radwell but never returned. She spared her young pupil nothing.

But Alec was aware very early on in his relationship with his mentor that she was not entirely the objective and selfless confidante of his young sorrows. She was steadily growing enamored of his budding manly charms and his undeniable good looks. And she had begun to drink in his presence and had urged him to take a "sip."

Growing up during Prohibition, Alec had first marveled at her regal disregard of the law in having liquor openly on the premises, and at the same time noticed, with involuntary satisfaction and even a kind of terror, that she smoked cigars. (It was shocking enough to him that his mother used cigarettes.)

There had come the night finally when bidding him good night, she had kissed him on the mouth, and though he felt he was not attracted to her by reason of her advanced age (Elaine had constantly reiterated she was old enough to be his grandmother), he returned her kiss and suddenly, prompted by the drink he had had, touched her breasts. She encouraged these overtures and allowed her hand to rest on his belt buckle. But instead of going farther, he had fled without a word down the long flight of steps leading to the front door and into the empty street.

From then on Alec had done something that he did not fully understand himself; he constantly encouraged his younger brother to run the endless errands required by Adele, who would, he assured Ned, pay him handsomely. And before many weeks had passed, Ned had almost entirely taken over Alec's position in the salon Bevington. Of course, Alec occasionally dropped in on Adele, brought her gifts and, if anything, was kinder and more considerate to her than before. But there was an unspoken understanding between them that Alec would be only a brief caller from now on, that he was no longer in her sphere of strong influence. On one of these brief calls he returned to her only half read an expensively bound copy of Daudet's *Sapho*, on the cover of which he had spilled a cup of hot Ovaltine.

But after all, he rationalized, he had given her Ned in return! He felt generous, and gradually Adele became more than grateful for the substitute. Only "little" Ned was completely in the dark as to the position he had inherited. He was performing the job of stand-in without quite knowing what that entailed.

Prior to Ned's coming to the supper table drunk, Alec had had other suspicions about his younger brother for some time, suspicions that inflamed and even maddened his own sense of laggard development with respect to girls. He was somehow positive that Ned had been intimate with girls who were, in the words of that era, "fast" or "loose" or downright rotters. One evening when he had picked up one of Ned's jackets by mistake and was putting it on hastily, a condom had fallen out of the breast pocket. Another time, when Ned had come home very late from working at the amusement park, Alec was positive there was the imprint of lipstick on the boy's neck and cheeks. Certain phrases and opinions that Ned let drop from time to time convinced Alec his younger brother had outstripped him sexually. He was deeply angry as a result, and resentful and ashamed, and his already smoldering jealousy of Ned kindled into open fury.

The night of Ned's coming home drunk from Adele's, after the culprit had been sent to bed, Alec stole into their sleeping room.

Lifting the boy's head from off the pillow, Alec spoke to him still asleep: "What happened?" He shook him now. "I said *what happened*?

Ned opened his eyes and looked at his brother.

"You can tell me, Ned," the older boy said more reassuringly.

"Oh, well, yeah," Ned muttered thickly.

"Say *yes* when you talk to me," Alec corrected. He was always nagging Ned to speak more properly, and had insisted that was one reason he had sent him to Adele Bevington, who spoke the King's English, according to Alec.

"Is there anything you need to tell me?" Alec wondered, letting the boy lay his head back again on the pillow. "Anything that weighs on you?"

"No," Ned answered. "I don't think so, Alec. I want to sleep the most of anything."

"Are you sure it was Adele who gave you something to drink?" Alec wondered. "And not some girl?"

"Well, if it wasn't Adele I don't know who it was give it to me," Ned mumbled.

Stung by this reply, Alec shouted: "Don't you talk sassy to me," and hit him.

"Now see here, Alec . . . you come into the room, wake me up, correct my English, and so on. And who sent me to Miss Bevington's house in the first place?"

"You should have refused the drink then. . . . She didn't mean for you to accept it anyhow. She is a generous woman, that's all." It was clear by his angry effusiveness he did not believe what he had just said.

Ned rubbed his eyes, and shook his head helplessly.

"I know you have been carrying on," Alec went on bitterly. "I hear it everywhere."

"Carrying on?" Ned wondered.

"When you're still only a baby," Alec continued. His anger that his younger brother was sleeping with girls maddened him to the point almost of incoherence. "Just watch out. I would if I were you."

Alec's words brought fresh hurt and resentment to Ned at always being picked on and bossed by his older brother, but Alec's warnings tonight greatly increased the worry he had had for some time about his relationship with a girl whom he had been seeing on the sly. He had been with her in an abandoned cottage near the millrace several times, and didn't wear a safety, partly because they would not sell contraceptives to him in the drugstore owing to his being underage, and partly because the girl, using a phrase that had shocked Ned, said she wanted him all raw down there. She was willing to take the risk, though look who was talking, he reflected, she was even more underage than him.

"Guilt is written all over your puss." Alec proceeded with his trial, when just then they heard Elaine's voice.

"Are you keeping that child awake?" They heard her footsteps coming up the carpeted stairs. "Alec"—the voice came closer—"will you answer me!"

"*Child*, my eye!" Alec spoke almost in Ned's teeth, and then without warning slapped him again smartly across the mouth.

As Ned rubbed the place where his brother had struck him, Alec said: "You'd better watch your p's and q's now."

"You won't tell Mama, will you?" Ned begged him, getting up and putting his bare feet on the Indian throw rug.

"So it's true then, isn't it?" Alec folded his arms across his chest and turned down the corners of his mouth. Just then Elaine entered the room, took hold of Alec's arm and shook him roughly, and then pulled him out of the room. But she had heard the last interchange between the brothers, and tomorrow at the latest she would want to know what was meant by "You won't tell Mama" and "So it's true then, isn't it."

For days after Ned's "revelation" that he slept with girls, the older boy nursed his resentment, his rage, his jealousy of his rival. While he, Alec, had been given all the responsibility as head of the house owing to the death of his father, had been made years older by reason of his mother's heavy reliance on him, had always held at least two jobs at once and cheerfully welcomed added responsibility and duties when called on, here was his little imp of a brother, who was always given the top cream, the favors, the excuses, who was always referred to as "the little boy," or "the child," as if he was never to grow up, never to be asked to shoulder any burdens, and now to cap it all—and this drove Alec to murderous ire—this child, this tiny boy had been lying in the tall grass with every girl he could unbutton his pants to. And Elaine had feared Adele might be a bad influence on him! Whereas if anything, he had ruined Adele, certainly driven her to drink! God knows what had passed between *them*. Alec shuddered.

But what tormented Alec even more than all these outrages, which he felt had been committed directly against him, was the burden of his own virginity. Yes, here he was, almost twenty, and he had only *kissed* a girl! While Ned—oh, to even think of it drove him to foam at the mouth—yes, the baby of the family had become a man before him. He wondered then what was wrong with him! And he blamed it all on Elaine, on Adele, on everybody he could think of, but finally like a swimmer coming up through a fathomless body of water where he has dived beyond his depth, he saw his dead father as the source and agent of all his woes, and he cursed Marius Cottrell for having the idiotic fondness for guns and hunting and being always away, cursed his dying and leaving him the unprepared head of the family. He decided then and there he would go to the local "bad house" and not waste any more time. He could not let the baby of the family go ahead of him an instant longer!

In the dead of night therefore he had sneaked out of the house, and crept to the local whorehouse, frequented largely by farm boys and an occasional traveling salesman. The madame in charge, a Mrs. Joceylyn, was upset on seeing him, for she knew Alec by sight, and she did not like minors or "good boys" to come to the house (Alec looked even younger than he was, but he became so obstreperous and flashed his money in her face with such vehemence, the poor woman decided that it would be wiser for the protection of the house to avoid a ruckus, and she accompanied him to a room at the farthest end of the establishment, where a young Mexican girl was waiting for her next customer. Alec stripped off his clothes with the speed and fierceness of a hero about to grapple with a foe who outmatches him. Hardly looking at the girl, he almost massacred her in his ardor to possess her. Then when the "deed," as he had so often called it in his daydreams, was accomplished, and his mission fulfilled, when he could no longer be called a virgin, when he had seen all of a woman, and had been initiated into the great secret, he burst into tears. Terrified at this unusual client, the young prostitute, hardly as old as he, tried to assuage him, rubbed his neck and back, and kissed him as one would an injured pet, held him to her breast, and then smiled when she saw he had fallen asleep in her arms.

But Alec's night with the Mexican whore somehow did not convince him he was now a man. He had done it, he could not doubt that, but the fact would always remain that his baby brother had done it before him. He would, therefore, he felt, feel forever outstripped by his younger rival, were he to lie with ten whores a night for the next twenty years. Yes, there would always be the recollection that a brat of barely fifteen years of age had beaten him to it, and that he was not a true victor after all, but second best. On this humiliating realization he would chew his ire for an indefinite season, and instead of glorying in a feeling of his own manhood and sexual prowess, which after all he had exhibited beyond any further proof, he felt like a soldier who, though severely wounded in battle, had seen the medal for bravery and the citation for excellence handed over to a raw recruit who had gone through the war without a wound or so much as a scratch.

Anyhow, whatever the case, he thought, he had done it, and no one could ever taunt him for not having done it; he had done it good and proper, and now he could forget about it and his having been a virgin for such a lengthy time. After all, if that was all there was to it, it was overrated. Indeed there was very little to it at all, come to think of it. Shooting a gun properly was more difficult and demanding.

An unwilling recognition had been taking shape in Elaine Cottrell's consciousness of late that she was not quite so attractive, certainly not so young-looking as she had been, say, even a few weeks before. While combing out her long yellow hair, she had found a few strands of gray. She sometimes paused as she caught a reflection of herself in the hall mirror, and would put her hand to her face as if to brush away the accumulated worry and the care of the years. But shortly after Ned's disgrace of coming home drunk, Elaine had an experience at the table as the evening meal was coming to a close that was as disturbing to her as seeing a ghost. She was presiding as usual at the head of the dining room table when, looking over at her two boys surrounded by boarders, she saw all at once not boys but men, and one of them was at that moment almost a photocopy of her late husband. This was the younger, Ned. Overfatigued by preparing one of her more elaborate meals this evening, she suddenly saw her two boys as grown men and strangers.

She kept studying their faces, hoping they would change back into the more immature countenances of a few weeks or months past. She had also gathered from her set-to with Alec, when she had stopped the two boys' wrangling, that Ned was seriously dating girls in the environs of the amusement park, a revelation that only bore out her own suspicion of Ned from some weeks past. But as she looked at her older son tonight, she saw not only a sudden vigorous maturity about him (this was taking place only a few days after his experience at the "bad house"), but another change in his physiognomy that was hard to particularize. His mouth looked entirely unlike the mouth she used to kiss good night only a few short months ago. Of course he had been shaving more regularly of late, perhaps every day now, and his beard was tough (so the barber had told him) for the rather unusual softness of his skin. But his mouth tonight did not look like Alec's mouth.

Elaine had warned Ned not to begin to shave too early, "like your brother," for, she had gone on, "your beard will probably be tough like his, and your skin is if anything even more tender." But tonight at the table, Elaine could observe that her younger boy's cheeks were getting covered with a soft carpet of down, and soon even she would recommend he take a razor to his tender skin.

"Do you have anything to tell me, Alec?" Elaine had said the same evening, after the table had been cleared and the two hired girls were doing the final clearing up of the kitchen.

Alec stared at her rudely. "I think that question should be directed to Ned, shouldn't it?" the older boy replied.

"You look so preoccupied of late, Alec. Tonight you looked very worried."

"Oh, those boarders make me tired," he snapped. "Why can't we eat alone like other families?"

Elaine assumed a hurt expression, but instead of quieting him, her wounded look drove him on: "Our house is overrun with strangers. They pick up the evening newspaper, take my books off the library shelf as if they were in their own home, and you can't hear yourself think for their big booming voices."

"If your father had left me any security, or property, Alec, you know perfectly well I would not have my house full of strangers, as you call them. But your father left us nothing."

"You can certainly say that again," Alec agreed, and looked somewhat shamefaced that he had spoken so sharply to his mother.

But even as this mild altercation (which occurred almost every few days) was in progress, Elaine still could not keep her eyes off his face, which, filling out so much, looked even more handsome. And his voice! It was attaining a resonance and masculine quality that even surpassed, she felt, her husband's, who had had such a fine singing voice. Alec's voice, she realized, must in part be changing so much by reason of his taking so many singing lessons with Paul Ferrand. Elaine felt a sudden flurry of jealousy then toward his singing teacher, who, now that Adele was no longer so much in the picture, took Alec away from home four out of seven evenings a week. Mr. Ferrand of course was, she felt, a better influence on the whole than Adele; he was trained in Europe, and had had a somewhat spectacular career in the Chicago Opera. And of course Alec wanted to be a singer, as he never let Elaine and Ned forget.

"The one you should keep your eye on is little Ned," Alec warned her. "I am doing all right."

"I hope you are," Elaine replied in a glacial tone which took Alec aback. She was thinking at that moment of Paul Ferrand, and his expensive twenty-room house, his two cars, and his extravagant ways, certainly extravagant for a mere voice teacher.

"But you know I am doing all right," he shot back. "Don't I have my nose to the grindstone seven days a week? Ain't I home every evening on time and sober at your supper table? Ain't I the model son?"

"Oh, Alec, Alec, that terrible tone of voice you take with your mother, and your purposeful bad grammar, which is, I suppose, to make fun of my own lapses in English."

Alec walked out into the hall and picked up a smart felt hat he had recently purchased on time from one of the few fashionable men's stores in the town.

"Alec"—his mother followed him on out—"it's very late, and it's Saturday night."

"Yes," he replied, not looking at her.

"Be careful," she added. He turned a look of calculated fury at her.

"You give that message to Ned, do you hear? He's the one who's . . . sowing the wild oats for everybody in this family."

Elaine now found herself almost more isolated than Adele Bevington. After all, Adele had her aristocratic name and her house, and although the town had moved about it and made it look like a commercial property, it still stood above most of the business "blocks" like a castle, besieged by progress, but still standing and intact like its owner. Elaine felt she had no solid support at all, and hardly any future.

The boys' mother had come from a much smaller town than Fonthill, a sleepy village nestling in the hills and overlooking tiny creeks and woodlands. Marius Cottrell had brought her almost unwillingly to the grimmer, less hospitable, certainly unpastoral boom town. And here in alien territory he had finally left her, with a substantial number of debts, a mortgaged house, and of course her two boys. A short while after Marius's death, a few eligible men in the town had shown an interest in Elaine, who was among the most beautiful women for miles around. But her financial plight, and her two boys' self-willed and arrogant natures, and her own rather grand ways, dampened their ardor. She was left to work out her own destiny alone.

Alec and Ned's regular visits to Adele Bevington's mansion put them—this was largely Elaine's thought—in a slightly higher social class than their mother could hope to aspire to, for Miss Bevington, despite her dubious early history, bore herself as if she were the very pillar of society. And although Adele was an occasional visitor to Elaine's supper table, she treated the young widow like her servitor rather than her hostess. And as a result of Alec's having been shown such special favor, he was invited frequently to all the best houses in town, while his mother found herself, attractive as she was, more and more in the company of Rita Fitzsimmons, the piano teacher.

The peculiar, if harmless, pleasures of the two women, Rita and Elaine, continued to consist of sitting in the piano teacher's large front room, smoking imported cigarettes, and telling of their early love affairs. They both admitted their present lot to be intolerable, denigrated Fonthill as a stifling place where only great wealth counted, a whispering-gallery of gossip, and with no future for anybody but the millionaire oil men, who still abounded, though in reduced numbers. Then after exhausting every topic of conversation and having rendered the studio blue with smoke, so that they could barely see each other's face, the two "girls" would go out to a Greek candy kitchen, Piraeus, where the owner, a hirsute brawny Greek, Nikos, served the ladies hot coffee and homemade sandwiches, and flirted with them both, and usually reduced their bill considerably, because, he said in his broken English, they were an advertisement for the place, a recommendation that left Elaine, at least, wondering. Then, after their refreshment, they would go for a brief stroll down Main Street, and return, often as not, to the studio, where Rita would get out the Ouija board and read their future.

So then Adele had gone on living in the same house where she had been born, the gabled mansion with its many rooms, its cupolas, its white pillars, its attic with the twelve-foot ceilings, and its basement like an underground fortress. Gradually, as the town had crept in on her mansion, and as her solitary state appeared to be permanent, she closed off all the house but the first two floors, and—as she joked once with Dr. Radwell— waited. Year by year the movie palaces began to appear on Main Street, one a few blocks from her house, with garish flickering bulbs spelling out its name, MAJESTIC. Across from it was erect- ed the mammoth Elks Lodge, with its eleven or so pillars and its countless steps, a vulgar display of oil fortunes, but since her father had been one of the most esteemed members of the order, she found herself more often than not taking one of her meals in its ostentatious gilt-filigreed dining room. The Royal Theater, directly facing her, she had come to consider almost her own private movie house, and the young men and women who streamed in and out of it, her specially invited guests. A few blocks away on the west side of the street was the Lyceum, which showed only cowboy movies and refused to admit women (Adele was always threatening either to enter perforce or to dress as a man and attend). Still farther north on Main Street was the Victory, which presented films that had had no success whatso- ever elsewhere in the nation, and which charged such low admis- sion every seat in the house was always filled. And finally far to the north beyond the river was the sprawling Elysian Meadows, which in good times had been the opera house, now reduced to nightly exhibition of photoplays. A small department store opened its door one day, very near the Royal, and then, soon, candy kitchens, chili parlors, florist shops, cut-rate drug stores, beauty parlors, and near the huge iron bridge that divided the town into north and south, a Negro-owned barbershop, hot-dog stands, and a showroom of used player pianos.

Far beyond the bridge and the muddy sullen river which flowed under it were the establishments that had since the Civil War been called saloons, and that now, under Prohibition, changed their names to near-beer parlors, and dispensed hot lunches, coffee, and pie, and occasionally played Victrola records. There were a number of banks, men's clothing stores, run by Jews and Syrians, and so many barber shops suddenly all in one block that one wondered if the men of Fonthill possessed one razor among them. Above all these thriving emporiums, finally, rose the lofty courthouse, with its copper dome, and atop it, the statue of one of the signers of the Declaration of Independence, and in its square, monuments to the brave youths who had died for their country in the Civil War, the Spanish-American War, and finally, green in memory, the Great War of 1918. Cannons pointed their black mouths in the direction of a ladies' ready-to-wear establishment, and a pawnshop. The only thing the street lacked, Adele pointed out, was a funeral parlor. The mayor had banned such businesses from Main Street, and the few that existed flourished at the very edge of the Poplar Grove Cemetery.

Adele often compared herself to a caryatid standing on high by her great oval window, looking down on the town, which still went on growing, to her dismay, despite the economic depression. And though it was hard times, people somehow found the spare change to go to the Royal and the Lyceum, and drink root beer and munch Cracker Jack and licorice sticks.

One evening seated in her accustomed place in the window, looking for, whether she was precisely aware of it or not, her boy, she had seen Ned's mother, arm-in-arm with a dark-complexioned man whom she did not recognize as a native of Fonthill. Mrs. Cottrell's familiarity with the gentleman in question rather shocked her. A few nights later, while taking a stroll in an unaccustomed part of town, Adele had seen Elaine driving with another stranger. Adele had stopped dead in her tracks. She felt these two glimpses of the boys' mother could mean only one thing, that Elaine "went with" men regularly.

Adele's own fall had not made her tolerant of other people's shortcomings, and she found herself highly incensed against the widow. So Elaine kept company with strangers, repeated she to herself.

A night or two later, Alec had called on her out of the blue, and complained, after an hour of their talking about nothing at all (the subject of Ned's drunkenness was never raised) that his mother was all of a sudden seeing "many beaux."

For some reason or other, Alec's choice of the word "beaux" caused her to break out into laughter.

"Well it wouldn't seem so funny, Adele, if it was your mother!"

She saw how deeply troubled Alec was that his mother should suddenly have other interests in life than her two sons.

At the same time Adele realized that if she breathed so much as a word against the boys' mother (whom both Alec and Ned adored deliriously, she was positive), she would lose them. So she tried to say nothing tonight, but when Alec's diatribe against Elaine went on rather too long, she said, "But, Alec, your mother has no husband. . . . And hasn't she the right to a little entertainment and relaxation?"

"Relaxation! Entertainment!" he shot back at her, livid with fury, so that Adele stared at him amazed and almost in terror. "I can't imagine what you mean, defending her!"

"But my dear Alec," Adele managed to say after a considerable pause in which she tried to assuage her own hurt feelings at being shouted at like this, "why do you begrudge your mother a few hours away from her kitchen and her duties as your mother?"

"Because these men are not gentlemen, don't you see?" He spoke darkly, and somewhat melodramatically, so that Adele had some effort now not to break into a grin.

"I suppose," he went on in his bitterness, "Rita Fitzsimmons is behind her going out with some of *her* traveling salesmen. . . . She is no better than she should be, if you ask me."

Adele now felt herself on very thin ice indeed. "But if she has *suitors*, Alec," she cautiously began and then stopped at the look of increasing choler on his features. "I mean, if she does see occasional gentlemen, I'm sure she's not serious about them."

"Suitors!" He grasped this word like a weapon to turn against her. "You would use such an expression!"

"Well, it's hardly any more serious than *beaux*, is it?"

Though still in a towering rage, Alec laughed in spite of himself, but Adele did not feel now like joining in. He had hurt her feelings very deeply, and she was also, to tell the truth, somewhat more disgusted with herself than with Elaine. Her beaux or suitors were obviously traveling salesmen, and he was probably right, were friends of Rita, whom she now despised more deeply than before.

"After all," Adele began again after a painful silence of two minutes, during which neither of them knew where to look, "your mother's real life is built around you boys. She has given up everything for you! A beautiful woman like her could have remarried, had she wanted to."

"You sound just like her," Alec said brokenly and bowed his head. He knew of course that Adele was as jealous of Elaine as Elaine was of her. Each woman secretly hated the other, but professed friendship and concern for each other. And always Adele had let it be known in strange little oblique ways that she would not judge a woman like Elaine, who had not had her own advantages.

"She is doing all she can do for you!" Adele almost shouted now, and this statement supremely irked Alec, for he saw in those harmless-seeming words another meaning. Elaine, Adele meant, had limited abilities and talents. She was not, in plain English, Adele's equal. So why shouldn't she go out with beaux and suitors, and seek her own level. Whereas if it were Adele who was the boys' mother, their fortunes would be dramatically different under such expert and imaginative guidance as the older woman would be able to give them, to say nothing of the financial aid that she could bestow.

"You expect too much of your mother," Adele had gone on, defending her rival while, to Alec's realization, making his mother at the same time much smaller of stature than she really was. "She does not wish to leave her home to make her own fortune. What would have become of you boys had she stepped out into the world? You would not have been the picture of robust health you both are today, showing as you do her steadfast and ceaseless care for you!"

Adele went on. She showed in her rambling speech, which Alec hardly bothered to listen to now, that she had always resented not only his mother's still-blooming beauty but her animal vitality and energy, and she was always shocked by a certain vulgar quality in Elaine's demeanor, which Adele excused in the boys. Elaine's laugh, she had once implied, was too loud, though musical, and her practicality, her very housewifely excellence, dismayed the older woman, who was useless in the kitchen and the laundry. Elaine was, in short, scarcely a lady, and so why shouldn't she treat herself to suitors!

On the other hand, it flashed through Alec's mind, Elaine had found Adele too pale and reeking of imported toilet waters, and too sedentary and idle, and finally, from the disaster of Ned's evening with her, too fond of strong drink. Elaine was as shocked that Adele did none of her own housework as Adele was shocked that she had seen Elaine "dating" traveling salesmen.

"I never go by her house," Elaine had said countless times at the supper table, "that I do not see Adele Bevington looking out her big front window. Evidently it is all she has to do!"

Adele realized that Alec had satisfied himself she was hostile to his mother by reason, queerly enough, of her very spirited defense of the widow. She had for a long time thought the boys must have got their brains from their dead father, if their looks from their mother, but now she wondered if the reverse was not the case, and that Elaine, despite her lack of education, had given the boys an acute knowledge of human nature at least. But then, too, Marius Cottrell had been handsome in a rough-hewn way and turned many heads when he had been alive.

Adele was too stunned by the bitter tenor of her meeting with Alec to weep. And this had been his first to her in weeks. She had realized for some time of course that his devotion to her was dying, if not entirely extinguished, and tonight's visit had proved it. At first (she could look back on it now) Alec had been jealous of her interest in Ned, and had discouraged his brother's visiting her. But she could see now all too well that, weary of the many demands she supposed she had made on Alec, he had surrendered his brother to her exigencies with a kind of irritated relief. "See if you can run your legs off for her, why don't you?" She actually imagined Alec saying to Ned. And had she only known, the older Cottrell had actually said something similar, indeed almost in the very words of Adele's bitter supposition.

She supposed Alec's singing lessons with Paul Ferrand were behind his neglect of her, and recalling some of the things Alec had let drop from time to time, she realized the boy had found in Mr. Ferrand a mentor superior to herself. And then the tears and the sobs came, and she shook with grief.

At first she did not hear the front door bell, engulfed as she was in her private sorrow over her hopeless love for Alec. But the bell continued to repeat its angry insistence, and she wondered why it sounded so much more ominous at this hour than during the daylight hours.

Then her face flushed with pleasure. It must be Alec come back to apologize, and to ask her pardon, to tell her Paul Ferrand had not replaced her in his affection and his need for guidance.

She went down the steps, and without now thinking it could be any other than Alec, she pulled open the heavy door. It was Ned.

She was too surprised to greet him.

"Have I awakened you, Adele?" he wondered. She was very grateful at that moment he had called her Adele. Still she stood on there at the door, almost shaking, and seeming to bar the entrance to him.

"You see," he went on, and without warning he pushed his way in, and closed the door behind him. "I mean, I had to wait until Alec had left. . . ."

"Of course," she replied. She was too upset to think *what* he meant, in fact.

"Come on in then, why don't you." And she turned up the stairs, with him first following and then going up a few steps ahead of her.

He faced her. "And we can talk then?" He touched the sleeve of her dress.

"Of course," she said. She was feeling better already, for if it was not Alec who had returned, it was at least his brother.

Inside the front parlor they both almost threw themselves into chairs. There was no doubt in her mind as she studied Ned just then that he had, she was convinced, a livelier intelligence than his brother, though his personality was not so fetching; he suffered from a fierce shyness, often blushing when anybody so much as spoke to him on the street, and, as Alec had complained about him to her so often, he was always curled up with his nose in a book, or exercising with ferocious determination at the local gym, but invariably, always alone.

"I don't know what I'd of done if you hadn't let me in," the boy had commenced when he saw she was not going to come to his aid with questions.

She had made herself a cup of her strongest coffee after Alec had left, for she knew she would not sleep that night anyhow. Without asking Ned if he wanted a cup, she brought him one, still steaming from the brew.

"I believe you sit up all night, Adele," Ned said after tasting the liquid with relish. It was almost as exciting as the brandy, and Elaine never served anything so strong or so tasty. He supposed Adele got it direct from Arabia, it was so unusual.

"I'm afraid youll be awake all night if you go on drinking that concoction," she joked. Then remembering the night with the Napoleon, she added halfheartedly, "Perhaps you shouldn't swallow down quite all of it."

"As a matter of fact, I've just been wondering if I'll ever have a good night's sleep again." He spoke with his lips almost inside the rim of the cup.

Adele stared at him. "At your age, I declare!" Then she poured herself another cup and stirred the liquid with a heavy silver spoon, though the beverage did not require stirring since she drank it black and without sweetening.

"I can't imagine what you can mean," she came back to his statement.

"Well, you see," he said, with his mouth still close to the inside of the cup. "I hardly know where to begin . . . but you're my only hope." He straightened up now and gazed at her. "I can't tell Alec, and I certainly can't tell my mother."

Adele waited a moment. "You were right to come here," she said softly. "If you wish, you can spend the night. And you poor boy, waiting outside all this time while Alec and I . . . quarreled."

He swallowed hard on hearing that. But since she said no more, he did not ask what they had quarreled over, and besides he wanted to deal tonight only with his own trouble.

"The reason I am here, Adele," he began in considerable fluster, the color coming and going in his face. "The reason is . . . I know that once, Adele, you were in a similar position!"

She almost spilled some of her coffee, and put the cup down with a heavy thump.

"Ned, I hope not," she said after getting hold of her nerves to some degree. She had no idea he had come with this kind of news. And she was almost sorry now that she had exchanged confidences with him, a mere boy. And she regretted the evening of the Napoleon. Yes, she should have kept her secret to herself, she should have gone and died with it, but then looking at his young face staring at her, the forehead wet with perspiration, the long black eyelashes sweeping upward and down, she was glad she had been indiscreet. Who else could be paid such a call in all of Fonthill but her.

"You can speak openly," Adele told him.

He beamed at her for a moment, then frowning, his lips twisting, he shook his head at the shame of saying it outright.

"Just tell it, Ned. Tell me, in plain English. It can't be that bad!"

He smiled feebly, and his eyes closed briefly.

"You haven't, after all, I'm sure, killed anybody!"

"No, that's true," he admitted, gulping audibly several times, but she could see that what weighed on his mind was nearly as heavy a thing perhaps as murder.

"There's no blood on my hands," he said with a hoarse loudness.

"Then, Ned, for heaven's sake . . . get it out! Of all people, you can tell me!"

"All right," he began, lifting his coffee cup up and then putting it down right away on the little stand by his chair. He wiped his lips on the napkin that she had handed him with the cup.

"I'll put it, as you say, in plain English. . . . I wish I could put it in Latin. . . . Well, then, I've gotten a young girl—she's a year younger than me—in trouble!"

For some reason, unclear even to herself, she smiled as she

heard him. It was a smile, she later tried to understand, that arose perhaps from incredulity, or perhaps from some sense of a lack of reality at that moment. But she kept herself from saying she did not believe him, for she did.

"You're sure that you are . . . the father?" Adele finally wondered aloud as he sat staring at her, perhaps because she had smiled, or perhaps because he felt now he would be tried and sentenced.

"The father?"

"I mean, are you sure you are the one, Neddy? Perhaps she's had others."

"Oh, no, I don't think so." He considered her statement. "I'm afraid I am the only one."

"She has told you this?"

"Not exactly. I'm sure of it, that's all. She had never been with anyone, you see, till me."

"Ah, yes," Adele said. She rose then and went to the window. The young couples were gone, and all the lights of the Royal were extinguished, so that it looked almost like empty space. Only the lights in the rear of the Kleitzer Bakery were burning, and she fancied she could smell the bread baking clear from here.

"She doesn't know where to turn," he went on, having wheeled about in his chair to say this.

"Of course, she doesn't," Adele said softly, and walked away from the window and took her seat again.

"One thing is certain, however, Ned. You cannot marry. If she is a year younger, or even a year older! Why, you're both practically in diapers yet." She remembered her own age when she had "fallen": *seventeen*. But she had certainly been no child such as Ned and his young girl were. No, Adele had been "old enough" when she surrendered to George Etheredge. She had been exactly sure of what she was doing.

"Did you know her well, Ned?" Adele came out of her reverie.

"Not very well," he replied. He was now close to tears. "It all happened last summer, you see, in those fields near the amusement park, near the apple trees, I guess. . . . She told me if I didn't come to her stepfather by tonight and admit it, she would have to tell him herself. Her condition is getting noticeable, to say the least."

"And did you go?" Adele wondered in a voice that had a little too much of the sound of the prosecuting attorney for her own liking.

"No. I came here."

"You poor dear." Adele spoke almost inaudibly.

"You're not mad then that I did?" he almost cried.

"You know me better than that," she replied instantly. "You did right. This is where you should be."

"Oh, thank you, thank you, Adele."

"You must always come to me in difficulties," she went on, and her eyes had a peculiar faraway look. "I am only trying to think, though."

Then they said nothing for a while, and were as still as if they were holding their breath.

"Perhaps," she now proceeded, "if the girl has told someone else by now, it may be better all around. But whether she has talked or not, you must prepare your mother and Alec for what has happened, Ned."

"Oh, I can't, I can't," he almost wailed. "You don't know them!"

She gave her strange smile again. "But who else is to tell them then?"

"Can't you, Adele?"

She stared at him pityingly.

"Of course I *can*. Can and will if it is necessary. But don't you see that if I go to Alec and your mother, it will look even worse for you. Your mother will also resent receiving such very delicate information from me. For I am, after all, nearly a stranger!"

"A stranger! Oh, Adele." He was hurt and bewildered by her words.

"Certainly, Ned, not a member of your family, after all, or even a distant relation. Of course, you and I are far from strangers."

"I should hope," he said brokenly, with his mouth almost pressed tight against his collar.

"If you think it will do any good, though, Ned . . . Please look at me! I will tell Alec. I will indeed."

He stared at her as he considered this possibility.

"After all, Ned, he is the head of the family."

"Yes, so he is," Ned said bitterly. He rose, but remained rooted to the frayed wool of the carpet.

"What else can I say, dear boy?" Adele got up too. He fell into her arms.

"If I could undo what has been done, wouldn't I?" She kissed his thick chestnut hair again and again.

"Yes, yes," he said through his tears. "But Alec. Oh, God, when you tell Alec!"

"I will see that he understands it all better than you may think. . . . He owes me an understanding of it indeed! I know you two boys are often on the outs. Brothers are like that," she went on. "But Alec cares deeply for you also."

"We'll see about that now, won't we?" He smiled and she let go of him. He stood now some distance from her.

"You can depend on me and on Alec to do the right thing. He will listen to me. I will see he does. He will pay heed to me."

She walked with him down the steps to the front door.

"It will come out all right, dear Ned. It is not the end of the world, remember. In years to come—oh, it will seem like perhaps nothing at all."

He threw himself again into her arms, and then, breaking away from her with a violent wrench, he ran out and had soon disappeared down the quiet street.

Despite her genuine concern and shock over Ned's fall, and her apprehension at the coming confrontation with Alec, Adele felt an unexpected surge of energy, even optimism. For no understandable reason she felt her own prospects were not so dubious, and Ned's obloquy in a strange way lessened her own burden of shame, carried all these years. She felt younger, blither, more confident. And she would fight for Ned.

She telephoned Alec. His voice was much more friendly than she could have hoped for, and he agreed to see her again that day. Perhaps he had felt guilty over their having quarreled, and was feeling remorse at having neglected her so long and having substituted little Ned as his stand-in. Hence his wish to be pleasant.

But Adele insisted on meeting him at the Elks Lodge. She could hear Alec's surprise, and a slight tinge of annoyance, when she mentioned this meeting place. For one thing the Elks had a stiff and stuffy atmosphere, and he would have to dress properly to go there. And though the tables were far apart, and there was an almost funereal quiet in the great dining room with its ostentatious chandelier hanging over the diners, one could not quite speak openly there. But Adele was unyielding as to their rendezvous. Perhaps she was not even sure herself why she had chosen the Elks, except that she wished to meet Alec on neutral ground, and was prepared to show him that she was aware he would never again be the very steady caller and friend he had been in times past.

Alec appeared a few minutes early at the Elks. His hair had been fastidiously brushed and pomaded with the help of Elaine, who was nervous about his appearing in a place where in her words "only millionaires congregate," and he wore his Sunday best. Much against his will, too, Elaine had insisted on putting a silk handkerchief into his breast pocket, where it appeared like a wilted lily (he removed it as soon as he was out of the house).

Adele, always punctual despite her grand ways, was already seated at a private table in the very rear of the enormous room, surrounded by ivory-colored walls and stained-glass windows on which were depicted stags, and maidens in diaphanous dress, and young huntsmen on black steeds brandishing bows and arrows.

Alec saw at once that she had chosen after all a fitting place for her confidential interview with him, and he wondered what in God's name he was to be held to account for now.

"Tea, I expect," Alec replied to her question as to what he might care to take for refreshment. (He only said tea to please her, since he had to order something.)

Adele herself was already drinking her second hot chocolate. A young woman in starched white apron kept refilling her cup and once she had brought Alec his tea, Adele asked the girl not to come back until she was summoned. "And please, my dear, stand over by that pillar there, for we are discussing, I'm afraid, a very private matter." The girl flushed and went off.

Alec studied his former mentor and friend. Was she about to be married? Had she by some miracle found her long-lost son? Or had the mysterious benefactor who had showered her with jewels seen to it that another great bequest, long deferred by litigation, was about to be hers? He could not determine from her face what her news was. He had to admit Adele would always remain a bit deep for him.

"I can assure you, Alec, that what I have to tell you will be as painful for me to divulge as it will be for you to hear."

He sighed deeply, and her eye moved anxiously away from him to the stained-glass windows and the severe ivory of the walls.

"I'm quite prepared, Adele," he said in a kind of grim encouragement. He loosened the tight knot of his cravat.

"It has to do with your brother, Ned." She spoke in an almost pious tone, inconsonant with her usual manner.

A flush of anger covered his face, which had been almost drained of blood a moment before.

"He has chosen me as his confidante, and his spokesman," she continued, but was interrupted by a glacial and cutting "No doubt" from Alec.

"I won't keep you in suspense," she went on with a hurt quality in her voice. "It is bad news, however."

He looked at her hard, then shifted his glance wrathfully away.

"Very bad, Alec." Adele was as near flustered as he could ever remember her.

"I said I was quite prepared," he almost snapped at her now, and they must have both remembered their quarrel of only a few days ago.

"It seems Ned has got some young girl in trouble. That is correct," she went on, now in possession of herself and fortified against anything Alec might say or do. "She is going to have a baby."

Alec's right hand moved abruptly, and as it did so he pushed off the solid silver knife and fork that had been on his place mat. Adele and he appeared to listen for the sound of the silverware's fall. He did not offer to pick them up, and the waitress, unbidden, came and performed the task for him, and then beat a retreat at a sign from Adele.

Alec was struck dumb, not so much at Ned's having got a girl in trouble as by his rush of blinding jealousy and rage that the "little boy" had again outstripped him in this new achievement.

Possibly Adele had some inkling of the depth of his feeling at that moment. Certainly something of her old affection for him came back to her from those days when he had been so faithful—before he had sent Ned to be his replacement.

"This will kill my mother!" Alec was finally able to say something out of the welter of all the feelings he was engulfed in.

"No, it will not." Adele spoke rather loftily and with a kind of authoritative severity that brought down his rising hysteria. "Your mother will be able to deal with it very well. She is a capable woman. . . . She is a strong woman. . . . But she has to be prepared, and you are the one who will have to do it."

"*Me!*" Alec cried. "Yes, it is always *me* who has to do everything in that house! Why can't the culprit tell her of his own disgrace?"

"Of course Ned can, if you wish it." She threw him this choice in a tone that cut like ice. "You have only to tell your brother he must do so and he will. But I believe you, being the older, know full well that only you can prepare Elaine for such a shock; you can't allow Ned to blurt it out to her without warning. Which is what he will do if you don't take over."

"To think that this is what he has been up to all these months!" Alec allowed some of his poorly controlled rage to come out, and again was overwhelmed by the galling recognition of how far the younger boy was ahead of him.

"I'm sure Ned isn't the first to have got himself in such a fix." She spoke with a kind of pitiless levity, and at the same time, languidly lifted her water glass and treated herself to a swallow.

He gazed at her wide-eyed and reproachful, but her own unblinking stare at him in return made him look away.

"I appreciate all the same your concern," he began, anger and humiliation making his voice almost unrecognizable. "I am indebted and grateful for your acting as an intermediary in such a shabby affair." He spoke now as Elaine's mainstay and as she would have coached him to speak.

Adele frowned, and was about to say he owed her no debt and no thanks when he blurted out: "I'm astonished, however, he came to you!"

"Astonished?" The hurt had come into her tone again.

"I suppose he had nowhere else to go." Ignorant perhaps of the blow contained in these last words, he likewise lifted his eyes to the stained-glass scenes of the hunt, and the unblemished ivory walls.

"When one is in trouble of this kind," she said, after a rather long silence during which her eyes rested on her two upturned palms, "it is hard indeed to know where one can go. Because you are still so untouched by life, you cannot know how hard! But I am rather proud he came to me." Her last words were pronounced with defiance.

"Oh, I am very glad he came to you, Adele!" Alec came to his own defense. "You were wonderful to hear him out. I thank you. I do," and his voice broke, and she saw the tears come to his eyes, but they were angry tears. "I must apologize for him disturbing you," he finished.

"Whatever you do, Alec, don't apologize. I don't need apologies. I won't have them in any case." She picked up her purse and drew out some bills.

"Let me pay for this, Adele," Alec beseeched her.

She handed the waitress the money as if he had not spoken.

"I am in your debt again, Adele," he told her as she rose. "I will always be grateful." He saw that he had offended her, that they were no longer close. He regretted her coldness and her dwindling affection.

"I hope to repay you one day for your many kindnesses," he mumbled, and looked up at her standing by one of the white pillars. Somehow he made no offer to rise, as if she had ordered him to remain seated until she had left the building.

"One is not kind in order to be repaid, Alec. Now please keep in touch with me, my boy. Do you hear?"

He took her hand almost convulsively and kissed it.

"If you will forgive me, Adele," he said after a moment, "I am going to sit on here. If you don't mind, that is, going back alone. . . . I feel so very much at sea. I can't explain it. I want to get hold of myself, I guess." Still seated he seized her hand again and pressed it to his face.

Very much moved herself, she pulled away from him, and without another word hastened out of his presence and the vulgar majesty of the dining hall.

The only way he could get hold of his emotions was to fall back on his habit of cursing his father audibly for having died and left him the man of the household. He dredged up again his bitter resentment that his mother expected everything of him and nothing of her favorite, Ned. There were times like now when he wished his mother had died also, so that nobody would expect anything of him, and he could go to Chicago and begin his singing career in earnest. He sat on in the dining hall until preparations were underway for the evening supper hour, and the immense chandelier began to shine with a resplendence it had not shown as they drank their tea. New waiters were arriving also and whispering about his presence. Rising awkwardly at last, upsetting as he did so the water glass by Adele's place mat, he snatched up his hat, and rushed from the place like someone who had helped himself to the cash register. He walked past Adele's house. Looking up at the big front window, he fancied he saw her purple silk dress moving about in the interior. He stopped. The rays of the setting sun had lit up the glass in front of which he waited, hoping to catch a glimpse of her.

He dreaded more than anything else having to tell Elaine—if indeed that was what he was now going home to do. For what purpose on earth was there in talking to that little sneak Ned? And again he was overcome by a blind hatred of his brother for having surpassed him with girls, for having, without a word to him or probably anybody else, suddenly become, for all his other backwardness, a man! And what was worse, about to be a father!

Alec took refuge for a moment under the canopy of a cut-rate drug store. He had to wait for his heart to beat less violently, and he had to make up his mind as to what to do. Of course he could just do nothing! Never let on to Elaine he knew, let the sky fall down on them in its own good time. But no, he realized, he would get a kind of grim satisfaction in taking the blinders off his mother as he let her know the truth, let her see her idolized younger son, her little dear, for what he was. Then would she dare to say "poor little fellow" or "he's after all only a young lad" when Alec pointed out some of his many shortcomings and secret deeds?

At the supper table that evening, Alec was still too shattered even to indicate he had some news for his mother. But Elaine noticed his pallor, his silence, and the unusually deep frown marks, always a warning of trouble to come. She sighed. She supposed he was going to ask her again for permission to leave home, and then, when she demurred, he would throw up to her how she was holding him back in his career. Or he would make some cutting remark, she supposed, about her "suitors" and "beaux," and say, as he had once done, "I would think you would finally settle on one of them, and marry him!" (He always said this deliberately, knowing full well all her suitors were married men, or at least poor matches.)

In one of their bitterest arguments, Elaine thought back as she studied her older boy at the table, she had reminded Alec that she could have given her sons away after Marius Cottrell's sudden death, and made her own career without their holding her back, a career like the one he sought, as a singer. She could have evaded *her* responsibility. "But my love for you came before everything else!" She had triumphantly ended the quarrel with this oft-repeated refrain.

"Then perhaps your love was misplaced!" Alec had shouted at her after this session. She had looked then so anguished when she heard these words that he had gone down on his knees and begged her forgiveness. Still, the words would always rankle in both their hearts, endlessly.

Instead of telling Elaine that evening of Ned's disgrace, Alec drove out in his broken-down little roadster to an out-of-the-way restaurant that had been both a saloon and a dance hall before Prohibition. The joint had atop its roof a mammoth electric sign, which dominated the landscape for some miles around, spelling out in queer blue lights: RUSSELL'S COVE.

Russell was a fairly young man, with sharp features, huge forearms always bare winter and summer, and hair so black it looked almost as blue as his sign. He always welcomed Alec, and sometimes gave him a drink of liquor if nobody "nosey" was around. Tonight two of Alec's friends were seated in the booth near the back exit, where the liquor usually flowed, and Alec walked over to talk to them, after having shaken hands with Russell what seemed a score of times. The friends were Mark Landon and Emily Gibbs. Emily taught school in a private institution nearby, and Mark worked in a hardware store while studying acting on the side. It was Mark, as much as Alec's singing teacher, who was always urging the older Cottrell to leave Fonthill and make it on his own.

All at once drinks appeared from nowhere, courtesy of Russell. The first illegal round was followed by a second, and then a third, and Alec had soon told Mark and Emily his news.

To his own considerable astonishment, Emily and Mark found Ned's predicament funny, and they laughed uproariously. Having been treated so many times in the past to Alec's censorious remarks about his younger brother, his two drinking companions now spoke of Ned in so contemptuous a manner that Alec, to his own surprise, found himself wincing and then doggedly defending him. Emily's attacks on Ned as "the little snot" and "I suppose he still wets the bed" had gone on to even more uncalled-for insults against Elaine herself until Alec said: "Of course you've never spread your legs to anybody, have you?"

In reply Emily threw a glass of liquor in his face. Alec slapped her, and Mark, his gallantry aroused, pushed and shoved Alec roughly until he fell out of the booth.

After a few more punches and insults, Alec, shouting and blubbering, ran out of the Cove.

Russell himself ran out in his shirtsleeves after him, shouting, "Don't you dare treat me like that, Alec, when I've been so damned considerate to you! You come back here, do you hear, you stuck-up little mama's helper!"

But Alec had already run out of earshot.

A kind of languor fell upon Adele after her "sessions" with the two Cottrell boys. She was conscious, of course, that her whole life now revolved around these two young men, and she wondered if their own mother was taken up as much as she was by their hopes and aspirations and sorrows. She supposed Elaine was so weighed down with her own burdens she was hardly aware that her boys had serious problems of their own, while Adele thought of almost nothing else than what faced her two young friends.

She bit her lip as she came now to a full realization of the emptiness of her life. For although she continued to be an omnivorous reader, books no longer filled her growing need for a deeper and more vital experience. She sometimes thought that all she accomplished was watching the procession of young people go in and out of the Royal and waiting for a visit or phone call from either Alec or Ned. (She could no longer expect much affection or communication from Dr. Radwell, who had all but disappeared from her life.)

Adele also mused that she was moved almost to ecstasy by Ned's trouble. She could not say, even to herself, that his calamity made her happy. But it filled her with a feeling of abundant energy and, odd perhaps to admit, hope. She was not sure what kind of hope, but it was akin to the feeling when in very early spring one knows that the snow and blasts of winter are over, and that no matter how many bitter fitful storms may still come from the north, soft breezes and the smell of blossoms will soon be the order of the day.

She also blamed the girl, whoever she might be, and despite her keen memory of her own fall, which Ned's trouble had brought back to her with fierce immediacy, she felt nothing but disapproval and dislike for the young minx who had got Ned to unbutton his trousers for her.

But most of all, as a result of Ned's disclosure, a kind of hysteria overtook her now, and conviction that somewhere, yes, beyond the shadow of a doubt, her own son moved and breathed and in some definite abode had his being!

Her vigil for her lost son had a timeless quality like eternity itself. She was certain that even in the afterlife she would go on expecting him, waiting for him there also, and sometimes she felt she occupied eternity already, for it appeared that all she did was wait, her door open, never locked, as the Royal across from her window kept its portals open for the endless streams of patrons attending endless matinees and evening performances.

She did not even know her son's name! And she was loath to give him one after all this time. She dared not give him a name even in her heart because if he should appear he would be bound to have another name. If only they had allowed her to bestow on him a name for the few weeks they had been together, or even on the day they had come to take him from her. She had protested at the last moment, but her sister, Jennie, had repeated to her the two choices dictated by her father and her lover, to take her son and earn her own living without a penny's help from her father and her seducer, or to come home without her son, and in comfort and security live down the obloquy of her folly. She had chosen what she felt was best for the child. She could not expect the poor boy to suffer total poverty and disgrace when, as her sister emphasized, a good family was waiting to take him off her hands.

"But where are they taking him?" Adele had begged to know. "And who are they, Jennie, these people who want him so much?"

That was part of the bargain. She was never to know, never to ask. It was more frightful, she often reflected, than if they had killed the child in front of her, for at least then she would know where to visit his grave. The *unknowing*, this absence of all certainty, was to become the tenor of her life, the dread food of her years.

Not to know! Never to be sure! Her eternity had commenced from the moment they had taken the baby away from her. She refused for a while to have her breasts pumped, until there had been the danger of abscess; then she had consented. "Why not cut my breasts off?" she had asked the nurse. Hardly a day went by when these scenes, which had occurred so long ago, did not appear before her eyes like the endless pageant of faces in the photoplay houses.

She would thus wait through all eternity for some word of this boy who had no name, whose location and least movements were forever to be unknown to her.

Once, some weeks ago, when she had drunk a bit too much of the "medicine" and was talking too freely with young Ned, she had begged him to be on the watch for her son. Yes, those were her words: "Can't you be on the watch for him, Neddy?"

"But you said you don't even know what he looks like . . . don't know his name. Did he have any mark about him that would make him recognizable?"

She had thought a long time before replying. "Yes," she had confided to him, out of a memory that she thought had gone extinct. "It was a breech delivery," she recalled, "and the obstetrician blundered. The poor baby's left little toe was, I feared, damaged. . . . And," she recollected feverishly, "the fingers of his right hand were slightly webbed."

That indeed had been the same evening Ned had drunk too much of the "medicine" and had gone to his mother's supper table drunk.

That same night Ned had touched Alec's sleeve upstairs and said through his liquor breath: "Adele's son had one of his toes injured in delivery, and the fingers of his right hand were webbed."

"You crazy bastard," Alec had replied in shocked horror. "Go wash your mouth out with carbolic acid, why don't you, before you tell anybody else your tales."

"Carbolic acid!" Adele had repeated Alec's words when Ned told her later of his fall from grace.

"It is all my fault, Ned," she had whispered. "You must never taste Napoleon again." Then: "Who knows what the authorities might do to us?" she had finally gibed. "Perhaps we'll be sent to jail together."

When the nurse was not looking, Adele had cut off a lock of the baby's yellow hair and had hidden it in her pocketbook. That lock was now preserved in a glass casket, hidden away in a cedar chest. She allowed herself to look at it only once a year, usually at the very end of the year, and once she permitted Ned to look at it. He had been at first afraid that perhaps along with the lock of hair would be the baby's toe. But as he stared at the relic, he had slowly agreed the lock was beautiful, golden as sunlight, and it seemed to fulgurate in its glass prison.

"He would be over thirty if he were here," she repeated always when she and Ned had their talks.

"You were a *young* mother," Ned had muttered.

"That was the trouble," Adele agreed. "Had I been strong as I later became, wild horses could not have dragged him away from me."

"Of course," her young visitor assented.

Adele smiled at him, and at herself. Taking a mere child into her confidence like this! And she thought of what the town would say, had it known. Oh, well, she considered it all, he would get over it. He would forget he ever knew her when he grew up and was married himself and had his own family. While she was destined always to remember, never to be given forgetfulness, living always in the endless parting from her only son.

Val Dougherty was the sole owner of the Ice House, which at the time of this story supplied nearly all the ice to the inhabitants of Fonthill. Years before, when he had not as yet become the owner of the Ice House and its adjacent quarry, Val could be seen alone delivering the cakes of ice to his customers. He had been an almost daily visitor then to the Cottrell house, and in the broiling heat of summer had sometimes made two deliveries; half-drenched with the dripping cakes and his own copious sweat, he all but terrified Ned Cottrell, then scarcely five years old, by lifting with the tongs the enormous pieces of dripping ice over his head, and when he had deposited the block in Elaine's refrigerator, he would turn his contorted features and bared teeth toward the young boy, who did not know whether he was smiling at him or perhaps about to attack him.

Now considerably better-off, perhaps even rich, with eight or nine young men to deliver the ice, Val would sit most of the day in his office conducting business, or, as some said, merely counting his money. Then when the counting or the rest of whatever he was occupied with ended, he would go to his stables, inspect the horses, and, more likely than not, saddle one of them and ride around his property on what was a kind of miniature race-track.

He was the foster father of Marilyn Dougherty, got in trouble by Ned Cottrell, and the husband of Maude, Marilyn's mother. Maude was a thin, nervous woman with beautifully silken red hair, and her delicate complexion was a considerable contrast to her husband's fiercely black beard, which, no matter how often he shaved, always appeared through his swarthy complexion. He had by birth the build of a wrestler, which had been further developed by his years of lifting the cakes of ice. When they were together, Maude and Val, she so delicate and fair, he so swarthy, almost black, people would wonder how such dissimilar persons could ever have met, let alone married. Maude Dougherty's first husband, Marilyn's father, had died in France, as an infantryman in the Great War. He had left her a little property and an insurance policy, from which legacy Val Dougherty had improved his ice business, but his wife's contribution to his business advancement had not improved their marriage. Man and wife seldom spoke to one another, in fact, and it was said they no longer shared the same bed, and only infrequently ever ate a meal in each other's company.

Val himself gave the impression of a man who never saw anything but the ice that he manufactured for his growing number of customers, and his horses, which he sedulously raised and cared for and constantly rode. With the years, as he grew richer, instead of getting sleeker he grew even wirier, more rugged, and if possible swarthier in aspect. He blamed his swarthiness sometimes on his Welsh ancestry and his coming from a long line of coal miners and seamen. His eyes, however, were of a bright blue; they looked often like glass eyes in so dark a countenance.

Dougherty saw his foster daughter, Marilyn, even less frequently than his wife, and had perhaps never said twenty words to her on his own in the past year. But he was not unkind to her, and once every few months would give her a gift of money, and then he would put his rough sinewy hand on her hair, as luxuriant and glossy as her mother's, and smile faintly as he did so.

"You've got to go to the Cottrells," Maude told him one intemperate winter day when she had convinced herself that Marilyn was really going to have a baby. After shaking and slapping her daughter, she had got the name of the culprit out of her.

Maude had felt that her husband would storm and rage when she first told him of their daughter's disgrace. But though she repeated her news several times to him as he sat sprawled out in his swivel chair in the ice office, he appeared not to actually hear her or at least not to take in the significance of her report. And when Maude began to be even more detailed in her description of Marilyn's condition he interrupted her with a gentle but slightly menacing "I heard you the first time you told me."

Stung by his calm, she cried: "Aren't you then indignant about it?"

He merely gazed at her with his cool light eyes, which shone now almost slate-colored at her.

"Tell me, Val, aren't you angry this has happened to our daughter?"

"*Our* daughter," he sneered. Picking his teeth with a toothpick he had split from some loose lumber, he went on: "Well, it ain't the first time a boy threw a girl on the grass and pumped some life into her." Offensive as his words were to Maude, the sleepy almost contented way in which he pronounced them was even more galling to her. She looked at his open shirt stained with sweat all about the armpits, and over his middle, and then at his unusually red mouth, from which a fierce energy, despite his dozing delivery, threatened always to flow. Indeed one of the things that had first attracted and finally repelled Maude was this ever-present, seldom-expressed strength of his body, a body that seemed impervious to any interruption of its own power by whatever currents might cross over to it from the outside.

"You can't let it go on any longer without doing something!" she warned him. There was the suggestion of a wail in her voice, and she attempted to stifle it, for the one thing he had always forbidden her was tears.

"What is there to do, since the damage is done?" He looked suspiciously at her eyes, and then threw away the makeshift toothpick.

"What is there to do!" She almost spat the words. "Get them to make it up to us. The Cottrells!"

"*Us*," he snorted. "She's yours, not mine. What's to be made up, since the damage is done." For a moment he almost looked riled, or at least behaved like a man about to spit out something that was lodged behind his tongue, and then relapsed quietly into the security, strength, and pride of his body.

"Val," she almost moaned against this stolidity, "you cannot *not* go! Do you hear me?"

He turned his full gaze on her as if she were some mere annoyance he might crush with the flat of his hand. "What am I to tell them?" he wondered in a terrible whisper, which made her go pale. He stood up, looking about for his hat, and appeared glad to be going anywhere to get away from the sound of her weepiness and the sight of her faded beauty.

"Ask them . . . for ideas." She finished the last words, wretched defeat spelled in her voice and her hands, which had fallen to her sides.

"Ideas," he mimicked, almost viciously pulling the hat nearly over his ears. "And what else?" he wondered, not looking at her, putting his hand on the doorknob.

When Maude said no more, he let out a string of curses, but without much force or meaning behind them, and slammed the door with such might that the room and its furniture continued to shake for what seemed minutes afterward.

Elaine had been told of Ned's "mischief," as she called it, only a few hours before Val Dougherty pulled his hat about his ears, prepared to have it out with the Cottrells.

If anything, Elaine had carried on in a more violent fashion than Maude Dougherty when Alec, after having gone over what he was to say to his mother a hundred times before the mirror in the upper hall, had asked his mother to sit down and be as quiet as possible, and then, in barely a sentence, had spilled out the worst to her.

"You go on as if I had brought you word of his death!" Alec had finally shouted at her, for instead of speaking, Elaine had screamed and wailed like a woman atop a burning house. Then becoming almost frighteningly still and deathly pale, she blamed Alec's poor judgment in having forced Ned to be the errand-boy and companion of that "old harridan" Adele Bevington.

"She has corrupted him with her influence!" Elaine flung these final words at her mainstay.

"I thought you'd say that. I'm totally un-surprised," he jeered, and took out a fresh package of Lucky Strike cigarettes, and lit one.

Although Elaine smoked in her kitchen and bedroom, she constantly spoke against the evils of tobacco for the rest of the human race, but more precisely, she forbade the use of the weed by her sons, of whom nothing short of perfection was required. Alec took out his cigarettes for the express purpose of defying and offending her. But in Elaine's distraught stage, she probably did not even see he was smoking.

"The girl, of course, is a slut, no doubt about that." The mother consoled herself with this statement, repeated several times.

"Marilyn Dougherty has no such reputation." Alec refuted her claim and gave his mother a look of total disapproval.

She walked in a circle around her kitchen, the site of so many of her pronouncements on life and people. "Adele Bevington gets him drunk, and before that, when he is still a child, hardly shaves his upper lip as yet, he's led astray by a common biddy."

Alec could not restrain a grin and then, tickled by his mother's choice of words and general hysteria, he burst out into a loud laugh.

"This is what comes of not having a man in the house!" She took up the hallowed refrain inevitably invoked in their many arguments.

"Thank you for that compliment, mother dear," Alec retorted, and blew one cloud of tobacco smoke after another. Not finding an ashtray he took his cigarette to the kitchen sink and put it out there, for the smoke was making him a bit dizzy.

"Remember, the world is not coming to an end," Alec tried to console her, and then moved toward the kitchen door and lifted the latch.

"Where are you going off to now, after dropping a bomb like this on me without one word of warning or preparation?" Elaine roared after him.

He reminded her of his voice lesson.

Wringing her hands at this new proof of his callousness and indifference, she struggled with herself for a moment, then said brokenly: "Very well, go on then, sing your head off while I try to pick up the pieces of our life alone as usual."

Alec hesitated a moment, then walked over to his mother and kissed her quietly on her face and then on the back of her neck. He took her hand and pressed it.

"Worse things could have happened, mother."

She nodded briefly, and allowed him to go.

When a few minutes later she heard the knock at the kitchen door and opened it on Val Dougherty with his hat pulled down over his ears and his white, gleaming, almost wolflike teeth flashing at her, she did not connect the iceman with what had happened to her son at all. She was both relieved and joyful to see him, for he had delivered to her door countless cakes of ice to keep her foodstuffs sweet and fresh for her persnickety taste. A kind of peace settled over the distracted woman as she saw a face almost as familiar as that of one of her family. The pleasure of seeing him made her forget the queerness of his call. Val had always acted before her, too, as a kind of social inferior and had punctuated his speech with countless "ma'am"s, and "Mrs. Cottrell"'s, and so forth, but now Elaine brushed that all aside by offering him the best chair in the room.

Elaine's friendly welcome reassured him also, despite the warning he saw in that her face was as swollen and red from tears as his wife's, Maude.

Without even asking him if he cared for something, she handed him a cup of freshly brewed coffee, a courtesy that in times past, when he was her deliveryman, on special occasions or in bitter weather, she had also extended him.

Tasting the coffee he muttered, "Maude's brew tastes like dishwater compared to yours, I swear."

Elaine laughed nervously, but stopped herself from commenting on Maude or her ability as a cook and housewife.

"I met Alec on the way out," Val said. "He's growing into a fine young man."

"Yes, he is, Mr. Dougherty," Elaine agreed, and then at the mention of Alec, blew her nose loudly, and sat down unceremoniously in the chair directly facing him.

"You shouldn't take on so hard." Val studied her. She was so much more beautiful than Maude, he reflected. In truth, there was no comparison between the two women. The fact that he had always thought Mrs. Cottrell so "above him" socially, too, made her for him even more imposing at that moment.

"You'll have to excuse me, Mr. Dougherty. . . ."

"Say Val, please, Mrs. Cottrell, like you used to. . . ."

"All right, Val," she said. "You see, I've had terrible news this morning."

He opened his mouth wide in puzzlement.

"But isn't your bad news," he wondered, "the same?"

She looked up in wonder at him, and he saw then that she did not know their two families were under the same cloud.

"Mrs. Cottrell, I supposed you knew right away when you seen me come in the door . . ."

Elaine, coming now to the realization of the meaning of his

being there, did not know whether she was relieved or even more disturbed.

"Your boy, and my girl," he began, and watched the wave of realization come over her face.

"She's the one?" Elaine finally spoke more sternly than she wished to.

"Marilyn," he assented, "yes. . . . My foster daughter," he added with a deprecation that almost made her smile.

"Thank God, then, Val, it's you. I can say what I feel, I don't need to hold back the tears or keep in my sorrow. If it had to be anybody, I'm glad it's with you, Val, that we share this sorrow together."

She gave him a look of such appeal, he dropped the cube of sugar from his thick fingers, which looked almost black against the whiteness of the sweetener. It had been so long since he had been near so beautiful a woman, all he could do was shake his head, and then, unaccountably he put the sugar cube directly into his mouth.

"I suppose you have decided what to do, Val," Elaine went on helplessly, and watched him chew the sugar. She pushed the sugar bowl closer to his coffee cup on the little table that was between them.

He chewed on for a moment.

"We haven't made up our minds what to do," he said at last.

"Thank God for you," Elaine kept saying, in the same tone she so often employed with her boys in her refrain, "If only there was a man in this house."

Beginning to recover some of her aplomb now, Elaine folded her hands in her lap, lost probably in the meshes of the problem she would never have dreamed would come to her family.

"One thing is abundantly clear, Val," she began. "They can't expect a mere child to marry!"

"Maybe the baby will die," the iceman volunteered.

Elaine looked up at him, a kind of flash of hope in her eyes, followed by a succeeding expression of horror: "Oh, you can't say such a thing, Val. We mustn't begrudge the poor little baby its chance now, can we?"

He studied her so closely, she flushed slightly and looked out the window, which she regretfully saw needed washing.

"I'll give you my idea, Mrs. Cottrell," Val said in a booming voice. "We'll send the girl away, and that will be the end of it. Finis!" He raised his right hand upward, and then helped himself to another cube of sugar and ate it.

"But what do you mean, Val?" Elaine wondered. She was suddenly as shocked by his cool indifference as by his mysterious assurance he could solve the problem by sending the girl away.

"I mean once she's had the abortion away from town here, we can all forget about it!"

Elaine's mouth came open and closed several times before she could get out: "Abortion? You don't mean . . ." It was the first time she had completely realized the seriousness of what Ned had done. He had created another life, and here the father of the girl, or the foster father, was coolly talking about getting rid of this new life.

"But they can't marry, and they can't raise a kid." He raised his voice until the glasses and plates in the cupboard rattled slightly. "You said that yourself!"

"But an abortion, Val. I didn't say that at all. Think of the risk of it for the girl if you can't think of the life of the unborn child. Think of—"

"For the moment, then," Dougherty said, rising, his enormous hulk seeming at that moment to blot out the light from the kitchen window. She stared at his arresting presence.

She now rose also and faced him.

"As I said before, Val," she began, trying not to look into his face directly, "if it had to be anybody in a situation like this, thank God that person is you. I feel I am in good hands."

"I think you are, Mrs. Cottrell, if I do say it myself. I've knowed your sons from the time they was babies . . . and I knowed Marius, too, if you will think back."

Was there a kind of invitation in Elaine's eyes, he now wondered, or was it only her look of helplessness, which his mention of the name of her husband enforced in her. It was perhaps many things, including the sweetness of the sugar and the heady brew of her coffee, which made him take her in his arms and gently, for such a rough man, kiss her on her brow. She trembled violently at his touching her, but she did not push him away.

Nestling, though somewhat rigidly, in his arms, she managed to say, "Are you sure, Val, that my boy is . . . the one?"

Dougherty nodded between his gentle kisses. "We're as sure as sure can be," he mumbled.

Almost abruptly, however, he broke away from her. Was it his disenchantment with his own marriage, or a fear of another dependent on him, or the very strength of his feeling for her that made him back away.

Elaine, too, felt a kind of relief that he had released her then, as well as a great happiness that he had taken her in his arms and kissed her. The last of her tears and sorrow were gone under his embrace.

"You've been quite decent about it, then, you and Maude." Elaine spoke softly.

He had put on his stained terrible hat, down again almost over his ears. His strange light eyes shone at her from out his dark skin, and then the very white teeth flashed at her like a sudden illumination in the night.

"We'll keep in close call, Mrs. Cottrell."

"Why not *Elaine* now?" she wondered, as he grasped her hand and then, turning, went out the door without responding to her somewhat feverish "Goodbye."

It seemed to Val Dougherty that Ned Cottrell showed up at his icehouse office a few minutes after his warm reception by Elaine, but as he looked back on it later he realized that several days had passed between his talk with the mother and his meeting with the son.

Winter was closing in. Val always visited his horses every few hours in the bitter weather, much to his wife's distress. He would rise sometimes three or four times on a very cold night to see if the horses were warm enough in their stalls, or if they needed a blanket or some other comfort against the rigor of the climate.

When he returned that night from the stables he sat on a high three-legged stool and went over his books. His thoughts though were not on his accounts, or even on his foster daughter's pregnancy, his scolding wife, or Elaine Cottrell's kisses. His thoughts were on his wish to run away. Nova Scotia was in mind. He wanted to go far north and live off the land. He would just leave his ice business, and all the money he had earned, to those two damned females, and decamp.

It was Ned's standing in the threshold of the door that brought him back to his present situation.

"You!" Dougherty greeted the boy, as one might speak to a ghost. Then: "Come in, Ned, why don't you." He pointed to a chair which faced his three-legged stool.

The Cottrell boy, however, went on studying Dougherty. He remembered him, of course, some years back, when he had delivered the ice to their house, and he had watched Val with curious admiration as he lifted what seemed to him then like hundreds of pounds of ice and deposited it in his mother's huge icebox on the latticed back porch. Tonight Dougherty looked, as he sat over his account books, even younger and stronger than he had as a deliveryman, and one could catch a whiff of his strong sweat again, as when he had lifted the huge cakes of ice.

"My mother said I'd better see you, sir," Ned began, but still did not take the proffered seat.

"You talked with her then," Dougherty mumbled.

"Oh, yes," the boy replied with appeasing eagerness.

Dougherty laughed softly, and Ned followed suit.

"I got to say it, and then I'm through with my comments," the older man began. "You and Marilyn are two of the unlikeliest candidates for having a baby in all the wide wide world."

Ned grinned cautiously then and sat down.

"But what's done is done," Val went on. "There's never any changin' what's done. By God nor man!"

Ned stooped down to tie one of his loose shoelaces.

"Your mom keeps you nice." Dougherty studied his visitor. "You can tell you get good grub, and she sees you dress proper."

"I work, too," Ned said, looking up with flushed face. "I mean I earn quite a bit of spending money. My mother is a widow," he reminded him.

"Oh, I don't doubt you ain't lazy." Dougherty appeared more grave now. "But you don't earn enough to keep the roof over your family's head and three hot meals on the table, that's for sure."

Ned nodded weakly.

"We was surprised about Marilyn, Maude and me, because she

was never out of the house, it seemed. . . . We wondered where
. . . you met!"

Dougherty took out his pouch of chewing tobacco but before
putting some of the plug in his mouth he offered Ned a bite,
which the boy refused.

The iceman's mouth, which was a handsome one, as Elaine
could have testified, was now disfigured with the chewing tobacco, so that his lips looked as if someone had smitten him with a
fist, so stained was his mouth with the brownish-red juice from
the plug. His teeth at the same time kept ivory-white.

"We don't want to pry, though." Dougherty chewed on
thoughtfully for a while. "You two young ones met, you did what
young ones do when they're not careful, and so it's done. Like
that." He spread his great arms as if to form with them the
measurement of a fathom for his backward pupil.

Ned had put his face in his hands and had leaned over as if at
any moment he might touch the floor with his forehead.

"You do admit you done it," Val said, and as he spoke, spat
right on the sawdust on the floor.

"I'm afraid so." Ned took his hands away from his face.

"Your two stories jibe all right," Val went on. "Yours and
Marilyn's. What's more, I can see by your face you ain't the kind
to do it for cussedness. You're not one of the pool hall crowd."

Actually Ned would have preferred that Mr. Dougherty punish
him rather than speak to him so dulcetly and understandingly.
His own memory of what had happened that first night and even
later nights in the meadow near the Roller-Skate Rink was almost
entirely dim in retrospect. It certainly had not seemed entirely
real at the time, despite the delirious pleasure, and today it was
not as real as some dreams he could also barely recall. And
besides, she had done it. He had told nobody that. Marilyn had
unbuttoned him after that long stint of kisses and hugs and bites,
even pulling him down on the grass. He would not tell anybody
that. He would remember her kisses forever, though, for they
had made him drunker than when Adele Bevington administered
the Napoleon brandy to him.

"Are you all right?" Dougherty's voice came somewhat far off
to him.

"Matter of fact . . . I feel a bit queasy," Ned responded.

"You better step out and get some air," his halfhearted interrogator advised.

Ned hurried toward the door, but before he reached it, he slipped and almost fell down. He was on his way to falling down in a faint, Dougherty saw, and taking hold of the boy's head, he pushed it down toward the floor so that the blood would reach his brain. Then waiting a bit, he helped Ned outside, where he could get a lungful of "Jack Frost."

"Just breathe in and out deep," Dougherty advised his charge and he filled his own ample chest with the bitter night air, while Ned followed suit. Dougherty spat several times.

"I don't have to marry her, do I, Mr. Dougherty?" Ned wondered when they had reentered the office.

"Marry?" His host scoffed, and closed the door behind him. "I wouldn't wish marriage on my worst enemy, let alone a young fellow like you that is only earning his spending money and living under the roof of his widowed mother. Married, hell. Nobody should ever get married, if you ask me. *Married* is for steers."

Ned opened and closed his mouth several times in considerable confusion.

"I'd give my right hand to be free," the iceman went on in almost savage vehemence. He picked up a penknife and began sharpening one of his pencils. "I'll tell you something, Neddy. Marriage is the end of a man, not the beginning of him. I was twice the man before I got spliced! I tell you, it's about as drastic as if the preacher cut off your two balls at the same time as he pronounced you one flesh. No, you stay clear of marriage. I'll see to that for you. You don't *want* to get married, do you?" He threatened the boy with his white teeth and his flashing eyes.

"No," Ned replied with alacrity.

"Good," Dougherty congratulated him with ferocious loudness. "I'll see to it then you don't."

"But, sir, what about the . . . baby?"

"What baby?" Dougherty scoffed with revulsion. "There ain't been one yet. A hundred things could happen between now and then. Miscarriages, abortions, or who knows, the poor tike may come out of her stillborn."

Net Cottrell had considerable difficulty believing that what had happened in the summer meadow could be the cause of all this talk about such fearsome topics as abortions and miscarriages, and Marilyn's own wails about periods and morning sickness, which she had also treated him to in the past few days.

It seemed to him then that all he had done was kiss a girl and lie down with her in the long grasses, and here he was to be held accountable by everybody he knew—by the whole town of Fonthill, indeed—when it was all he could do to get through the day by himself.

In his desperation he did a thing that surprised both himself and Val Dougherty. Without permission he seized the plug of chewing tobacco from out the iceman's rugged grasp, and putting some of the plug in his mouth, said: "I think if you don't mind I'll try a bite of your tobacco after all."

Dougherty stared at him for quite a spell and then let a wide grin spread over his dark features.

"I'll let you in on a secret of my own," Val told the boy. "I think I'd have gone over the hill long years ago if I didn't have my chaw. It's better than whiskey or corn liquor and they ain't made it illegal yet neither, by Christ, those damned preachers and pikers makin' our laws. . . ."

"Isn't that the damned man for you!" Elaine had cried on hearing from Ned concerning the content or lack of content of his talk with Val Dougherty.

"He couldn't care less what happens to his own daughter! And I wonder, come to think of it, how many bastards he has sired in all the neighboring towns and counties!"

"Marilyn is not his own daughter," Ned said soberly, a bit surprised, too, at his mother saying "damned" and "bastard," words she forbade him and Alec. He finally sat down in the cretonne-covered overstuffed chair. They were in the kitchen, where all the great confabs, arguments, and decisions usually took place. Elaine was cutting up a dozen or so vegetables for one of her thick, hearty winter soups.

Every so often, brandishing the little sharp knife, she would look over at Ned and exclaim something, and shake her head. "I can't believe this has happened to you," she moaned. "It seems only yesterday I was holding you on my lap. Now, thanks to that horse breeder and his family, see where they've put you. Oh, Neddy, Neddy. I think my heart will break."

Ned stuck out his chin in a manner somewhat reminiscent of Val Dougherty, and pulled tenaciously at his left shoe.

"Your brother feels disgraced, too. People are talking about it all over town, you can be sure. I hope Adele Bevington is pleased with what has happened to this family!"

"Adele?" Ned wondered. "What has she got to do with it, will you tell me?"

"Probably everything," Elaine almost shouted. She began almost stabbing the bunch of parsnips to fine bits. "After all, she followed the same path a generation ago. . . . Yes, she must have been as loose as Jezebel in her day! She's no fit influence for you, Neddy, and I wish you'd quit going there."

"But it was you and Alec told me I could work for her," the boy responded with some heat and indignation. "You told me yourself she would add to my 'general culture.' " He quoted what he thought had been Elaine's exact words some time ago. "You don't think I thought up going to her old mansion on my own, do you?"

"Mansion, my eye!" Elaine scoffed. "It's falling to pieces like she is. . . . Getting you to drink at your age! What will she think of next? Why, for years people crossed over to the other side of the street when they saw her coming. She was notorious. I'm sure she was Dr. Radwell's . . . concubine."

The last word hung in the air for a moment like a cloud of black smoke. "But what riles me most is Val Dougherty's attitude." Elaine surged back to the topic of the iceman.

She had advanced to within a few inches of her son, still carrying upraised the vegetable knife in her right hand. "You actually mean to sit there and tell me he had no ideas at all as to what should be done in a case like this? No *suggestion* even?"

"He told me," he said, looking at his mother with considerable misgiving, "he swore, in fact, he would like to pull up stakes himself and go to Nova Scotia and hunt caribou and grizzly bears."

"Where have I heard that before!" she said bitterly and returned to paring some huge potatoes. "And why doesn't he go to the North Pole! You mean to tell me he didn't even scold you, didn't set you straight on what you have done?"

"But I haven't committed a crime, Mother, have I?" Waiting for her to cool down a bit, Ned added, "Val Dougherty, I think, thought it was amusing."

"Amusing! Amusing to bring a poor child into the world without a name or a father!"

"But you said I was the father!"

Hearing this statement brought her again to deep sobs and tears.

"If Marius Cottrell hadn't been more interested in guns and hunting than in his own flesh and blood, none of this would ever have happened. And you say Val Dougherty is thinking of going to the Far North also! Yes, if your father had done as he should have done, we would not be having this conversation right now. He would have kept you two boys in line, and there would have been no midnight rendezvous with that little slut of a Marilyn Dougherty. Ned, you have taken twenty years off my life, I can tell you. I will never get over this. And he had *nothing* at all in the way of advice or proposals? What a brute he is, after all. But what can you expect, he was just an iceman for years, with his horse and truck. Then he got a little money from some relative of his wife who had died and he bought the whole icehouse and quarry to boot, and they threw in the horse stable. I think he makes moonshine liquor on the side. Of course he wouldn't care what happens to a decent family! He acted pretty fresh, too, when he was here the other day, I can tell you."

Elaine stopped now, however, for she did not want to compromise her own moral elevation in the eyes of her boy.

"I'll be blamed for your fall, Ned, until the end of my days, I suppose," she went on in a less vociferous tone, blamed if I do, blamed if I don't. They'll say, I know, that I was a bad example. Oh, I can hear them now!"

His mother, nonetheless, was gradually winding down. Actually she was relieved that Dougherty was not going to take any action against her and her boy. And Ned's having revealed that the iceman had mentioned miscarriages and abortions, although this horrified her, also, in some way even she could not understand, calmed her.

"I feel I have lost you, Neddy," she said when she had finally put the soup on to simmer. "I feel you are no longer mine." She wiped her hands on her apron again and again.

"Well, why do you want to say a thing like that for?" Ned wondered, and rose from the big chair. He stood facing the outside door.

"Now don't get up and run out on me like your older brother always does when I am trying to tell you something."

"I have to go and work at the candy kitchen tonight," he reminded her.

"Yes, I suppose you do. . . . I'll get you some early supper then. But Neddy, don't you understand what I mean? I feel I've lost you."

She went over to him and took him in her arms, and succumbed to a fresh outburst of tears.

"No, you haven't, Mom," he said. "You ain't lost me," and he sobbed a little himself, probably more from confusion than anything else. "Ain't I here with you? I'm not leaving, am I, Mom?"

"Let's hope not," she whispered, and held him to her more tightly than before.

"To think my dearest and youngest son. . . ." she began, but then could not get the remaining words out.

"I don't exactly know how it did happen," he said lamely, as she began to prepare him a cold roast beef sandwich.

"I'll never blame you again, Neddy." She spoke with a faraway look now in her eyes. "But I do blame the Doughertys, especially that great hulk of a Val."

Ned studied his mother's features. She was a very pretty woman, even in a housedress scrubbing the kitchen floor. But she did look a fright when she bawled, and she bawled rather frequently.

"He's nothing but a baby still himself," Elaine said to herself aloud after Ned had eaten his early supper and gone off to his work at the candy kitchen.

Adele had not cut herself off completely from any social life since her retirement as a newspaper writer. She attended rather regularly the sessions of the fastidious if suffocating literary club of the town known as the Altrusa. In fact the club often met at her house, always on Thursday evenings. The Altrusa usually invited a well-known writer or sometimes a United States senator or congressman to address the members on some topic of significance. But since these great authorities and public figures were not always able to find their way to the backwater of Fonthill, Judge Hitchmough, now retired from the bench, was frequently invited to address the women—much against Adele's wishes, for the judge was old enough to remember "as if it were yesterday" her "secret" and her years of obloquy. Before her "fall" indeed he had been a constant caller at her father's house. It was perhaps because he had never condemned her, but pretended to admire her, that she disliked Judge Hitchmough so thoroughly. And always, at the beginning and again at the end of the evening, he would press Adele's hand and hold it for what seemed an endless time in his ice-cold grasp. And often during one of his lengthy talks to the Altrusas he would turn his moist brown eyes upon her and smile, as much as so say, "You and I, my dear, know what life is all about."

The only person whom Adele felt close to at these absurd sessions was Melissa Deedes, who taught English at the local junior high school and was at the present time Ned's teacher. Adele had never been certain whether Melissa was aware of her own disgrace of so many years ago. Melissa was after all only twenty-five, and even the Great War was a bit cloudy to her, let alone Adele's fall.

"I can't bear Judge Hitchmough," Adele confided to Melissa one evening when she had insisted the teacher remain after all the other Altrusa members had departed.

Melissa smiled nervously and looked away, for the judge was a trusted adviser to her father, and a former member of the school board.

"Melissa, may I suggest something to take our minds off that cumbersome session." Adele changed the subject when she saw Melissa's reluctance to hear her on the subject of Hitchmough. (Adele had lectured Melissa on the old man countless times.)

The schoolteacher nodded, for she knew what Adele meant.

"A drop of something as a reward for our boredom?"

While Adele went to her special cupboard, which contained the greater part of her "cellar," she tried to admonish herself not to say too much in front of the youthful teacher. Melissa still lived at home with her parents and her two brothers, and these visits to Adele were almost her only escape from strict family surveillance. Melissa often complained about the tyrannical supervision exercised over her, especially by her older brother, Jasper. Melissa was still rather a handsome woman, so people described her, though a bit too stout, and her having earned a Ph.D. in English letters had scared away, finally, the last of her young suitors. She was firm about not allowing anyone to call her Doctor, but her advanced degree and her family's strict watch over her had caused her to feel—and to dread—the prospect of soon becoming an old maid.

Adele handed Melissa the snifter of French brandy.

She had drunk her second glass when she said, as if alone now: "I feel I will scream when Judge Hitchmough touches me."

Melissa did not seem to hear her friend, so absorbed was she in the pleasure of inhaling the warm aroma of the grapes, which rose to her from the glass.

"I have never seen such a bestial look on a man's face at times," the older woman was going on. "He makes advances to me . . . because he knows my secret. . . ."

A painful silence ensued. Adele realized that so far as she knew, Melissa had never been told about her past, and knowing how strictly Melissa's family kept her from any direct contact with life, she supposed the young woman was entirely in the dark about Adele's "secret."

"What I wanted to talk to you about, however," Adele went on in a kind of fluster, "is the news about Ned. You have learned about it?"

"Yes," the schoolteacher replied, like a witness in court. "I have."

Perhaps Ned's disaster moved her so much not because she was appalled by his action but because, like Alec Cottrell, she felt Ned's giving a young girl a baby made her own virgin state still more oppressive and burdensome to her.

"I thought"—Adele watched Melissa—"that perhaps you could do something for Ned."

"I?" Melissa wondered. She smiled strangely, then twisted her lips down.

"Oh, I realize there is perhaps very little *we* can do. I have talked with him, of course."

Melissa had emptied her glass, but she indicated by shaking her head she would not take another, not immediately, at any rate.

"I don't know what I'd have done without those two Cottrell boys." Adele now gave out this refrain, which often came from her lips when she was alone.

"It's fortunate at least, Adele," Melissa opined, "that it is summer, and school is not in session. Talk and insinuations may have died down by fall."

"Talk and insinuations, my dear, never die in Fonthill."

When Melissa said no more, Adele, prompted by her drink, almost called out: "I was wondering, Melissa, if you might not be able to talk with Ned. . . . I understand he does not know where to turn." Adele paused as she heard herself make this statement. For one thing, she realized, she knew nothing of the kind. She supposed, actually, Ned had *everywhere* to turn. And she did not understand why she wanted Melissa, virginal Melissa, to speak with Ned about such a delicate matter.

"Please forgive me, my dear." Adele spoke up when she saw the flush of embarrassment spread over the schoolteacher's features. "I know how closely your family protects you, especially Jasper."

In her extreme discomfiture at this turn in the conversation Melissa, almost without realizing it, extended her empty glass. The older woman lost no time in refilling it. They allow her to drink, provided she never sees a man her own age, Adele reflected bitterly.

"I want you to listen to something," Adele said. Something told her she should stop now, should not pursue the drift the conversation had taken, should find refuge again in palaver about books and movies and the coming speakers for the Altrusa members.

A kind of rapt but fearful look came over Melissa's face.

"Ned's bad news," she began, "has taken me back thirty years. . . ." Adele's right hand trembled so violently at that moment, that she put down her glass. As she did so, Melissa caught sight of a diamond brooch under her lace collar.

"Thirty years," Melissa prompted her friend.

"The gulf between you and me, my dear," Adele went on, "is you are so protected, and what is worse, so pure. I will not say more."

"But you act as if it were my fault, I am . . . what I am."

"I mean nothing of the kind."

"I am doing all I can do," Melissa said bitterly.

"Until I met the Cottrell brothers," Adele went on like someone who is reading aloud a play script and has decided, for a reason not clear even to herself, to skip several paragraphs, "I was beginning to forget the kind of woman I was."

"Adele!" Melissa spoke so softly perhaps her friend did not hear her.

"I have been living my life all over again, don't you see. All due to Ned's disgrace. His predicament has made me live *my* predicament all over again."

"You have always treated me as if I did not know what you have been through," the younger woman was able to say. "You should have trusted me more."

"But you seemed so surrounded by brothers, father, mother, that house you live in. . . . I was once housed, jailed, kept under lock and key just as you are! You see, it is all coming out." Her voice broke and a kind of thick, heavy salt tear fell from one eye, a tear as hard and unrefreshing as a hot cinder.

"Why should Ned's case open my whole life up to me again? I have not slept for nights! I have been brought awake again."

It was Melissa who was weeping now, as if she were required to do so for her friend.

Adele knew in her innermost consciousness that Melissa was perfectly aware of her history. That was, however, the game Adele constantly had to play with herself. She expected people both to know of her long-ago disgrace and not to know of it. Since the disgrace had become an integral part of herself, she could not be recognized unless people knew of it, and yet her whole life, until perhaps Ned's fall, had been lived as if there had been no fall of her own, no baby, no exile, no humiliation, no "ruin" of her father's house and reputation.

"It was only when I was pregnant, and later when the nurse presented my boy to me, that I was alive. . . ." The whole story was coming out now, the first time she had told it complete to anybody, the first time, too, that a woman as virginal now as Adele had been was hearing it told.

"Then when they took him from me, when, through my cowardice and obedience to my father, I let them take my baby away from me, I died. . . . I have been dead ever since. Ned's disgrace has brought me to life again."

Adele scarcely noticed that Melissa was helping herself to more brandy.

"I remember," she went on, watching her guest drink, "when they had taken him away, how my breasts flowed so painfully with milk, and then—this is so important—they flowed also with blood. . . ."

Melissa sighed and attempted to say something in return, but a kind of hurricane of words was coming out of the woman, who would not give up the memory of her sin or her loss.

All that had kept her among the living, she confided to the schoolteacher, was the hope that one day she would meet her son. Her standing at the high arched window that overlooked the main street of the town was, without her always being aware of it, part of her "watch" and vigil. Her presence had gradually become noted by the passersby, especially the young men and women who attended the movies at the Royal. So she had put up for a while, as a consequence of her being "spied upon," a great white silk curtain, from behind which, like an opera singer waiting for her cue, she could survey the stream of the young below, unobserved. But finally she had pulled back the curtain and kept up her "watch" in full view.

In the late afternoon, Adele told Melissa, she sometimes slipped downstairs and went into the Royal itself, walked down its dark aisles, and seated herself in the section that was surrounded with dark velvet curtains, reserved for "special patrons." A young man with the down just beginning to appear on his cheeks usually led her to her special seat. Here, despite her rather deep reading of the great French novelists, she partook of the melodramas and romances of the silver screen, as engrossed as the manicurists and the salesgirls at Woolworths who sat a few rows away from her. And always with the feeling that perhaps her boy might be—who knows?—among the spectators who sat in darkness.

I had to give my child away!

The long rhapsody was over. She did not even want to taste more of her brandy. She was totally exhausted from her own narrative, given at last in full, before this untried, untouched virgin. But the strange realization was now coming to her full force that Melissa, like everybody else in Fonthill, had already known it all. Adele, alone among all the inhabitants of the town, felt the secret she carried was her own, when the very paving stones she walked on knew it.

"You will talk to Ned, then?" Adele said as the two women were parting, and Melissa kissed her on the mouth.

Then as she was already holding the teacher to her breast, she said: "And everybody knows what happened to me, Melissa?"

"It is not talked of, my dear. Believe me . . . it is almost never mentioned."

"Almost never." Adele smiled.

Sitting later by the dark aisle of the Royal or sipping her "medicine" Adele would repeat Melissa's words: *It is not talked of . . . It is almost never mentioned.*

"But it is known," Adele would say aloud, in the theater or at home. "It is known."

That night, after Melissa's visit, Adele had a very severe nightmare that left her prostrate for the rest of the night's slumber and for most of the day that followed. In her dream Mayor Grosvenor had come to pay her a call. He was a short, squat man with a huge mop of white, dead-looking hair and tiny almost purple eyes that never looked at the person he was speaking to. He had been mayor of Fonthill for so many years that people had the impression his office had been conferred upon him for life, or was perhaps hereditary. It was a hot summer day in the dream and the mayor entered her room hat in hand, fanning himself vigorously and all the while looking about the premises as if seeking somebody or something. He reminded her in a hollow voice of a proceeding at which he had officiated, when Dr. Farquar of the library board had presented his charges against her for having withheld information from the library board that she was the unwed mother of a boy, and also for giving forbidden books to minors and unmarried women of susceptible temperament.

Mayor Grosvenor then presented her with a legal paper, perhaps a subpoena. He was serving her this paper, however, he said, as a warning, not as a writ of arrest. Adele's father, he pointed out, had been one of his closest associates, and without the elder Bevington, he would never had secured his present office.

"Yes," Adele had shouted in her sleep, "had my father been living when the library board met to hear Dr. Farquar's charges against me, I would never have lost my post as librarian. I would never have been summoned to hear such charges!"

"Granted." The mayor had smiled and placed his hat over his chest, and then turned it with the hollow side up like an inept magician who cannot produce the most elementary feat of magic.

"But the charge this time, my dear Adele, is more serious. It is a federal case, I am afraid. Not only have you served liquor illegally, you have served it to minors and virgins, who have no protection against your influence. And there is more!" he now warned her by lifting his right hand upward as if somewhere in her many rooms he saw in all its awesome splendor the unfurled Stars and Stripes. "Not content with plying young boys with liquor you took them to your bed. Old as you are, Adele, for you are not young."

Adele wakened on the words "not young."

So real was the dream to her that she looked down at her hands to see if they bore handcuffs.

She rose, slipped on her satin carpet slippers, and turned all the lights on in her sitting room. There stood the illegal brandy bottle which, though marked "Medicine," defied the federal law and probably the flag itself. Infuriated against Mayor Grosvenor as if he had actually been there to arrest her as an enemy of the Constitution of the United States, she poured herself at once an ounce of the illicit distillation of the grapes. It was of a sweetness not far short of the far-off night when she had pressed her mouth against George Etheredge's naked breast.

Walking up and down, entering one room after another, she wondered aloud why after all these years had she not outlived her shame and her anger against her principal accuser, the Reverend Farquar, long interred in Poplar Grove Cemetery. Why did she still think everybody smiled and smirked when she walked down the main street when all they saw was a forgotten old woman. Even virginal, untouched Melissa had not taken the story of her shame very seriously. It was ancient history, and she would not be far short of ancient, should she survive a few more weary years. A very old woman who nonetheless took sin seriously in an age when sin was no longer real, who went to motion pictures incessantly, and who had young men in to ply them with booze against the laws of the land. But no one, not even Mayor Grosvenor in real life, or the dead Reverend Farquar, if he returned from the grave, could have foreseen she would go into the bedroom with the young men from the Royal. For even with all her diamonds on, she would not tempt the most desperate day laborer! *Or would she?*

She stopped before the hall mirror. Her white hair in this light looked like the dazzling blond color then in fashion, shimmering, and deceiving the eye. She had almost no wrinkles. All at once she hurried to the drawer of her dresser and drew out one of the longer diamond necklaces. Yes, she thought, there was beauty when she put on the gems. Strange, inexplicable, and even unearthly at this hushed hour of the twenty-four—certainly not daytime beauty. And was she waiting with her diamonds and her beauty only for her son, who had never come, despite all her pleas to every power that ruled the universe? Was he, after all, the only person she was living for? And how could her son find her even if he wished to, when every thread binding her to him had been snapped? She put on another necklace, a bracelet, and, trembling, some earrings. Yes, only these precious stones understood her and her loss, testified to her pain and her constant death-in-life. There had been times when she felt she would grind them to powder so that she could be free to forget who she was and so die. But now, in the awe-inspiring hush of this hour, she kissed the stones. They had not forgotten who she was and the price she had paid. They told her to be hopeful, to wait, to be beautiful.

A day or so later, still meditating bitterly on her dream, she heard the persistent knock on the back door. In her still unclear mind the knocking appeared at first to be some fanciful echo of her nightmare. Then she heard the words, from a familiar voice: "Are you at home, Ma'am?"

Adele had been dumbfounded on opening the door to a strapping Val Dougherty. Years ago, as he had been to Elaine Cottrell, he had been her ice man, and had always taken time off from his route to repair something broken or leaking or malfunctioning about her house. But she had not seen him for some years.

Adele had never been completely easy with Val, despite his faithfulness and dependability while he had been her deliveryman. At the same time, though, she had blurted out to him things she would never have dared utter in the presence of anybody else.

Today he was unshaven and there was a strong smell of liquor on his breath, but she asked him in. He proceeded to sit down without being invited.

She was still too unnerved by her imaginary interview with Mayor Grosvenor to think his visit strange.

"It's nervy of me to come in like this unannounced, Miss Bevington," he began. "If you want me to go, I will. Understand?"

"You'll do no such thing, Val." She surveyed her caller. "You wouldn't have come if it wasn't important. I know you."

He smiled. Val Dougherty's smiles were more terrible than his customary dour and frowning expressions. His smiles gave the impression his entire face would crack and fall off.

"Can't we go though into the kitchen proper, ma'am? . . . This little anteroom, as you call it, is so formal. And I remember the kitchen."

Adele Bevington laughed. "We can go anywhere you like, Val."

She led the way to the kitchen, almost as ample as her front sitting room.

"Yes, this is where I used to deliver you your ice," he commented in a voice almost out of earshot, once they had settled down in their chairs, facing one another.

"You speak as if it was ages ago," Adele scoffed.

"This room," he began looking about, "is big enough to have a banquet in! It all comes back to me again," he went on. His eyes fell on a piece of apple cake which she had purchased from the Kleitzer Bakery. He stared at it until she said: "Go ahead, Val, and have a taste of it."

He took it immediately in his hands and tore off a piece with his teeth. His loud chewing both amused and comforted her.

"There's coffee, too, on the stove over there." She pointed to a steaming graniteware pot. Without waiting to be urged, he went to the stove, poured some coffee into a cup from which she had drunk only a few minutes earlier, and swallowed loudly. Then he helped himself to more of the apple cake and wiped his mouth with the back of his hand.

"If you ever need me for anything"—he spoke softly now, cocking his head as if he was listening at the same time to the sounds of his own digestive system—"no matter what the hour or the occasion, Miss Bevington, call me. . . . I've felt kind of hurt you never did want me for anything after I quit the ice route."

"But for heaven's sake, Val Dougherty," Adele began, drawing around her a shawl she had put on against the coolness of the kitchen, "you've gotten to be a big, successful businessman these last few years. How could I call you up for a leaking faucet or broken pipe when you're making money hand over fist?"

He whistled. "That might have been so two or three years ago," he mused. "Not now. . . . I'm near to being busted like the rest of the country."

He hurriedly told her then of all that had gone wrong, of the extravagance of his assistants, but she understood at the way he brushed off this hard-luck story that his ruin was not the subject of his visit.

"So I may be fetching you your ice again, you see." Val summarized the chronicle of his change of fortune.

"But something must be saved of your enterprise, Val?" she commented, and rose to close the window, which had been open a crack, letting in a steady current of cold air.

He nodded gently, the disfiguring smile playing over his lips. "Yes, the quarry itself. I can jump in it and know it's still mine if the worst comes to the worst." He let out a guffaw so strong some of the dishes rattled in her china closet.

"But I come with a different tale to tell, ma'am." His eyes beseeched her for complete attention.

"Adele . . . can I call you Adele, at least for what I'm going to say?"

She nodded her assent.

"Adele, then . . . my wife's daughter, for I have no kids of my own. Marilyn." He gulped, and shook his head, drank more of the coffee, gulped again, and was helping himself to the sugar when he heard her voice: "Val, I already know!"

"She's in the family way, Goddamn it," he informed her anyhow.

He looked at her, disappointed that she knew. "News travels fast, don't it."

"It does in Fonthill," she agreed.

He nodded, watching her closely still. "I had forgot," he said. "You're close to the Cottrell boys."

"They're like my adopted sons, Val."

"Now here I thought *I* was your adopted son," he cried. She was grateful for his joking at that moment, and he was getting to be more like the old Val she had known, despite the grimness at the seat of his nature.

"Ned came to me, you see . . ."

"Ned Cottrell," he mused aloud, as if he found the boy a poor substitute for himself so far as Adele Bevington was concerned.

"I should never have got married," he went on in a loud voice. "I should have stayed what I was, an iceman. . . . Then I'd not be in the fix I'm in now."

"Val," she began when she saw he had fallen into a reverie almost as deep as those she was familiar with, "I want you to let me help you!"

"No," he almost screamed. "I didn't come here for help, and I won't take it."

"But you came for something, Val. You didn't come for . . . breakfast . . . surely."

"No." He grinned. "I expect not. Forgive me for what I'm going to say . . . Adele. You can order me out of the house after I say it if you want to. Forgive me now in advance. But I know, you see, once you were there, too . . . where Ned and my daughter are. I've pretended to my wife and to him, the little simp Ned, it don't afflict me . . . but matter of fact, I can't sleep over it. Adele, I know what you went through so long ago. You're brave . . . and tough. Don't order me out for speaking to you like this. I come here because I knowed you had been through it."

He was alarmed by the expression on her face. He did not know what the expression meant. She rolled her eyes, until sometimes they were all whites only looking at him. He took her hands in his. He had said the unspeakable, that was all, and she was not angry. She was moved but not mad, and she would not order him from the premises. But he knew her secret.

"Go on, Val," she encouraged him. "You're pale as a sheet. . . ."

"My mother once told me I was too dark-complexioned to look pale or to . . . blush."

"There is no color in your face now certainly, Val. . . ." Then: "Don't hold my hand so hard, if you please."

"I didn't even know I was grasping it." He smiled, looking down at their two hands. He let go of only some of the pressure, and kept her hands imprisoned in his.

"I never thought you knew about me," she confided.

"Oh well." He grinned. "I loved you for it. . . . I knew back then you knew everything, but you see I wouldn't let myself speak. I thought you would order me out of the house. You were pretty grand. Now I'm too wrought up to care. . . . I mean if you order me out now, it's all right. . . . but I had to tell you. You went through it then. Help me now . . . help us."

"But my fall was years ago." She spoke now as she often did when alone. "Years and years ago."

"Help me with my wife's daughter, if you will . . . or help with your boy, Cottrell."

He waited, brushed his mouth with his great right hand, and sped on: "Oh, it's not the money so much, though we don't have no money now. I didn't come here, Miss Bevington, for money . . . but where to go . . . if there is a doctor maybe . . . what to do. . . . Don't you understand? . . . You see at first it didn't dawn on me, what was in store. Then it thundered and lightened and blinded me. What to do, and with what?"

She wanted now to be angry. She wanted to tell him he could leave, that he was mistaken, that she had never been "there," that he had listened to gossip. But she brushed aside all her old attitudes and pretense. She was glad, glad another person beyond Melissa knew what she was, someone strong and manly and proud knew her, knew it.

"That was so long ago, Val Dougherty. . . . I barely remember the place. They took my baby away from me."

"Yes," he urged her.

"The agreement with the man . . . who got me in trouble . . . George Etheredge . . . Well, after all, I was barely seventeen. Hardly older than your daughter. But I let them take the baby away from me . . . that is the mistake I can't get over."

"But where is he?"

"You tell me!" Her voice rose in anguish and astonished him.

"Why, he would be a man by now," he muttered, his astonishment, if anything, growing.

"Oh, certainly." She had pulled her hands away from his, but he took them again in his rough grasp. The very impetuousness of his action made her accept it.

"You lost him forever?"

She nodded. "You see what poor help I am to you, Val. . . ."

"No, this talk had to take place. . . . You don't know how much it had to."

"But money, Val . . . I'll give you money . . . I'll give you a lot."

"Oh, money." He let go of her hands and flung his own two open hands outward as if to throw all the money ever printed to the winds.

Then all at once he was smoothing her hair, and she was falling gently against his chest, which rose and fell tumultuously as if he had again, as in old times, lifted the massive cakes of ice up to his shoulders.

She broke away from his embrace and signaled for him to follow her into the main body of the house.

She sat down at her desk and began to write something.

"Oh, no," he warned her. "I won't take any."

"Oh, but you will." She looked up, holding the check toward him.

"I didn't come for the money," he went on.

"Don't you know I know that?" She waved the check in the air.

"I can't be beholden," he whined.

"Well, after all," she told him, coming closer to put the check in his shirt pocket, "it's not for you, is it? It's for them, your daughter and, as you call him, the Cottrell boy. . . ."

"I suppose." He touched his pocket that contained the check. "I didn't come here for money." He repeated his statement like an oath.

His lips moved spasmodically; then he managed to say: "What if in return, Adele Bevington, I was to find this son of yours for you?" He spoke sleepily, with a queer grin on his face.

"If anybody could have found him," she began, after a long pause during which she watched him as if to memorize every particular of his face and figure, "it would have been me. I've sent a score of persons to search for him. . . . No stone has been left unturned. . . ."

"But someone must know—somewhere."

"Oh, Val, that was over thirty years ago. A whole age has passed, another come . . ."

"But what if I was to look . . . and find him?"

Without warning he took her in his arms. He put his mouth to hers. She had not been kissed so since that night, now also an age past, when she had fallen, as from a great height, a fall deliberately taken, nonetheless. After all, she thought, she was old enough to have given birth to this man who now pressed her to him in such mindless abandon. She almost felt at first he meant to wound her with his teeth. Yet his kisses were certainly not his thanks. She felt he had a desperate need at that moment to possess her, that he could not leave her until he had, could not, indeed, take her money, until they had had this union. He carried her into her bedroom, where only she and her diamonds ever kept count of the long hours of the night. Then she felt the full weight of his desperateness, his need for some immediate human closeness, while she experienced, along with the vehemence and wild pleasure, the sense that lightning had struck her in a deep forest, that she was buried under countless trees, branches, leaves, from which she would never rise.

The next day she could not remember much of it, except for the actual wounds he had left on her body. And where he had not cut her flesh with his kisses, she felt undetectable cuts far below the surface of the skin. It was more unreal than the photoplays at the Royal, but the cuts and abrasions from his mouth were real. She must have dreamed it, she kept saying. Her iceman had brought her fire.

But one thing out of all the hours in one another's arms kept coming back to her, more clear than the ferocity of his embraces, his last statement to her before he went out the door: "If he's alive I'll find him for you."

She felt some new kind of life stir within her as she had so long ago when George Etheredge had undressed her with a deliberate if equally delirious ardor in the fashionable Chicago hotel.

Valentine Dougherty's visit had destroyed a certain idea that she had had about herself. For years now she had thought that everybody knew and dwelt on her sin, that wherever she went people immediately raised in their own mind images of her nights with George Etheredge, and of her illegitimate son. But, as she had tried to point out to Dougherty, a whole generation had come and gone since then, since the days when, in the words of the popular song of the era, *My sin was loving you.*

The sin she had been punished for at the beginning of the century was today something to yawn over, yet her sin was the only thing real to her. Despite all her frenetic activity since then, her accomplishments and victories, only her fall and her lost boy had any reality for her. The rest was numbing boredom and sleep.

As Adele's idea of what other people thought of her was being destroyed by Dougherty, her own idea of herself was also being altered. Dougherty had taken a great deal of the very substance of her life away by his unexpected appearance, and his still more improbably passionate caresses and final embrace. She had been, if anything, raped, but it was a rape she had accepted as not to be resisted—foreordained and unavoidable. She had *sinned* then with Dougherty—she fell back on the meaningless concept—at a time when there was no sin and at an age it would be unlikely indeed she would again conceive to bring forth a child in shame and disgrace.

But if he had destroyed so much of herself and her past by his words and action, Dougherty had also given her a fearful and perhaps after all unwanted hope. He had told her he would find her son. He had destroyed the reality of her sin by his passion and he had promised, so to speak, to raise the dead. It was as though through her intimacy with Dougherty she was about to give birth again to her long-vanished boy.

She admonished Dougherty he would never find any trace of her son if the most expensive detectives and police agents had not been able to. He had replied, "Of course they didn't find him. . . . They didn't know where to look."

She had fallen under his influence. After the chaste if intense and incestuous love she had felt for both the Cottrell boys, Dougherty's famished, almost degrading outpouring had all but done away with the "old Adele." She spent, as a result, more and more of her time in the late afternoon in her special reserved seat at the Royal. The melodramas, which had seemed ridiculous and exaggerated lies about love, now sped past as the very essence of truth. She wept and laughed. Dougherty had both killed what she was and restored her to another life. She felt both revitalized and annihilated. She also knew that he would never return again to bestow love on her.

A strange and incomprehensible dread now took possession of her. She feared that Dougherty would find her son! She, who had lived so long in the reverie of finding him in some sun-drenched kingdom beyond the present, now trembled at the possibility of his being restored to her by the coarse brute who once delivered ice. She shrank with terror from the prospect of meeting her own flesh and blood.

And along with Dougherty's last whispered words to her—*I'll find him for you*—came the strains of music from her Victrola: *My sin was loving you.*

Shortly after her intimacy with Dougherty, unsigned letters were thrust under Adele's door. They were contained in large thick envelopes, and both the envelopes and the paper on which the letters were penned had been burned by matches or candles to give them, one supposed, the look of antiquity. The letters told of Adele's being a votary of vice, and of operating a house of "malodorous fame" in which she was both the madam and the principal whore. The writer claimed that Adele came to the door so slowly (a fact attested to by all her friends) owing to her having to extricate herself from the naked embraces of one of her many customers (whereas she came to the door slowly owing to frequent onsets of rheumatism).

She was struck dumb by reading the first of these epistles, but her stupefaction began to diminish on second reading, and by her third and fourth perusal of its contents she began to experience a kind of exaltation rather than her first seizure of panic and terror, although pain and terror remained also. But the letter, perhaps even more than her sexual abandon with the iceman, was filling her with a new and abundant vitality and a sense of well-being she had not known since her early youth. The anonymous letter completed her rebirth, begun by Dougherty's clumsy, animal, and all-too-welcome ravishment of the "old" Adele. So she was a whore! She read and reread this section of the letter. She kept a bawdy house for young boys. She was damned at last forever. And her happiness knew no bounds. The peculiar letter somehow at one strike freed her from all the years of cringing and hiding, worry and bewailing. The letter even made her forget her son, at least temporarily. She had no son because she was a whore. Whores have no sons. So the letter said, and so she now believed.

At first she thought a woman had written it, and she went over in her mind several suspects. But it was too crazy for a woman. Only a boy could have written it. A boy who had read too many of the books she had given him. She held the letter to her face and caressed it. Only a boy, and only one boy. Ned, she was positive, had penned the letters, but to be sure she would have to see Alec and Melissa. They would be certain, especially Alec. It would be a pretext also for calling him back to her.

But before laying her case before anybody, she must enjoy her triumph as a bad woman and a "votress of vice." When night came after the fourth or fifth letter had arrived, she lit only her candles for illumination, and putting aside all of her clothing except a thin shift, she adorned herself with all the diamonds that had been sent to her over the years—sent as anonymously, she reflected, as these inspired letters. Looking in the tall pier mirror, she saw reflected there now not an old woman of fifty, but a woman of incalculable age, resplendent with precious stones, the precious stones of her Chicago sin. Her son now seemed far away, never to have been born. She barely thought of him before the spectacle of her new-found youth and beauty and her iniquity celebrated by an unknown writer's hand. Why, she reflected, had she not gloried in her fall from the beginning? Why had she not taken her son and become then and there a woman of pleasure, and so kept both of them in plenitude and ease—as the words of the letter described her as doing now, and praised her for so doing!

So she was a whore, if so late. She would not dare tell Melissa that, would she? She was certain Melissa knew no more about life than what she had culled from books, or overheard from conversations. But Melissa's imagination was sinful even if her body was that of a virgin. Reverend Lilley would have understood that perfectly well! She then thanked God for Melissa in any case. And thanked all the gods of all the world's pantheons for these letters. And if Ned had written them—who else could have, with their childish belief in the beauty of vice, in the glory of fleshly expressions?—she thanked every god who had ever breathed for Ned. She could hardly wait until the next meeting of the Altrusa Club to show the letters to the teacher of English. Meanwhile she could glory in her wickedness and her newly realized abandon.

Under the pretext that he would do work "around the house," Dougherty became almost a regular visitor now to Adele's—much as he had when hardly more than a boy himself, he had fetched ice for her. But those far-off visits when he had been just beginning, had lasted at the most only three or four minutes. Today he stayed with her for hours, sometimes all day and into the night. Adele wondered what his wife must think when he was gone from home so long.

"Maude is glad when I'm away and out," he told her. "Besides, she's getting ready to take our brat away soon so she can have her baby, you know."

One evening Dougherty arrived half-drunk, with a strange, mournful, and yet cunning look on his face.

"What do you have up your sleeve this time," she wondered. She was engaged in a bit of crocheting, though actually she seldom finished the pieces she worked on. Tonight it was an elaborate doily destined for her kitchen table. She was determined to finish this one.

"I have been thinking about your big secret," Dougherty began.

Adele's hand stopped crocheting for a moment. She looked over at the desk, where the "anonymous letters" were left lying.

"Did you hear me?"

"Of course I heard you," Adele replied, still looking at the letters. "You have a voice that reaches to the fairgrounds."

"Adele, he has to be one of the boys in the Soldiers' Home."

Both her hands fell to her lap and the crochet hook dropped to the floor. He stooped down and picked it up.

"Do you remember our talk?" He watched her. "You told me how much you would give if someone found your boy."

"Dougherty . . ." she began, but he stopped her with a scowl.

"He has to be one of the boys at the Soldiers' Home, I said." Dougherty spoke like someone giving a backward pupil a lesson in arithmetic. "Has to be."

"Nobody knows his whereabouts." She defended her reluctance to hear more. "All investigations have long ago been closed! There is *no* evidence . . ."

"I've done a lot of diggin' and thinking'. . . . I even talked to Dr. Radwell."

"You should not!" she cried, and put down her crocheting. "Leave him out of this. . . . That's all over," she said brokenly.

They exchanged looks such as only people who have been recently intimate are capable of.

"Soldiers' Home," she said. "That's nothing but a county infirmary. A poorhouse!"

"Go ahead. Call it anything you like, but it's full of young guys from the war."

"But what proof have you *he's* among them?" She spoke almost in a wail.

Dougherty could see then that she did not want to find him, did not want to have him restored to her, especially if he was one of those in the Soldiers' Home.

"I'll take you there, Adele." She had never heard him so gentle. She found she did not like him this way. She walked over to the window and looked out.

"I'll go inside with you," he went on, standing now beside her and looking out also at the Royal. "We'll walk down the corridors together, you see." He tried to hold her hand but she pulled away from him.

"No," she said in fury.

"No!" His old mean side came out again, and she was glad.

"It's one of those soldier boys that's yours. Has to be. I done my investigations."

"But how will I know which one it is?" She allowed him now to take her hand.

"You will, Adele." He sounded almost like Dr. Radwell. "You will know . . . your boy." His voice broke off like a person falling asleep.

He saw then what she was feeling as clearly as if she had spoken—it was the same thing he had suspected from the beginning of their talks about her son. She loved the "dream" of having a son somewhere or even of having a son who had died, but to walk through rooms of men badly disabled, no longer themselves "among the living," and pick out her "dream"— wouldn't that spoil everything her life was built on? And her whole life was dream.

"Granted you have to be prepared for some sorry sights, Adele."

"You forget I was a newspaperwoman for twenty-five years." Her voice, however, had lost its usual resonance and command. "I've seen things in my day," she finished in a querulous tone.

"Yes, you've seen everyday casualties that were picked up and carried away immediately. . . . These are worse. They sit in one place and stare at you."

"I don't know how you can be so sure one of them is my . . . is . . . mine!"

"I told you I've made investigations."

Ordinarily she would have demanded what investigations, with whom, when. But she did not want to know the source of his knowledge. He had destroyed her entire way of life, first by his one night of lovemaking and now by his role of omniscient detective who was to bring her secret into the light.

"I don't know what to say or do. I declare!" She moved away from the window. She walked over to the armchair but did not sit down in it. She merely looked into the big green cushions of the chair.

"If you don't go, you'll feel worse." She could feel his breath, like that of a horse, she fancied, upon her neck.

She wheeled around.

"Why couldn't you have let me alone. . . ? Why did you have

to wake me up, I mean? Why, Dougherty, oh, why." She fell easily into his arms.

"Take your time then about coming there with me," he comforted her, but his voice was hard, almost nasty again.

"But why do you want me to do it? You do want me to!" She wept now in the almost sickening strength of his arms. She felt both security and loathing in his nearness.

"You set the ball rolling," he mumbled, but she could feel he was far away from her. She knew their "love" was over. "You wanted to know if he was alive. I wanted to give you something for what you done for us. . . . And I got sort of deep into the inquiry. . . ."

"How deep?" she wondered.

"I paid some people."

"Oh, Dougherty . . . why couldn't we just have let it rest!"

It was he who now broke away from her embrace.

"They're expecting you at the Soldiers' Home," he finally announced. "I've made the appointment for you to go look at the boys. . . ."

"And you say they're in pretty bad shape," she almost shouted.

He waited a moment. "Well, they ain't picture postcards, that's certain. Some is out of their minds, others have legs and arms and eyes missing. Then there's the ones who was gassed. . . . But they're not all that terrible to look at . . . They're young still. They look younger than they are, too, on account of I suppose they just sit there doing nothing. . . . They say, the nurses and doctors, they can't *remember*, most of them."

She nodded.

"We'll go Thursday, Adele. OK? Thursday next at eleven o'clock a.m.?"

"Thursday," she repeated bemused and icy. "All right, if it must be, it must."

She wondered, that dreadful morning when Dougherty came to take her to the Soldiers' Home, if she herself were not perhaps going to be committed, and his coming for her was perhaps some ruse of the mayor and the city officials to "put her away." At any rate she was in a state of terror and extreme weakness. She brought along a flask of brandy, and Dougherty laughed when he saw it half-concealed in her handbag.

"There ain't that many to look at, after all." He tried to cheer her up.

She found riding in a delivery truck with him degrading perhaps, but she had the conviction at that moment that she had only Dougherty to rely on, only the iceman for her trust. Besides, his quiescent kind of brutal nature always calmed her.

The edifice that finally loomed in front of them was queerly reminiscent of George Washington's country house. The pillars, the huge windows, and the greensward surrounding the main building somewhat reassured her.

They walked right on in. Dougherty signed a slip with a guard at the desk, and they were ushered down a long poorly lit hall to a large room with barred windows.

"Now act your age." Dougherty tried to joke when he saw how pale and drawn she was.

"If I had acted my age, I would never had said ten words to you, Dougherty," she snapped. But his insolence made her feel better.

Miss Loughty, a registered nurse, now appeared. She peered at Adele Bevington while Dougherty explained in his booming confident voice that they were looking for a relative of the family.

Nurse Loughty reminded them that they would be permitted to stay only fifteen minutes, and not a second longer.

"That will be more than an eternity, I'm sure," Adele replied.

A gong sounded and they now walked past the first room into another, even more spacious one, which gave out the usual institutional odor of carbolic acid, sweat, and stale food.

Two long rows of chairs and beds dividing the room faced them.

"This is inspection day for the M.D.," Nurse Loughty explained. "We run our establishment very much like the military," she went on, permitting herself two or three inordinate yawns. "Yes"—she looked about with satisfaction—"our boys are all spruced up for today, and are unusually bright and cheery, don't you think? Come this way, please."

The men, whether lying in the beds or slouching in the chairs, only barely looked up as Dougherty and Adele Bevington walked past one bed or chair after another. Their faces and lips gave no flush or movement of life. Their hair, almost meticulously combed and brushed, looked entirely artificial. The waxen nails and hands threatened to melt in the incoming rays of sunlight. Even their eyes barely moved or scintillated as the visitors passed among them.

But Adele found each and every one of the "destroyed" men handsome. They reminded her of effigies of saints in a cathedral she had once visited in Italy. They looked as if they were praying, praying for her. Each soldier or sailor she passed looked more beautiful than the last.

"We should have brought flowers, Dougherty." She repeated this several times.

"Don't talk," he instructed her irritably. "Look! You're here to look, remember?"

"Yes, yes."

When they had finished the tour of inspection, she turned to Dougherty and said recklessly: "They *all* look like my son!"

He grasped her arm painfully. "Then go back there and take another good look," he growled at her. She bowed her head.

But what she had said was true, true for her. They were all in her eyes golden-haired, blue-eyed, with high foreheads, and kissable mouths.

"We'll go back again," Dougherty told her when they had returned to his truck. Out of breath, she leaned against him all at once for support.

"We'll keep going until you recognize him." He looked down at her as she rested her head against his chest. "We'll go and go and keep going until you recognize him. One of them is yours."

He pushed her away from him then, and got into the vehicle.

Ned's full baptismal name was Russell Edward Cottrell. After his "trouble" his mother for some reason began to address him as Russ, and finally everybody followed suit. But soon, as if nobody could believe he was a "father," the old name crept back, and soon he was Ned and even Neddy all over again.

"Russell simply does not fit him at all." Adele was speaking to Alec one evening about Ned, and specifically about the anonymous letters he had been putting under her door.

Tonight was the first time she and Alec had had a "good talk" in some weeks. She handed the older Cottrell boy a sheaf of the strange documents. He laughed and giggled in a manner she had never observed in him before. The letters released some inner spring in his being, she saw. He guffawed, and turned red in the face, and even drooled as he perused one letter after another. Alec's laughter was like music to Adele, and his response made her admire the "terrible" epistles even more.

"He's always writing awful things like these . . . since he was a brat, he's done it," he informed Adele. She had feared up till now that Alec might have had something to do with the letter-writing. Somehow it would have upset her even more.

"He writes things like this to his mother," Alec went on, sobering up a bit as he thought back on his brother. He blinked at Adele.

"And she doesn't correct him?" Adele wondered.

"No," Alec said thoughtfully. "She says he's uncorrectable . . . because he has no dad, she says. If he had a dad, she believes," and Alec's own voice slowed down, as if he were thinking of something he had never thought about before, "well, if he had a dad, you see, he wouldn't write them."

Adele shook her head and sighed.

"There are rumors," Alec went on darkly, "that he has got other girls in trouble too, but the only one who has squealed on him is this Marilyn."

Adele closed her eyes.

"By the way," her visitor went on, "they are sending her away to live with an aunt in Denver or some place way out west. . . . We'll probably never hear of her again, if you ask me."

"And the baby?" Adele inquired in a muffled voice.

"Oh, yes, the baby." Alec seemed to jog his memory on this point. For him, Adele saw, only the disgrace was real: there was no baby. And his brother still could not believe Ned was a father, or anything but his baby brother.

"So I suppose there is nothing to do but get used to these letters." Adele pretended Ned's singling her out for his "attacks" was a great cross to bear, whereas she delighted in each succeeding communication.

"You have to admit they are funny," Alec commented. "They're the only good thing he does."

"Oh, he has other talents." Adele spoke up in the younger boy's defense. She was angry still that Alec had neglected her over the past months and had turned her over, so to speak, to his brother.

"Melissa Deedes even thinks he will be a writer," Alec scoffed. He looked up and around Adele's sitting room, then went on reading and rereading with grudging admiration the "terrible" epistles.

Probably without his being aware of it, Adele watched his every expression, gesture, movement, as he read the accusations leveled at her by a boy with the down still on his cheeks, a boy about to be a father.

After Alec had gone, "deserted" her again, as she called it, and when night had come and the lights of the Royal invited passersby to come in and partake of the theater's fare of romance, Adele put on just one of the more resplendent diamond necklaces and read and reread "poor" Ned's letters to her.

"The strange thing," she said to herself, "is they are all true. Shortly after he began to put them under my door, Dougherty, as if he had read one of the letters, makes his appearance. . . . My God, will there be *more*? At my age?"

But if Dougherty desired her, even if only for that one time, might there not be others? She was suddenly afraid. She tasted the "medicine" bottle now too often, she knew, and put in her appearance far too many times at the movies. In fact, she saw all the films now which the Royal presented. The titles of the photoplays no longer struck her as ridiculous or in bad taste. Gradually, like the shopgirls and Woolworth salesclerks, she took in with a kind of dead earnestness the feature of the week, sensational hits such as *Shoals of Desire*, *Secret Husband*, *Forbidden Trysts*, and *Garden of Remorse*. And very often she found herself attending the same film two and three times. The woman who sold the tickets, heavily rouged, with mascaraed eyes, and purplish-black eyebrows, often waved her on in free. "Go on in, my dear, since you enjoy it so," she would whisper to Adele.

Widow Hughes's property directly adjoined Elaine's house. Most of the land surrounding the widow's twenty-five-room mansion was given over to apple orchards, which she had allowed to run wild. Mrs. Hughes herself was, even in the opinion of the most charitable observer, "far gone, far from being herself." There were very few in the town who could actually remember that far back, however—to when she had been herself. The widow of the Congregational minister, she had always claimed that her husband had married her for her wealth (she still owned nearly half the farmland in this county and neighboring counties, and a considerable number of oil wells), and that once he was sure of her by their wedding bond, he had disgraced his calling by philandering about with every woman who would allow herself to be alone with him. Several lawsuits had been instituted against the preacher by irate fathers, husbands, and brothers, and Widow Hughes had had to put up for sale several farms to pay for all these legal proceedings. As soon as her husband was dead and buried, she refused to attend church any longer, took up pipe smoking, gave up almost all contact with society, and until recently insisted on keeping a horse and buggy, hiring unemployed young men to drive her on her occasional visits to her attorney or to one of her farm bailiffs. The crowds of loafers around the courthouse would stare and jeer when they caught sight of the buggy, but a wrathful look from the old woman quieted them, and a hoarse cry from her lips of "Scum!" carried for blocks. She had long ago lost track of time, and was often seen prowling about her orchards dressed only in a thin negligee or a teddy.

The only person in all of Fonthill Mrs. Hughes showed any liking for was in fact Elaine Cottrell. She would enter the back door (seldom if ever locked) and prowl through Elaine's house at will, at whatever hour, looking like a veritable phantom with her disheveled hair and pale wasted face, sometimes with an expensive handmade white shawl her only garment. Somehow she had got wind of Ned's disgrace, and had come over even more frequently of late to comfort and consult with the "bereaved" mother.

"You know, my dear, you are in my will," Widow Hughes had begun one afternoon, addressing Elaine. "But as I may outlive you, my dear—who knows?—I am quite prepared to help you now in this period of bad sailing."

Elaine had burst into tears, whether at the thought of such unhoped-for generosity or because poor Ned's mistake was now providing talk for the entire town.

Widow Hughes opened her mammoth purse, and brought out several rolls of bills.

"Widow Hughes, put that money right back, my dear." Elaine pretended indignation at this offer of such largesse.

"What would your son think, dearest, if he knew you were giving away your money?"

"My son can rot in hell," Widow Hughes replied acerbically. "Do you think he cares a tinker's damn what becomes of me? He is even worse than his dad was. . . . You are looking, Elaine, dear heart, at a martyr. My husband was not even faithful to me on our wedding night. I found him in bed shortly after supper in the St. Louis hotel with one of the chambermaids. . . . I was glad, later, however, that awareness of what I was in store for in our marriage came at the very beginning of the race. From then on my wedded life was one long mockery of the sacrament of marriage. . . . I recorded well over a hundred adulteries on the pastor's account before I left off keeping a list."

Elaine had heard the story of Reverend Hughes's dissolute career so many times that she could have written it all down from memory, word for word, but now the pastor's immorality made her terribly uncomfortable. It reminded her somehow of her own boy Ned, and his fall.

"Have they caught the girl who led him astray?" Widow Hughes wanted to know, sensing where Elaine's thoughts were.

"They are going to send her away shortly, Mrs. Hughes." Elaine smiled wanly.

"My husband would have never gone to the dogs had he not been tempted." The old lady resumed her favorite subject of discourse. "You have no idea what young pretty women are really like under their silks and satins. There is nothing they won't do to ruin a man, and a man of the cloth is a specially tempting target for them. . . . Had he never seen a fetching pair of legs, he would have been all right. But the minute one appeared, and you know how many there are everywhere, he was a goner."

Elaine now handed the roll of bills back to Mrs. Hughes for the second time. The old woman, rising then with difficulty and making a great fuss over "false modesty," pushed the bills into Elaine's bosom, where they then remained.

"You must put a guard over Ned," the widow went on. "Can't you send him to a military school where they will keep him away from women altogether?"

Elaine shrugged her shoulders helplessly, and quoted the saying that after the horse is stolen, what use is it to lock the barn.

"I wish to have a long heart-to-heart talk with our Ned." The older woman spoke with mysterious emphasis, and took Elaine's hand in hers. "At the very first opportunity, my dear, send him to me! Agreed? I must counsel him."

Elaine winced, for she knew how difficult, if not impossible, it would be to persuade Ned to go to the old woman's house and hear her lecture him, but of course, more likely than not, it meant Mrs. Hughes, after the "lecture," would slip the boy ten or twenty dollars from her limitless resources.

A long silence followed, punctuated occasionally by Elaine's sighs, and the old lady's "Now, now, my dear."

"You don't have a drop of something in the house, do you, angel?" Widow Hughes whispered.

"I do, sweetheart, but please don't let out to anybody that I have it on the premises, will you?" Elaine replied with all the mystery and secrecy she was capable of when the mention was made of illegal beverages.

"It's still against the law of the land to have it?" the old woman queried when Elaine brought her a small glass of her best home-made wine."

"I believe it is allowed in one's own house," Elaine reassured her. "But we mustn't noise it around in any case," she cautioned, knowing what a gossip the old thing was.

Widow Hughes drank two glasses of wine, each sip followed by loud smacking sounds of enjoyment. She had to be helped down the kitchen steps then by Elaine, and finally all the way to her apple orchards and back to her own kitchen.

"After all, my precious, there's lots of pleasure in drinking something you know is forbidden, isn't there? And forbidden too by the damned breed of men who keep us all in shackles, damn their eyes!. . . But I outlived the dirty lecher, and I kept every cent my daddy and granddaddy willed me, though he would have spent it like water.''

She made kissing sounds now to Elaine through the screen door, and then, waving to her "dearest friend," the old lady closed both the storm door and the inside door against robbers.

Widow Hughes, also known by older residents of Fonthill as Widow Birdie, had been a kind of hermit for nearly a generation until young Ned's disgrace galvanized her into coming out again into society. Her bewilderment at first was considerable, for after consulting her address book, dated 1905, and having a boy drive her to the addresses of friends and relations recorded in the book, she discovered to her total dumbfoundedness that the people were for the most part dead or "unknown," and that in many cases the houses themselves where they had lived had been torn down. Indeed whole neighborhoods were no longer in existence, and trees of heaven, poison sumac, Scotch thistles, and milkweed alone thrived in their stead. To those few who remained among the living, the widow announced herself as the Mrs. Reverend William Hughes, but the persons who greeted her at the door were, in the old woman's phrase, "mere descendants—or new-comers" and had never heard of her or her pastor husband. In some cases those who came to the door were the grandchildren of the persons whose names were inscribed in Mrs. Hughes's ad-dress book. To these, and the few others who were among the living, she gave her "news," that young Ned Cottrell had been led astray by a scapegrace girl, and needed money to pull himself out of the slough he had been lured into. Any contribution would be welcome, for the boy's mother was a penniless widow who had to scrub floors. Many who opened the door on her were speech-less, more at her outlandish appearance and out-of-fashion cloth-ing than at her queer request for Ned, and rather than argue with the "old rip," they gave her money to get rid of her. She insisted on giving the donor a receipt. Encouraged by the generosity of the few who remained this side of the grave, she canvassed whole sections of the town, raking in the money, as her husband years before had passed the collection plate in church.

Mrs. Hughes was better than trumpets, megaphones, fire en-gines, or sky-writing in apprising Fonthill of the fall from grace of a promising young man. Whereas, had the widow never learned of this fall, few persons might have ever heard of it. And as she quickened to the drama of the story she was awakened by memory back to the days of her "hell on earth" and martyrdom to a preacher of the gospel who practiced fornication more regularly than he administered the sacraments. To the persons she canvassed in behalf of Ned, she also now reeled off the names of the young women, married, unmarried, or widowed, who had so long ago lured her husband to his own moral destruction. Most of these strumpets and harlots were unknown to her auditors. But to the widow, nothing had changed since 1905, except, when she gave it careful thought, that her husband was no longer subject to her jurisdiction and she could no longer threaten him with refusing him her purse strings and warning him that if there was one more breath of scandal, she would turn him out of house and home to beg in the streets.

After one of her rounds of visits, Widow Hughes would return in triumph to her own neighborhood and immediately inform Elaine of her progress. She failed to understand why Elaine did not wish to receive the collection of dollar bills, nickels, dimes, and even pennies that she had so laboriously solicited for Ned and his child-to-be. Only the thought that the widow might possibly after all remember her in her will made Elaine put up with the old crone, though Elaine begged her practically on her knees to cease and desist from informing the quick and the dead of Fonthill of her boy's ruin.

"Silence, my angel, don't you see, is the only method to adopt in these circumstances," she told the old woman again and again.

Bemused, Widow Hughes retorted: "You sound exactly like my husband. . . . Silence, my foot!" Then looking all about her anxiously, struggling with one of her frequent lapses of memory, she whispered: "What is your name again, my child?" She studied Elaine's features with a kind of rapt adoration. "You are so beautiful, my girl . . . a sight for sore eyes. . . . Your name comes back to me . . . Elaine . . . Elaine, you will be remembered, no question about it. Your name is written down."

"In heaven, I suppose, Widow Hughes."

"No, my dearest. On earth. There is a copious reward coming to you on earth."

Elaine smiled and shed a few tears.

"No one will ever know what I went through with that man,"

she had begun again. "You *are* my dear friend Elaine, aren't you." She again struggled with her decayed memory. "I can't tell my secrets to strangers, you know."

"I am Elaine. I am your Elaine."

"He finally unbuttoned himself right in the pastor's study in the church and ravished them within arm's reach of Holy Scripture. I believe he will burn in hell when he is called by his Maker . . . or is now burning. . . . Yes, yes, I recall now he is dead, though it seemed this afternoon on my rounds he would be waiting for me in the pastor's study. . . . What time is it?" The old woman roused herself from her reverie.

"It's five o'clock." Elaine consulted her tiny wristwatch. "The factory whistle will blow at any moment, and I must get supper to going, or my boarders will have nothing to eat. . . . You'll have to excuse me, Mrs. Hughes."

"Go right ahead with your preparations, dear child. Pay no attention to me if I watch you at your hive of activity. Might I ask, though"—she lowered her voice—"if you have any more of that elixir of life you treated me to last?"

Elaine thought for a moment, then spoke in a sorrowful voice: "I will get you some, darling, if you will promise me something. Swear to me you will stay to home and not go informing all the neighborhoods of poor Ned's trouble. It creates such a bad impression. Promise me you will stay home and not go bearing these awful tidings to the whole world."

"I will." The old woman spoke with great reluctance. "I will give up my tidings-bearing as you call it, if I may have a drop . . ."

"You will swear it on the Bible, then?"

"Oh, leave the Good Book out of it, please. Pastor Hughes swore on it just before he ravished the choir mistress and I surprised both of them naked in the choir loft. . . ."

Elaine had already gone to the buttery and opened her secret cabinets where the bottles were under lock and key. She brought back a flask and showed it to her visitor.

"Now let me hear your promise, Widow Hughes."

"For that elixir of life, I'll never go out again, Elaine my own dear girl! You know, that's the one thing I miss since the Reverend left me. He did stock a good cellar, angel. It saved our marriage. . . . Of course it was legal then, wasn't it? . . . Do you think they are burning him in hell?" She grasped Elaine's arm.

"I think his sins were forgiven him, Widow Hughes."

"That would take an eternity all by itself," the old woman said after musing for a moment.

She stood up then and took Elaine in her arms and kissed her many times.

"Complexion like peaches and cream, strawberries and snow!" The old woman went on kissing Ned's mother.

"There, there." Elaine extricated herself at last, and wrapped up the bottle of wine in pink paper.

"Now drink this sparingly, Mrs. Hughes," she cautioned. "And remember, tell nobody who gave it to you. It's no longer legal, as it was in the days of your husband."

"Why not?" The old woman became suspicious and truculent.

"An amendment to the Constitution. Surely you remember that," she said jogging Mrs. Hughes's memory.

Cradling her in her arms, and helping her hold the wine bottle, she chided, "You wouldn't want to be arrested at your age, now, my dear. . . . You've had enough troubles."

"Oh, jail might be a good rest," Widow Hughes quipped.

The two widows walked arm in arm toward the apple orchards, and then up the many steps to the old woman's mansion.

"I'll be a good girl for you," she told Elaine. "Give me one more kiss before I go back into my dark lonesome dwelling. . . . There, thank you, my sweet. . . . I'll take the bottle. . . . I won't go out anymore, I've promised. . . . I'll stay here in my lonesome dark old fortress . . ."

Elaine waited until she heard the door lock behind the old woman.

"God seems to spare me no punishment at all," Elaine sighed.

Back in her kitchen, she counted the money the widow had raised for Ned's disgrace, and then burst into tears, whether through gratefulness or shame, or both.

One of the continual sources of wrangling between Elaine and Ned had always been her younger boy's reluctance—often refusal—to carry hot dishes of food to Widow Hughes.

"Why is it always me who has to visit that old scarecrow?" This was how the argument usually began, but today, to his mother's considerable puzzlement, Ned agreed without a murmur to take the preacher's widow her evening repast. Elaine did not even have to add this evening, "Remember, Neddy, she might remember you in her will," or hear his rejoinder, "Oh, I bet!"

The front door to the mansion was open, so that Ned walked on in and called out to Mrs. Hughes he had brought her a hot meal.

Widow Hughes appeared at once. She was wearing a fairly unsoiled white silk dress, an amber necklace, topaz earrings that hung almost to her shoulders, and she had daubed her face with Dorin rouge. Even her hair had for once been rather neatly dressed.

"Come into the dining room with that treat, dearest," she said.

Ned now laid the covered dishes, which he had carried on a tray, on the scarred and battered walnut dining table, long enough to seat twenty persons.

"Your mother is such a wonderful provider," the old woman was saying as she peeked into one dish after another. She screamed with pleasure. "Go out into the kitchen, handsome, and bring me a napkin and some utensils."

She went on gazing at the dinner Elaine had prepared for her. She sighed and shook her head. "Why couldn't I have had a daughter like your mother," Widow Hughes remarked, accepting the napkin and silverware from Ned, and beginning at once to taste the casserole of noodles and ham even before she sat down. "Mmm, heaven," she said, chewing loudly. She still had her own teeth, though they were little more than black stumps.

"My daughter-in-law is a devil," Widow Hughes went on, seating herself at last at the head of the table and looking down its long expanse as if many persons were seated listening to her. "A hardened rip, that's all she is. Sits in her front parlor down there with the spyglass in her hand"—she pointed in the direction of her son's house only a few doors away—"and waits for me to have a stroke or fall down the front stairs to my death. But I mean to outlive her, the trollop. Anyhow, she's not in my will, and Christ and his angels couldn't persuade me to remember her. I've disinherited her. . . . I told my lawyer how she had tried to kill me several times by putting the slop jar on the staircase."

Ned nodded sleepily. He had heard all these stories a hundred times or more.

"My son is even worse," the widow continued. "He don't dare put on his suspenders until she tells him. Most men, as a matter of fact, have no character. The world would come to a grinding halt without us women. . . . Mmm, such grand victuals. Makes my eyes water, it's all so good!"

She held her hand over her brow as if in silent prayer.

"Divine food. I wonder you boys don't get fat eating your mother's cooking. You're all muscle and bone, I guess. You run it off, I suppose."

She stopped chewing, thinking of something.

"You're in trouble again, I hear." Widow Hughes spoke omnisciently now, craftily. She put down her fork, and masticated more slowly.

"Always come to me, Ned, when you're in deep like you are now. . . . I know life. Your mother doesn't . . . she's a wonderful woman but should stick to the kitchen. She doesn't know how to raise boys, poor darling. . . . You see, I was married to the most terrible man who ever drew breath. But it was an education, an education in deviltry. I could write a book about men, and women, too. He had countless sweethearts, or paramours, as they said then. He was a man who was nothing but appetite. When he just saw a skirt he became inflamed. Beside himself. He often wanted to go to bed with me at noon, whenever he got aroused. Being a preacher he was home all the time. But you see, I learned to know men. And of course women. The women he ruined. I hated him, but what could I do? In a small town when one is as well-fixed as my daddy left me, I couldn't just throw him out on the street. But I should have, Neddy. I shouldn't have had to put up with him. But it taught me about human nature. I could write a book about it, but nobody would dare publish it. . . . Men are no good, take it from me. It's women who keep the home fires burning. Men do nothing but impregnate us and fight wars. . . . They're all bluff and noise!"

"But I'm a man," Ned got in finally.

"Yes, dear heart." She considered his retort. "But you see, you're different. You Cottrell boys are smart and talented. That makes the difference. I'm talking about the run-of-the-mill type of man, such as my late husband. He had no talent except to go to bed with women, and brawl. Being a preacher, however, he couldn't go to the saloons and knock men down, but he had a punching bag out there in the carriage house which he finally wore out, and he went hunting every fall and killed enough animals to populate the ark. . . . No, you are different, Ned. . . . You are Ned, aren't you, and not Alec? I always get you two mixed up, but if you're Ned I like you better. Alec is not too considerate of me, Neddy. I wish you'd tell him so. He's trying to live above his station. Stagestruck, stars in his eyes, and all that. Takes singing lesson with that sissified Paul Ferrand. . . . But to come back to you, Ned. Don't marry that whore who got you into trouble. I know her family. They're backwoods trash. I know you're not to blame. When women want someone the man hasn't a chance. They'll get his trousers off him if they have to cut them off with razor blades. So don't marry her. Let the baby be adopted or let it die, but don't ruin your youthful promise by marrying some slut. Let her starve to death on the streets with her baby if necessary, don't you get mixed up in matrimony. Besides, you're too young. The milk isn't dry on your mouth yet. . . . Now I have a little something for you, Neddy."

The widow rose, and went to a large Chinese porcelain vase. She turned it slowly over and brought out some bills.

"No, no, no!" Ned cried when he saw her coming with the money. "My mother won't allow it!"

"Now, you hush, Neddy," the old woman warned him. "This is my money and I am in my right mind, though my daughter-in-law pretends I'm nuts so she can send me away and get my property. But let me tell you something. She will die long before I do. I see it in her skin and the whites of her eyes. Bright's disease. I shouldn't be surprised if she was lying over there dead now with the binoculars in her hand, having watched me all day. That's all she does from sunup to sundown. Watches this house with her blamed binoculars. So afraid I'll give away money and my antiques. Now I won't take no for an answer. You take this money, Neddy, and don't marry that whore. . . . Another thing that has bothered me"—she had put the money in Ned's shirt pocket and now returned to the table to finish the casserole—"is this." She wiped her mouth and hands on the linen napkin. "It's that awful Adele Bevington you work for. Do you have to work for such a creature? She is one of the most abandoned women in the nation. She went to bed with every married man in town in her day. Had many illegitimate babies. Was ordered out of the church, though they've let her back in again because the new preacher is a dimwit. She has had the gall to go on living here after the scandals of her youth. Went away for a while about once every spring to drop one of her bastard babies, and then would rush right on back here to start all over again. You don't have to work for such lepers, Ned. Even if she is one of the old families here. She disgraced her daddy. He died of the shame. Her sister, Jennie, also never got over it. Disgraced her whole family and she thrives on it. Is still going strong, while her family lies in the churchyard. Her first paramour gave her enough diamonds and emeralds to fill Cartier's window with. . . ."

Ned had stood up, had begged to leave. Widow Hughes paid no attention to him. She went on chewing and talking and laughing and scolding and gossiping. Perhaps she barely noticed he had left, but when he was going down the front steps she appeared behind the inner door, and shouted out to him: "I'll do the dishes tonight, and bring them back to Elaine in the morning. . . . I have some more advice for her about your future, honeybunch. . . ."

Ned came back to the house from the widow's swearing and stomping, he took off his cap and threw it to the floor and jumped on it, and then in his fury he seized one of Elaine's hand-painted china cups and dashed it against the wall.

Elaine stood perfectly silent in the center of the kitchen watching him.

"You always break something of mine when you are in one of your rages, don't you?" She spoke with an ominous coolness that all at once made him uneasy.

"And I'll tell you another thing," she went on in her new detached manner while Ned stared down at the pieces of the broken china. "If you don't quit smoking and what's worse, chewing tobacco, you are not going to have any wind to compete in the swimming matches next summer!"

"The swimming matches!" he exclaimed, as if they were the

last thing on earth he could be concerned with. "All right then, since you mention them . . . I'll tell you why I chew and smoke and the rest." He stopped on the last word and gazed at his mother. "You and Alec boss me from morning till night. Making me pay calls on that old hellion next door. She's insane, if you ask me. Do you hear? Don't you realize she is? She's an old maniac, that's what, and I have to go over there and tend to her. . . ."

"It won't kill you to be nice to an old woman like that, especially in her case when she might remember you. . . ."

"If you tell me one more time about some old woman with one foot in the grave who is going to remember me in her will, I am going to smash all your china!"

"Oh no, you won't, young man." Elaine now raised her voice. But studying her son's distorted features and wild eyes, she said more softly, "Ned, Ned! You are not yourself anymore!"

"I want to be let alone by you and Alec . . . do you hear? I want to lead my own life and not be ordered here, ordered there. Told who will remember me in their will, who to softsoap and be nice to, who to smile and grin at, and kowtow to . . ."

"Alec and I never told you to get a young girl in trouble, though, did we!" Elaine burst into tears on saying this, and began gathering up the broken pieces of china.

"I'll pay for the damage," Ned said with forced penitence. He began picking up some of the smaller bits and pieces from the accident, but his mother pushed him away.

"Pay for it!" she began. "You can't even buy a cup and saucer like this nowadays. It's beyond paying for, you thoughtless, selfish scamp, you!"

Still holding some of the bits of the broken cup and saucer, she sat down at the kitchen table. "My own mother hand-painted this china, and see what you've done in one second of temper!"

"I'd rather be horsewhipped than go to that old hag's house, and you know it!"

But Ned's anger had passed, and he sat down across from his mother at the big pine table.

"If there were a man at the head of this house, you would be whipped, you can depend on it. . . . And you'd not be in trouble with that slut of the Doughertys' either, I can vouch for that. And you'd not be allowed to stain your handsome mouth with chewing tobacco either. Do you realize what it will do to your teeth and gums? Go look in the mirror, see what it's doing to you."

"Mom," Ned said in supplication, rising, and almost kneeling before her at that moment. "Don't make me go to that old woman's house again. It gives me the willies, let me tell you . . . to have to hear her and see her—and smell her!"

"You'll be old someday yourself," Elaine went on, softening a little. "Widow Hughes thinks the world of us. I don't know why you can't be a little considerate of the poor thing."

"Let Alec go, then, if someone has to be considerate. Let him put up with those sessions of hers."

"I don't know what is going to become of you." Elaine shook her head. She wiped her eyes on her apron. "I thought you were settling down and getting to be a champion swimmer last term, and now look at you!"

"If you keep harping on what I've done, I'm going to run off, do you hear me? That's right. R-u-n off! Don't look at me like that, either, as if I'd killed somebody. . . . All that's wrong with me is I got caught. The other boys do it and go clean. So I'm to be hung for a horse thief. I tell you, I have my own life, too. Widow Hughes, bah!"

And leaping up, he rushed out of the room, and then out the back door, from whence he had stormed in, and on out through the big back yard and through the opening in the hedge he invariably used.

"I've prized this hand-painted china cup since I was a girl." Elaine looked at the broken pieces of china. "It seems that everything in life is parting with something. Every day we part with something precious. It all seems to be steady loss. He'll find out, though, when he leaves home, how good he had it here."

She walked over to the large cupboard and took out a piece of freshly laundered cloth and blew her nose on it. And then she wept even harder.

"I could have screamed with dread when I saw her coming up the walk to my house. . . . Maude Dougherty herself! I've always hated that woman. . . . And to think I'm now involved with her."

Elaine was reeling off the "minutes" of the meeting with her "arch enemy," which she felt Maude Dougherty was at that moment, to Alec, who grumbled and mumbled and occasionally giggled as he studied his mother. Her tirades aroused in him a kind of sickening bewilderment and also a sneaking admiration. He decided on such occasions he must get his energy from her, for all his dad had ever liked to do was solve difficult problems in mathematics, go hunting, and clean his guns. The rest of the time he dozed and loafed. He barely knew Alec was his son.

Elaine was so occupied with her encounter with Maude Dougherty that she did not notice at once that Alec was sporting a black eye. He had got it in a scuffle with a "smartass" (he used the word "bully" with his mother) who had taunted him with being a telephone operator. Sid Green, a former football player of local fame, told Alec no man could do that kind of work and have his self-respect. Alec had got up from his table at the Star Restaurant and hit his detractor. Sid had struck Alec across the mouth, and then, surprise of surprises, Alec had knocked the quarterback down, and in his sudden uncontrolled rage had jumped up and down on his prostrate foe, cracking several ribs. The local constable had had to separate them.

"By God, if I am a phone operator, I am a *man* phone operator," Alec said again and again, interrupting constantly his mother's recital of her showdown with Maude Dougherty.

"She said scarcely ten words about Marilyn's pregnancy and coming abortion," Elaine Cottrell went on while trying to take in Alec's account of his knocking Sid Green down at the Star. "All she talked about was something else, though I finally did get out of her she and her brat are leaving for the West for good in a day or so. . . . And that *something else*—Alec, are you listening?— concerns, indirectly, you."

She took in then his black eye, and made a loud sound of horror, but the urge to finish the news Maude had brought sped her on: "Perhaps I shouldn't repeat it, though." She stopped mysteriously as if an eavesdropper were listening at the door.

"Oh, mother, please!"

"Your eye, really, Alec . . . I don't know what to say. . . . What Maude told me concerns your Adele Bevington." Elaine had put on her "church" face, as Ned once described her expression. She would have to be coaxed to tell what she knew. But when Alec only looked pokerfaced, she went on: "It seems Val and Miss Bevington have been . . . intimate. So Maude thinks."

"Oh, rot." Alec flashed a scornful look at his mother, but the color drained out of his face. "I don't believe it," he went on, coming to Adele's defense. "Why, Val Dougherty, though he's hardly young, is still young enough to be . . . her own son. And besides, she wouldn't lower herself . . . to the love of an iceman."

The thought of Adele and her diamonds in bed with Val Dougherty suddenly made Elaine burst into a fit of laughter.

"Well, I don't see what's so funny." Alec was indignant and close to tears.

Elaine's mirth died away when she saw how seriously Alec was taking it all.

"You seem to forget Adele Bevington has quite a past," Elaine began, her bitterness against the older woman's long influence over both her boys now coming out. "She was the first really notorious woman of this town, owing to her social standing. Her liaison with George Etheredge has never had its equal, not only because he was nationally known in financial circles, but because she bore him a child and then went on living here in Fonthill, kept all the while by her lover in unheard-of luxury. Indeed, all her present wealth, many think, came not from her family but from her seducer. . . ."

Elaine was becoming increasingly uncomfortable, however, because of Alec's reaction to her rehashing of the scandal of Adele's past. She saw even more clearly now how greatly attached he had been—and still was—to the Bevington woman. And she was very angry and jealous that such an old "girl" should have become "intimate" with Val Dougherty, whom, as a matter of fact, she had felt drawn to herself. If Val had to have somebody else beside that frump of a Maude, why had he chosen an old woman! Obviously it must be her money, or, to be more exact, her diamonds.

"Well, Fonthill has a new scandal on its hands, Alec, and it promises to be a big one." Elaine spoke with diminished indignation, however, for she saw the storm that was coming over her son's features.

"How can you, of all people, believe such gossip," he shot back at her. "Especially from a woman like Maude Dougherty. You talk about bad reputations! Please, for Christ's sake!"

"Well, she's at least a married woman, Maude is."

"But what about before she married Val Dougherty? She had to marry him because she was pregnant by someone out of the score she had been partying with in those cottages by the mill race. She had to, and Val wanted a woman to keep house for him!"

"You seem to be very well-informed for such a high-minded boy!" his mother scolded, but she was already losing interest in the conversation, and besides, she greatly feared Alec's evil disposition. He had a temper as terrible as his late dad's.

"At least Maude married," Elaine pointed out. "She didn't continue to flout the laws of the community and accept diamonds from the man who led her astray, or create—only yesterday—a disturbance during the sermon at the First Presbyterian Church!"

Alec was inconsolable. The thought that his Adele, even though he had cooled toward her lately, was the "mistress" to a coarse, brutish roughneck like Dougherty deeply hurt him. He realized how important Adele had been in his life. Still, the story was beyond belief, and yet he believed it. He hated Adele at that moment and he loathed his mother. Besides, his cheek and black eye smarted horribly from the fracas he had been in at the Star Restaurant. But he could feel proud anyhow that he had knocked down Sid Green, who was his superior in strength and athletic ability. He bet that little snot of a Ned could not have done it, even if he was going to be a father.

"The little prick!" The words slipped out.

"Who on earth are you talking about like that in my house?" Elaine pounced on him. "How dare you employ such an expression in front of your own mother!"

"Oh, forget it, why can't you. . . . I've heard you say worse when you're riled."

"Who were you referring to, if it isn't too much to ask you, Mr. High-and-Mighty?"

But all at once she took in completely the state of his face, the many cuts and abrasions and the black eye which was seemingly growing blacker by the instant.

"Who but your other, your favorite, son! Isn't it what he's done that has turned everything topsy-turvy in town. If he can't keep his pants buttoned . . . and he has written Adele such terrible letters he has driven her to . . . to . . . prostitution!''

Elaine slapped Alec across the mouth, causing his already stinging face to smart even more intolerably. As a result he burst into a series of sobs and groans.

"I don't know what you can mean, accusing poor Ned of driving an already lost woman to prostitution. What letters are you talking about anyhow?''

Alec pushed away from her, and Elaine decided that whatever the letters were he was referring to, she wanted no more additional burdens or worries heaped on her at the moment.

"Now, now, Alec, dear heart.'' She rose and put her hand on his hair and smoothed him gently. He was too weak to repulse her.

"We must all stick together, Alec.'' She went on standing patiently by his side. "You know as well as I do that Maude's daughter must have used all kinds of tricks and blandishments to get that poor boy to work her will!''

Alec smiled through his tears, despite his bruised mouth and lacerations.

"She raped him, if the truth were known . . . for before he was with her, poor Ned hardly knew what time it was if he heard the courthouse clock strike the hour.''

"You can say that again.'' Alec grinned desperately.

"Maude's daughter led him down the path to his ruin as sure as the sun rises in the east. . . . Oh, the slut, the filthy common minx, just like her mother, who had the nerve to sit down in my house just a short while ago. . . . I should have the place fumigated! It serves Maude right if Val is out philandering with . . . others.''

"I wish you would never refer to that subject again.'' Alec had gone deathly pale. "It just *cannot* be true.''

"Now, now, Alec. All right, I won't speak about it ever again. . . . I'd like to see those diamonds, though, someday,'' she added in a dreamy, meditative mood. She walked toward the big cupboard in the next room, within which were displayed some of her own heirloom china, solid silverware, pearl-handled knives, antique tureens and turkey platters. She stared at her own small inheritance from her past.

The thought of Adele and her diamonds and her albeit illegitimate son became, all at once, for at least a moment fully real to her.

Alec had once said of his mother that if Widow Hughes died and left her all her stocks and bonds and farmlands, and if Adele went into a nunnery and bequeathed Elaine all her diamonds, and were she likewise a millionairess in her own right, she would still hang out her clothes to dry on the line, scrub her kitchen floor, and wash her own windows upstairs and down until they shone like the sun at noon.

Elaine was hanging her sheets and pillowcases out in her spacious backyard when Sheriff Will Greaves, dressed this time in his civvies, sauntered up to her, and although trying to draw a long face, smiled in spite of himself, partly, one supposed, because Elaine looked so fetching even when doing hard manual labor.

"Might I have a word with you, Elaine, my dear?" the sheriff asked, doffing for a moment his big-brimmed bandbox-new hat and grinning sheepishly, his gold fillings flashing, and then plumping his hat back on, and the smile and the teeth vanishing in a trice.

They stepped onto the sprawling back porch screened off from view by latticework.

"Now don't tell me you are here to arrest me for selling liquor, Will, because I do no such thing. You yourself have told me a score of times there's no law against making one's own for mince pie and plum pudding and an occasional glass to a friend."

"I'm not here as your peace officer," Will told her, trying not to smile again. "I'm your friend, Elaine. . . . I was Marius's friend also, don't you forget that. I'm also a friend of your boys."

"Yes, I know you are, Will." Elaine sighed and wiped her perspiring face with a fresh tea towel she found on the green wicker table. She sat down, and motioned for him to do likewise.

"I have just one word of warning, my dear, and then I'll be off without taking you any longer from your household tasks."

"Oh, for heaven's sake, Will, not another word of warning!"

She smiled one of her irresistible smiles, causing a dimple in her chin to appear. "All right then, out with it!"

He looked past her out toward the apple orchards of Widow Hughes and beyond to the wide unpaved road that led to the river.

"You've got to keep a tighter tether on them boys of yours . . . and that's gospel . . . or there'll be hell to pay. That's all I have to say."

"That's all! And I suppose you think that's little, for a woman in my situation to keep a tether on them. . . . You know they're uncontrollable at that age. You've got boys of your own."

"But I keep a tight rein on them, Elaine." He took off his hat and fanned himself, though the big latticed porch was cool as one of Dougherty's icehouses.

"It's different when there's a man in the house, Will," Elaine reminded him. "It's the man who knows about tethering and reins."

"I suppose you've got something there, sure you have. . . . But, look here, this fighting in restaurants . . . that's the last straw."

"Sid Green taunted my boy with doing a girl's work at the telephone company," Elaine hotly defended Alec. "Do you expect my boy to take a taunt like that, and then thank him for it! Why don't you call on Sid Green's mom and dad, and rake them over the coals, instead of coming to a widow woman's back door."

"I have done just that," the sheriff almost whimpered. He had just looked at the declivity slightly revealed between Elaine's breasts. He dared not look up at her again for a moment.

"My boys have never had any dad to advise them, to teach them to be men," she went on when she saw the sheriff's head lowered as if in prayer.

"Well, they're men all right, Elaine . . . little Ned and Alec!" He shook his head. "But jumping on a man's ribcage when he's already knocked out cold . . . Don't you think that's going a bit far now, my dear?"

But Elaine was, if anything, growing more irate at this intrusion upon her home by the officer, who was the agent of the outside world, the world she despised, which she had always felt was her personal antagonist.

"My boys are never the ones to start the trouble, Will Greaves," she went on now, recklessly, in view of the sheriff's backing down. "Take Maude Dougherty's daugher, Marilyn, for I suppose you'll be coming to Ned's case since you've brought up Alec and his fight. The Dougherty girl as good as unbuttoned Ned's trousers, Will Greaves. I think you know the Doughertys, though, better than me. I need say no more."

"But, Elaine, it takes two to make love as well as engage in fisticuffs. And your Ned may be underage, but he ain't no babe in swaddling clothes."

"A woman is always older than a man, Will, you take that from me! Always more cunning, more full of tricks and deceptions. I think a girl comes into the world with all that. Ready to trap a man is her born nature."

"Now, Elaine, you shouldn't ought to be so hard on your own sex."

He stood up, nearly put on his huge hat, and then instead allowed it to cover his belt buckle. He looked worsted, or as Elaine would put it later, he went out of her house with his tail between his legs.

"Let me tell you something, Elaine," the sheriff said bashfully. "You're a wonderful woman. And a good mother, I think." He looked about him. "You keep a fine house here. . . . But for God's sake, try to keep them in line, Elaine, for all our sakes."

There came then a strange moment. Their eyes met, and somehow they could not stop gazing into one another's pupils. In one of those unexplained impulses Sheriff Greaves, probably before he knew he was going to, had given Elaine a quick brush of his lips on her forehead, a kiss that was chaste but impassioned.

The stolen embrace made her features soften. She closed her eyes briefly, for she could feel Will's eyes on her bare white arms and the curve of her bosom under her thin cotton dress. She almost wished he would take her in his arms, too. There would be then no more talk of tethers, or keeping her boys under lock and key.

"Will they have the baby?" Will wondered, somewhat official again, then turned to go down the steps, smartly plumping his big hat on his head.

"Mother and daughter will handle it their way, Sheriff. They've cut me and my boy off from all further responsibility, you see. . . . And after all, how do we know Ned is the only one Marilyn has grass-stained her skirts with?"

The big man laughed then so that he could be heard down the block.

"I'll remember that when someone else gets in a similar fix," he quipped, waving goodbye. "Grass-stained her skirts," he muttered to himself as he passed out of earshot.

Elaine stood on the back steps watching him depart.

"It's a sad thing we have to depend on men." She spoke almost loud enough for her voice to reach the officer. "I don't mind sons, for they're a comfort as well as a trial, but those big grown-up fellows. I don't know. You want them, but then you'd like to be rid of them once the want has passed, and their damned pigheaded blind selfishness sweeps over your life like a cyclone. I think I prefer being a widow than have to take my orders from a big strapping bluff of a know-it-all like him. . . ."

Usually a young man from the telephone company or a recent college graduate who was "reading law" in one of the countless attorney's offices would pay a call on Rita Fitzsimmons about the time her last piano student was about to depart. This would be around nine p.m. The young men enjoyed smoking imported cigarettes with an older woman in a day when no lady smoked unless she was a member of the highest society—or if she had intellectual pretensions. Rita always inspired these young men with a desire to leave Fonthill and go to a great metropolitan center, where they could find themselves. She considered herself a rival in a way to Adele Bevington, but though the two women lived only a block or so from one another, and Fonthill was certainly a small place, their paths seldom, if ever, crossed. "Ah, yes, Rita Fitzsimmons was born on a farm," Adele had once remarked to Alec when the piano teacher's name came up in conversation. And this was the only mention anybody had ever heard come from Adele concerning her supposed rival.

Rita, however, had more to say concerning Adele. All Rita's

young male visitors learned through her of Miss Bevington's Chicago past, the scandal of her having a bastard son, and giving it away, the diamonds, and so forth, and the long years of struggle to regain her standing in a prudish and vindictive society. Rita's description of the life of Adele was tinged with admiration, even envy, though she claimed she would not want to know the older woman. (Adele could not have allowed herself to know Rita under any circumstances, for the rather ironic reason that she considered Rita a loose woman, and of too plebeian an origin.)

Young Allen Mowbray was "sitting at Rita's feet" the night Elaine decided she must go to the piano teacher's studio to unburden herself. The evening's lessons were not quite over when Elaine arrived. She nodded to Allen—he was an acquaintance of Alec's, and had once called at her home. A young woman was playing Schumann's *"Träumerei"* at too rapid a tempo, and Mowbray was perusing an old copy of *Vanity Fair*. The air of the studio was blue with cigarette smoke.

After dismissing the interpreter of *"Träumerei"* and quickly putting the seventy-five cents the girl had paid for her lesson in a tall vase, Rita did not accept Elaine's offer to go out with her to the Greek restaurant, as was their custom, but, moving her head in the direction of her young male visitor, indicated Elaine would have to be content with saying whatever she had to say with a third party present.

When Elaine showed hurt and disappointment by pouting, Rita spoke up: "You're among friends, dear. . . . This young man knows all there is about life and its sorrows, don't you, Allen?" Mowbray blushed a furious beet-color, and smiled feebly under his new-grown mustache.

Mowbray was only a couple of years older than Alec, Elaine recalled, but according to Rita's "advertisement" of the young man, he was a world traveler (actually he had never left the United States, but had once gone to San Francisco). He had "lived," in one of Rita's favorite expressions. Nonetheless, despite his worldly experience, he had never been in any of the trouble Elaine's boys always found themselves in. Certainly the sheriff had never called on his family. But then, his parents were well fixed and owned their own home.

"I have taken the liberty of telling Allen about Ned's dilemma," Rita said, by way of concession to Elaine's disappointment in not getting to talk to her friend alone.

"I'm afraid there is nobody in Fonthill who has not heard of Ned's dilemma, as you call it."

"The story has spread like wildfire, no doubt about that." Rita offered Elaine a very long gold-tipped cigarette, which she drew from a box decorated with an Egyptian sphinx.

"And it's not only poor Ned now." Elaine thanked Rita for the smoke. "I was visited only this morning by the sheriff. . . ." Elaine confided this bit of information directly to Allen Mowbray, who sparkled with interest at the mention of Will Greaves.

"Alec was in a fistfight at the Star Restaurant," Elaine added with cool, sophisticated nonchalance, which caused Rita to drop her cigarette.

"Alec?" The piano teacher was incredulous. "I can't believe it!" She did not picture Elaine's older son as a pugilist, since for one reason if not another he was a steady caller at Adele Bevington's.

"Sid Green made fun of his part-time job as a telephone operator."

"Good for Alec." Mowbray was livening up even more considerably, and had turned noticeably away from Rita to give his full attention to Elaine. "Sid Green deserves a thrashing."

"But there must have been more to it, wasn't there, than Sid Green's taunting Alec with being a telephone operator? I mean . . ."

It was evident that Rita was annoyed that Elaine was monopolizing her visitor's attention so completely, for she had wanted to have a private talk with Allen tonight.

"Oh, I won't say that Alec is a saint." Elaine's voice shook a little, for she had not liked Rita's being so "surprised" that Alec would engage in a fistfight. "He and his younger brother come to blows all the time. Their dad was an amateur boxer, after all." She stretched the truth here a bit, though Marius was known as always having a chip on his shoulder, resulting in frequent scraps.

Everybody laughed then at this last remark.

"I believe both your sons have been fortunate in enjoying the friendship of Adele Bevington," Mowbray brought out when the laughter had died down.

Rita frowned deeply on hearing the name of her "rival," stamped out her cigarette, and coughed several little "stage" coughs, which, finally, by their very artificiality embarrassed everybody. The evening was going very badly.

"But I think I should be going." Allen rose with peremptory haste. "You two ladies, I am sure, have something particular to discuss."

"Not at all," Elaine said in a shaky high voice, rising also, and moving toward the door. She had realized almost from the moment she had entered the studio that her unannounced visit was not welcomed by the piano teacher tonight. "I don't want to intrude, and besides I cannot stay a moment longer." She gave out this obvious alibi.

"Oh, but Mrs. Cottrell." Allen went over to her and took her hand in his. "We can't let her just walk out on us like this, can we, Rita, when I have brought a special gift which has to be enjoyed as soon as possible." He went over to the oval table in the middle of the room and picked up a large package covered with wrapping paper decorated with flamboyant pictures of candy sticks and roses. He drew out a bottle of imported gin.

Elaine shot an inquiring look at Rita, and Rita nodded to her, meaning she should stay.

While Rita went through the portieres to the adjoining room and began chipping ice and arranging glasses on a tray Mowbray moved his chair closer to Elaine and whispered: "If I can ever be of any assistance to you, Mrs. Cottrell, I hope you will call on me. . . . I admire you so very much." He got out this last sentence rapid-fire, as if he feared Rita might come in and overhear it. He blushed to the roots of his hair.

Elaine was unprepared for such an overture. She smiled her gratitude while wondering how Mowbray expected to help her.

"It's outrageous that the sheriff should visit you," he went on. "I will speak to my father about it. You know he is quite a prominent attorney, if I do say so myself."

"Yes," Elaine said uneasily as she saw Rita advancing toward them with their drinks. "I should think the sheriff could find more important things to do than threaten widows and orphans."

"Exactly," Rita said in a thunderous, slightly hostile note of agreement, and she handed them their gin and ice.

As they sipped their drinks in the dark little studio, they had a satisfying and even comforting sensation of breaking the law. Drinking was a kind of accomplishment all by itself.

"There are no charges being brought against young Ned now, are there?" Mowbray began, loosening his tie, and speaking more confidently, but with his best attention still directed toward Elaine.

"No, it's all over, I am told by Mr. Dougherty and his wife. They will do nothing. The girl is to be sent away—is already probably on her way west, to some relatives, I believe, in Colorado."

"The Doughertys," Allen mused. Without warning he burst out into what was nearly a guffaw. Elaine and Rita, despite their irritation tonight with one another, exchanged looks.

"I heard the most awful story about them the other day." He snickered behind one hand. He had drunk most of his gin and his voice was booming.

Rita gave Allen a look of inquiry, but then smiled for him to continue.

"Well, if you ladies won't be offended. . . . It's not exactly a story one would repeat just anywhere. . . . It should probably go no further, you understand, than within these walls."

He laughed uproariously, at the same time struggling to decide how to tell the ladies what he knew.

Both women nodded now for him to go on. Rita kept tasting her drink sparingly, almost as if she had decided not to finish it.

"I heard this from a lawyer, an associate of my father, who assured us it is absolutely bona fide true," Allen commenced. "It seems that the present Mrs. Dougherty had a rather unusual past history . . . certainly profession. . . . Mr. Dougherty is said to have met her in a sporting house in Toronto. . . ."

Elaine spilled a bit of her drink, and Rita in great if pretended concern rose to hand her a larger napkin, perhaps hoping the story would not be elaborated on. But Mowbray went on: "It seems Mr. Dougherty was so taken with her that he would return every Friday to the *house* in question. They said he often did nothing but just gaze at her for hours, he was so smitten. Then he sued for her hand in marriage in the very house! He would not take no for an answer . . . categorically not!"

Mowbray had helped himself to more gin, without offering the ladies a refill, and he had great difficulty now in controlling his laughter.

"It was not a very long engagement!" he finished.

Finally the ladies joined in with his laughter, though since the story came from such a very young man who was from a good family background, and owing also to Elaine's rather shaky present standing in the community, the merriment was accompanied by some embarrassment and occasional pauses of discomfort on the part of the two women.

"This would be my luck," Elaine Cottrell kept saying to herself after finally leaving Rita and Allen Mowbray in the Bower of the Muses, as the music teacher on festive occasions called her studio.

"She hadn't a minute for me, her best friend!" Elaine continued to speak out loud. "Just when I needed to pour myself out to someone!"

Though it was now very late, Elaine found herself walking down Main Street in the opposite direction from her home. It was at that time not exactly decorous for any woman, married, unmarried, or widowed, to be seen unaccompanied on the streets at that hour. But Elaine was so flustered and angry, so beside herself with confusion and helplessness (both her sons frequently mimicked her, even to her face, by quoting her incessant refrain: "If only there were a man at the head of this house!"), and tonight with no one to hear her, she was muttering, "If I had a strong and reliable helpmeet, I would know what to do and how to proceed!"

She had become aware of a car horn honking and following close beside her, but she barely looked at it, so consumed with sorrow was she, and stung by the rebuff which Rita had given her this evening. But as the car kept honking its horn, Elaine at last stirred out of her reverie and, looking up, recognized Freddie Yost at the wheel of his new car.

A feeling of blissful relief swept over her at the sight of a familiar face, and without realizing how her actions might look, she hastened over to the car, whose door was wide open and the driver's hand extended to help her inside. She threw herself into the seat as if she had been waiting for him for hours.

She had no more sat down beside him, and saw the car moving rapidly down the deserted street, than she burst into sobs and weeping.

"What's wrong with my little girl tonight?" Freddie wondered, and put his free hand on her neck. She could not have chosen a better way to break the ice than her flood of tears. Keeping his hand resting lightly on her, he drove off at an increasingly high speed, turned right off Main Street, down West Main Cross, and headed for the outlying section of town like one pursued by the state police.

Freddie had only "dated" Elaine once or twice, some years ago, but he, like many other men of the town, had always kept a roving eye on this good-looking prize beauty and neglected widow. Freddie had watched and wanted her for time out of mind. A widower himself, he had a very good position at the Electric Light Co. as an engineer, but he had poor luck with the girls, as he often said. And tonight here she was, leaning against his chest, with his arm about her, helpless in some sorrow, asking for his comfort and protection.

He had never counted on such a meeting, let alone so dramatic a surrender as Elaine now afforded him, and she would never have dreamed of allowing herself to be comforted and caressed in a virtual stranger's car at midnight. But her grief over Ned, her feeling of rejection by Rita, her long years of fending for herself and her boys, all at once caused her to give vent to every hurt and disappointment of the past years. The continuing warmth of Freddie's caresses, the fresh aroma clinging to him of some pungent after-shave cologne, comforted her as no other encounter had for many weary years. With the support of his right arm, she told him nearly "everything" about Ned, Alec, her dead husband, Marius, her mortgage, her hard work, Rita, even Widow Hughes, and at last Rita's "bitchy" coldness tonight.

Unlike any man she had ever known, he welcomed all these confidences, and the more she told him of her troubles, the tighter his powerful right arm caught her to him.

"You should never have to lift a finger, my darling." Freddie spoke soothingly, giving her quick kisses whenever he could spare his attention from driving.

Elaine now looked out the car window and saw they had come to a landscape totally unfamiliar to her. The car stopped. They were parked in a lonely area near the forest preserve. There were no lights of any town, not even a remote farmhouse nearby. The surrounding sky itself seemed bereft of light. It was as if they had traveled all night through many towns and villages and farmlands to arrive finally at the edge of a wilderness. But Elaine was too weak to resist his affectionate and beguiling nearness. She surrendered first to his lips with their sweet peppermint taste, and then to his importunate throbbing desire. She had not known such impetuous hunger in any man. Freddie Yost took her to him as if he had been waiting for her love from time immemorial. Her own husband's caresses seemed now as far away as her girlhood. Even her boys appeared to vanish from her consciousness, together with the crushing weight of her heavy responsibility for them. There was only the inflamed and consuming presence of this man, who had appeared as if by a spell, out of her hopeless need for love. His masterful desire kindled her own sleeping and stifled emotions as no other man of her acquaintance ever had.

"Let Rita Fitzsimmons have her Allen Mowbrays with their mealymouthed subservience," she thought as she fell back in helpless surrender to Freddie Yost, and let his massive hands touch her throbbing breasts. His fierce male insistence swept away any impulse she might have had to deny him.

"I have outlived everybody to whom I could go as an equal."

Adele Bevington had written these lines not once but several times in succession in an old tattered cookbook of her mother's during one of her fits of depression.

Even as she wrote these words down, everybody in Fonthill had become aware that something had "happened" to Adele.

"Something has snapped in her," Rita Fitzsimmons reported. The music teacher resented the fact that Adele sneered at her for "always being on the street," and had asked Ned and Alec: "Does she *have* to go to her pupils' houses on foot?"

Rita had retorted angrily: "Doesn't that spoiled heiress know that I am too poor to ride? I cannot even afford the shoe leather, let alone a taxi."

Now the tables were turned, and Adele was seen frequently on the street. But something else even more inciting to gossip had occurred.

There was a growing number of unemployed in Fonthill at this time, especially among young men. The jobless either congregated near the courthouse or spent their days and early evenings in the reading room of the Free Library.

But quite a few of the young unemployed men were aware of what once only schoolboy truants had known: that there was a secret rear entrance to the Royal Movie Theater, reached through the men's toilet, and one could simply go into the movie house without paying if one entered the theater from this "comfort station."

Adele now attended the Royal Theater every afternoon, whether she had previously seen the current film or not. She became aware of the presence of young out-of-work men in considerable numbers scattered among the audience, and she observed that they were entering from the rear of the theater without paying. During one of the waits caused by the film's breaking while the movie was in progress, Adele had struck up a conversation with one of these youths, and after the movie was over, she had invited him to her home for coffee and a sweet. She had seen the young man in question lounging about the outside of the theater many times from her "post" at her window. His name was Bert Jeppson. He was only the first of many whom Adele would "corral," in the phrase of one of her detractors, and "drag" to her domicile.

There was still the thought, too, somewhere in the recess of her memory, that one of these unemployed young men might be, after all, hers. Certainly those veterans at the Soldiers' and Sailors' Home were not.

Word of Adele's new interest in bringing young strangers to her mansion made the rounds of Fonthill's supper tables.

"Someone should speak to her." Elaine was discussing the matter at her boardinghouse evening meal, after hearing the new gossip repeated about Miss Bevington.

Both Alec and Ned exchanged looks. They felt a shared responsibility toward Adele, but they did not see anything so reprehensible about what their "benefactor" was doing.

"But she's always helping someone." Alec contradicted his mother.

"Helping people, you call it!" His mother pretended to be offended. "Do you call taking young tramps, which is about all they are, off the streets and bringing them home with her, *helping*? It's a wonder they don't murder her!"

A more serious discussion was going on at the same time at the home of Melissa Deedes concerning Adele's new "proclivities." Judge Hitchmough had dined with the Deedes family this evening, and as was his custom, he spent a half hour or so chatting with his goddaughter Melissa.

Judge Hitchmough himself brought up the "question of Adele," much to Melissa's discomfiture. As a matter of fact, she had grown tired and weary of these after-dinner dialogues with the old justice. Melissa's parents believed Judge Hitchmough was rounding out Melissa's education, not only by his talks to her on the legal system of the English-speaking world, but also by entertaining her with his memories of his travels in Europe and Africa some forty years ago. Whereas the truth was, Melissa was bored to extinction by the judge's company, and found his ideas and his travels beneath contempt.

Indeed so bored was she with him this evening that her mind had wandered to such an extent that when she heard him say, "I wonder if *she* realizes the impression she is creating!" Melissa had to say, somewhat abashed: "About whom are we talking, Judge Hitchmough?"

He exchanged a peculiar look with her.

"Who, my dear, but Adele Bevington." He spoke quietly, as perhaps he had done many years before when he had pronounced sentence in his courtroom on someone found guilty by a jury.

"You must have heard some talk of her past," the old man went on. "I mean, my dear, even you, in your sheltered family life here, cannot be unaware of the disgrace of thirty-some years ago. . . . But this new chapter in her career is altogether, if you ask me, more inexcusable! Indeed, indeed!"

The schoolteacher sat down in a large wicker armchair at this point in the conversation, and the old man, sensing some kind of loyalty Melissa must have for the person he was raking over the coals, approached her chair.

"What is this *new* chapter, Judge?" Melissa spoke with a kind of controlled menace that made the old man stare at her hard for a moment.

"I hesitate to go into details, but it appears that she is engaged in the practice now of bringing young out-of-work men right off the streets to her home. Often at an advanced late hour!"

"Adele is extremely kind and charitable. . . . It does not surprise me," she said with lofty coolness.

The old man stopped. Words formed themselves on his lips, but he did not utter them. He was amazed, and certainly riled, to see that Melissa Deedes was not shocked by Adele's conduct. She was, it was clear, a partisan of the Bevington woman.

"Melissa, my dear girl, pardon me," he began patiently, and the schoolteacher could imagine herself being brought now before his bar to face a number of charges. "You must be aware precisely of her scandal of years ago."

"Adele has told me all about it," Melissa replied, not looking at the judge, and retaining her frigid, barely courteous demeanor.

"Told you all about it? I see." He paused. "But you also realize, I am sure you will agree with me, that her present conduct is, if anything, much more reprehensible than her first fall from grace—when at least a man older than herself may have led her astray."

When there was no response from Melissa, the judge hurried on: "Of course we have all forgiven and forgotten that," he went on, and he began pacing up and down on the rather frayed carpet, which was old even when Melissa was a child.

"Adele has not forgiven or forgotten those who persecuted her." Melissa found herself raising her voice so that it must have reached her parents and her brother, Jasper, in the next room. "Her whole life was spoiled by what happened to her as a young woman. . . ."

He stopped his pacing. It was clear that what he had been about to say, however, was cut short by this surprising turn in the conversation by a young woman he had thought he could be sure of.

"Nonetheless," he said indecisively, and touching the tight knot of his cravat, "if you could be persuaded to go to her at this time, and point out to her, if you will, that her present behavior is as little acceptable today as her great mistake of so long ago!"

"Her mistake?" Melissa flared up. She quickly drew down the edge of her dress, which had come considerably above her knee, with an abrupt motion, at which the old man averted his gaze. "What about other people's mistakes?" she chided. "Must one solitary woman be put on trial again and again?"

Judge Hitchmough removed his glasses, blew his breath upon the lenses, and wiped them with a silk handkerchief.

"I am sorry, sir, but I cannot go to her about such a thing."

"But I am speaking to you about her . . . friendship with these young men she meets . . . on the streets. I am not reviving her sin of so many years ago at all."

"Her sin? Oh, Judge Hitchmough, how can you, in this day and age, use such a term. I am surprised at you. A world traveler, an omnivorous reader. Please!"

Stung, the old man smiled, showing his broken black teeth, and then retorted: "What would you call it then, Melissa? Her achievement? Let me say at once, however, I do not condemn Adele. I have never condemned her. Even after her fall I was a welcome visitor to her father's house. I have used the word 'sin' because it was the word the town used at the time of her disgrace. Her fall made a great deal of hubbub. It was the scandal of that decade. It has not completely died down now. She has not let it die down for one thing. That is correct . . . Adele Bevington has fanned the fires of her own disgrace!"

Melissa had gone very pale. The muscles of her throat and mouth moved spasmodically, but she could not form any words. She made a kind of choking sound at last, and the judge, turning his back on her for a moment, continued: "That is why some-one"—he spit something into a handkerchief and then turned to look at her sideways—"someone, if not you, then another person, should warn her that her behavior, if it continues, may spoil her present position in the town."

"What is her position, after all!" Melissa spoke in a voice so altered by indignation Judge Hitchmough stared at her in incipient alarm. "She is nearly a recluse. She has no position!"

"Adele Bevington is the last remaining member of a family which was known even nationally in its day," he corrected her. "Her father and grandfather were among this community's most illustrious citizens."

"So they were then!" Melissa went on hotly. "But I cannot go and speak to a woman old enough to be my mother and scold her for a few charitable hours spent with young men who are out of work, and hungry! How would I dare, even if I wished to play the Pharisee! She has earned her freedom to act and say what she pleases!"

"But I don't think you still quite understand," Judge Hitchmough went on patiently, and with all the craft which he had once used to deal with an uncooperative or hostile witness in the courtroom. He sat down heavily on a small cushioned stool within arm's reach of her. "She meets totally unknown young men at a movie house, young men who have entered the theater through the toilet without paying their admission fee. She brings them, one and all, home with her, like a . . . Pied Piper! She has also, which may be worse, kept company with the former iceman Dougherty, whom she meets frequently in the back room of the Star Restaurant."

He waited for some registry of shock to show itself on Melissa's face.

"Remember, Melissa," he said when she showed no sense of shock at his revelations of Adele's actions, "she is a member of the Altrusa Club."

"The Altrusa Club?" she almost thundered at him. "What has her being a member of a club got to do with her seeing whomever she wishes to!"

"A great deal, my dear!" He had stood up now when he said this, and gazed at her with flashing eyes.

"Are you not aware of the stipulations and requirements of members in this club? Have you recently read its constitution? It is not an organization open to anyone!"

"Adele is certainly not just anyone, Judge Hitchmough. She is above all of us, in my opinion."

He stopped for a moment.

"Very well, granted," he said with portentous smoothness. He looked at his watch. "Granted she is above all of us, certainly in pedigree," and he held on to this last word as Melissa scowled at him. "All the more reason, my dear girl, why she should be warned of the peril she is in. . . . Now, let me say it, and have done with it. Either you will go to her and let her know the danger she is facing, or I shall go and tell her in a forthright manner."

"I will go," Melissa moaned. "It will not be necessary for you to see her."

Judge Hitchmough smiled broadly then and nodded several times, or perhaps his head merely shook so that it resembled nodding. He had been positive Melissa would say just what she had said in any case.

"Adele would not be happy to see you," the English teacher said in dry, almost menacing accents.

"Probably not." He coughed into a soiled handkerchief. "That is why you will be doing us all a favor, my dear . . . and especially those of us who have been life members of the Altrusa Club, on whose behalf I have been speaking to you tonight."

Melissa looked him full in the face.

"In fact," he went on, "the president of the Altrusa Club, Widow Hughes, instructed me that if you were unwilling to go to Adele, I would be entrusted with that duty."

"Widow Hughes." Melissa considered the way the cards were now falling. "I doubt, though, that anything I or anybody else can say, Judge Hitchmough, will make Adele change her ways. She will continue to do just as she pleases."

"Then we shall be compelled to drop her from the Altrusa Club's membership," the judge announced with sudden acerbity.

Melissa stood up. "Then you will have to drop me from membership also, Judge Hitchmough." Her voice was barely audible.

"Now, Melissa. You cannot mean what you say. You are overwrought!" He attempted to take her hand, but she broke away from him, remembering at the same time Adele's description of the loathesomeness of his very touch.

"Melissa," he began again. "Let us discuss this at a later date then when you are calmer."

"I am perfectly calm now, Judge. And I wish to repeat, if you drop Adele from membership in the club, I will also resign at once."

Judge Hitchmough picked up his walking stick and his large, rather grimy yellow hat.

"I didn't hear your last remark," he said in hoarse rage. He turned then to look her full in the face, his own eyes blazing so that they looked red as fire.

"Think it all over, my dear," he began, approaching her. But, at the sight of her face he drew back, as if by mistake he had touched a live wire. She had flushed scarlet, and her lower lip was trembling, and in her eyes he saw the kindled anger of a Melissa he had never known or suspected existed. He was more than troubled.

"Forgive me if I have upset you," he added, thinking it would be all that would be said today.

"You have bitterly disappointed me," she remarked, and she folded her arms as she went on glaring at him.

"I am greatly disillusioned in you. I thought you a kinder and more tolerant man. I see I have been mistaken. Good evening, Judge."

He twisted his lips in a queer grimace, which was perhaps meant to be a smile.

Then bowing his old-fashioned way, he turned his back on her and disappeared through the gloomy aperture of the front door.

Even in the dead of winter, in Fonthill, the Church of the Disciples of Christ was accustomed to erect a great tent on the outskirts of town, and invite young unknown preachers and singers with untrained voices to take part in a month-long revival. The congregation was composed largely of middle-aged to very old women, a few young farmers and their wives, and because the meeting was free, a sprinkling of the curious, the unemployed, and even a number of wastrels. Among the latter there was always someone who had to be ushered out because of his being drunk or obstreperous. The singing did not amount to much, and the only accompaniment to the hymns was a badly out-of-tune piano, with some of its keys missing. The ventilation in the tent was so poor that one might have thought it a hot evening in July, and even the young farmers found themselves fanning their faces and chests with the mimeographed programs they had been given by the ushers.

Distracted as she had not been for many years, Adele Bevington found herself on this particular oppressive, chilly night taking a longer than usual walk—past the gas works she went, past the closed and bolted beer factory and the glycerine works, almost spectral at this time, and then finally, directly in her line of vision, appeared the bizarre lights of the revival tent, the strains of its music drifting out to her blocks away.

Adele's upbringing had made her despise such demonstrations of unbridled piety and hysterical fervor. The people who attended such meetings pained her by reason of their wretched attire, the despicably ugly coiffure of the women, but above all by reason of their loud credulity and spiritual malleability.

She never understood at the time or later why she stole into the tent and took one of the back seats. Beside her was a program, which she picked up and fanned herself with assiduously, as the others near her were doing. Perhaps it was the voice of the young preacher that had drawn her in. Perhaps it was merely her dogged boredom with everything and everybody, which welcomed even the ongoing display of what she thought was vulgarity and muscular and perfervid evangelism. At least it was no worse than Reverend Lilley and his dessicated propriety!

At first she heard only the preacher's words calling his flock to repentance, asking them to put aside their old life and lack of commitment, to become new creatures in Christ Jesus, but gradually she took in his face and form. Around his fair hair and white brow moved something almost like a halo in sacred pictures. Something stirred in her, like a memory of some other time and place; indeed some other person not herself seemed to be sitting in the seat she occupied—some older, greater consciousness came over her of a better and happier time. She heard the preacher's voice as if it were music. She wanted more when it stopped and only the *amen*'s of the congregation took its place. Then her own voice was heard crying: "More! More!" The auditors heard her cry, then turned back to stare at her, and some even repeated what she had said, echoing her "More!"

Adele had risen at her own foolish audacity. She stood, so conspicuous, for she was surrounded only by empty seats. She bent over slightly, the program she had used for a fan slipping out of her right hand to the sawdust at her feet.

"Do you wish to testify, sister?" It was the voice of the young preacher conveyed to her in thrilling loud resonance.

"I . . . I only wish to hear . . . more," she responded, but this time in too faint a voice to be heard. "More, more," she whispered to herself.

The choir now raised its deafening metallic voice, and the procession of those who wished to be saved began to move toward the center of the tent, on to the platform on which the young minister stood. Adele found herself moving toward him also, though she would be the last, the most laggard of all those seeking salvation.

He had almost turned away now from the host of those whom he had blessed, when she reached him. His powerful upper body, clothed only in a blue shirt, was wet with perspiration. The veins about his eyes stood out like the tiny roots of plants. His strange almost violet-green eyes met hers. They stared at one another for an inordinate time; then he said the words: "Sister, welcome. Welcome."

Adele took his hand in hers.

"Give the sister some water," he addressed to his assistant. Adele took the tumbler from the man who held it for her, and drank audibly, greedily, till there was no more to drink.

"Blessed is she who thirsteth for the water of life," the preacher said to her in an almost harsh threatening cadence.

"I will be back," she cried after his retreating form. "I will be . . . back." She spoke almost idiotically. Turning around she saw that everybody had left. She was not certain how long she had stood there alone.

Then, without her knowing she was doing so, she hurried toward the exit through which the preacher had disappeared. There was a smaller tent beside the great one, with a half-opened flap. She walked on through.

Standing in the middle of this smaller tent was the preacher. She was unaware at first that he had taken off all his clothes. He was drinking something out of a bottle, that was all she was aware of.

"May I?" she said, and took the bottle from him. She drank even more thirstily now than she had from the tumbler of water. She saw nothing contradictory in the fact that what she drank now was whiskey.

His arms moved backward in unison as though they were wings and he would perhaps move upward into the air.

She handed him back the bottle. They both looked at one another. She could not read the meaning on his face or mouth. He seemed unconcerned that he was naked or that she had discovered he was in possession of an illegal drink.

Then she took his face in her hands and pressed her lips with all her strength and desire against his mouth.

"I will be back." She suddenly heard her own voice repeat the refrain, and she swiftly turned away from him and walked on back into the larger tent. "Yes, I will come again," and she burst into a strange, hysterical laugh, which shocked her finally into silence. It was the oppressive air of the tent, she thought to herself, the suffocating heat of the awful brown tent.

A great pennant in scarlet and black letters moved all at once in an unexpected current of air. She read its letters again and again: I KNOW MY REDEEMER LIVETH.

Then she hurried out into the night.

At first Melissa had written Adele a letter in which she outlined Judge Hitchmough's charges against her without mention of him by name. She spent hours composing the letter, but when she had finished and read and reread it, she realized she could not send such a document. It sounded like some official account of a trial held in absentia, with a guilty verdict attached. She was at the same time a little peeved that Adele had not let her know earlier that she was in the practice of inviting young unemployed men to her home for food and drink. She would have been a little more prepared for Judge Hitchmough's blistering attack on her. But then, to whom did Adele ever tell her troubles, unless it was the Cottrell boys.

She would not post the letter, and for fear her brother, Jasper, or her parents might see it, she tore it into fine bits and flushed it down the toilet. She would follow the old judge's instructions and see Adele in person, though she had never dreaded anything so much. Poor Adele was to be found guilty again after having paid for her first misdeed.

"Why, Melissa!" The older woman's delight at seeing the schoolteacher, however, died away on seeing the expression on her caller's face.

Melissa kissed her friend on the cheek.

"Something is wrong," Adele said, ushering her into the front parlor.

"No, not exactly," Melissa told her, trying to gain time to find the words to begin.

"Yes, there is. I can read faces even better than a book. I know something's wrong, so let's have it, my dear. No ceremony is needed here."

When there was no further response from the teacher, Adele wondered: "Are you in some personal difficulty of your own?"

"No, but I feel as bad as if I were!"

Adele realized then that it was something to do with her. "Well, well." She spoke in a jocular manner. "I suppose then that I am to be arrested for some new misdemeanor."

Melissa smiled faintly.

"I'm afraid I made an awful fool of myself the other evening by going to a prayer meeting, and accidentally entering the dressing room, if one can call it that, of the evangelist. . . ."

She saw, however, that Melissa had not even heard her.

"What are they saying against me now?" she brought out in an almost irate loudness.

The schoolteacher came out of her lapse of attention and stared at her friend. "To put it bluntly, Adele, they are thinking of forcing you to resign from the Altrusa Club."

"*They*, you say?" Adele spoke throatily after a pause of at least a minute.

"Judge Hitchmough," Melissa barely whispered. "And Widow Hughes perhaps."

"Widow Hughes?" Adele looked astonished. She rose, went to the front window, looked out, seeing probably nothing, and returned to her chair and sat down abruptly.

"I don't want to pry into your private life," Melissa fumbled, and colored. "But there has been talk about you . . . all over town . . ."

"Talk concerning the long-ago?"

"No."

Melissa's attention had been gradually turning to Adele's diamond necklace, which she had never seen her wear before. Adele's right hand held the jewels in a tight grasp, and as she did so the gems appeared to shimmer.

"Adele! Adele!' Melissa had risen as she said this and was coming forward to her friend.

"No," was the response. "Go back and sit down, Melissa. I urge you. Just tell me what are the charges."

Melissa remained standing. She hated herself, for she felt she was at that moment the judge's talebearer, spy, informant. Or she was the forewoman of a jury bringing in the guilty verdict.

"They say you bring young men home with you." The schoolteacher spoke dryly, almost antagonistically. "That once they are here, you all drink. . . . Sometimes you dance."

"Yes."

"That you do this constantly, at all hours. . . . You find them on the streets. . . . You find them in the movie theaters."

Adele moved her head in assent several times.

Still standing, her lips dry as ashes, the schoolteacher went on: "They feel you are a bad example."

"*They* again," Adele mused. Then, going on somewhat inconsequently: "There is so much suffering today. . . . I hardly knew of it. . . . A good deal of hunger, too." But Adele spoke these few sentences with the complete disinterest and expressionless tone of someone who has been asked to read aloud an item from an old newspaper.

"But, Adele, do you . . . *know* these young men whom you bring here?"

"I know them now, Melissa. Yes. I know them."

"And Mr. Dougherty?"

"Have they dragged his name into this also?" She dropped her hand from her necklace. She laughed bitterly.

"Judge Hitchmough . . . Widow Hughes." She shook her head. "They were my secret, my hidden, accusers of so many years ago! Though they always pretended to be my friends. But Judge Hitchmough was the worst. He was always one of the principal talebearers at the time I had my baby . . . the baby I gave away."

She waited for some time, then almost spat out: "How I loathe that old slinking sneak. Under his prim exterior must lie the heart of a rotter—a lecher of the first magnitude. I would rather lie down with spiders and bats!"

"Adele, if you are read out of the Altrusa Club, I will leave also."

"I don't think that is wise," she said firmly. "After all, consider. You are a teacher. Your reputation must remain what it is . . . spotless."

"I have already told Judge Hitchmough I will resign if you . . . are dropped."

Adele smiled in spite of herself.

"Oh, if we could only unmask all of them, my dear. They must have, every one of them, done something grimy and low once in their lily-white lives! But, Melissa, you must not defend me. . . . Let me go. Nobody can save me, nor never could."

"Do you think it wise, my dear, to bring the young men home with you?"

"Wise? Why should I be wise at my age?"

"But if it is misunderstood, my dear."

"Let it be misunderstood. I can't care any more. . . . I paid for my sin once. I refuse to pay for it again. There is no law that says I cannot feed and comfort young men who are out of work, discouraged, and haven't had a mouthful to eat for days."

"But you have given them . . . brandy."

"Oh, well," Adele said. She rose and went over to the door.

"Don't send me away," Melissa cried, getting to her feet. "Don't make me feel I am one of them!"

"You aren't one of them, precious, but you aren't one of my sort, either."

"You must not send me away, Adele," the schoolteacher almost begged, and threw herself into Adele's arms.

"Who said anything about sending you away." Adele comforted her, smoothing her hair, and kissing her forehead again and again.

"I believe in you thoroughly, Adele. . . . I love you . . . I love you more than I do my parents."

"You must not say that."

"I do say it."

She kissed the teacher again. "You've said words tonight I desperately needed to hear."

They slowly broke away from one another's arms.

"Oh, please be careful, Adele," the younger woman urged her as she stood at the open door a few minutes later. "Don't be . . . too conspicuous, dearest."

Adele smiled and shook her head.

"I'll try to be careful for you," she promised, and kissed the teacher goodbye. Then they held one another again in a last passionate embrace like two friends about to separate forever.

A kind of bittersweet satisfaction came over Adele now that she was aware of her new disrepute. When she had ruined her reputation and that of her family so long ago, she had been surrounded by those whose task from then on was to protect her from her own ignominy and loss of honor, and also save her, if at all possible, from further calumny. They were kind but strict jailers. They loved her despite her moral obloquy.

But today, in the cloud of her new shame and ruin, she had no one to whom she could truly turn. She was completely responsible to and for herself. Hence her bitter feeling of "satisfaction." And her new disgrace in many ways was much graver. For when she had "fallen" before, she had been, after all, a girl. And her seducer had been a man of high position, much older than herself, who also, like her family, volunteered to protect her from any future suffering and scandal. But now—and here again the strange sense of satisfaction came over her—she was her own seducer, her own source of disgrace. She had willingly broken the rules of society, a society less censorious and straightlaced than the one she had grown up in, but still hidebound and unsympathetic. She had gone out into the highways and byways and brought young men to her chambers, so said the gossip, had plied them with strong drink and then taken them to her bed and showered them with the suffocating love that life had so long deprived her of.

"Why doesn't she go to some great city, where her kind are permitted, or at least ignored?" one housewife commented, on learning of the growing scandal.

People walking down Main Street would now look up at her high second-story window overlooking the Royal Theater in hopes of catching a glimpse of the "bad woman." Often, to their glee, they would see both Adele and some young day-laborer looking down absentmindedly upon the street below.

Adele was not only disappointed in Melissa, she was angry with her. She found her kind of sympathy and commiseration insipid, flat, fundamentally shallow, if not insincere. What did Melissa know of life? How could she teach Shakespeare and Marlowe, living as she did in the safe gray maw of her middle-class family?

But she was no better herself! She had allowed her own family, after her sin, to cloister her as securely as if she had been a nun. And she had let them take away her son, who by now might have stood here today and defended his mother, have made her secure against the scandal that was now falling upon her unprotected head, for his love would have been enough to silence all malicious tongues. And didn't the fools see that when she allowed young men to visit her in her sitting room they were there only as an embodiment of her son, and not her lovers! And the few drops of brandy that she had let them have, was not that too only some form of communion and nothing more, some balm of comfort which Our Lord himself had given to his weary disciples.

She could think of nobody to whom to turn now but Charles Radwell, who lived some fifteen miles from Fonthill. She had once thought she was in love with the doctor, but she knew in her heart he did not care for women. He lived alone, or shared his bachelorhood with some rough young farm boy, who acted as his chauffeur and handyman. He had been saddled with his old mother most of his life, and used her miserable invalid existence as an excuse for not marrying until it had got "too late," and he was too old. Once, long ago, a few years after her disgrace, she had told Charles she loved him. He had stared at her as if she had confessed to poisoning someone. His discomfiture at her confession of love had, however, only made her care for him the more. She had indeed pursued him in a vague, inconsequential manner, but at last, seeing he could never belong to anybody, engulfed in his obsessive devotion to his medical practice, as he had been earlier bound over to his ceaseless devotion to his mother, she made herself forget him as best she could—until now. Yes, until now. She knew he would not welcome *her*, but he would welcome her trouble, her disgrace, her problem. He always welcomed tragedy, illness, desperate sorrow. She would bring them all to him today.

She called a livery company, which charged excessive prices, and told the driver an emergency compelled her to go at once to Dr. Radwell's house in the country.

In the car she thought back to her unsuccessful courtship of him. Perhaps she had been drawn to him because he knew her story and because she was sure that he could never be hers. Never be any woman's. During the period in which they had seen one another frequently, he had, in an undemonstrable, almost undetectable way, encouraged her advances to him. "Encouraged" is perhaps too strong a word. But he allowed her to touch him, to praise his beautiful hair, which she once told him was "hyacinthine." He had wondered what that actually meant, and she was unable to explain its meaning except that it came from the Greek myth concerning the boy whom Apollo had loved.

"But does it refer to the color of his hair or to its curliness, or what?"

That was when Adele had taken his hand in hers.

"You are a cold fish," she had once said to him in a voice trembling with anger, when he had merely allowed his hand to rest in hers for all of a half hour, without returning any pressure of his own.

But as in her case, his dead family still ruled his life. His mother would not have approved of his getting married, and he obeyed her command from the grave.

Now here she was, years later, seeking out this cold, inscrutable man whose hair was still beautiful, perhaps more so now that it was snow-white. Yes, she wondered, what on earth did "hyacinthine" mean. Certainly Hyacinth, at any rate, had not had white hair at the age of fifteen.

She had forgotten how old Charles Radwell was. But when he came down the steps of the front porch to help her out of the livery cab, she saw how much he had changed. He was so much older than she! And his house, which she remembered as huge, looked small and mean, its roof in a state of disrepair, the tall, blackened chimney about to topple.

"I have all but given up practicing medicine, Adele," he told her once they were comfortable in his front parlor.

"I should slap you for that remark, Charles," Adele chided. "I didn't come here for medical advice. In fact, now that I'm here, I don't know exactly why I did come. . . ."

He laughed at that, and since he so seldom ever even smiled, let alone broke out into laughter, she was heartened after all for having come.

"But you must be here for something specific, Adele. You're not exactly known for your social visits."

"True," she agreed, and closed her eyes and brought her lips into a thin line. "I suppose I came here for something."

"To ask my hand in marriage, I presume." He laughed again.

"And why not, Charles? You might do worse!"

"We would make a fine pair," he said softly.

She began tugging at her white gloves, and then pulled them back tight on her hands.

"To come to the point of my visit, though, Charles . . . whatever I may get up the courage to say to you today—you are expected to do nothing about what I will tell you. . . . I have, however, I will tell you, disgraced myself again, Charles."

"Oh, nonsense."

"You remember my first disgrace?"

"I remember you had a baby out of wedlock."

She was a bit hurt by his abrupt frankness—the typical abruptness of a doctor.

"So I did, Charles. I think you are the only person living who knows it, though, for a fact."

"But you are surely not going to have another baby now, Adele?" He spoke now very slowly, almost sleepily, like the Charles of many years ago.

"So far as I know, I am not." She spoke in a kind of coquettish way, but her voice was too sad for that of a flirt, and it made Charles Radwell look at her carefully. "But I've set all tongues a-wagging again. It seems, Charles, I have a practice of filling my rooms up with young men who have no place else to go. Out-of-work boys."

"Well, what is so odd about that, Adele? I've always filled my home with young people. They come and go at all hours. Why shouldn't you?"

"But I have no profession to practice such as yours, Charles. No waiting or consulting room."

She watched him now as if for a sign to tell more. When he said nothing, she went on: "They feel I've overstepped the bounds, Charles. I'm to be read out of the Altrusa Club . . . dropped, as an undesirable. Judge Hitchmough and Widow Hughes are behind that move."

"The Altrusa Club." He could not conceal his scorn. "Why you ever belonged to such a thing is beyond me in the first place. I should think you'd be relieved to be dropped. And by Widow Hughes, and Judge Hitchmough! Good God, Adele."

He could not help showing, however, a certain annoyance that she was in "trouble" again.

"You've always worried too much about what people say, Adele. You should have left the damned town of Fonthill when you had . . . your trouble. I always said so!"

"I sometimes think," she began, searching in her purse for a smoke, "that if I could only find my own boy, everything would be different. I would be happy, that is, caring only for him, working for his welfare. We would have been out of reach of the Altrusas!"

He came over to her, shaking his head as he did when he saw the condition of one of his patients, and offered her one of his own Turkish cigarettes.

When he had lit it for her, he said: "It isn't very likely you will find him now, Adele."

"I suppose that is why I seem to think about him all the time."

"The war took so many of our young boys from here," he went on in what at first seemed to be one of his inconsequential remarks, so characteristic of him. But then he added: "He would have been the right age to have been a soldier, and gone across."

She nodded, and extricated some of the bits of tobacco that had come loose in her mouth.

"Don't you ever long for something, too, you have missed, Charles?"

"I won't let myself, Adele. That's why, old as I am, and God knows I am old, I keep on doctoring. Or to put it more exactly, my patients insist on coming back to me, without me having to tell them to . . . as if I knew anything really. But they get comfort out of just telling me they ache here or have a stitch in their side there, and so on. . . . Most of being a doctor, Adele, is letting them tell you how they pain."

"It's all mostly pain, isn't it, Charles?"

"Well, Adele, you have always exaggerated."

"But if you *let yourself*, Charles, wouldn't you feel perhaps you had missed the important something in life?"

"I've never let myself dwell on that, Adele, to tell you the truth . . . or the minute I began to do so, *think*, as you say, how much I have missed, I'd get on with my work."

"I walk up and down the streets at night looking at the faces of the young men. . . . People think I am looking for a lover . . . but I am looking for him."

He had come over to sit near where she sat, and he took her hand. Then after a while she saw he was only taking her pulse.

"Adele, if you will allow me, I am going to give you something to take for your nerves. Will you let me give you something?"

"Oh, Charles, yes. I would take anything you gave me, I suppose."

Before he could leave the room, however, Eddie Pomeroy, his hired man, came in with muddy boots and said something in a whisper to the doctor.

"I'll be back directly," Charles told her in an almost unfriendly voice, and he left the room with Pomeroy, who tipped his hat at her in a manner that she found offensive.

She began to cry a little now that she was alone. She had made a fool of herself by coming, and by telling him what she had told him. She was old, too, like the doctor, though she appeared so much younger. And perhaps there was no real disgrace to her life, after all. She was too old to be disgraced. She was only foolish, that was all.

She saw Eddie Pomeroy standing before her, extending to her a small, carefully wrapped bottle.

"This is the medicine, ma'am," he said. "The doctor has an emergency call in his office, and won't be able to see you out."

The hired man had almost to force the bottle into her hand.

"The doctor is very sorry," Eddie went on. "He says he will phone you tonight or tomorrow for sure. . . . The instructions are on the bottle, ma'am."

Still she could not speak, but she held the bottle and stared at it.

She sat on for some time after the hired man had left the room. She rose then, and walked toward the front door, but on the way she saw a door that she had not remembered from her visits from times long past. Something made her push the door open.

Within was a very spacious sleeping chamber, in the center of which rose a king-size bed, with rather resplendent comforters and two pillows.

She saw that the bed had been hastily made and a comforter merely thrown over the rest of the bed clothes. She walked on into the room. There were the imprints of two heads on the two pillows. On the bedpost over the pillow with the deeper imprint hung the hired man's rugged outdoor jacket and his hat. She stared a long time at the imprints of the two heads, and then hurried on back to the livery cab.

The true repercussions of her visit to Charles Radwell did not come to her until that night, when she was to remember again and again the one "detail," the detail of the imprint of the two heads on adjoining pillowcases.

But without warning, remembering what she had seen in the bedroom, her torment made her cry out in the rented car on her way back home, so that the driver turned around and said, "Did you say something, Miss Bevington?" And when there was no reply, he called out: "Are you all right, ma'am?"

"Don't worry about me, Elmer. Even if you hear me give a shout or scream, pay it no attention," she assured him. "I've just had a very disappointing meeting back there," and she waved her hand in the direction of Dr. Radwell's house.

At home that night, sleepless despite having treated herself to the doctor's medicine more times than the instructions on the bottle called for, she finally put on her dressing gown and sat down at her writing desk. Since she could not "sleep on" her chagrin and disappointment, she would write it down. The hours went by, and her writing continued. She would tear up one sheet and begin another. The wastebasket was soon full of the discarded versions. Finally she finished one that seemed right. Yes, this was the one she would send, even if it might prove the end of her friendship with Charles.

The younger Cottrell happened in as she was studying the envelope as if it were a winged messenger that, were she only to loose her fingers, would take off at once and drop into the doctor's hands.

Pouring Ned a cup of her morning coffee, she said: "I have written a terrible letter to Dr. Radwell."

He nodded, wanting to hear more.

"Would you care to hear me read it, Ned?"

He grinned assent.

"Very well." She pretended she would read the letter only because he desired it, and much against her better judgment. "If you must hear it, you must . . . but I warn you. The contents are dreadful."

Sitting down near her, Ned brought his legs up, locked his hands around his knees, half closed his eyes, and smiled as she read:

> *My dearest Charles,*
>
> *I cannot begin to tell you of the anguish I felt at seeing the imprint of two heads on your pillowcases. It is so unlike you, so unworthy of a man of your intellect and breeding to sleep with a common groom.*
>
> *I can tell you now what you have already known or suspected over the years, that after my annihilating experience with the man who abandoned me, it was you who occupied the central position in my life. I see my love for you, call it, if you will, my passion, was absolutely misdirected.*
>
> *What is worse, even after seeing the proof on your bed of what you really are, I still love you, hopelessly, unavailingly, certainly foolishly. How foolishly and unavailingly, those imprints on your pillowcases well reveal. If the world could see that bed, all the whisperings and talk directed for so long a time against me would be as empty air compared to what they could say about you. But you are a man! You are protected against the world. I never was, and can never be.*
>
> *Nonetheless I long to see you again, perhaps only to be treated to even worse humiliation and suffering.*
>
> *Forever yours,*
> *Adele*

She felt a kind of outraged amusement when she looked up from her reading and saw the expression on her young listener's face.

At the look she leveled at him, he opened his eyes wide, then closed them long enough to say in a hushed voice: "And that is all of it?"

She looked at him fiercely.

"I mean," he tried to explain, "you won't add more?"

"What more, in God's name, could one add!" She licked the envelope and pressed it and its contents against the table. She got up and handed it to him.

"Mail it when you go out." She addressed him as she might have spoken to Val Dougherty.

"Adele," Ned said turning his face directly toward her. "Do you think it's smart to send it? I mean," he hastened to assure her at the sight of the thundercloud coming over her face, "it is a wonderful letter, or epistle, I guess you could call it."

"Why not call it an epistle," she said acidly. "By all means, call it an *epistle*."

"But, Adele"—he spoke to her now as if he were the older one—"won't it ruin everything? Don't you think he'll think you're a—"

". . . a fool? Of course he will! I am a fool."

"Well." Ned looked down at the envelope, straightened his sleeves, and smiled. "It's a damned grand thing. I wish I could write somebody a letter like that."

"If you live long enough, precious, you will."

"But"—he made the mild protest—"if you want to go on knowing . . . Charles Radwell, Adele?"

She had risen and was walking around the parlor, smoking one of the doctor's cigarettes (she had carried away the package with her).

"He sleeps with his groom," she said. "Can you beat it?"

"But maybe he's so old, he needs . . . attention."

"Attention! My Christ! Oh, Ned, really."

She disappeared into the next room. He went on looking at the letter, as if the very words put down there might suddenly speak out again with her voice.

When she came back into the room he saw she had put on one of her diamond bracelets. She looked, somehow, he thought, taller and more confident.

"Nobody sleeps with his groom." She spoke in such a deep

voice, in such positive, judicial tones, that had he not been looking directly into her face he might have thought a stranger had entered to pronounce judgment.

"Nobody could do such a thing! It is entirely appalling. And then to allow the bed to be unmade, staring at one like that. . . ."

"Adele, are you sure it's not him that is the father . . . of your boy?"

She came toward him as if she were about to strike him.

"Good God in heaven," she said at last. "I thought I told you who was the father. A *man* was the father," she added bitterly. "A man . . ."

"I see." Ned wilted under the weight of her rage. "Of course he couldn't be the father."

"But I think now I loved him more than the real man . . . who ruined me."

She almost sang out the words.

"I'll mail it, Adele. . . . This very morning, I'll send it off."

She nodded, the grief beginning to rise up in her, making her bosom heave and shake.

"But I bet you'll regret it."

"I haven't the slightest doubt you are right. But if one contin- ued to act sensible, where strong feelings are concerned, wouldn't one go mad? Or shoot somebody? After all, a letter like this is better than a gun or knife, or setting the house on fire. . . . Mail it! Go to the main Post Office, better still, hand it to the postmaster himself."

She came up to him and held him to her, and then bestowed a long wet kiss on his lips.

"If one must sleep beside his groom, one should close and lock the door, Ned. Close and lock it. That sight was worse than a whole counterpane covered with . . . condoms!"

The last word spoken by a woman who, after all, was a lady shocked the boy. He would have thought she would not know such a word, despite her "history." For her history had always seemed to him like something pretty well romantic, even poetic.

He turned his face away from her, and putting the "terrible" letter in his breast pocket, hurried out of the room, at the same time uttering a choked "Goodbye."

Both Alec and Elaine wondered whether Ned had been drinking again as they all sat assembled that evening at the supper table. The younger of the Cottrells sat unusually straight in his chair, but his face was flushed and he would snicker occasionally without warning, and several times he held his hand over his mouth, suppressing, one supposed, his merriment over some dark secret he knew.

"Well, what's so funny, will you tell us?" Alec inquired at last, when there was another tremolo of laughter coming from Ned. Alec slapped his napkin against his thigh. "Will you let us share the joke?"

"It's nothing at all, Alec." Ned pretended now to be serious and he turned slightly pale. He knew even then that unless he was careful he would give away Adele Bevington's secret.

The special guest at the dinner table that evening was Keith Gresham, a young man who worked in a lawyer's office and had been "across" in the war, in fact was said to have been seriously wounded in France, but his sturdy build and steady eye and pink-colored cheeks disputed the story that his health had suffered from his war experiences. His hands were even more massive than Val Dougherty's, and he allowed them to rest on the white Irish linen tablecloth tonight as if he held the reins of decorum and order in his place at the head of the table. But he winked at Ned, whom he had always favored over Alec, and he said in a voice a bit too high for his rather brawny build: "Can't you let us in on what you're keeping up your sleeve, Neddy?"

"Don't encourage him in his wickedness, Mr. Gresham," Elaine entreated the boarder in a voice that wavered between anxious supplication and irritation. "He's only too eager to tell something unsavory."

" 'Unsavory' isn't a strong enough term for what he's thinking," Alec snorted, toying with his food. He was seldom hungry at supper, but around midnight he worked up a voracious appetite and then either rifled the ice box or went off to the Star Restaurant, where he had run up a considerable bill.

"Now let's have no unpleasantness when Mr. Gresham is

present," Elaine begged her sons. "After working hard all day in a law office, I'm sure he's in no mood to have to hear you boys scrap and argue."

She turned then an almost beatific look on the young veteran.

"I wish you would call me Keith, Mrs. Cottrell," he responded to her entreaty.

Elaine was about to say she would welcome calling him by his Christian name when Gresham looking straight at the younger boy said: "All right now, Neddy, quit teasing us; and let's have your secret! We know you've got one, so out with it!"

Elaine and Alec exchanged glances with one another.

Ned, coloring violently and looking sideways at the boarder, finally got out: "It's about Adele Bevington, of course."

"But why 'of course,' Neddy?" Gresham spoke with pretended naïveté.

"Keith, don't egg him on now," Alec implored weakly. "He's done enough to ruin that poor lady already. Don't get him started!"

"*I* ruin *Her*!" Ned almost let out a war whoop. Then, picking up his fork, he attacked with fury the stuffed pork chop on his plate.

"I think we should change the subject," Elaine proposed, "and change it at once. I'm sure Mr. Gresham has a score of topics he can discuss that are of more interest than where the conversation is going at the moment."

Keith gave a few mumbled remarks on how "the law" was boring enough to have to "read" in an attorney's office without burdening the supper table with it in the evening, and then, as he reached for his water glass, his right hand trembled so badly that everyone at the table turned their eyes away in embarrassment. In fact, Keith Gresham had considerable difficulty in bringing the tumbler of water to his lips at all.

Then, setting down his water glass without drinking, Keith said: "Just the same, if Mrs. Cottrell will not be angry with me, I'd like to hear what Ned has say about Miss Bevington. I'm sure she's a lot more interesting than my law office. She's someone, in fact, I have always wanted to be introduced to."

"Well, that can certainly be arranged, Keith," Ned said with impudent loudness.

"Ned, I will not speak to you again, young man," Elaine warned him.

"But what have I done, Mother?" the boy asked with an injured "noble and innocent" tone. "I merely mention the name of the person I work for, Miss Bevington, and I get all these nasty glances and warnings and scoldings."

"We'll let the subject of Miss Bevington rest for once and all at this table," Elaine intoned as if saying an extra blessing. "Mr. Gresham will understand, I'm sure." She attempted to smooth over the awkward turn the conversation had taken.

"Adele has had to go to see Dr. Radwell, that's all there is to my secret," Ned said angrily. He noted in the silence that followed that everybody wished to hear more of this meeting with the doctor.

"Is she ill, by chance?" Elaine inquired indifferently. She picked up a piece of her pear salad, and tasted it critically.

"Well, she certainly *was* after her visit to the doctor's house, to hear her," Ned went on in a casual, bored tone. He leaned back in his chair and looked from one person to the other. His glance then rested on Keith, whose expectant countenance encouraged him on.

"She was terribly upset by something she saw at Dr. Radwell's house, so that she was, as Mother might say, quite beside herself. I was upset, in fact, for her."

"I bet you were!" Alec said acidly, but even he did not forbid the younger boy from continuing.

"Her emotional turmoil, you see, stemmed from the fact that on leaving the doctor's house, where she had gone to have a private talk, she saw that the bedroom door had been left open." Ned kept his eyes glued to Keith, and Keith, like a prompter, never let his eyes stray from the boy. "She walked on into the room. Then she saw that the two pillows on the doctor's bed had the imprints of two separate heads. . . ."

Still watching Ned, Keith raised his water glass, this time with his left hand, and drank. His left hand did not tremble.

"One, of course, was the imprint of the head of the doctor," Ned went on, speaking directly to Keith. "The other imprint was that of the doctor's chauffeur, or as Miss Bevington calls him, his groom."

"Well, that's quite natural." Elaine now spoke up, her cheeks a flaming red. "The doctor is very old and has to have constant attendance. He might have a heart attack in the middle of the night, and Eddie Pomeroy is right there at arm's length, as he should be."

Ned, however, had given the boarder such a look of devilish mischief that the young lawyer's assistant burst into a raucous guffaw.

"I'll speak to you after the meal," Alec told Ned with a murderous look.

"If you young men will excuse me for a while," Elaine announced, standing up, "I'll go out and see to our dessert, which is a sort of 'special' tonight in honor of our guest of this evening." She looked straight at Keith, who flushed and bowed a little. "I promised Mr. Gresham I would prepare him the 'special' some time ago, but with one thing and another, I was not able to until tonight."

Elaine, hardly taking her eyes off Ned, however, hurried then out to the kitchen.

"You low-down little cad," Alec remarked when his mother was out of earshot, addressing Ned. "Have you not one shred of decency?"

"Excuse me, Alec," Keith butted in. "But we did sort of worm it out of Ned, didn't we? At least I did, and I apologize for it."

"Your apology, Keith, is not going to let the little bastard off the hook all the same!"

"Oh, now, Alec," Keith implored. "Go on. Please! You can punch me in the kisser, see, but don't take it out on him."

Alec now turned his full scrutiny on the boarder. This speech, proving Keith's preference for his younger brother, brought to the fore all his feelings of jealousy and envy. He jumped up, threw down his napkin, and rushed out of the room.

"Good riddance," Ned sang out, and beamed at Keith. But Keith, without so much as a glance at Ned, carefully putting down his napkin by his dessert fork, hurried on out after Alec.

"For pity's sake, where has everybody gone?" Elaine wailed as she brought in a tray of the "special" dessert, a gigantic huckleberry pie with a monument of stiff whipped cream rising in its center. She put down the heavy tray on the little sideboard and looked at the empty seats in anguish. Her eye then slowly fell on the "guilty" one.

"I don't know what is to become of you, I swear, Ned. Now see what you've done. Ruined the pleasant evening meal with your scandalous talebearing . . . stirred your only brother up again to fury, and now one of our nicest and best-paying boarders has left the table without finishing his meal!"

Elaine now followed after the two young men and began calling out their names—"Alec!" and "Keith!"—from the threshold of the front door.

Ned helped himself to a mammoth piece of huckleberry pie and was nearly finished downing it when Elaine, Alec, and Keith reentered the dining room more or less arm in arm, and then all sat down somewhat stiffly, like guests who had just arrived.

Elaine, ignoring her younger boy entirely, served helpings of the huckleberry "special" to Alec and Keith in a churchlike silence.

Ned stared at his brother's face. Alec had been weeping and his eyes were quite red and puffy, while Keith looked very fatherly, and a bit stuffed-shirt-like, as he sat down in the big chair at the head of the table.

But soon nothing was heard but *ah*'s and *oh*'s from Keith and Alec as they ate mouthful after mouthful of the huckleberry surprise, which should have been, after all, the main event of the evening repast.

Elaine had dried the last of the dishes, and thrown the sudsy dishwater down the drain, and wrung out the last of the many tea towels.

As she walked through the hall on her way to the front sitting room she spied Gresham's new spring hat. She picked it up cautiously and looked inside the crown to see his head size, seven and a fourth, and noted the name of the Chicago store where he had purchased it. She caught a fleeting scent like nasturtiums from the inside band, coming, she supposed, from some hair oil he used. She did not let go of the hat, though, and finally raised it to her face and touched it to her lips. Her misfortune, she often thought to herself, was that she loved almost all young men.

Keith had gone home. Ned and Alec had disappeared, she thanked fortune, and she could sit now in the front parlor and collect her thoughts without their constant yapping and snapping at one another, and the silence would allow her to forget Ned's infernal, outrageous fabrications about people.

She had hardly begun to settle down with some mending when, looking up, she caught sight from the front window of Keith returning in quick, if uneven, strides toward the house. Elaine put down her sewing, pulled her skirt down a bit, and pushed back a lock of her hair.

"You forgot your new hat, Keith," she greeted him.

"You found it!" He blushed faintly under his last summer's tan.

"Won't you sit down, though, a moment?" Elaine said softly. Away from her duties as hostess and mother of two obstreperous boys, she was now, though nearly ten years older than he, like a high-school girl, he thought.

"I believe it's going to storm, Mrs. Cottrell," he said, and his eyes strayed over to the socks she had been darning.

"Oh, I think so," she agreed. "It's much too sultry and warm for this time of year, isn't it?"

"I'm sort of glad I forgot my hat." Keith looked toward her now. "I wanted to say something, if I may."

Elaine touched her imitation-pearl necklace. "Go on, Keith." She gave him her full smile now.

"About Ned," he began, and Elaine, scowling a little, got out: "Well?"

"I hope you won't be too hard on him, Mrs. Cottrell, after tonight's little upset. I don't think he quite realizes sometimes what he is telling us."

"I expect he doesn't," Elaine said composedly, and let her hands fall idly to her lap.

"He's such a fine boy, really."

"Oh, thank you." Elaine's face brightened, and then melted in softness. "It's not easy being both mother and father to two such scamps, I can tell you. And Ned is, of course, the wilder of the two, even though he's the younger, as you know."

"That's the best time of all." Keith's voice was as soft now as hers.

"What time, Mr. Gresham?"

"Their time of life." Keith's voice rose now like a soloist's. "When you're their age, you know, fifteen, and twenty . . . After that, what is it?" He passed his hand over his face.

"But you're hardly more than a boy yourself," Elaine protested.

"Oh, no, ma'am . . . I'm thirty-two almost."

"That's terribly young for a man."

"Well, I suppose, if you compare it with a hundred."

Elaine gave out a short unmusical laugh.

"If you ever felt, though," he went on, "that you needed me to help you with—Ned, at least . . . I don't know about Alec. He's already a young man. But Ned . . ."

"To straighten him out, you mean?" Elaine's voice fell to a whisper.

"I guess that's what I mean."

"I'm afraid the damage has been done." She sighed. "Wasn't that perfectly awful what he said tonight about Adele Bevington, though? Poor Adele!"

After a moment's pause, they both burst out at the same time into what was little less than a guffaw, and then caught themselves and tried to restrain their mirth.

"He makes up stories about people, you know." Elaine covertly studied her visitor, then looked away.

"I have no doubt." Keith grinned.

"He's quite wicked, in fact," Elaine went on. "And he looks so like a little angel, but he's an imp. A true imp. Even his dad used to say that about him. 'We have a little imp on our hands,' Marius always said."

Keith's eye fell now on her wedding ring, which, worn though it was from use, appeared to shine in the darkness of the room.

"Oh, but you're blessed, you know," he told her. "Think what a future you have—in them."

Elaine became somewhat uneasy now. She did not quite know where the drift of his visit might lead. It was more than the hat, she saw.

"I'm sure," she said weakly, "that one day you will settle down and raise a family of your own."

An awkward lengthy pause divided them from one another then.

"You were in the war, I believe." Elaine hesitantly broke the silence.

He started a little. "Oh, well," he nodded, "yes, I was—across. . . ."

"And were wounded?" She was frightened by her own boldness.

He nodded.

"I hope Ned will never have to go," he muttered, and then sprang to his feet.

"Let me go get your hat." She hurried into the adjoining hall.

She returned so quickly that she surprised him in the act of wiping his eyes with his pocket handkerchief.

He hastily took his hat, which she held out to him, and as he took it she noticed for the first time what strong, heavily veined hands were his. They did not look like those of a young man who worked in a law office.

"If I can ever do anything to put young Ned straight, at any time, please call on me." He spoke confidingly to her.

She was a bit taken aback by hearing her own phrase, "put straight," but his willingness to do something for her pleased her greatly.

"I suppose a good whipping a few years back might have been beneficial," she ventured, and her face took on a look of harassment.

They both found themselves looking at one another in a kind of frightened, eloquent manner.

"May I kiss you good night, Mrs. Cottrell?" He choked out the words.

She put her face up to his, and he kissed her chastely, dryly, almost coldly. But his eyes flashed. He put on his hat all of a sudden, and then as suddenly took it off, for he probably remembered he was still in the house.

"Good night, Keith." She spoke in a hushed, perhaps matronly way.

Still he did not move to leave.

"It's so wonderful to come here—to a real home."

He pressed her hand, and she felt the trembling in his fingers as he let go.

She thanked him. She whispered, "Much obliged, my dear,"

as she saw him go out and down the walk. She watched him out of sight.

He was a kind of young giant of a man, but she noted there was something not quite right with the way he walked. A little zigzag toward the left, and a certain dragging of one foot.

"He said he was across," she whispered aloud. "He sees me as a mother, I guess," and she turned away from watching where he had disappeared into the dark.

As to his straightening out poor Ned, she thought, and she sat down at her desk, sighing, and shaking her head. He'd spoil the boy just as we have all spoiled him, and though he's a big strapping fellow and a soldier at that, he'd let Ned get away with murder just as I've done. . . . Keith Gresham. She smiled, and the tears stood in her eyes.

A black cloud lifted from Elaine's house, as she put it, when one morning, after having cooked breakfast for everybody (a few boarders showed up occasionally for this meal), she opened the pages of *The Courier* to the section called "About Town and Country" and saw as if in letters of flame the notice:

> Mrs. Val Dougherty and her daughter Marilyn have gone for an indefinite stay to Mrs. Dougherty's parents in the vicinity of De Beque, Colorado. Mrs. Dougherty is the former Maude Renshaw.

She could not contain her feeling of relief. An iron thong holding her since the day she had found out what Ned had done was broken.

"My family and my home are saved," she kept repeating on the telephone to all and any whom she could reach. Rita, Widow Hughes, even Adele, were all rung up and given the joyful tidings. Rita, almost as relieved as Elaine, called back several times, in hopes of hearing additional good news. Adele's reaction was more measured, but Elaine was too buoyant probably to notice such moderation.

"It is also conclusive proof," Elaine told everybody, "that my boy is not the guilty party. Else why would they have fled like this, and to a part of the country one has never heard mention of?"

She shed over her ironing board so many tears of thanksgiving that she sprinkled shirts, sheets, with this dewy expression of happiness, and in her rapture she scorched several of her brand-new tablecloths.

As she quieted down a bit, she would repeat every so often under her breath: Little do they know of what a mother goes through. They will never know because they are men. Excruciating as the pain of giving birth is, the sorrows that come from then on are even more immeasurable. That is why, no matter what a mother may do in this life, our Savior will welcome her with open arms at the gates of Heaven, for He alone of all the men who were ever born knows what a mother goes through.

Ned, though clearly shaken by the news, in contrast to his mother's open ebullience, was sober as a judge, and dry-eyed. Alec appeared totally indifferent, even contemptuous, and soon after left the house for what he described as an important engagement.

After having read the piece in *The Courier* enough times to memorize it, Ned sauntered out to the backyard, and though the evening was drawing on, and it was still chilly at this time of year, he sat down on the old swing attached to an elm tree, which he seldom used now since he was growing up so fast. Elaine watched him from the kitchen window, and finally catching sight of her face, he smiled at her. That smile brought her more happiness than anything she could remember for some time. And though Ned did not resemble her husband in any one particular, his smile at that moment brought back Marius's own face to her, clearly and painfully.

Drying her hands, and throwing on a sweater, she drew up a chair and sat down beside Ned in the backyard.

"Don't you feel relieved, dear?" she wondered.

"I guess I do." He smiled broadly again.

"You don't know how handsome you look when you smile, Ned. You should do it more often. Scowling don't become either of you boys, you know. I have thanked God all day, though, that you are not guilty after all. And you are now scot-free."

She laid her hand on his arm.

"I have one favor, though, to ask of you, Neddy. Please now don't be short with mother when you hear what it is, but I do hope you will comply."

"Yes," he said dutifully.

"I think it would be wonderful if you went over and called on Val Dougherty this evening."

"Me?" he exlaimed and pointed with his index finger to his chest.

"Yes, Ned. . . . You like him, you told me."

"That was when I was a little boy," he retorted in a contemptuous tone that recalled Alec's way of speaking. "Why, Mom, should I go?"

"For one thing, he must be terribly lonesome tonight, with his wife and daughter gone for good."

"How do you know it's for good?"

"I have my source of information." She spoke somewhat primly. "Besides the very fact the newspaper would print it meant they would never return."

"But if someone has to go, why don't you go see him, Mom—if he needs cheering up, that is. After all, I am only a kid, to quote you. What cheer could I bring him?"

"A lot. . . . After all, Neddy, wrongfully or not, you were implicated in his life, and now, partly because of you, he's left high and dry."

"Just a while ago, you said I was innocent. Now you say I am implicated!"

She crossed her arms and shook her head.

"Please go, for my sake, Ned . . . won't you? Maybe we could persuade him to board with us too, now, once or twice a week."

"Oh, so that's where the wind is blowing from!" Ned grinned, and then gave out a low whistle. "So that's what it is."

"No, it's not my main reason for sending you, Ned. You know me better than that. But, for heaven's sake, I can't go to see him. How would it look? And he's always liked you so much. Remember when he used to bring the ice and let you ride with him on the truck. You were so crazy, too, about his horses, and he let you ride them. . . . Go on and see him tonight, Ned, dearest."

She rose and bent over and kissed him on the mouth, and Ned took the hand that bore the battered wedding ring and held it tight, and muttered he would go.

That was one evening Ned would not only remember, but strange to say, it was also an evening and an event about which he did not tattle and gossip and "tell."

What he saw that evening ended his days perhaps as a talebearer and town tattler.

"I am not the same fellow," he said aloud when he came home so late that night after his visit to Val Dougherty. "Maybe I am not even me."

He had walked all the way to Val's because his bike had a flat tire and Alec would not allow him to have his roadster ever. The long walk had tired him, and when he got to Val's house, he could see no lights anywhere, and there was a stillness about the whole place that made Ned uneasy.

"He's probably gone off to the bad house," Ned muttered, using Elaine's term.

Ned strolled over to the fence beyond which the horses pastured.

Then he saw the horse coming round the little bend in the track. At first he thought it was riderless, it was so dark now; then, as the horse approached nearer he saw Val was the rider. Ned was slightly hidden by the big cottonwood tree that grew by the side of the road. As the horse came closer, he could hear Val's husky voice saying something. He was somehow, though, not prepared to see the former deliveryman stark naked, and both the mare and he showed the effects of extreme exertion, the mare snorting and letting huge strings of white stuff fall from her mouth, and Val in a state of near collapse, wet with sweat, his thick curly hair a sopping mess, the hair on his chest dripping visibly.

Only a few yards from the cottonwood tree, Val dismounted, and Ned observed he had ridden the mare without a saddle. All at once he took the horse's head and brought it to him. He kissed her and held her tightly against his chest. Then it appeared that he covered her eyes with kisses, as one would a person who was dearer to a man than the whole world. Ned held his breath, relieved that the heavy branches of the tree kept him from view. He felt both acutely embarrassed and exuberant. But he did not want Val to know he was a witness to this demonstration of closeness to his mare. He supposed it must go on all the time, the way both the animal and the master acted, or maybe it was going on tonight only because he had lost his wife and daughter. Then the man and the mare walked together for a while listlessly, aimlessly, stopped as if they were imparting some message to the other, and then they both went resolutely to the stable. After a short while, Val came out, locked the door, and sauntered on into the kitchen entrance of the house.

Ned waited in the dark. He felt he could smell both the mare and Val and the wet earth about him. He knew he must be in no hurry to break in on the iceman after what he had been a spectator of. Val must certainly never know he had seen him show this strong feeling for his horse.

As Ned knocked feebly on the kitchen door, he heard Val's voice say: "Just a minute, will you?" He hurried into the next room, and put on his pants.

Val came to the storm door and said through the glass, "Oh."

"Shall I come in?" Ned wondered bashfully.

"The door ain't locked" was the response.

"Do you mind if I see you?"

"Suit yourself."

"Then I won't come in!" Ned spoke sulkily.

"Oh, come on in. Suit yourself means that."

"Does it?" Ned snapped, but he opened the door and entered, and walked straight to the circular table in the middle of the room and sat down.

The smell that came from Val was overpowering. It was a mixed odor combining the elements of the stable and something that was him, which was maybe more animal than the horses. He was also still wet from his exertions from riding.

"It was Elaine's idea," Ned finally brought out rather bitterly.

Val went on looking at him.

"I hope you got an eyeful tonight," he said in a strange choked manner.

"What do you mean by that?" Ned whispered.

"Just what the words say. I seen you spyin' on me, watching . . . but I wasn't goin' to stop what I wanted to do just for a snot like you. Now you know."

"Know what, Val?" The deliveryman's breathless way of speaking was in Ned's own voice now.

"Oh, don't be any worse a dunce than you already are."

"I don't know, Val," Ned implored him. A kind of queer gasp escaped from him then.

"Now we are goin' to bawl in the bargain?" Val spoke viciously, and went over to the cabinet and pulled out a bottle of liquor, took off the top with his teeth, and then had a swig. He put the bottle down on the circular table with a bang.

"I've loved horses all my life."

Ned felt then that it was all worse than he had supposed after all, and he was all at once afraid somehow of Val, whom he had looked up to all his life. He was even afraid the man might hurt him, might, that is, kill him, from the way he talked.

"I came here on my own," he began. "Though Elaine did tell me to come, but I would have come, Val, without her saying I ought to."

"Good, good boy," Val said nastily.

"You looked grand riding around tonight," Ned said in desperation.

"Thanks, thanks. . . . Now go back to town and tell everybody what you seen."

"But I didn't see nothin!'"

"No?"

Choking down his fear and rage, he went on: "But even if I had seen you kill somebody tonight I wouldn't snitch on you, Val. . . . I've been your friend ever since I can remember." And he wheeled around in his seat to look at the iceman full in the face.

"Well," Val replied, swallowing some more booze, "I can certainly remember you back far enough, you crafty little bugger."

Another sound escaped from Ned—whether of grief or rage, who could know?—and this sound evoked a sneering laugh from the older man.

After a silence, he went on: "A horse is the best thing there is in the wide, wide world." He drank repeatedly from the bottle. "A little city crud like you wouldn't know that though."

"I always knew you liked horses, Val. Why do you scold me like I was guilty of something against you, will you tell me?"

"Horses is my all, do you hear?" He spoke savagely. "Do you think I care that those two whores left me? *Care*? I'm relieved. I'm delirious, limp with relief! They left me the house and the stables and the land. What do I need them for when there's all that and the mare and the rest of the horses? You tell me."

There was a silence except for the partly suppressed groans of Ned.

"You quit makin' them sounds," Val warned him.

Attempting to silence his sudden onslaught of tears, which came from he knew not where, Ned only succeeded in letting out a series of wails.

"I said quit it!" Val strode over to where Ned was seated. He struck him once, then again, then several times. The blood rushed to the surface of the boy's cheeks.

"Good . . . You look better with the blood running over your face."

As he stared gloomily at the boy, something seemed to break in the horse fancier. His pupils narrowed, his mouth worked violently as if a torrent of words was struggling to rush out.

Without warning he picked the boy up by the scruff of the neck and held him up as one would a doll, and gazed into his eyes. Then he lifted him high in the air and looked at him as he held him aloft. Then almost dropping him, he quickly shifted him so that Ned was sitting on his lap. The boy's groans and sobs ceased as quickly as they had begun.

"All right, all right, Ned," the stable owner said softly. "All in the day's work."

He sounded as if he was going to fall asleep with Ned on his lap.

"Suppose you'll tell it all over town tomorrow." But these words were pronounced without feeling or revilement, peaceful words spoken in a doze.

"No, I won't tell, Val . . . cross my heart."

Val's huge rough hands with the blackened nails moved idly, indifferently, over the boy's face and hair.

"But tell what, Val? I don't understand, I swear I don't understand." His hot tears fell over the heavy hands of the delivery-man.

"Why, that I love horses the way I do," Val replied in a drowse.

"Oh, I see," Ned responded in a deep quiet and in a kind of paralysis of understanding.

"That's why she left me, among a hundred other reasons. . . . But I can't help bein' me, now can I?"

Ned knew he should feel terrified and sick at what he heard, but whether it was because he had never known his own father, or whether he could remember Val more clearly from further back even than his own so-often-absent father, he felt now totally at peace with this wild unbalanced man who had punished and abused him, then petted and comforted him, and who now held him tightly to himself as if he were his own.

"Tell it all over town now, see if I care, I won't lift a hand against you if you do." Val went on talking in his slumberous bass voice.

In a few minutes the older man's snoring rose out of the silence of the room. The sound was nearly as frightening to Ned as when Val had raised his fist against him, but the hands of the iceman were loosening around his arms, as he sank deeper and deeper into sleep, and finally, extricating himself cautiously, Ned was able to stand up. The snoring abruptly stopped, and the sleeper moved convulsively on his chair. Then the snoring began again, even more stertorously.

Once free of the man's grasp, Ned stood some time looking at him with a kind of wonder and gradual kindling admiration. Yes, he was sound asleep.

Looking about the room, Ned saw a frayed Indian blanket. He threw it over the sleeper, and then went on watching his "captor."

"I won't tell nobody you love horses," Ned said in a whisper. "I crossed my heart I won't, didn't I? And I won't."

For a long time now Alec had objected to having to sleep in the same bed with his brother, although, as Elaine always wearily pointed out, the bed itself could easily sleep three or four giants, let alone two young fellows not fully grown. Alec complained that Ned snored, talked in his sleep, and kicked him in the groin repeatedly during the night. But the worst affliction was, after all, the younger boy's continual talking in his sleep. "He must have nothing but nightmares once he gets under the covers," Alec harped to his mother.

But the night after Ned's visit of condolence to Val, Alec was treated to such an outpouring of moans, groans, wails, garbled messages as if sent from hell, the mumbled horrors of his dreams, that the next morning a haggard Alec drew his mother aside to read her the riot act, as Elaine later described her older boy's harangue and ultimatum to her.

Elaine promised she would move Alec to the little spare bedroom down the hall, which was more soundproof, and she would borrow a bed for him from Widow Hughes, who would be more than happy to do them this favor (Widow Hughes's spacious attic was full of beds).

But what Alec had told her about Ned's nightmares and his talking in his sleep had disturbed Elaine so much that when Ned came down to breakfast she gave him a long and searching scrutiny, which caused the boy to say, "Well, what have I done wrong now, Mother?"

"It's not what *you've* done wrong, dear," she said sadly, and hurried out into the kitchen to fry his eggs and bacon.

"What does that mean?" He followed her, holding his glass of tomato juice and sipping it while he spoke.

"We are going to have Alec sleep in the spare bedroom from now on, dear," Elaine informed him in a soothing, cautious, under-the-breath tone, which recalled the way she had addressed her mother some years back after the old lady had had her stroke.

"What's wrong with him sleeping with me all of a sudden?" Ned asked with a kind of bitterness, which made his mother look up from her preparation of his breakfast.

"Don't you think you're a little too old to sleep with one another, in any case?" Elaine spoke with cool matter-of-factness.

"And he just discovered this today?"

"No, no," she went on soothingly, "he's mentioned it before . . . but it came to a crisis last night evidently, when you had a nightmare, and shouted and swore and said a lot of things which woke him up."

"A nightmare! I don't remember any nightmare." He raised his voice, and drained off the last of the tomato juice.

"Go back into the dining room, dear, and I'll bring you your breakfast."

Ned sauntered on back in and fell heavily into the big chair that Keith Gresham had occupied a few evenings before. His eye roved to the corner of the dining room where his little high-chair stood, which for some reason Elaine had allowed to remain there unused, unoccupied except when occasionally she placed on it some silverware prior to its being polished, or a vase to be filled with flowers.

Ned had gone very pale.

He stared at his creamy scrambled eggs and slightly overdone bacon.

"So what did I shout and swear and say in my sleep?" he wondered.

"Oh, like all nightmares, it didn't make any sense." She tried to dismiss the whole subject. "So enjoy your breakfast, Neddy, and we'll not think about it again. . . . It is high time you boys had separate beds in any case."

"But *what* did I say in my sleep?"

"As I already told you, it was something didn't make any sense, like dreams usually don't, but you'll have to ask Alec, dear, for he was the one who heard you talking in your sleep."

"Ask Alec! He would never tell me what I said if it was to kill him."

"Well, it did upset him very much or he would not have insisted he have his own bed from now on," she admitted.

"But he certainly must have told you what I said in my sleep!"

Ned had not touched his breakfast.

"Ned, darling, it is not something I want to repeat."

"Did it have to do . . . with Val?" he kept on.

Elaine dried her hands on her apron, trying to collect her thoughts.

"Yes, in a way, I suppose it did. . . . But, Ned, you haven't told me a thing about your visit to Val when you went to see him last night. Perhaps you'd like to tell mother now."

She was very disturbed to see he had not touched his breakfast.

"Are your eggs and bacon all right?"

"You know they are," he said in a choked voice.

"Well, you did see Val last night, I gather," she went on.

"You gather from my talking in my sleep, you mean."

"You need not tell me if it bothers you, dear. We will forget the whole thing. . . . But you did see Val, you say?"

"Yes," Ned admitted. He made an attempt to eat a portion of the eggs, which had gone cold. "He was out in the pasture when I got there. We had a friendly talk, and that is about all. . . . He's my friend."

"Good—good." Elaine sighed. "You see there's nothing in nightmares really, my dear, to have to think about them. You saw Val, and he was friendly. . . . I suppose he was sad his wife and daughter had gone away, though?"

"Oh, a little." He went on forcing himself to eat some more of his breakfast. He smiled queerly at his mother.

"Val has a lot to tend to on his place," he added languorously.

"His horses," Elaine said coldly.

Ned dropped his coffee cup and spilled quite a bit of the liquid on the tablecloth.

"Never mind about it, dear," she consoled him in almost honied tones, and went out to the kitchen to get a cloth. She returned to wipe up the spill without a word of reproach.

"What did Alec say I said in my dream?" Ned turned sharply to his mother.

"Ask him, dear." Elaine pretended total innocence. "I didn't understand exactly what he did say."

"But he said I mentioned horses?"

"Something like that." She walked in the direction of the kitchen, and then stopped and looked back sideways at her son.

"Alec may have misheard you, Ned."

She waited there between the two rooms, then got out: "Perhaps you should not go to see Val again if you are going to be so upset afterwards this way. I should not have made you go to see him, perhaps. I am to blame, I see. . . ."

He pushed back his unfinished meal.

"All that happened when I got there," Ned began, trying all the while to remember his oath to the deliveryman, "is he had been working hard and was tired out, you see. . . . We went inside his house and had a nice talk, and he told me I should not worry about a thing. You see, Val is somebody special, Elaine."

She permitted him to say "Elaine" in this familiar way. Perhaps she did not even notice he had taken the liberty.

"I have always looked up to Val," her son went on, as if reciting from a lesson. "I do still. As I say, he is something special. No, Elaine, I will go there again and call on him. I want him to be my friend. I don't know what I could have said in my sleep, but it is not true anyhow, whatever it was."

"But if you don't remember what you said in your sleep, dear, how do you know then it's not true?"

"I mean Val would not do anything I would feel ashamed of him for."

"I see," Elaine said. "Of course, of course."

"I want to look up to him still," the boy went on in a strange, almost childlike confidence.

"Then we won't talk about it anymore. . . . In a few minutes, after I do the morning chores, we'll go over to Widow Hughes and get a bed for Alec—agreed?"

Ned moved his lips, and then nodded. Then, putting his head down on the linen tablecloth, he burst into the same kind of groans he had demonstrated before the man he said he would always look up to.

"It will be all right!" his mother said almost fiercely. "Do you hear me, Ned? It will be all right," and she hastened out of the dining room.

"I know all about it, Ned, because I know all about everything."

Widow Hughes addressed these words to him as he entered the trellised back porch that led directly to the old woman's pantry and kitchen.

She took both his hands in hers, as her late husband, Reverend Hughes, might have done. She closed her eyes and shook her head. Two tears dropped down on her furrowed, rouged cheeks. She was wearing a long green silk dress. Her hair had been partially coiffured, and a great tortoise-shell comb hung loosely from the back of head.

"My mother thanks you for letting us have the spare bed,

Widow Hughes," he greeted her, and attempted to extricate his hand from her firm grasp.

"You face shows, my dear"—she studied him—"the strain that man has put you to."

When he looked inquiringly at her, she added, "Val Dougherty."

"Oh, do we have to talk about him?" Ned implored. He stared in sudden disbelief at the "road map" of her face, as Alec had once described it.

"I mean, Widow Hughes, I've had enough trouble over this case already!"

"Case is the right word, my boy. Case it is, and will be."

She patted him on the shoulder, and again shook her head at his predicament.

"We fall among wicked men when we are young, my dear," she went on, ushering him into her kitchen. "There are snares everywhere for youth. . . . No one knows better than I, my dear Ned, how we are beguiled and trapped by evil. You are looking at a supreme victim of those snares and traps."

"Sit there," she said abruptly and almost pushed him into a chair with huge hand-carved arms and a velvet back.

"Look here, my boy. I know everything. You need not speak, even!" She held her right hand up, the palm facing Ned, adjuring him to silence, or perhaps confession.

"I knew it all even before I overheard your mother (bless her beautiful face) and your brother Alec speaking of the monstrous thing you witnessed as I sat on my iron bench in the orchard. . . . I hear so much, Ned, dear. It is a burden I have to carry. But burdened as I am by people's secrets, and they are legion, I never reveal them. I bear them silently."

"Where is the spare bed, Mrs. Hughes, and I'll go up and get it," Ned blurted out.

This abrupt interruption confused the old woman, breaking her train of thought. She looked about the walls of the room and to the oak table in the center of the room, as if somewhere she could find the thread of her discourse.

"It's upstairs," she finally replied, and put her fingers to her lips. "It won't walk off on its own legs, though," she whispered. "It will wait for us, my child. But before we talk of beds or go to move them, we have a greater matter to deal with. Horses, and a rider!" she concluded in prayerful sorrow, and she stumbled over to one of the overstuffed chairs and sat down with a heavy sigh of weariness.

"You were a witness then to this deed, Ned?"

He looked blank at her.

"Oh, the innocent," Widow Hughes cackled. "You saw Dougherty at the devil's work?"

"I only saw him riding. . . . What is all this, Widow Hughes?" He began to rise, but she motioned him to keep his seat.

"Be calm. I have heard what your mother and Alec said, but you forget I know Dougherty! So then, it's true?"

Ned almost felt now he would cry out from sheer vexation. God, he thought, she must be a hundred, and like the very dead, she walks in her orchard, listening to all who disclosed their secrets to the wind and the air.

"He is a lover of horses."

"Yes," Ned incautiously agreed, and then stopped. Very slowly the pieces of the puzzle began to fall into place for him. He went quite pale, and the old woman moved closer to him as she glimpsed his discomfiture.

"He's . . . a great horseman," the boy said incoherently.

"There can be little forgiveness for such a deed," the old woman remarked gravely, and she kept peering at Ned, as if his least motion would confirm what she now charged Val Dougherty with.

"I know nothing bad about him." The boy began his defense, but slowly it was all coming over him that whatever he said now in favor of his friend, Widow Hughes, Alec, his mother, all had, by some kind of magical appropriation of his words spoken in sleep, convicted both Val and him. Convicted him because he had talked in his sleep, and convicted Val for being a lover of horses. Of mares, more exactly.

With his head swimming, and his fingers almost tearing off the pretty pearl buttons of his shirt, which his mother had sewed there from an old discarded dress of hers, he caught snatches of the old woman's rambling:

"I do not know exactly what his punishment must be, but I will tend to that later. . . . I will go to him today. . . . I'll get my old buggy and my horse from the farm. That will make him pause. Yes, I will ride up to him and offer him the choice of repentance, provided of course he admits his crime . . ."

"Oh, don't go, Widow Hughes. He will think I talked . . . when I've sealed my lips and promised to protect him."

"Of course he would force you to silence." Widow Hughes spoke with the understanding and patience of a great jurist. "You are not to blame at all for his iniquity!"

"But don't you see, I don't know about his iniquity!" He jumped up. "Don't you see what you are doing to me?"

"What *I* am doing to you, cherub! Don't *you* see, *he* has made you party to his vile wickedness? And that must not be allowed! By reason of my having been wife to a minister of the gospel, I will go to him today and make him confess. We will not arrest him, yet. If he repents, we will perhaps take no further action at this time. It's not ripe for the sheriff as yet. I will go today. . . ."

"But don't you see, Mrs. Hughes," he beseeched her, "I've said nothing, told nothing. I didn't squeal on him!" He now appealed, it seemed, to the very walls and empty chairs of the room. "I know nothing against him."

Her eyes, enfolded in so many wrinkles that they resembled tiny bullets, stared at him unblinking in glee.

"He swore you silent allegiance, and that is *guilt*. If he hadn't done nothing, why were you sworn not to talk, then? Answer that!"

"I saw nothing, Widow Hughes," he almost babbled. Then, as if speaking in his sleep again: "He was naked, of course, and was leading the mare around the track. But Val likes to be naked."

She nodded solemnly.

"I tell you, I swore to nothing, for I seen nothing!" He almost screamed out the last words as his hands flailed about.

Then, as he protested again and again his own innocence and that of his friend, the horror of what that friend was now being charged with came home to him like lightning over his exposed head. Val did it with horses. He was one of those men he had read about in those books on ancient myths he had borrowed from Adele. He saw dimly now what Val had made him swear to. He understood then just as vaguely what he might have told

Alec as he talked and babbled in his sleep.

"Val is a good man, Widow Hughes." He began a kind of defense again in hushed tones. "He is a prince of a man, I do believe. . . . Don't go to him. Don't tell him. He'll think, don't you see, that I tattled. . . . He is my close, close friend."

Almost methodically, as if he was at church, he got down on his knees then before her and cried: "Don't tell him. He'll kill me! He has such a temper. After all, all he did was lead the mare about the track when he had no clothes on. Who else saw it but me? Don't go. . . . I'll work for you, be your servant, hired man, clean your cistern and cellar, and dig up all the dead stumps in your orchard. I won't charge you. I'll do it for nothing. But don't go to Val, do you hear? Don't. . . . I can't lose him."

Widow Hughes touched Ned's touseled hair, and smiled.

"Have no fear. You won't lose him," she said coquettishly, and fell into a reverie.

"You would do all those things you enumerated for me, for nothing?" she queried, half shutting her eyes as she thought of the tasks he had volunteered to take care of.

"I will work my fingers to the bone," he responded, using a phrase of Elaine's.

Her smile broadened.

"Well, let me think about it."

"No, no, you must promise me now you won't see him, won't go to his place, won't get me in trouble with him."

"You are so fond of Val's companionship? I see . . . I see."

Ned stared at her. He felt then that she also associated him with some wrongdoing alongside of the deliveryman, but what it was he could not fathom.

"Your poor mother," the old woman muttered, and then after a long wait: "The devil's work is never done. Never done."

"You won't go then?" he begged her with more sobs and groans.

"I won't," she said resolutely. "If you plead for me not to, I'll obey you. . . . I'll forget it."

He grasped her old, veined hands, kissed her rings.

"There, there, my darling, we'll go upstairs and get the old bed then."

"Good, good, Widow Hughes," he sobbed on.

The next day Ned could not get out of bed. He had a high fever, and the doctor feared for a while it might be meningitis. He prattled a great deal in his unconscious state, but now he slept alone so nobody heard what he prattled, though Elaine tiptoed in every so often to change the cold compresses on his forehead.

"Poor little chap," she would mutter. "I don't believe he still knows the time of day about so many things, but thank God he is out of danger, the doctor says. . . ."

Val Dougherty was arrested just a little after dawn on an unusually cool spring day (the thermometer had broken all records by going down to 20 degrees Fahrenheit), and a few hours later Ned Cottrell, whom Val called the "misprized calf," was taken from home by a deputy for questioning, though Elaine did all she could to prevent the boy's being taken from her, struggling with the deputy to break his hold on her boy, and according to one report even tearing his shirt half off and biting him, but Ned was hauled away nonetheless.

Actually what had occurred was never quite clear to the town. There were as many different versions of what had transpired as there were people who listened to the versions.

But had Widow Hughes not been listening in her orchard to Alec's graphic account of what Ned said in his sleep that morning, and had the old woman not gone to the sheriff with her accusation, certainly Val Dougherty would not have been arrested, and above all, Ned would not have been taken to the police station for questioning.

The sheriff had handcuffed Dougherty only because he had struck the sheriff when he had asked him if the report was true.

"Did you, and are you in the habit, Val Dougherty, as is claimed, of mounting your mare only a few yards from the public highway?"

That is when Dougherty is said to have struck the officer.

Handcuffed, Dougherty was asked again: "I will put the question to you again, and you'd better answer this time. Did you commit an act against nature with one of your horses in view of any and all passersby?"

Dougherty raised his handcuffed hands as if to strike a whole auditorium full of accusers, then letting his hands fall, he replied. "No." But the *no* was followed by hundreds of curses and words so vile and obscene that even the law officer was fazed. The turbulence of Val's foul mouth filled the old deputy with a kind of grateful respect for such an outpouring, words he had not heard since he was a young man, when the country was rougher and more colorful.

"Bring in that boy, then, if you have got him here," the sheriff said to the deputy.

"Oh, no, no, not that one," Dougherty had cried, which the officer took for an admission of guilt.

Ned was hustled on into the same room where the interrogation of Dougherty was taking place, and was slammed down smartly on a little stool facing both the accused iceman and the sheriff. The deputy was asked to leave the room during this inquisition.

"Now, my boy," Sheriff Greaves began, but his words were almost inaudible because of his heavy breathing and the sounds of his chewing wet snuff. "Did you see Val Dougherty here doing anything which you would say was out of the ordinary the night you paid him a visit? Did you observe him," the old man went on when the boy did not immediately reply, "performing any act which you would call downright low or against nature?"

Ned thought for a while, but instead of looking at the sheriff he was staring straight at Val.

"No, sir, I did not," Ned finally answered the officer, and Dougherty went limp as a rag doll.

"Then what did you see him doing the night you dropped by his place, Ned Cottrell?" the sheriff wondered in a honied, drowsy inflection.

Ned began to look in Val's direction, and then instead he turned his face toward the barred window, and then straight back at the sheriff.

"He was leading the mare back to the stable, sir."

"Yes," the old man encouraged him. "And what else?"

"That was about all, sir. He gave me good evening and inquired about my family, and said he would be through with his chores in a minute and could talk to me. So he put the horse in the stable then, and I followed him on into the house."

The sheriff picked up one of the empty chairs and slammed it down on the floor until it was a wonder it didn't go to smithereens.

"Then what about the story that is going the rounds like wildfire," the officer roared, "that you seen Dougherty, that man over there, having sex-u-al re-lations with his mare? Will you tell me?"

Ned turned first a furious beet-red color, then pale as one of Elaine's fresh-laundered sheets.

"I only know what I saw, sir. Which is what I said."

The sheriff stood over the boy for a long time, his breathing and chewing making the only sounds heard in the room. Then he rang for the deputy and instructed him to remove the "accused" from the room.

When the sheriff and the boy were alone, he began putting to him the same question again and again, each time in slightly different phrasing.

"Were you intimidated by the presence of Val Dougherty in the room, Neddy?"

"No, sheriff. He is a good friend of our family."

"And is his bein' a good friend of your family the reason why you have told me one barefaced lie after another, Sonny?" The old man suddenly screamed his head off.

"No, sir, not at all, sir." Ned had begun to quail a little nonetheless.

"Then God damn it"—the sheriff threw caution to the winds—"tell me exactly what you seen that night or you are going to live to regret it. Do you understand me?"

Ned Cottrell had inherited from his mother a very emotional disposition, but he had received from his dead father—without his knowing it—a cool, collected calm under pressure. He now replied with glacial aplomb: "Just what I told you before, Sheriff. He was leading the mare to the stable, which he presently done, and then he asked me to come into his house for a talk."

"What did he have on when you seen him leading the mare?" The sheriff had moved directly over him.

"His work clothes." Ned lied brazenly, evenly—*divinely*, the old lawman thought—and then the boy gulped so violently one would have thought he had swallowed all the lies he had ever told in his nearly fifteen years.

"His work clothes! His *birthday clothes*, don't you mean, you God-damned little perjurer, you? You are a liar past shame! A hardened practiced prevaricator of the first water! By Christ, you are a caution. God pity your poor mother and your brother Alec! Yes, you take the cake, by God!"

The old man walked around in a circle, swearing and grunting and chewing, but Ned also observed that his interrogator could barely control himself from laughing also.

"Ned Cottrell," the sheriff said after a long time spent in cursing and walking, "I'll tell you what I will have to do. I will have to let you go, yes, though you're guilty as sin, black corroded sin. But I have to let you go. *This time*! This time . . . but by Christ you better watch out the next time, do you hear? The next time might see the jailhouse door slam on you for good."

"There ain't going to be no next time," Ned responded.

Stung to even greater fury by this response, the sheriff came up to within an inch of the boy's face and cried, "You watch that God-damned tongue of yours."

Then, grinding his teeth and coming eyeball to eyeball with the brazen Ned, he whispered: "He didn't stick it to the mare?"

Ned shook his head countless times so that he resembled a speeded-up pendulum.

As if he had been waiting all this while to enter at that precise moment, the deputy opened the door and stood before them with folded arms. "See this one here goes right home, Sy," the sheriff commanded. "Better drive him there. You know where he lives."

It was already dark when the deputy brought Ned home. Supper was on the table, and there were no boarders present tonight.

Elaine looked rather old and pinched, and had sprinkled face powder rather carelessly on her cheeks and throat, while Alec was all dolled up as if he had come out of a bandbox.

Ned spilled everything immediately he had sat down, saying: "They didn't get a thing out of me because I didn't see a thing."

"You bet you didn't," Alec sneered.

"Let the little fellow eat his supper in peace," Elaine adjured. The poor woman did not know what to think anymore. Since Ned had lost his reputation by becoming the unwilling father of a child about to come into the world, she was at sixes and sevens as to everything concerning her younger son. She believed on one hand that what Ned had babbled in his sleep was true, and on the other hand she did not believe such things happened anywhere. But she never wanted to hear about it again, and warned Alec that if ever he so much as mentioned the subject, directly or indirectly, that big as he was, she would personally thrash him.

Just as the moon was rising (it was a little past full), Ned got his bike and began riding slowly, indolently, sometimes stopping along the side of a ditch, or a clump of trees, as if meditating not going any farther, then abruptly putting on the speed, as he drove inevitably to the stables.

As on the night of his other visit, the lights were on in the kitchen, but this time there was no sign of a horse anywhere or of Val. A queer stillness was everywhere.

Ned waited outside the glass door for a moment, then pressed his nose against the door itself. In a far corner of the kitchen, he spied Val curled up like a small boy on the dilapidated davenport.

"Will you take your God-damned nose off the glass, and come in, or get your ass home, why don't you." Val's voice could have reached the stone quarry.

Ned came on in, scraped his feet on the welcome mat, took off his cap, and held it in front of him as if before a priest or perhaps another sheriff.

"Well, did I do all right, do you think?" Ned inquired, breathless.

"Oh, you done fine for you . . . fine!" Val's anger welled up out of him fearfully.

"But I wanted to . . . save you," Ned explained.

"Oh, you did, did you? After you damned me, you mean!"

"What do you mean, Val, damned you?"

"Oh, you don't know, do you. Well, ain't you a innocent

angel boy come down from the clouds! *Don't know how he damned me!*"

Val had stood up now from the davenport, and to Ned's genuine horror he saw he was stark naked, as he had been the time of his visit before. Val reached for his trousers and stepped into them gingerly.

"I never spoke against you." Ned defended himself, and he kept repeating the words over and again, like a refrain.

The tea kettle began to whistle—Val wanted some hot water with his whiskey tonight—but in his rage at seeing his accuser and defamer he let it whistle on; then, when its shrill cry was intolerable, he sauntered over to the gas stove and shut it off. He poured the hot water into a mug with the booze and sipped it without even blowing it cool.

"I should pour the scalding water down your throat," he cursed.

Then going closer to his visitor as he sipped the brew, he said: "Somehow I can't hate you. Why is that? I should choke you to death and throw you into the quarry but all of a sudden I just can't be mad anymore."

He threw himself down again on the davenport and ran his fingers through his matted coal-black hair.

"I tell you I told Alec in my sleep," came Ned's defense, which was followed by Val's ear-splitting rejoinder, "But you didn't see nothing that evening because I was only taking the goddam mare for a walk."

"You kissed her a lot, though," Ned whispered.

"But you didn't see the other because there wasn't no other that particular evenin'. I have quit it, don't ask me why. I have quit it."

"Quit it?" came the supplicating querulous muttering.

"I used to do it, may as well tell you. Used to, every so often." He looked out the window in the general direction of the stone quarry, a dreamy expression in his eyes, and his mouth all at once relaxed in soft lines.

"No, no, you didn't." Ned stood up and tiptoed as if on hot coals over to the davenport. "Tell me you didn't, Val. Tell me you didn't."

"But I did."

Ned had fallen on his knees beside the iceman and was making strange little cries, but the older man still kept his eyes fixed on the window, which faced the quarry.

"Take that back, please," the boy said. "Say you didn't do it," he implored.

"What do you want me to do." He studied his visitor now, his big gray eyes without definite focus. "Want me to lie like you lied to the sheriff?"

"I thought I told him the truth."

"Except you didn't. I thought you knowed I did it. I thought you knowed . . . I was with the mare every so often."

Ned's cries began to rise in volume, and he held on to Val's trouser legs like someone who is holding to the straw he hopes will save him from the flood.

"Take it back," he kept repeating.

Moved by something he could not quite understand in the boy's anguish, Val sat very still, scrutinizing his accuser, his defender.

"If I say I won't do it no more, will you quit bawlin'?" he proposed. But there was missing in the older man this time the usual curt and brutal cadence.

"Put this down the hatch." He handed the cup to the boy, who at first turned his face away. Then slowly he grasped the cup from Dougherty and drank a little.

"You got to get the stardust took out of your eyes some day anyhow," Val said, drinking. "People can't help bein' what they are. You expect too much from your elders. People have got to be what they are. . . ."

Without his being quite aware of it, he saw that his free hand was imprisoned in the boy's. Ordinarily he would have pulled away from anyone who took his hand, for the very thought of tenderness of any kind had always scared him, but somehow he could not tear his hand loose from Ned Cottrell, and though it was a pain he could not define, this closeness from a boy, he did not have the heart to break the pressure of his handclasp.

"He looked up to me, I guess, the poor bastard," Val said after Elaine's younger son had gone home, and he put on the kettle again to have more hot whiskey.

That night, even though now he slept alone in perfect repose, Ned dreamed that Val, surrounded by many horses, had turned into a huge sugar loaf, white and bare, and that the animals he tended were all busy licking and eating him. Despite the inroads they made on him, who had turned to this terrible white sweet, he remained whole and recognizable but also seriously changed and diminished in some hard-to-understand way.

Elaine Cottrell talked from sunup to sundown. Hardly had her eyes opened in the morning than she began to speak in a running stream of words, which covered every aspect of her own life, the lives of her sons, neighbors, and all those who happened to come within her orbit. She called up to her boys from the basement, from the front porch, from the inner recesses of her many pantries and butteries, from every part of the old echo-chamber of a house, she talked on the telephone, and in the evening she often continued her confabulation on the steps of the back porch with whoever happened to pass by. Like her younger son, Ned, she was also known to talk in her sleep, so that one might wonder when she was ever silent.

The disgrace and scandal of Val Dougherty's "terrible deed," however, galvanized Elaine into even more lengthy, continuous rapid discourses and harangues. At first she blamed Dougherty for having done what, after all, the law had decided he had not done, or could not prove he had done. Then, although she concurred with the courthouse and the sheriff that there was no proof he had committed an unnatural act, she blamed the iceman for having corrupted and misled her younger son, who was already, by inheritance from his dad, possessed of "bad blood" enough.

Then the wind changed without warning, and Elaine blamed the whole affair on the evil, demented mind and vile tongue of Widow Hughes, whose pastor husband had been one of the greatest scapegraces who had ever drawn breath.

But whether Dougherty had mounted one of his mares or not, he might as well have mounted the whole stable of his horses, so far as the town was concerned. He was singled out by all who passed him in the street, and schoolboys jeered at him. Some called him names. Val's maternal uncle (also a breeder of horses) had always said his nephew should have been a prizefighter and not an icehouse entrepreneur and raiser of horses, and the town may have been reminded of the uncle's characterization of his nephew when Dougherty began beating up on all who called him names or even scowled at him. There was many a broken head and black eye in the aftermath of Dougherty's arrest.

Ned, too confused by the conflicting accounts, was as much at sea as ever over what Val was innocent or guilty of, but gradually the iceman's "confession" became blurred in his mind, and he found himself looking up to Val more than ever.

Alec stuck his nose in the air even higher when the name of Dougherty was mentioned, and warned his mother never to admit him to the house, and admonished his younger brother he would bloody his nose on every pavingstone in town if Ned so much as spoke to that lowdown runagate.

But as talk died down, and as the realization grew that Val Dougherty was not going to be put in jail for life, that all and any proof was lacking that he had committed acts against nature, and that after all, he was, like his father, his uncle, and his grandfather before him, a breeder of horses, a kind of crabbed grudging reinstatement of the name of the iceman came about.

And since somebody had always to be blamed, blame therefore fell on Widow Hughes, who lived, after all, in a twilight world of infernal dreams about man's wickedness and impurity. "Her mind"—Elaine continued her ceaseless discourse—"must be as untidy and disarranged as her mansion. She sees the worst in everybody, and if she cannot find the worst, she invents it out of whole cloth. I will have to watch my step even more now that I know she is traipsing around in the orchard and listening at the door! I wonder what stories she has carried to the church and the lodge and the Sunday school about me and my boys. God knows why we are not all in jail with her mouth and tongue going at both ends." As Elaine washed the clothes in the basement (it was "blue Monday"), and then hung them out to dry in a fitful sun, she reflected on her unfortunate lot. She was the true widow, while the old woman across the way in the sprawling estate adjoining her own modest house was more like a celibate queen who, it is true, had given birth to a son (he hated his mother and never communicated with her unless some legal business forced him to), but remained to this day untouched by real love or charity. The one thing that had been granted the old woman by an "unjust Providence" was wealth. Whatever she touched multiplied and remultiplied, until even her bankers and brokers had lost accurate account. Elaine often enumerated, however, as she worked in the laundry room or over the ironing board, the old lady's holdings. She owned most of the farmlands in this section of the state. Most of the business blocks in the town of Fonthill were hers, including the movie houses, most of the candy kitchens, and, it was said, the pool parlors. She had lost track of all the tenants who rented from her, and many of them lived without paying her a cent. Once the widow had discovered a safe upstairs that contained stocks and bonds purchased a generation ago, which she had forgotten she ever owned. But like Midas of old all her wealth had brought her little but misery, loneliness, isolation, and madness.

While she was hanging her wash out to dry, Elaine practiced the speech she intended to deliver to the widow. How, she would begin, dared you destroy the reputation of my boy, linking him to acts which you falsely ascribed in the first place to young Val Dougherty! Acts which even that cretin of a sheriff was unable to prove against him! How dared you, you old rip, listen at the doors of my home, behind walls, hidden in your orchards or among the mass and tangle of trees and weeds run wild, feeding your insatiable appetite for gossip and scandal, or, to put it in plain English, dirt! Oh, indeed the wicked flourish like the green bay tree, for you are nothing if not wicked. Your icy disposition made you refuse to be a wife to your husband, and that drove him to lust, concupiscence, and lewdness, and finally resulted in a mob burning a fiery cross on your front lawn long ago to protest his having lost his head over a girl of thirteen and led her to perdition. You and you alone were to blame for all of that!

Her washing on the line, the boys' shirts and work pants and her own hand-stitched tablecloths and pure linen napkins, and scores of handkerchiefs (one would have thought they did nothing but weep in that household from the numbers of them), Elaine Cottrell marched toward the mansion to bring her enemy to the bar of justice. Usually Elaine entered by the back door. Today she resolved on going in by the mammoth front portal with its frosted glass. She knocked. No answer. Then she shouted. Silence. Recalling how deaf the old recluse was or how deaf at least she pretended to be, she simply walked on in, went down the long dim corridor, hallooing and calling out the old woman's name.

A pale mahogany door opened, and Widow Hughes, dressed in what she called her traveling costume, a taffeta gown of more than a generation ago, stood before her.

"Daughter!" She welcomed Elaine and took her hands in hers. "You are remembered in my will, sweet child, never forget that!" She kissed the astonished Elaine on both her hands. "I know what you have suffered. You have done right to come here for solace."

"Do you now indeed know what I have suffered!" Elaine cried, some of her righteous anger emerging from the surprise of her welcome. She scrutinized the old dame's face. "Widow Hughes"—she tried to remember her age and infirmity—"do you know who I am? Do you, my dear?"

"Call me Rosa . . . always call me Rosa. 'Widow Hughes' is for the congregation, not for a dear thing like you."

"Who am I then, Rosa?" Elaine cried in exasperation. "Tell me who you think I am."

The old woman smiled with forbearance. "Why, you are Alec and Ned's dear mother," the old woman chided.

With great velocity, she tore off an emerald from her finger, and tried to force the jewel on Elaine. "Take this ring, dear heart, for I won't last out the month, and you must wear it in my stead."

"Oh, Widow Hughes, please consider what you are saying and doing, my dear! I cannot accept your jewels. You know, too, if you saw this ring tomorrow on my finger you would call the sheriff, and have me arrested for robbery. Put it back now on your own finger. You have caused me such sorrow . . ."

Putting her mouth to Elaine's ear, she whispered between

kisses, "Sit here, my lamb," and motioned Elaine to a green silk settee. "Sit where I can admire your beauty . . . oh, you are beautiful. If I were as beautiful as you, my darling, I wouldn't care what people said about me. I would go to jail gladly if they called me 'Beauty,' and I would dance from morning till night."

"Where would you dance, my dear?" Elaine wondered, and sighed and seated herself in the depth of the settee.

"Dry those tears . . . and listen, *you are in my will*!"

"I'm afraid it is a will, then, that will be broken."

"Never!" the old woman shrieked. "Do you think one cent of my wealth will go to that milksop wastrel waiting down the street for me to die!"

"Are you speaking of Barney, Widow Hughes?" Elaine shook her head, with a wry smile. Her anger was diminishing, and with its departure she could no longer get out the speech of denunciation she had rehearsed for the widow.

"Call me Rosa, my name is Rosa . . . you goose!" The widow allowed her own irritation now to come out. "I am Rosa to you."

"Very well," Elaine agreed.

"Blow your nose," Rosa ordered her.

"I only asked you who you meant by the milksop." Elaine's curiosity had to be satisfied, for the mention twice today of her being in the old woman's will had changed the entire tenor of her visit.

"Who do you think I meant but my son, Barney," the old woman snapped. "I have disinherited him, and let me tell you why. . . . Now listen well, my child. Barney, my milksop son, was got upon me against my will that fearful damnable wedding night. I was violated!"

"Violated?" Elaine was now dry-eyed. "What are you telling me? That he is not your son . . . by the pastor?"

"Oh, of course by the pastor. But he was drunk that night when I conceived Barney. . . . He took me by the throat into the front hallway while he was in his cups. I begged for pity, or the decency of the upstairs bedroom—the conjugal suite, you know. Do you think he would listen? He called me prude, Miss Ice-Floes, Mealy-Mouth, Butter-Won't-Melt-in-Your-Mouth, oh, a hundred names. Then he tore off all my wedding clothes, and laid me under his lust on the hardwood floor. . . . He beat me until I was unconscious . . ."

Elaine had narrowed her eyes to mere slits.

"You think I am mad, too, I can tell. I know the expression! Of course what I've told you is so, you goose girl. . . . I could weep, too, but I'm not like you. I'm turned completely to ice and rock salt. I've wept several hundred rivers, and those rivers are now either all dry or turned to ice and salt. So I don't sleep. . . . I walk up and down the orchard, I walk through people's houses also, as they accuse me of doing, listening, listening. . . . What am I listening for? Love! I'm listening for someone who can tell me of love. But all I find is bestiality!"

"But by reason of this practice of listening, my dear Rosa, you have caused me and mine great harm and suffering."

"Listening for love, and hearing only loathing and horror, my dear," Rosa went on ignoring Elaine's interruption.

"Do you realize, Rosa, you have ruined the reputation of my younger son, Ned, and that of poor Val Dougherty?"

"So it's *poor Val Dougherty* is it now?" Rosa retorted. "My dear, you are sheltered from the world, and from stark reality! Good . . . it has kept your beauty intact!"

"My boy was taken into custody by the sheriff all because you *misheard* what I said by the orchard wall."

"I've heard so much by the orchard wall—Rosa has." The old woman pondered. "If walls could talk! If orchards could give out their secrets! God would have to destroy Fonthill! Of course He will have to presently in any case. . . . But how have I brought your son to prison?"

"Oh, Ned's free now, Rosa, but you should not go running to the sheriff talebearing! Do you hear me? And Val Dougherty is ruined as a result."

"You are in my will, my darling." She petted Elaine. "You are my favorite heiress, precious . . . so let us forget my folly in going to the sheriff because *you* are remembered!"

"Promise me, though, you won't go to the law again, at least not about my sons and me!"

Rosa Hughes smiled beatifically, which swiftly changed to a crafty smile. She held out in her hand her emerald ring.

"You won't take this ring, sweetheart?"

"No, no, please."

"Then I will disinherit you! Either take this ring for your own, or be stricken forever from my will."

"But tomorrow when you visit me and see the ring on my finger, Rosa, you know you will threaten me with arrest. It's your way."

"Never . . . never. . . . You don't know Rosa Hughes."

"Then write a paper to the effect the ring is mine."

"Oh, very well, darling . . . presently. But turn on the little lamp on the stand there so I can admire your beauty. . . . There! That's good. . . . Now, lift the shade a bit. . . . Good. There is nothing like a beautiful woman. All the rest of God's creation you can keep . . . but a beautiful woman, that is the treasure."

"My sons are quite handsome too—you've said so yourself, Widow Hughes, or rather, Rosa."

"Did I say they were handsome? Only because they look like you, dear heart. Only because they resemble their gorgeous mother. But like all the breed of men, they have that hanging between their legs which gives them and us no rest or peace or even a good night's slumber. Pastor Hughes insisted on putting it into me every few hours. That's why I still can't sleep, Elaine, dear girl. What do you start like that for now? Be tranquil when I stroke your hair. I've had no sleep in forty years because I keep fearing he will put it in me again."

"Oh, Rosa, let's not think back to the old days." She moved away a little from the old woman's caresses.

"Except that's all I do think about, my angel. He marked me. He branded me for all eternity. They won't let me through heaven's gate because there was that between him and me. No, he is waiting by one the blackest rivers in hell for me, and there by its waters, when I join him, my torment will begin again. He will insist on spearing me once I reach the dark shore where he wanders forever. He waits for me there with his javelin and pike, with his forked instrument . . ."

"We won't think about it any more, dear frend." Elaine looked at her ring and smiled. "Rosa, oh, Rosa. Thank you!"

"I'm glad that ring fits you so well, Elaine, my child." The old woman quieted down now. "Of course I'll write a letter to the effect it is yours from now on."

Widow Rosa now stood up and beckoned Elaine to come near her. She showered the younger woman with wet terrible kisses.

"There is nothing like a beautiful woman . . . nothing. Not

even the peach tree when in blossom can rival it. Kiss me, like a dear . . . kiss me, dear child. You are remembered in my last will and testament."

Adele Bevington had begun going every evening to the Star Restaurant shortly after she learned of Ned and Val Dougherty's arrest. She was too shocked by the event even to discuss it with anybody, and at the same time she did not feel like staying at home. She had the strange apprehension that she too might be arrested, and she felt somehow she was implicated in both Ned's and Dougherty's "guilt." Even when they were freed, and the matter dropped, she felt too nervous to stay at home. The Star Restaurant with its ample rooms, its private dining quarters, and its cheerful, obedient young waiters became her refuge while the scandal raged.

Adele was especially fond of one young waiter, who often acted as the manager when his boss was absent. He was Stacey Winant, and he had a crush on Adele—it was a standing joke to the other personnel of the Star. If she merely sipped from her water glass he refilled it to the brim. If she dropped her napkin he replaced it with a fresh one. Her coffee cup was never allowed to contain anything but scalding hot liquid, and each morsel of food she touched had to win her total approval, or it was carried back to the chef. All that Adele lacked from Stacey, as one waitress put it, was for him occasionally to kiss her feet as she reclined at the table. Stacey also permitted Adele to smoke, though cigarette smoking was forbidden to ladies.

Tonight, however, Adele noticed that there was something on Stacey's mind—he seemed preoccupied and nervous. His face was pale, there were dark circles about his expressive green eyes, and his lips were always forming words, which he then would not allow himself to bring out.

"You have something troubling you tonight, Stacey," Adele said when he handed her the bill. She had never said anything so personal to him before. He flinched.

"I hope, Miss Bevington, I haven't made your meal disagreeable by my manner." His hand shook as he took her money.

"Why don't you come to my house when you are through here?" She lowered her voice so that no one else in the restaurant would hear.

If she had asked to marry him, he could hardly have been more surprised. The son of an unemployed factory worker—his mother had died when he was two—and with little education except for what he had picked up himself by going to the library, he considered Adele as far out of his sphere as a member of royalty, certainly as removed as one of the reigning motion-picture stars.

"Don't fail me now," Adele commanded him when she saw the consternation her invitation had put him in. "I will be waiting for you."

When he arrived she saw that he must have gone home to put on his Sunday best. His hair had a rather thick pommade and was skinned back, and he was freshly shaved and reeked of witch hazel.

"You will never know what this means to me," he began.

"And you will never know, Stacey, what your kindness and considerate treatment of me has meant over the past few days. If everybody was as kind and considerate as you . . ."

"But I only do what is owing to you, Miss Bevington."

She was completely won over to him now, even more than when he served her at the Star.

"If you are troubled by anything, Stacey, I will gladly hear you. . . ."

He shook his head.

"What is it?"

"Miss Bevington, I promised the person who shared his secret with me never to divulge it."

"I see." She was disappointed somehow.

"But since it touches on you, I will break that promise if you think it right."

"Who is it who has made you promise, Stacey?"

He struggled a little more with his conscience, then began: "Do you know a young ex-infantryman—he was badly wounded in France—named Keith Gresham?"

For some reason she started as if he had touched her with a hot iron. "I know of him from Ned Cottrell," she said finally. "I believe he boards at Elaine's."

Stacey nodded. "But before I begin," he said, "I have a small confession to make." He saw nothing but encouragement and compassion in her glance, and went on: "In order to make ends meet I tend bar at the Iron Kettle, where we serve liquor—against the law, of course."

She smiled.

"Young Keith Gresham was there the last time. He got fearfully drunk, and then sick. I felt somehow responsible for him, and I took him home with me to my father's house. . . . Miss Bevington, I don't know how to continue. . . . I don't want to hurt your feelings. . . . I have no right to say what I am about to say. It's only because I admire you so much."

"You must continue, now, Stacey," she said, but she was as frightened as he was alarmed at going on.

"The long and the short of it is, he told me that in France he had known a young soldier who said . . . he was your boy."

Her face drained of blood. She rose and went to her cabinet and took out the bottle. He welcomed the "medicine" almost as much as she did, and they both sat silent drinking from her heirloom glasses.

"And did . . . this boy he said he knew die then in the war?" she finally asked.

"Oh, no, I don't believe he did. I believe he is here."

"Here?" she wondered in a kind of rising hysteria.

"In the vicinity, ma'am."

"From now on you are to call me Adele, and nothing else," she warned him.

"Have I hurt you so very much, Adele?"

"Yes, yes, you have," she replied with dry bitterness.

"I feared so telling you, but on the other hand . . ."

"You did perfectly right. Perfectly right."

Like so many others before him, Stacey Winant stayed the night, and like the many others, he spent it, in contradiction to Fonthill gossip, in chaste, if slightly inebriated, slumber.

Coming home sometime after midnight, Ned found a note addressed to him on the little stand in the hall. It was from Adele.

On very thick robin's-egg-blue stationery, it read:

> *What do you know of Keith Gresham? It is urgent you tell me as soon as
> possible.   With love, ever, A. B.*

Staring at the note in the dim light, he suddenly heard his
mother call from the floor above: "I would like a word with you,
young man!"

He did not even have time to put Adele's note away when she
had reached the newel post on which he was leaning.

The clock in the parlor chimed one. Elaine's face was covered
with cold cream, and her hair had been combed out long so that it
reached almost to her waist. Only a very good-looking woman,
Ned reflected, could appear so attractive in such a state of
disarray and bad temper.

"I want to know where you have been! Coming home at such
an hour at your age."

He had seldom seen her so fierce, and in his flustered state, he
handed her the note from Adele as if it would explain his actions.

She barely scanned it contents, handing it back to him. It was,
he saw at once, not Adele she was worried about.

"I thought you knew where I was." He kept his voice low.

She went on waiting for him to continue, like someone who
also held over him a yardstick in her hand.

"All right, then, I've been to see Val Dougherty, where you
told me to go in the first place, remember?"

"Val Dougherty indeed!" she burst forth, and Ned could tell
from her eyes that she had feared he had been to some worse
resort, such as the Carlyle House.

"I don't want you to go there anymore, do you hear?" She
came down the one remaining step of the staircase and stood
directly facing him. "He's not fit company, either, for you. He's
old enough to be your father."

"So he's old," Ned taunted her, for Dougherty was the most
youthful man he knew, younger than Alec in his energy and
quick way of moving, younger than Elaine, who smoked too
much and didn't watch her diet. Then looking down at Adele's
note, he corrected himself. Keith Gresham, he guessed, might be
younger.

"What on earth can you have in common with him?" Elaine
was going on. "He's a coarse, uncivil brute, and you know it."

"No, no, that's where you're wrong." Ned defended the man who, if no longer his idol, was in some way he did not understand his close friend.

"And it's not true what you and Alec and that old hag across the way have been saying against him, I'd have you know!" He spoke with an almost laughable forensic orator's ring.

"Well, I'm glad to hear you reinstate him morally."

"He can't help if it he likes horses, and horses like him." Ned immediately realized to judge by his mother's expression, how damning was the remark he had just made.

"I won't have you seeing him," Elaine remarked after catching her breath, but somehow there was no conviction or real prohibition now in her voice.

"Who else do I have?" he snapped.

"Who else, he asks!"

"Yes," he almost roared. "I can't count Alec, with his voice lessons and his primping. And you're always either busy or out with one of your boy friends!"

She fell back a little.

"You watch your tongue," she warned. "I tell you, your mouth will be your own destruction one of these days."

"Then you *don't* have boy friends?" he went on, all but crowing at her discomfiture. "You mean you sit home and crochet. Ha!"

She put her hand on the newel post and looked away.

"Ned, Ned, what is to become of you. I ask you!"

"What is to become of you, you might ask. After all, the day is coming when Alec and me will be gone. Then who will you quarrel with? Who will you scold and nag and preach and harp at? Tell me who!"

"You insolent little pup! What you've needed all these years is a man's firm hand over you. Well, I've tried my best to do all I could for you, but I've failed." She began to wail a little. "My boy friends, indeed! Would you have your mother do nothing but cook and sew and clean house for you boys, and never have a moment's relaxation or diversion? I know that's what you expect of me! To be nothing but a household drudge. . . . And yes, the day *is* coming, as you say, when you boys will leave, and then what will I have to show for all my labor and care and worry and sorrow? You'll be gone, and I'll be an old woman."

"Well, I won't give up going over there . . . to Val Dougherty's, no matter what you say. If you can date your boy friends, I can pay an occasional visit on the horse trainer if I want to."

"Oh, Neddy, you have broken my heart more than any other person in my entire life." She raised her eyes to the upper floor as if to place her case before silent witnesses up there.

"I don't tell you what to do, Elaine," he finished abruptly, partly because his voice suddenly cracked in the heat of argument, for it was beginning to change.

"A grimy coarse man like that," she said under her breath. "God knows what he is teaching you!"

Her tears had dislodged the cold cream on her face, some of which was about to fall on her pretty cerise-colored nightgown.

"I wouldn't go there, Elaine, if he was a bad man," he said, beginning to relent a bit himself. "Don't you have no trust in your son? I wouldn't see him if he taught me bad things. . . . I think he is a fine man."

His mother hurried up the stairs now to her bedroom, but Ned followed, defending himself in a string of garbled words, after her.

She was wiping her face on some unmended tea towels when he came into her room and continued: "I want you to tell me, Mother, I can go there."

"Go," she sobbed, "go . . . for you'll go in any case. You and your brother, Alec, don't love me. Alec loves that awful old Adele Bevington more than he ever did me . . . and you love the horse trainer, if you ask me, to judge by your defense of him."

"Love him?" Ned was scandalized.

"Look up to him, then." She amended her phrase. "You never look up to me because all I've been in this house is the woman who cooks for you, washes and mends your clothes, keeps you clean and neat, and watches out for your health and security. Beyond that, I mean nothing to you."

"Why, you know that's not so," Ned said feebly.

"Yes, as you say, you'll soon be gone and what will I have to hold on to? . . . A few memories, a snapshot of when you were little and really loved me, and the constantly fading memory of your dad." She now burst into a terrible storm of sobs, long put off perhaps, suppressed until this moment.

"Oh, don't carry on so, Mother, or I'll be breaking up too!" He went up to her and touched her gingerly. She started under his touch.

"Just do as you please, Ned. Do as you please."

"But I want to *please you*, too, Mother." He put his arms around her neck and she allowed him this privilege, but did not return the pressure.

"I appreciate you." He spoke huskily. "I love you."

She took one of his hands in hers. "I expect you do, Ned," she said between her eloquent sobs.

"I don't begrudge you going out with your boy friends." He yielded.

"Oh, they mean nothing to me compared with you boys," she testified. "Can't you see that?"

"I do, Mother," he admitted, close to sobbing now himself. "I do."

"Well, for heaven's sake," came a scornful hollow voice, and Elaine and Ned looked up from their embracing one another to see Alec standing on the threshold of the room watching them.

"We've had a good talk, Ned and I, Alec." Elaine made an effort to break away from her younger son now, but he held her to him. "It has done both of us a lot of good." She smiled peacefully at Ned, who pressed his head still against her bosom, and was crying also, and by reason of his tears not daring to look up at Alec, whom he still feared and before whom he was bashful of displaying his feelings.

"So I see," Alec responded, but some of the scorn and anger had gone out of his tone.

He moved a little closer to his mother and brother.

"Things will be all right yet, boys." She comforted them. "I know you both will find careers and make all of us happy one day. But we must stick together as a family, and show our devotion and love of one another. We must not have quarrels and disagreements and wrangling. No, we must not."

Somewhat astonished still at the spectacle of his brother and mother in such close and tearful embrace, Alec stayed on for a while, as if soothed and softened by so many tears and so much penitence. Then, after kissing both his mother and Ned good night, he went off whistling to his own room and closed and locked the door.

Alec Cottrell, despite his friendship with Adele Bevington and a fistfight or two, was considered by the citizens of Fonthill as a model son and brother and the mainstay of his wretched mother's life. Everybody knew he had decided not to go to college in order to keep the family together, though the truth was closer to the fact that he did not care about books, and prolonged study of any kind bored him. Unlike Ned, Alec was thought to be orderly, conscientious to a fault, and consistently dependable. And whereas at one time tongues had wagged with respect to Ned's dancing attendance on Adele Bevington, the same tongues had had only praise for the older son's waiting on the "old sinner" hand and foot, and had seen in his constant visits to Adele another proof of his charity and self-sacrifice. Alec was the town's Sir Galahad. Indeed there was practically nobody in all Fonthill to speak against him, and his very perfectness made him, finally, all the more vulnerable to mischance, and temptation.

The path to his temptation was prepared for him by the fact that his singing teacher, Paul Ferrand, had moved to the outskirts of town while his own family property was undergoing extensive repairs. In order to reach the new residence, Alec borrowed Ned's bicycle, against the latter's loud wailing and complaint.

"Learn to be generous where generosity costs you nothing," Elaine had chided her younger boy.

"The bike always comes back with something wrong with it when he rides it," Ned complained. But the chief reason for his not wanting Alec to take his bike was simply that he could not bear this additional proof of his older brother's appropriating to himself everything he had or might one day possess.

The first time Alec returned from one of his jaunts to his teacher's house he wore such a strange expression on his face that Ned rushed out to the garage at once to see if he had not broken some part of his wheel. It was, alas for his wish to complain, in perfect condition. In fact Alec had even filled the front tire with air.

At the supper table that evening Alec behaved, in fact, more like Ned than like himself. He sighed frequently, shook his head, and ate very sparingly from his plate, all of which infuriated Elaine. She considered anything short of a ferocious appetite an insult to her cooking, and she had in time past refused to keep as boarders some young men whose taste for her victuals was persnickety.

"What is wrong, Alec?" Elaine spoke frostily toward the end of the meal. "You have picked at your food like a canary."

"I think I am exhausted from my singing lesson." He offered this weak apology.

"Well, you do want to be a singer." Elaine was almost threatening. "But I never heard of one that ate like a bird!" Alec excused himself politely, and left the table.

After the dishes were done, with his assistance tonight, Ned sauntered upstairs. Alec's new bedroom, where he now slept alone, had its door open, and the younger boy peeped in and stared at his brother, lying down on the freshly laundered bedspread. He had not even bothered to take off his shoes, which would certainly have brought down on him Elaine's wrath had she happened in.

"What's eating you?" Ned inquired, sounding more like Alec than himself.

Alec gazed dubiously at his brother.

"Shut the door, why don't you, Neddy," he said in an unaccustomed civil tone, sounding for almost the first time like Ned's equal instead of the supercilious "little father" speaking to his "brat brother."

Ned uneasily closed the door.

"I've set eyes on the most gorgeous girl I ever in my life did see."

Ned sat down unbidden now on a small child's rocker. Usually Alec would not permit him to seat himself until he gave permission but tonight he ignored his brother's breaking of the rules.

"Well, where did you see her?" Ned inquired in a kind of throaty growl.

"Way over at the edge of town. Paul, you know, lives near the fairgrounds now."

"Oh." Ned spoke with conspiratorial encouragement.

"She seems to do nothing but sit on her porch swing all the time," Alec went on, not even looking in Ned's direction, and working one finger into his ear. "She looks like she had dropped from the sky, I'm telling you."

Ned gaped at his brother. No, he could not be drunk, or crazy, yet he was as different from the old Alec as frost from burning sunlight.

"I'm telling you, I rode past her house ten times, staring at her, until, my God, how I did it I will never know, but I parked your wheel and went right up to the porch and said hello. And she answered me back without batting an eye. . . . I've never seen such a beautiful girl. I'm telling you." He bowed his head as if he had a sudden bellyache.

"How old did you say she was?" Ned wondered.

"How old is she?" Alec cried with some of the old rancor and ill-temper common with him. "How should I know." He lapsed back into his new mooniness.

"But she's young, ain't she?"

"Well, of course she's *young* . . . sinfully young . . . and she lives there all alone. She says it's her brother's house and he's often away. . . . There's such . . . *sleep* in her eyes, Ned . . . such deep pools of sleep!"

"Sleep?" Ned spoke now in the magisterial, sneering way Alec usually used on him.

"She's the original Sleepy-time Gal, I do believe, come to life."

Alec's mooniness, his "slush" as Ned later was to describe his brother's talk, nearly elicited a sarcastic cutting comment from the younger boy, but he decided to keep this new and unforeseen sentimentality and weakness of Alec's to himself for later on when he might need it. He therefore let Alec "drivel" on.

"Did she give you her name?" Ned finally wondered.

Alec hesitated. "Her first name, yes, of course." He spoke evasively.

Ned waited to hear it.

Alec looked at Ned sharply, then: "It's Enid." He spoke in a confidential whisper. "But for God's sake don't tell Elaine."

Ned rose as if on cue, and slightly curling his lips downward, remarked, "I'm surprised you'd think I'd break a confidence with you, Alec . . . expecially on a matter like this."

Alec was evidently still too moonstruck to notice the sarcasm of Ned's words. If he had only thought for a moment he would have known that Ned was never in times past capable of keeping any confidence whatsoever. When had he not blabbed to anybody once he had heard a secret? But Alec had gone blind to all Ned's past betrayals. He could feel only gratitude that he could share his secret with a sympathetic ear.

"It must be the end of the world," Ned said half aloud as he softly closed the door of his brother's room behind him. "Christ Jesus has come down to earth," he mumbled to himself, "and has found out what it's like to be made of flesh and blood!" He stopped by the balustrade and let out a soft chuckle. So that perfect young man he had always to look up to in times past, the little plaster saint after whom he was to model himself, was all at once calf-sick in love!

Ned, however, did not need to blab to apprise Elaine that something was wrong with her mainstay, the "little father" of the household, as she sometimes referred to Alec in her talks with Rita Fitzsimmons.

Alec now consistently ate almost nothing, toying with his food, or when Elaine was not looking, putting the larger portions of his victuals on Ned's plate. His necktie was now only half tied and hung loose about his starched collar, and tiny blue circles appeared for the first time around his eyes. His hands tightly grasped the silverware or the beveled drinking glasses until his knuckles went white.

Even more watchful of him than Elaine, if possible, was Ned, who, gimlet-eyed, took in every motion, sigh-faltered sentence, or movement of lip or brow of his brother.

"What in the deuce are you staring at me like that for?" Alec cried out one evening at Ned while Elaine was in the kitchen dishing up the dessert.

Then, perhaps remembering their new relationship, and a secret shared, a trust consecrated, Alec softened his remark with, "Go ahead, if it gives you pleasure, stare away, why don't you?"

"You must go to her, Alec," Ned whispered.

"What?" the older boy almost shouted.

"Go to Enid. Tonight. Just tie your tie, put some hair oil on that cowlick of yours, get out your new hat and the patent-leather shoes you never wear, and go to her house. Don't wait for her to invite you. Go. Just walk on up to the front door, but don't ring, go on in like she was expectin' you. And then when you're once in, just take off your hat like Prince Charming and throw your arms around her like you were expected. Then, you see, you'll have your wish."

Alec stared dumbfounded at his brother. He could hardly have been more astonished if the devil himself had been sitting there in Ned's place conjuring him. He knew Ned was ornery, often incorrigible, in fact, but he had not quite suspected he was wicked. But then, after all, had he not got Maude's daughter in trouble, the little sneak! As if for the first time the scales fell from his eyes. Yes, in so many ways, "little" Ned was his elder, and much more practiced in cunning and wiles. Witness that awful speech he had just delivered him! But instead of being angry and scolding him as usual, Alec was grateful for the daring of his advice, and he smiled at his brother in a fashion totally out of character with the old Alec.

"What are you two whispering about now?" Elaine pretended to grumble as she brought in the pineapple upside-down cake, smothered in the inevitable fresh whipped cream and topped with red cherries.

"At least you're speaking civilly to one another, thank the Lord."

She motioned to Alec to come help her serve the dessert, and she portioned out the sweet on handsome old china, the largest helping going to Alec, the next largest to Ned, and only a small helping to herself, who was always pretending to watch her figure.

"Oh, go on, Mother," Alec coaxed her, "take a real portion. We like our women a bit on the plump side, don't we, Neddy?"

Elaine's face brightened with smiles, and she leaned back in her chair. These all-too-rare sessions alone with her boys at the supper table (there were no boarders present this evening) were her deepest happiness. Indeed she had once said that her idea of Paradise would be to sit at a long, beautifully appointed table like this, candles glowing, glasses and silverware resplendent, attended only by her sons.

"Sometime, and perhaps in the not-so-distant future, we may all go our separate ways." Elaine gave her little after-supper speech now. "Then we will think back on these times, and realize how happy we were!"

The two boys looked down at their plates as she said this,

embarrassed by their mother's emotion, but somewhat frightened, too, by the warning in her words.

When Elaine had dried her eyes, and gone to the kitchen to get the coffee, Ned kicked his brother under the table, and muttered: "Don't wait for the coffee and the mints, Alec, go now and do as I told you!"

But Elaine was already handing Alec his cup of freshly brewed java.

"I declare you two have more secrets tonight than a couple about to elope."

Looking at Ned in a sickly, almost hypnotized, way, Alec slowly rose, put his napkin in the silver ring, and excused himself.

"Don't tell me you are taking two voice lessons in a row, Alec!" Elaine called after him as he repeated his excuses and left the room.

"You'll stay, I hope, Neddy, and help me with the dishes," Elaine said softly. Ned nodded. She reached for his hand and pressed it to her.

"Do you suppose he is in love?" she inquired after a few minutes of silence.

They heard the front door slam after him a moment later. Elaine walked over to the window and looked out.

"He's taking your wheel again, Neddy. Did you know that?"

"Oh, yes, Mother," Ned answered drowsily.

Coming back to the table, Elaine let her eyes rest on her younger boy, and then said good-humoredly, "You two boys have something up your sleeve! I know it, I know it! Well, have your little secrets, why don't you. A mother can't know everything about her sons."

Stung almost as much by Ned's patronizing advice and his abject surrender to such advice as by his sudden infatuation for the unknown girl who lived at the edge of Fonthill, Alec soon had worked himself into such a crescendo of emotions that he was ready to attempt anything. Perhaps even to kidnap by force the "girl of his dreams."

"By Christ, she shall be mine," he kept muttering, the phrase coming to him out of one of the novels Adele had lent him last winter.

A fine rain was falling as he approached the porch where Enid usually sat. The lights inside were on, but for a moment he could see no sign of her on the porch, which was being pelted with the rain. Then directly beside the front door he saw her. She was curled up with a blanket over her, but the rain was falling there also.

He brought his bike to a stop and called, "Aren't you afraid to get wet?"

"No. Aren't you?" her rich voice came back to him. He was struck by the sound. Her voice was richer than a girl's, and it completed his captivation, if that was possible.

"I have got myself a bit drenched," Alec said, and he brought his wheel up to the front steps of the house. He shook his head free of the drops of rain, for in his haste he had forgotten to wear his new hat.

"Well, step in, why don't you." She spoke rather curtly.

"My name, remember, is Alec Cottrell."

"Come on in and dry off, Alec Cottrell."

He kept looking at her with open-mouthed disbelief. He thought for a moment he was still at the supper table with Ned and Elaine, daydreaming.

"You don't think it rude and bad-mannered, me coming here like this?" Alec inquired.

"I'm sure I don't." She had stood up now, and was folding the blanket neatly. "I had hardly noticed the rain was coming down so heavy."

Without another word she went on inside.

He stood on there on the front porch, nearly motionless.

"Are you going to stay out there and keep your bike company in the rain?" she finally called to him, in that silvery voice which made him shiver.

"Hey, Alec Cottrell, *come to*!" She held the door open for him.

He walked inside cautiously, wiped his feet, and looked about him.

The room was nearly bare of furniture. There were no pictures on the walls, which were a freshly painted white. No rugs on the floor. Only four chairs, all of different kinds and makes, all new, large, and of stout, durable leather and wood.

In the next room he caught a glimpse of a long table such as people might use for meetings rather than dining. But there were no chairs around the table.

A brand-new floor lamp in the front room gave the only illumination.

"Do you live here alone?" he wondered, slowly taking off his wet raincoat and then, at a motion from her, putting it on one of the chairs, and sitting down on another.

"I have been keeping house temporarily for my brother. He's with the merchant marine."

"I never noticed this house before until I saw you sitting on the front porch," he explained.

"You certainly have gone by here enough. I decided you were a prospective buyer, but I see closer up you are too young for that."

"Too young to be a buyer?" he said, and he sounded as silly as Ned.

She smiled and lit a very long cigarette.

"So you smoke, too?"

"Why too?" she wondered, and he saw that her eyebrows were carefully plucked and painted.

"Oh." He colored. "My mother also smokes. On the sly, that is."

Alec could not take his eyes away from her. She looked only about fourteen, but her voice was not fourteen, and the way she looked at him and the words she used were not those of a young girl. He shivered suddenly.

"You see," she said, "the rain makes your teeth chatter."

"Oh, go on." He grinned at her.

They looked at one another then for a long time.

"Oh, Enid," he said all at once, and he felt again that he must be still at his mother's supper table, and Ned had handed him one of his crazy letters.

"Yes, Alec," she said in a comforting kind of voice.

"How did you get so beautiful," he mumbled.

"Oh, please," Enid said. "Don't talk like a calf."

"But you are, you know." He kept staring at her helplessly.

"And am I ever tired of hearing it," she grumbled. Looking at the end of her cigarette, she said, "I don't have anything in the house to eat or drink."

"Oh, don't even think about anything like that," he said.

"It gives the hands something to do when conversation don't come easy," she went on still looking at the end of her smoke.

"Is your brother gone a good deal?" Alec wondered.

"My brother?" She started a little. "Oh, yes. . . . His boat trips last anywhere from a month to two months. On the Great Lakes, you know. . . ."

"So there's not a lot of housework to worry about when he's gone so much," Alec suggested and he looked around again.

"There's nothing to do at all here, I find," she agreed. She stared down at his feet, where a puddle from his wet boots had been accumulating.

"Just sit still. I'll take care of the wet." She went out of the room and came back with a mop—brand-new also, like everything else in the place.

As she was mopping up the puddle, Alec, as if prompted now by Ned, rose and caught her in his arms and kissed her twice on the cheek.

She pushed him away, and with one hand on her hip, flashed a look of displeasure.

"I guess I can excuse that in you," she told him. "Or can I?" She studied him disgustedly, and then went out into the next room carrying the mop. He could hear her wringing it out in the toilet bowl.

When Enid returned to the front room she looked, he thought, even more gorgeous than before. The exertion of wringing out the mop had brought a faint pink flush to her face and bosom. Her eyes, which were greenish-blue, sparkled like one of Adele's gems.

"Peaches and cream," Alec muttered between his teeth.

"Oh, stop it, for Pete's sake," Enid sneered. "You don't mean a word of it. Or do you?" She flashed her eyes at him angrily again. "I must admit you have been giving me the go-over for days now."

"*You* should wear diamonds from head to toe." Alec spoke now in a stupefied manner. "You should be all jewels and diamonds, and wear a crown."

Enid made little clucking sounds with her tongue but he could see to his delirious joy that she liked what he was saying.

"Where did you get this line?" she wondered after a bit, trying to look serious.

"I don't have any line, Enid. You are so beautiful I can barely breathe." He shook his head again and again.

"I notice," he went on in short gasps, "that you don't really smoke your cigarette. You just hold it. That makes quite a picture."

"That's so," she agreed. "I don't want to stain my teeth any more than I have to. Yet I like to hold something, especially when I'm nervous."

"Do I make you nervous?"

"I don't know what *you* make me." She smiled at him.

"You wouldn't let me have one real kiss before I go?"

"Who said anything about you going?"

"But I thought I make you nervous. I'll leave at once if you say so."

"You dunce," Enid flared up. "The milk is certainly not dry on your lips."

"Tell me I can stay, then, and I'll stay."

"I thought when you came in so brazen tonight you had come to stay."

"Would I stay near you, if I did stay?" He was gasping now for air, it appeared.

"You can stay any place you want, near or far or in between far and near."

"It's only near I'd want, Enid."

He jumped up and came over to her chair, and agitatedly took one of her hands.

"It's just as soft as I thought it would be," he said. "Eiderdown." He touched her hair. She sat as composed and sleepy as usual. One would not have known he was anywhere near her to judge by her placidity.

Kneeling now before her he began kissing in a famished way both her hands. "It's all too wonderful to be true," he would comment after every few kisses.

"Your hands are as rough as sandpaper," she said. She leaned over just then and gave him a fierce kiss on the mouth.

He touched his lips now with his fingertips, and stared in amazed concentration at her. His head was swimming, and his heart could be heard pounding, probably as far away as his parked bike.

"We'll turn in early," Enid promised him. She got up and extinguished the front-room light and returned to her chair. He began to moan softly.

"Stop that confounded sound," Enid warned him. "One would think a two-year-old was in the house."

"How did you get so beautiful," Alex kept saying, recalling this phrase from a movie Adele had taken him to.

"Yes, yes, how?" she mimicked him. She gave him another of her suffocating kisses, and when she withdrew her lips, he let out a succession of coughs and gasps. Alec's hair was wet from excitement as much as from the rain, and she stroked his head with her white hands. His phenomenal excitement began to make its own impression on her. She was not any longer the complete mistress of herself.

"We had better go upstairs, I think, before you rupture a blood vessel."

"A blood vessel?" he protested. "How could you think such a thing at this time?"

"Get on your feet, honey. I don't want to have to carry a big boy like you to bed."

He did not remember anything more until he was in the king-size bed with her.

"I believe I like the sight of you hanging around my neck better than those diamonds you keep talking about," she told him.

Later, he stared at her naked form under him, he stared even at his own nakedness, and then he enveloped her, he felt, as if he had dived into all the clouds of the rain-heavy sky.

Ned had barely begun to eat his dish of hot mush and milk when he heard Elaine's screams from upstairs. His hand froze over his silver spoon. The cries came again and again. Then he heard his mother's footsteps coming downstairs.

Holding his napkin to his mouth, he studied Elaine as she entered, flushed and distraught.

"His bed has not been slept in!" She spoke accusingly to him. "Did you hear him come in last night?" Again her tone was accusatory.

Ned shook his head.

"You're sure?" she went on.

"We don't sleep in the same bed anymore, Mother," he reminded her.

"And a lot he minds about my having to do more sheets and comforters because of that change, doesn't he?" she went on, and then sat down at the table by Ned and put her hands over her eyes.

"Where do you suppose he is?" She spoke now in a more collected, cold, and angry voice. "Do you think I should notify the police?"

"No, no!" Ned rebuked her, and spilled half his water glass. Elaine barely noticed the mishap today, and he soaked up the spill with a fresh napkin.

"But what if he has been murdered, Neddy? Or had a terrible accident?"

"Well, then the police will notify us," her younger son replied stoically.

"You would say that!" Elaine scolded, and then let escape a sob or two.

"I know he's in love." Ned could have bitten his own tongue off for saying this. And his remark had the effect it would have had if he had told her of the "secret" on purpose.

"In love with whom?" she stormed.

"I don't know any more than what I've said. He told me he was in love."

"Well, he can't have meant that terrible Adele Bevington, can he?"

Ned saw that Elaine would have almost preferred Adele at this moment to some new, unknown object of his affections.

"I'm not supposed to tell anybody." Ned now turned to his mush and milk again.

"I see," Elaine said, and rose to go to the kitchen. Turning around she said rather sweetly: "How will you have your eggs this morning, Neddy?"

"Why, poached." He spoke as formally as if he were in a restaurant.

Elaine searched his face for a moment. "Poached then it shall be," she said, honeying him.

Ned stared at the damp place by his place mat and cursed himself for having let out Alec's secret.

Thinking about Alec's being smitten, thinking always too about Val Dougherty's midnight confession, and still wondering about Adele's note asking about Keith Gresham, Ned forgot it was breakfast time, forgot almost where he was when he heard Elaine cry: "Now, if that doesn't look delicious then I can't boil water!"

On one of her best china plates she had placed three poached eggs dotted with paprika and fresh parsley, and surrounded by golden-brown potatoes.

Ned's face softened, and he began eating.

Elaine did not wait long. "Now, darling, tell me, who is this woman he has fallen in love with?"

Ned told her the little he knew, and gave the name of Alec's crush.

"Enid!" Elaine repeated and blew her nose. "At the edge of town, too! Wouldn't you know! Of course I've seen for some time now he would up and leave us. . . . There'll be nothing for me to do then but turn this place into a regular boardinghouse. Or get married."

"Get married?" He opened his eyes wide.

"Yes!" She shouted back at him. "Don't you think I am marriageable?"

It was obvious from his expression he did not, and Elaine went off into one of her customary under-the-breath strings of exclamations and inaudible mumblings.

"A young boy staying out all night like a common roustabout with no family name to uphold."

Taking off her apron and folding it with ceremonious slowness, she said: "Well, let Enid cook and scrub and wash and iron and slave for him. Let her see how she likes it!"

Ned kept his eyes averted and swallowed the last of his breakfast. "I'm working today at the fairgrounds," he reminded his mother, getting up. He kissed her swiftly, and then ran out the back door. But he was soon back again. "My bike is gone." It was his turn now to show emotion. "How will I get to work?"

Elaine shrugged her shoulders. "If *he* misses work today," she went on, "and is fired because of it, all because he is soft on some slut, I'll tell you, hell will be to pay in this house."

The whole thing struck Ned as so ridiculous he began to laugh uproariously.

"I suppose, smarty," Elaine retorted, "if I was to ask you what tickles you so much, it would take you a month to think up an alibi, wouldn't it?"

However, Ned's laughter snapped the tension somehow, and Elaine began her morning housework with some slight degree of equanimity.

Ned walked the two miles to his work.

One did not need to be present at any event in Elaine's house in order to be in possession of the latest news. Elaine's telephone conversations to friends were more comprehensive than a radio news broadcast, for they not only went into minute details as to what had happened that day, but reviewed the events leading up to the occurrence.

That evening, back from the fairgrounds, Ned heard: "You will never know what I've been through, Rita. Thank God, you never married. I don't believe unmarried persons know the hell a married woman goes through. Not to mention a widow."

Ned turned his chair a little more in the direction of the telephone to catch his mother's talk with Rita Fitzsimmons. It tickled him more than anything now to hear of Alec's disgrace for a change. He had eaten his peck of dirt with regard to his own shortcomings, and now it was old Alec's turn, damn him.

"Yes, he finally showed up for an early supper tonight." Elaine's talk with the piano teacher went on while Ned muffled his gleeful laughter. "He looked the spit and image of his late dad, if God will forgive me saying so. You remember, I'm sure, how Marius often came in the house with his nose in the air as if he was a Morgan or Rockefeller. . . . I see now Alec is just like Marius. Never gave me one word of explanation—Alec, that is— as to where he had been. His face was all puffed up and red as if he was coming down with the mumps. . . ."

Elaine, however, had considerably glossed over for Rita a good part of her confrontation with Alec, Ned noted, and his glee and satisfaction redoubled.

"I don't ask you questions when you're out with one of your many boyfriends, do I?" Alec had roared at his mother when she demanded an explanation of his absence the night before. (This was not conveyed to Rita.) "And I don't ask what you do in the back seat with Freddie Yost, do I, Miss Piety?"

"I wish your dad were here just to hear how you talk to your mother!" Elaine had shouted at him so vociferously that Widow Hughes, deaf as she was, heard, standing on the back porch, and debated whether she should intervene personally, or merely call the sheriff.

But becoming uncertain how to proceed just then, Widow Hughes was able to arrive only after Alec had left the premises, and she overheard Elaine's conversation with Rita:

"He claims he is in love with this perfect stranger, and what is more, says he is going to marry her. . . . I tell you, Rita, this all stems from Adele Bevington's influence. Before my boys knew her, they were model young men. . . . Now look at both of them."

"Thank you, Elaine!" Ned called down from the upstairs bannister, and then saw—not to his very great astonishment—that Widow Hughes was sharing the "performance" with him.

Whether it was because of the memory of Widow Hughes's recent generosity in bestowing on her an heirloom ring, or the fear of the old woman's double-dealing and vicious tongue, Elaine offered an apology to Rita that "company next door" had arrived, and hung up.

"Now, now, my angel." Rosa Hughes approached Elaine, and took her in her arms. "You must not take Alec's carrying-on so seriously."

Elaine appeared content to be petted at that moment by Rosa.

"How lovely my emerald ring looks on your hand," she noted, and she kissed the finger that held the gem. "And it is yours, don't start so, Elaine. It is all yours, and there are more where it came from. . . . I know you affect the friendship of Adele Bevington, my dear, leastways your boys do, but her jewels all came to her through crime and prostitution, whilst mine, dear heart, come from inheritance. Always remember that when you hear the name Adele Bevington, and say either to yourself or better aloud: 'Of course, her jewels came to her through vice.' But what do I hear, daughter, about Alec leaving you?"

And worn out by her worry and the burdens of being both mother and father to her sons, Elaine poured out her vexation, grief, and anger against Alec, Ned, the dead Marius, and the torments of poverty and hard work, while Rosa Hughes caressed and kissed her, and kept winking at Ned, who stood rooted to the spot, disgusted but too fascinated also to leave off gaping.

"Should young Ned be present, Elaine, while you are confiding to me your secrets?" Rosa inquired when there was a slight indication of a pause on the young widow's part.

Slightly freeing herself from Rosa's embrace, Elaine cried: "Ned Cottrell knows more about life than a man of forty! He could have us go to school to him and we'd come away bowed down by life's secrets, I'm afraid!" As she finished this sentence she let out a kind of snort of anger.

"Who is this woman he is spending his nights with?" Rosa now turned to the younger son.

"Don't tell any more than you know," Elaine remonstrated now. "And leave the house! Do you hear me, Neddy. Leave us to our grief."

Ned rose with lordly deliberateness. He was reluctant to get too far beyond earshot, for he knew there was bound to be a rich confab between these two women, who in the end always said the unsayable, for it was they, he was positive, and not he, who knew everything there was about "life."

He went out on the back porch, where he could hear bits and fragments of the two ladies' confidences.

"It's in their blood, how many times do I have to tell you." Rosa Hughes's deaf-woman's voice reached out as if it would penetrate to the very edge of town, where Enid could hear her. "It's like a boiling burning lake of naphtha in their blood. . . . Remember when all the oil wells caught fire here? No, that was before your time. Or can you recollect when the nitroglycerine factory blew up? The whole town was nothing but sky-high flames. I thought it was the Last Judgment, my lovely. Yet those oil and glycerine explosions are as nothing to what is circulating in men's veins. Look nowhere else for the bottomless pit and the river that is never quenched. What is beyond the universe, do you think? I know now. It is the unquenchable lust in the veins of men. Nothing can put it out. Nothing. Don't fight it, my beauty" (and here could be heard the delirious sounds of kisses bestowed on his mother by the old harridan). "Yes, if a thousand women were to sacrifice their chastity, say, to one young hearty like Ned out there, that fire between his legs could still never be put out. . . . I believe men burn even in the grave. . . . I believe the fire that is in them may indeed be behind the makeup of our entire universe."

"Ned, I can hear you out there by the latticework," Elaine now called out to him, but in a somewhat calm and collected manner for her. "This is not for your ears, do you hear? Leave the premises at once. You may as well go the way of your brother to perdition, so follow his footsteps."

Obeying, Ned slammed the door behind him, and Widow Hughes's orotund forensic utterances proceeded apace.

To the surprise, indeed the consternation of the Cottrell household, bright and early one morning, before breakfast had been served, a telegram was delivered to Elaine by a Western Union messenger boy, who looked at least four years younger than Ned.

Elaine called to Alec, holding the yellow envelope as far away from her as possible.

"Open it, Alec, and then tell me what it says. It's bound to be bad news."

"Oh, Mother," he replied with lofty pity for her ingenuousness. "Very well, then." But it did not take any close observation on anybody's part to see that Alec was as frightened as his mother as to what the telegram might say.

"Well!" Elaine exclaimed after her son had read and reread the message several times without speaking.

"Why, it's from, of all people, Adele Bevington." He began to hand her the message.

"No, no, read it to me . . . I have mislaid my glasses."

"One hardly needs glasses to read it, Mother." He looked at her with a wondering expression in his eyes.

"Well, then, read it, for God's sake!"

Alec cleared his throat, and held the telegram in both his hands before him as if it were sheet music and he was about to favor with a solo. "My very dear Elaine," he read. "It is a matter of the most pressing urgency that I see you this afternoon at three o'clock. Unless I hear from you to the contrary I will send a rented car to your house at about half past two. You will be conferring on me the greatest of kindnesses if you will accept. Gratefully, and very sincerely yours, ever, Adele Bevington."

"Why on earth she would send me a telegram just to invite me for a talk!" Elaine began, and sat down to catch her breath. "Frightening me to death like this, when nobody sends telegrams in Fonthill except to announce death or disaster. She would. She must be grand!"

"Mother," Alec began reproachfully as Ned entered the room and snatched the telegram from his brother's hands and perused it.

"Well, you're going, aren't you, Mother?" Ned inquired as Alec glowered at him for his rudeness.

"Of course she's going," Alec snapped, grabbing the telegram away from Ned. "What excuses could Mother give not to accept such an invitation?"

"Oh, I can think of a thousand excuses, Alec, for your mother to give . . . and I am the one to decide whether I will accept or not, not you!" Elaine gave her son a withering look. "One would think she was the Queen issuing a summons! And both you boys have visited her so many times that you regard her behavior as normal. That is what galls me so much. You condone anything and everything she does, both of you!"

The two young men stared at one another.

"I don't know what on earth I could tell her she does not already know," Elaine went on, but one could see that she was gradually coming around to accepting the invitation as unavoidable.

"I have nothing nice to wear, and besides what am I to do about this evening's supper. I'm expecting three boarders, at least, and perhaps four. . . ."

"You must close the boardinghouse tonight, that's all there is to it," Alec advised her.

"All there is to it, he says. And do you know how much money is in my purse at this moment? The trouble with you, Alec, is you live with your head in the clouds, and Ned is no better!"

"Mother," Alec said in his most conciliatory tone, "I will

telephone every one of the boarders and simply tell them an emergency has come up, and that we will be closed. As to money, I have more than enough."

"Adele Bevington better have something really important to tell me," Elaine grumbled.

"I'm sure she will," Alec comforted her. "If you will allow me," he went on in a humble and comforting manner, "I'll help you pick out a dress that will suit you, and you can wear the necklace and earrings Grandmother willed you, which you seem never to wear."

Elaine pouted now like a young girl, but allowed Alec to go on encouraging her.

"One would think I was going to be presented at Court the way you carry on, Alec," she cried as he led her upstairs.

Ned, scowling, read and reread the telegram and then with fury threw it on the floor, and left the house without his breakfast.

"One would think I was about to be married, instead of visiting poor disgraced Adele Bevington!" Elaine exclaimed, looking at herself in the mirror under the admiring glances of her oldest boy. Alec grinned, for he saw that his mother was pleased with her appearance. Indeed she looked radiant in her pretty shimmering homemade yellow dress, her pearl necklace, and her new silk stockings and high-heeled shoes.

"Adele will adore you," Alec beamed at her. "And it will do you good to be away from the boarders one night. They will appreciate you all the more!"

"I think you do love your mother a little bit, don't you?" Elaine said to him. He kissed her on the mouth, and for a few moments her worry about him and his new "flame" was absent from her mind.

The sound of the hired car driving up in the alleyway roused them from their reverie.

Elaine ran down the front steps like a young girl, threw a kiss to Alec, and got into the taxi and was off. Alec shook his head and sighed. He was sure he would be the topic of conversation at Miss Bevington's, though their tongues would wag about Ned also, needless to say.

Elaine felt a secret dread all at once, and the queer idea

invaded her mind that her sons had sent her away, and that she would never see them or the boardinghouse again. Or if she did return she would find both Alec and Ned married, and their wives would bar the door of her own house to her. She was sorry she had accepted the invitation, yes, it was a mistake, but there was no point in turning back now. She had never felt comfortable in the presence of Adele Bevington, but she had never before been alone with her, and this time she was to see her, as it were, by command. She would be at her mercy, without counsel or defense.

But when Adele opened the heavy frosted-glass door, Elaine saw at once that Adele was if possible even more distraught than she, indeed nearly desperate.

"Thank God, you've come, Mrs. Cottrell!" She kissed the boys' mother on the cheek several times. "Come in and get comfortable. I hope I have not inconvenienced you too much by asking you here. I tell you, Mrs. Cottrell, I do not know where to turn!"

Elaine looked about her, taking in the magnificent imported furniture, the ceiling-high bookcases filled with beautifully bound gold-lettered books, the priceless (or so she thought) vases, mirrors, crimson curtains, and elegant rugs. And this was where Ned and Alec paid court to her! No wonder their heads had been turned. She felt slightly dizzy herself.

When she brought her glance back from surveying the room she saw Adele handing her a cup of steaming hot tea.

"It will relax you from the ride," her hostess said. Adele continued to stand up, and every so often made a few steps around the chair Elaine was seated in.

From somewhere not too far from them came the sweet, heavy odor of baking, which all at once became cloying in its pervasiveness. Had Adele been busy in the kitchen preparing her something? The odor of flour, sugar, spices was suddenly everywhere.

"I hardly know where to begin, my dear," Adele said at last. Elaine's attention was diverted from the odor of baked goods to the fact that Adele had put on her lipstick carelessly that day, so that indeed she looked as if she had been bitten on the mouth. As if reading her guest's thoughts, Adele took out a pocket handkerchief and wiped her mouth.

"Would you allow me, Miss Bevington," Elaine ventured with considerable trepidation.

"Oh, would you, please."

Elaine put down her tea cup and, rising, took Adele's handkerchief and wiped away the excess of lip rouge.

"Oh, thank you. You are so thoughtful." She went over to one of the smaller mirrors and wiped the last of the lipstick away.

"First of all"—Adele came back to Elaine, and helped herself at the same time to her own tea—"I want to tell you here and now that without the kindness and courteous consideration of your sons, I think I would either have gone mad these last years or died!"

Elaine began to say something, but Adele raised her hand and went on: "You will never know my gratitude to you. . . . But I did not bring you here just to tell you I am grateful. Someday I hope to give you tangible proof of that gratitude, tangible thanks. . . ."

"But you have already," Elaine responded, and any ill will or jealousy she had ever had for Miss Bevington seemed at that moment swept away forever.

"I have done nothing. But I have accepted a great deal. We will say no more on that score—at present." She sipped more tea.

"Allow me, Mrs. Cottrell, to take up the least of my problems. I shall be very quick. I am to be ruled out of the Altrusa Club."

Elaine had her cup raised to drink, but at the mention of *ruled out* she put the delicate china cup down, and waited.

"But why?" Elaine finally was able to inquire.

"The personal animosity of one person and one person only, Judge Hitchmough. He has always despised me since I was a young girl. And it was my father who was one of the founders of the Altrusa Club! It has nearly driven me to running through the streets screaming. No wonder I put on my makeup crooked. But crushing a blow as my dismissal from the Club is, we must go on to more important matters. I will take up the next matter briefly, though it has broken me, and then we will pass on to our main business, which concerns you, and, if you will allow me to say so, also me. . . ."

Elaine appeared like a woman who has finally come into a day of sunshine after a bleak and cloudgirt winter. Her winning smile at that moment gave Adele the courage to say: "Word has come to me from a reliable source that one of your young gentlemen boarders, Keith Gresham . . ."

A look almost of panic coming across Elaine Cottrell's face made Adele stop for a few seconds.

"You do know Mr. Gresham?"

Elaine could only nod several times.

Mr. Gresham has told my informant, Mrs. Cottrell, that he knows the whereabouts of my *son*, who was taken from me in infancy. . . . I am sure you know, of course, of my principal misfortune. It is what is behind Judge Hitchmough and the Altrusa Club ruling me out, if the truth were told."

"Keith Gresham!" Elaine could only repeat in a murmur.

"I thought that sometime you might ask him to come to see me. . . . The rumor has revived so much that I thought was buried and forgotten. . . . That is one favor I would like to ask of you."

"I shall speak to him at once, depend on it."

Adele beamed her thanks, but like a woman who has been given official duties to transact and who cannot pause on any one matter of concern or business, she went on to what she had called the "principal purpose and consideration" for which they had come together.

"The reason, my dear, I have taken the liberty of asking you to pay me this visit, at a time I realize is not convenient for you, touches on you directly, and as a friend of your sons, I hope you will see that it touches my loyalty and affection for you and your family."

Having said this, Adele sat down and helped herself to several hearty swallows of rather tepid tea.

"I am talking about Enid Beauregard," she said in what was almost a bass voice at that moment, owing either to her having swallowed so much tea or to the unpleasantness of the name and the subject now introduced.

"I see that name is as much a source of pain to you as it is to me," Adele continued, studying the different changes of expression on the part of her guest.

"Alec is no more the same boy he was since he fell under her influence than night is day." Elaine spoke woefully.

"All I require from you, Mrs. Cottrell," Adele said, sitting back in a regal posture, holding both her hands together, which allowed one to see her many rings blazing away in the failing afternoon sunlight, "and all I will require in the way of assistance is your permission for me to proceed."

"To proceed?" Alec's mother blinked at her.

"To rid ourselves of her!"

Elaine's eyes opened wide—she even paled á little.

"Oh, nothing violent, have no fear of that, though she deserves to be killed!" Elaine laughed her musical nervous little laugh, and Adele rose and filled her visitor's cup with hot tea. "I could kill her with my own hands and sleep soundly forever after."

"I am afraid she is a much worse sort than I realized." Elaine heaved a great sigh, such as Widow Hughes herself might have expelled on hearing one of her own worst suspicions confirmed.

"She was in love, you see, with her half brother before either of them knew they were blood relations."

Elaine leaned forward, then, taking in what she had heard, leaned back, and her cup and saucer jangled together until she put them down.

"You said her half brother?" Elaine inquired.

Adele nodded.

"Furthermore, though she looks under twenty," Adele continued, "she must be over thirty, for thanks to her half brother, she has never lifted a finger all these years. He keeps different houses for her to live in, one in Chicago, one in New Orleans, one here. . . . She lives in a perpetual prison, a prison, true, with quite a few luxuries, but her brother is her jailer.

"And poor Alec has fallen for such a creature!" Elaine apostrophized the walls, picked up her cup and saucer and took a long swallow.

"All I need from you, Mrs. Cottrell, is to tell me I can proceed now in my own way to make her leave, and not return."

Perhaps Elaine Cottrell did not hear this last sentence, at least not at the moment Adele pronounced it. Her mind was in a turmoil. *If he had to fall in love with someone, why did it have to be of her sort* was a sentence that kept revolving about in her head.

"Mrs. Cottrell!" Elaine heard Adele's voice coming as if from a block away. "I have upset you, my dear. Pardon me."

"How will you effect this," Elaine said, coming to herself.

"First of all, Mrs. Cottrell . . ."

"Oh, please, call me Elaine, for heaven's sake."

"Elaine, then," Adele agreed rather condescendingly, "Elaine it shall be. But listen, dear heart, you will let me go ahead at my own speed, and in my own way . . . for you do want Alec freed from her, don't you?"

"More than anything in the world. You know that."

"But I had to hear it from you. . . ."

"Of course. Do what you think proper and best."

"That is all I need to hear. When you leave here, my dear girl, you can leave with the assurance that Alec will soon be free."

Adele rose, eyes flashing, jewels blazing, hands clasped over her heart. She gazed at Alec's mother with the satisfaction, pride, and affection a teacher might show who sees that a backward and not over-bright pupil has mastered a difficult problem in higher mathematics.

She walked to a screen, which Elaine had hardly noticed before, and with some effort pushed it away. Behind it was a kind of butcher-block table on which rested three enormous cakes—wedding cakes one might have thought them to be. They were, of course, the source of the tantalizing odors of baking that had reached Elaine's nostrils so persistently.

The beauty, the sumptuousness of the cakes, caused Alec's mother to let out a cry. She rose and went over to the table.

"I would never dare to compete with you as a cook, or a baker, my dear," Adele said softly and took the mother's hand in hers. "But I wanted to please you!"

"You baked . . . these?" Elaine cried.

"Yes. For you. Only for you."

"But it must have taken you days."

"Yes, perhaps days." Adele laughed. The admiration of Alec's mother for her cakes had made her already feel rewarded.

"At first I had thought of going to Aunt Willy down the road—you know, the old black woman who claims she was a slave and is perhaps the finest cook in town after Alec's mother. . . . Then I said to myself, 'No, Adele, you must roll up your sleeves, go to the kitchen and prove to Mrs. Cottrell you can be of use for something after all.' "

Adele was already busy cutting a slice of each of the cakes, for her guest.

Then Adele waited. As Elaine munched and nodded, however, she could tell she had triumphed. She could tell the cakes were all she had hoped they would be.

"I could not have equaled any one of them!" the mother cried. "You are not flattering me?"

"Indeed no. They are of supreme quality. . . . But you must have used four dozen eggs at least! They are elegant enough for royalty. . . . And your frosting! Your . . ."

No expletive was spared. The two women were finally seated and went on tasting and commenting, occasionally even smacking their lips, eating some of the frosting and crumbs from their fingers.

"My dear Adele, you have no equal!"

Elaine's praise soothed and comforted her. She repeated what Alec's mother had said in praise of her again and again that evening: *No equal! No equal!*

The cakes were good, if I do say so myself! Adele repeated in the darkness, hours after the mother had gone home. *But baking is sure slave labor! And the poor thing does that every day for her boys and her boarders! God pity her, God take care of her.*

Her happiness at pleasing so severe a critic as Elaine Cottrell was a kind of ecstasy all that evening, all that night.

"I will destroy Enid Beauregard," she said in her half slumber. "Utterly destroy her."

A few days after Elaine's five-hour meeting with Adele Bevington, Alec returned to the fold. He had not slept in his own bed at his mother's for over a month.

He returned just before nightfall as if nothing had happened, and Elaine tried to pretend he had never been gone, that there was nothing unusual in his sitting down to late supper. When a few hours later she heard him go to his own room and close the door, she stopped breathing. If he stayed, she knew, it was over. If he merely packed some more things and went out, then Enid would have him forever. But he stayed. Night after night he stayed under her roof. It was over.

Elaine did not dare ask Adele what she had done. She had always been in awe of the Bevington woman, but now she was almost terrified of her, as one feels a kind of superstitious aversion to a saint who has granted a special favor. But she must have gone to Enid! She must have done something to effect this change.

When Ned came down to breakfast, she said very little to him about the prodigal's return, studying her younger son's face as if to find there the answer to her many questions. But she was sure from the way Ned kept his lips tightly compressed and averted his eyes from her direct glance that he knew "something."

Ned had for a long time had the "abominable" practice (a word of Elaine's) of going through Alec's private letters. He had once found some love letters from a girl several years older than Alec, but they were of little interest to Ned. Alec's private diary, penned in violet ink, however, arrested his undivided attention. Since Ned prided himself on being smarter and more literary than his brother he found the moonings and musings of Alec amusing, when not laughable or tiresome. But he was not quite prepared for the outpouring and intensity Alec put pen to with regard to Enid. He wondered how Alec had the nerve to put down all he felt, all he had done. I have to hand it to old Alec, Ned reflected as he went over all the entries.

But the most interesting thing was that Enid had disappeared. Alec had slept on in the Beauregard house for at least a week waiting for her, until he caught sight of a large piece of cardboard he had observed many times but had never examined. On the face of it was written, "Alec, I am leaving forever so don't wait for me to return. I do not love you, and never did. You were so eager I wanted to see how far it might go. It didn't go far, so goodbye."

Alec must have looked at that piece of cardboard a hundred times and never thought the handwriting scrawled with a pencil stub was a message for him. He thought it was something she had written to the milkman.

"I will never get over it," the diary continued. "I don't care she didn't love me, only that she left me. I will go back to the house every night, just to catch maybe a tiny whiff of her person, or remember the coral of her nipples. . . ."

But after a while he no longer went to the house at all. But he was no more like the old Alec than up is down; he had lost a good ten pounds, dark purple circles rimmed his eyes, and his hands shook a little.

"Well, he's back to stay, Ned." Elaine initiated the conversation that morning.

Ned shrugged his shoulders, aware his mother was studying him.

"You might try to be a little more sympathetic from now on to your brother, if you ask me." She spoke with cool confidentiality. She went on to prepare him an unusually sumptuous breakfast this morning, whether because of her joy in having Alec back, or because she was about to ask a favor of her younger boy. The repast this morning was a Western omelet, French toast, crisp bacon such as he loved, and she had both heated and whipped the milk for his coffee.

"What does the big splurge commemorate, Mother?" he said uneasily as she brought in the victuals.

"For our mainstay's return." She smiled. She had on a fresh apron, and had brought in a bouquet of nasturtiums, wild roses, and some late violets for the table.

"You would think to look at all this grub that I was being sent off to join the army." Ned now looked his mother straight in the face.

She watched him eating the breakfast she had prepared with such care, nodding in silent satisfaction at each bite he took into his mouth. She smiled constantly. When she filled his coffee cup she touched his soft hair with her hand.

Finally, then, it came out.

"Ned, dear, you are keeping something from Mama."

He let the heavy silver fork fall to the plate.

"Mom!" He warned her, and wiped his mouth angrily.

She turned tearful then.

"Why is it I am the last ever to know anything about my own sons! Answer me that! I bet Adele Bevington knows more about you both than I do. . . . For, Ned, you know something! I am positive."

"About what?" He pretended he was completely in the dark.

"You know perfectly well what I am talking about. I can read your face like a book. After all, who knows you better than your own mother? . . . Yes, you are keeping something from me. . . . After all, you knew about Enid Beauregard long before I did, and you never said boo."

"Oh, Mom, God in heaven!"

He stared balefully at her, but she could see his features relaxing, his hands unclenching.

"Just tell me, Ned, darling. I have the right to know the secret, don't I? And it will go no farther."

"Well, his affair with Enid Beauregard is over," Ned said dryly.

"But that's hardly news. After all, he's sleeping and eating here again after a month away. I mean, Ned, the *real* news. You've heard something! Or seen something! Or read something." She said the last words in a whisper such as Nazimova might have envied.

Ned colored on the last words, and she had him.

"What have you read, dearest?"

"Enid Beauregard left him because she found him too . . . boyish." Ned spoke in the way he had so often spoken in his sleep while in bed with his brother in days past.

"Anybody could have told him from the first it was mere puppy love." She spoke with such sweet, reasonable kindness Ned could hardly believe his ears. His mother was a deep woman, all right. But, as Adele had taught him, women were deep. And dangerous.

"He's brokenhearted over it still. He even thought of . . . killing himself."

"Oh, God, Ned . . . how do you know that?"

"I told you not to push me now! I won't have it!"

"Ned, I have kept a roof over your head ever since your father died. Don't I have some little right to know what goes on under that roof. Tell me!"

"It didn't go on under your roof."

"Don't you sass me . . . Ned, I am telling you, it is my right to know. He is my son."

"We don't demand to know everything about you, Elaine." He spoke rather bitterly.

"There's nothing to know," she almost whimpered. "I'm your mother . . . I have devoted my whole life to you. . . . What else is there to know but that?"

"Well, you do have . . . gentlemen friends," he reminded her.

"Oh, those occasional visits to a movie house or an after-hours dinner café . . . Am I never to be allowed to leave my own house?"

"Anyhow,"—Ned found himself now going beyond what he knew was prudent—"our Alec can never complain he knows nothing about life again, can he? I mean he's had it with a girl, and good!"

"Ned, I'm surprised you would speak so before me. Are you sure you are not just talking out of your imagination?"

"Would imagination cover a whole month being away?"

That frenzied, waiting expression on her face propelled him forward.

"I saw something . . . Alec had written, if you have got to know."

"A letter?"

"I can't tell you any more, Mother, dearest. I've got to be off to this job at the Amusement Arcade, remember."

"Ned, what did you read? And where did you read it?" She put her hand about his neck.

"Mom, that was the best breakfast you ever cooked me," he told her, looking away.

"Where is this thing you have read, Ned? Just tell me."

He waited a minute. Then his struggle was over.

"I think you'll find what he's written everywhere, if you have to know. Under the bedclothes, in commodes and bureaus, inside of books. He's been molting with bits and pieces of writing about his love. . . . Now leave me alone, do you hear? Leave me alone!"

"Thank you, darling." She insisted on kissing him, though he tried to draw his lips away from her. "I think I will take just a peek at the things you mention." She spoke with calm piety. "After all, Alec needs all our love and protection now. . . . Imagine Enid Beauregard jilting him, Ned. That's a hard blow for a young fellow even though it's only, as you said, puppy love."

"Did Enid Beauregard jilt Alec, or did Adele Bevington run her out of town on a rail?"

Elaine went an ashen white.

"What do you mean?" she said, gasping.

"You are the one who put your head together with Adele. Why don't you tell me!"

He saw what he felt was her guilt.

"We must keep this to ourselves, Neddy," she implored him.

"I don't know what Adele did, believe me. And it was I she summoned, after all. . . . We will keep this close now, do you hear?' We must not drive Alec out from our midst again! Thank you, Neddy, for standing by me . . ."

He broke away from her, and went out the back way, but instead of slamming the door as usual, he closed it as noiselessly as if it were made of gauze.

Had God wanted to deprive the women of Fonthill of the main substance of life, he would have removed their ability to speak. Elaine came from a long generation of farmers' wives, some rich, some impoverished, some fancying themselves grand, some pitying their hard lot on stubborn unyielding pastureland, but all, from sunup to sundown, like the birds in the myrtle and ivy and poplar trees, talking incessantly. Only at night did their tongues show signs of abating.

When Elaine had visited her grandfather's farm, as the wives' talk slackened with the fall of darkness, the men—threshers, farm hands, hired help—would sometimes gather outside the big back porch, and in the summer night talk softly among themselves, sounding in the blur of the landscape like tree frogs or crickets. Their low chuckles and stifled laughter gave indication they were speaking of something the womenfolk could not and dared not share.

But in the daytime the women were masters of speech, and their tongues never stopped.

It was Adele, indeed, who had shocked both Alec and Ned when she had once remarked that perhaps God had formed the world out of his spit, for his prime creations talked so much. "And without that *spit*," she had said, shocking the boys again by the use of a word that was faintly indecent at Elaine's table, "we would not be women or indeed men. Though no man," she predicated, "can talk as well as a woman. And the only reason women are not greater writers than men is that God has imprisoned women in the sepulcher of their own bodies, from which new life of course springs forth." And Alec and Ned had stared at one another in shock, if not horror, at Adele's speech.

Immediately, then, that "little Ned" had skiddooed from the

house, Elaine rushed to Alec's solitary room and began rummaging about among his "things." Drawers were flung open, commodes rifled, bureaus ransacked, closets (the room had two spacious ones) looked into, old shoeboxes inspected, even the chamber pot under the bed (seldom used nowadays) picked up and given the once-over. Then, under his pillow, where he must have left it after his last entry, she found the cheap Woolworth *A Diary of My Year 1930*, which she opened with the desperate concentration of a prisoner who expects to find in a secret place the key that will release him to freedom.

Poring over the handwriting of the diary, she forgot her housework, her preparation for the boarders' evening meal. She did not even hear from below the voice of Rosa Hughes calling for her dearest, her only friend, her daughter—more a daughter than her own flesh and blood, and so forth. No, Elaine heard nothing now, took in nothing but the outpourings of a lovesick boy, which would have made any reader laugh outright except a mother like Elaine. She read, as she would later say to Rita Fitzsimmons, her own death warrant.

In page after page of the Woolworth diary, she found the unknown, obscure, but irresistible-as-sin-itself Enid Beauregard extolled to the heights, while her own devotion, sacrifice, unstinting labor, and ceaseless love were ground into the dust under his feet. For Alec loved only a common slut named Enid, and his only home was her white frame house at the edge of town.

So stricken with countless conflicting emotions that she could barely see the page before her, and staining the ink with her tears, so that Alec's outpourings would be nearly illegible to any reader who came hereafter, Elaine was especially annihilated by an entry in the last pages of the diary which read:

> The greatest happiness of my entire life was the night you allowed me merely to rest my head upon your uncovered breast. If we could only have slept on like that together forever and a day, never to awaken to the rest of the world . . .

At that moment Elaine threw the book clear across the room, breaking its cheap leather spine and allowing all the pages to fall in disarray on the highly polished wood floor.

"Is that a housebreaker up there?" The cries of Widow Hughes at last reached her.

Elaine went out into the hall, but she was still too overcome by her reading to reply to the old woman standing at the foot of the stairs.

"If you are a robber up there, admit it!" Rosa went on. "I fear nothing, least of all death."

"Amen!" Elaine answered back.

To the mother's surprise, the old woman now almost raced up the steps. "My precious Elaine," she addressed her. "What on earth has occurred? You look so beside yourself . . ."

"Hold me to you, Mother," Elaine said to a baffled Rosa. "Hold a dead woman to your cold breast."

"Now, now, my favorite girl." Rosa held her and smoothed her hair.

"My son is in love with a bad woman," she said in a collected manner.

"Naturally," chuckled Rosa Hughes. "I told you they were all alike, but you pooh-poohed me at the time. All alike, my pet, beardless, bearded, or old white-haired goats. All have the mark of the devil between their thighs, and they can be nothing but horned beasts. . . . Accept the inevitable, and accept my love instead."

"Don't ask me to tell you what I have been reading, Rosa." Elaine spoke in a tone unrecognizable as her own. Indeed she cooed almost like a small girl now. "I must erase from my brain and heart what my eyes have been subjected to. . . . I have nothing now . . . nobody. My sons care less for me than the scraps left over from last week's supper table. Val Dougherty cares more for his mares and ponies than they do for me!" She added this last thought as if it too came from the scrawled words of the diary.

"Val Dougherty and his mares indeed!" the old widow cackled. "Care is hardly the word!"

The old woman allowed Elaine to whimper and moan against her bosom, and then gradually from her dress pocket pulled forth a paper, legally executed and notarized.

"What is it, Rosa, you are holding up for me to see, for my tears have blinded me."

"Proof positive, angel, that you own my emerald ring. I have just come from the lawyer's office, where, by the by, I caught sight of one of your boarders, young Keith Gresham. . . . There's a prize for some woman, if you ask me. Ready for the snatching, my dear, and overripe at that."

Elaine was sobered up by inspecting the rather lengthy legal document giving her possession of the old woman's heirloom ring.

"You thought I didn't remember about handing over to you the emerald, didn't you. You see me as older than I am. . . . Now let us go downstairs together and have a taste of one of your wonderful desserts. I hope you baked the suet pudding with the wine sauce for me. . . ."

"I will bake you anything your heart desires," Elaine said, and gave a last look back at Alec's room, where the diary lay scattered in shreds.

"So I have lost my mainstay, the prop to this household," Elaine rambled on in a calmer if more bitter tone. "And before I lost Alec, of course, I had had to bid goodbye to little Ned. . . . They will both be gone now any day, and what will I have to show for my life . . . tell me!"

This "tell me" was not so much directed to the venerable Mrs. Reverend Hughes as perhaps to God himself, who, having given women the burden of their lot, had, as Adele Bevington once remarked, bestowed on women as a kind of booby prize the gift of tongue to tell from early day to nightfall the story of their sufferings.

"So your firstborn has betrayed you." Rosa comforted Elaine with such statements, and followed these statements with kisses and praises of the younger woman's beauty, and promises that she would be remembered now even more generously in her will (she drove the lawyers to distraction by changing it every fortnight).

Unsoothed by the old widow's kind of comfort, once she was left alone, Elaine hesitated for a few moments, then swallowed her pride and called Rita Fitzsimmons on the telephone. For indifferently as Rita had treated her on the last visit to the studio, who else would bend an ear to her woes now?

"If you are troubled, this is the place you should be. For God's sake don't stand on ceremony, but come over at once." Rita's voice, however, sounded more professional than friendly, but Elaine hugged the receiver of the phone to her cheek, and forgot how cold Rita had been to her on her last visit.

"Whatever you may think of Adele Bevington," Rita began after the two women had embraced and kissed and were seated so close together their knees touched, "you can thank her for Alec's rupture with Enid Beauregard."

Elaine stared at the music teacher. She could not tell her that the rupture meant very little after what she had read in her boy's diary, for wherever Enid Beauregard was, Alec loved her best.

"How do you know Adele had a hand in it?" Elaine spoke coolly, and accepted an imported cigarette from Rita.

"You remember the young man who was here on the occasion of your last visit . . . Allen Mowbray?"

Elaine blew out a cloud of smoke and nodded.

"By the way, he was terribly taken with you," the music teacher added, then rushed on: "It seems he was walking past the Beauregard house one evening, and he could not help noticing in the front room the two women going at it hammer and tongs, Adele Bevington, and Alec's girl friend. He stopped, and caught snatches of conversation."

To her own surprise, Elaine felt more anger against Allen Mowbray for having eavesdropped than gratitude to Adele for having made the rupture. For the real rupture after all was Alec no longer loved his mother! Nothing would ever make up for that, even if Enid Beauregard were burned at the stake and her ashes thrown to the four corners of the earth.

"Evidently our Adele had enough against Enid to drive ten girls out of town on a rail. . . . So rejoice, Elaine, rejoice. It's over."

"Oh, of course." The mother tried to brighten a little. "Yes indeed, it's all over," she went on. "It's only a question of time now until Alec leaves . . . us."

"But at least he won't be leaving with a woman who has led such a . . . life." Rita tried to speak cautiously, but saw she had said the wrong thing in any case.

"All that I know, Rita, is that I have lost him. He will never be mine again."

Usually never at a loss for words, Rita could think of no phrase to offer as balm for such passionate possessiveness.

"There is something about one's firstborn." Elaine began to unburden herself, and then suddenly stopped. She could not tell what was in her heart to Rita because, she told herself, Rita was not a mother. Even Widow Hughes, mad as she was, Elaine saw, was a little closer to what she was going through than the music teacher. For the great part of what it was to be a woman, or even human, had been denied Rita. She could only express what came out of her head. And if there was anything in the world Elaine Cottrell despised, it was common sense. Only flesh and blood knew the truth. The mind could only babble.

"He will forget Enid," the music teacher rambled on, when Elaine told her finally in a very indirect way of what the diary had conveyed. "But he is so part of you, you will always be first in his heart. . . . Can't you see that?"

"But I've lost him." Elaine repeated this phrase again and again, as a convicted person will tell judge and jury he is innocent.

When the air of the studio was so blue with smoke they could barely see one another, the two women parted. But it was a parting almost as close to distrust and bitterness as when they had come near to quarrelling in the company of Allen Mowbray. Their goodbyes had almost a ring of final parting.

The phrase "firstborn" left Rita meditative, with perhaps a feeling of unfulfillment. Then she had her own sorrow, which she had not been able to broach tonight owing to Elaine's own overpowering disillusionment. She kept looking at a newspaper clipping, picking it up, and then putting it away in a box decorated with seashells. She envied Elaine, she realized, because the young widow was completely herself. She admired Elaine's beauty, however faded it was beginning to be, for it was still beauty. And she was nearly in awe of Elaine's strength and resourcefulness in raising two boys to the threshhold of manhood without a husband to lift a hand. But she was also aware of Elaine's unspoken criticism of her, that she could not understand what a mother felt for her boys. Yes, Elaine had everything, the teacher grudgingly acknowledged, and she considered Alec's mother's ceaseless energy in cooking, housekeeping, washing and ironing, and supervising her boys, whom she loved to idolatry, as compared with her own dry life with her piano students and her sterile pursuit of books and operas and the events of the world of sophistication.

But Rita was not completely taken in by Elaine's somewhat evangelical portrait of herself as living only for her boys. She had seen Elaine too many times in the company of handsome, often rather young men driving in expensive cars, or taking a late snack at the Star Restaurant with one of her occasional men boarders. No, her heroine was not exactly a saint, certainly not spotless. She had *some* love from sources other than her idols, Alec and Ned.

Elaine on her way home that evening was also considering Rita's life, and came to the conclusion the music teacher was not quite the nun that Fonthill required its piano instructors to be. Once, she recalled, while passing the music teacher's studio in the evening, she had looked up and seen the silhouette of a youngish man standing behind the green blinds of Rita's bedroom window. Elaine had stopped. The silhouette had been joined by another, that of the teacher. The man had taken the cigarette out of his mouth and put it into the mouth of Rita. Then Rita, having taken a draw, put the cigarette back in his mouth. They kept up this game for what seemed minutes, until, with the cigarette nowhere in evidence, they pressed their lips together in a fervent kiss while stray whorls of smoke escaped from their close-pressed mouths, until the man's hand reached out and extinguished the light by pulling on a long cord, also in perfect silhouette.

"Wouldn't you know, I've forgotten my gloves!"

Elaine was nearly halfway home when she was aware of her forgetfulness. The gloves were specially prized, for they were a gift from Alec. She almost ran back to the studio, despite her high heels.

She had to knock many times before she heard Rita come to the door, and then the voice of the music teacher was almost unrecognizable. Indeed for a moment Elaine thought some other woman was in the apartment.

Even more astonishing was the fact that Rita attempted to hand her back the gloves through an opening only large enough to hand them over to Elaine. But the aperture was large enough for Elaine to catch a glimpse of Rita's face. It was swollen almost to the point of disfigurement, and several strands of hair had come down, so that in the few minutes since Elaine's departure she seemed to have turned into a different woman, of a different age, as if the Rita who had presented herself to Elaine had been nothing but a mask.

"What in God's name is wrong?" Elaine cried with such vehemence that Rita allowed the door to come wide open and admit her friend.

"Something has happened." Elaine spoke almost as if to herself. She was terrified at her friend's appearance. "Shall I call the doctor."

Smiling now, and wiping her face with cold cloths, Rita struggled to say something, and then was able to get out, "A doctor wouldn't have the faintest idea how to proceed." She sat down and motioned for Elaine to seat herself also.

"I thought of telling you earlier this evening," the music teacher went on, growing calmer now. "But I did not feel strong enough to get the words out. . . . And you have troubles enough of your own."

"You poor darling, keeping it all in like that. You know you can trust and depend on me, Rita. You must unburden yourself at least now." She smoothed the gloves in her hands as she spoke. "Please trust me! For your own good, Rita, dear," Elaine urged her when there was no sign the music teacher was about to talk. Elaine moved her chair closer to her friend.

"It's hard to tell even a bosom friend like yourself that one has been such a fool as I have been. . . . I remember once reading in a newspaper about a man who had defrauded many middle-aged women out of their lifetime fortunes. The judge in the case is reported to have said at the trial's conclusion: 'There is no law on the books which can protect fools from themselves.' " She gave out a little cry when she had said this.

"I suppose you remember Kenneth Craig," she began.

Elaine nodded. The depth of Rita's suffering made her forget all her own chagrins and heartaches at that moment.

"No, I'm not going to have a baby"—Rita gave a short little laugh—"like poor Adele so many years ago. I wish my trouble were that simple. I would have nothing to worry about." She stared at Elaine's gloves and smiled again.

"Kenneth Craig," she went on now in icy self-possession, "promised he would marry me last September. It was just before I was going to New York City." She smiled again as if remembering that time in detail. "You must have noticed how happy I was then."

"We all noticed it, certainly, Rita."

"Good," she said, and continued to smile. "That was the time of my fool's paradise. . . . I felt at the time I was *too* happy! I said it to myself, 'Watch out, you're too in love!' I know now how true that was."

Elaine took Rita's hand in hers, as a nurse will take a patient's when she sees the approaching wave of a paroxysm of pain, but Rita gently disengaged her hand.

"I wore his engagement ring until last week. It lies in the little bureau drawer over there along with my mother's own wedding ring. It will lie there now till it turns to dust. Yes, we were very happy. . . . Then Kenneth confided to me about six weeks ago that he was in rather serious financial trouble. . . ."

Elaine let out a little cry of foreknowledge as she sometimes did at a movie whose outcome suddenly became clear to her.

"He told me finally, after I had begged him to explain his difficulty, that he needed twenty thousand dollars, and that would clear up his financial problems and we could be married at once. At the time he mentioned the sum—twenty thousand dollars—I had forgotten he knew that was the exact sum of money Papa had left me when he died a couple of years ago. Twenty thousand dollars! Kenneth Craig knew I had that in my possession. . . . Yes, it would tide him over, he promised, and his troubles would be at an end. . . . I never doubted Kenneth Craig," Rita said after a solemn pause. "I have trouble doubting him now. When I remember his smile, his soft gray eyes . . . I fall into the same trap all over again."

Rita got up with stately slowness and self-possession. She went to the bookcase built into the wall. She took out a large scrapbook full of mementos, and from it she extricated a newspaper clipping already yellowing. She looked at it briefly, returned to her chair, and held it in both her hands.

"Doc Grover down the hall brought this in a couple of weeks ago. . . . I'm glad a doctor brought me the clipping, Elaine, for I felt so light-headed as I began to read it"—she tapped the clipping—"I might have fallen to the floor had he not helped me to a chair."

She handed Elaine the clipping.

KENNETH CRAIG ARRESTED ON SEVERAL FORGERY CHARGES
WAS MARRIED, FATHER OF FOUR

"Father of four," Elaine repeated carelessly. She only skimmed the article, but her gaze lingered on the photo of Kenneth, with his open countenance, warm full mouth, and weak chin. He did not look like her idea of a crook.

"Married." This word too escaped from Elaine before she could suppress it.

She was thinking back, as she pretended to read the clipping carefully, to her own recollection of Kenneth Craig, who had come to Fonthill at least twice a week in connection with his work as salesman for a paper company. He wore flashy neckties, sparkling stickpins, shirts that resembled silk, and shoes so brightly shined they could have reflected every passing object. She had never trusted him, she recalled. And she had always wondered why a woman of "artistic and cosmopolitan" tastes could have let herself be smitten by a man who might have been a barker in a carnival, or a bartender.

"And the twenty thousand dollars?" Elaine urged her on, for Rita sat like a person entirely alone looking out on empty space.

In reply Rita blew out a ring of cigarette smoke, and then with fierce energy blew the ring until it disappeared into nothing.

"Oh, it's God awful," Elaine muttered, and rose. Rita also now got up unsteadily, and Elaine put her arm around her. Then they hugged one another passionately, and kissed, and uttered exclamations and even curses. It was so late when Elaine was finally ready to leave that Rita had to phone the livery to call for her.

"But why, oh, why did you not tell me before?" Elaine repeated constantly while waiting for the hack to arrive. "When you know I would understand."

"Understand, yes, I suppose . . . but the shame was so

keen. . . . Papa's fortune!" She let out a dry hard gasp. "I'll never see a cent of it now, of course. He was, after all, nothing but a common crook. I wonder how many other women he has deceived . . . lonely, unwanted women like me."

"I won't let you say such things about yourself!" Elaine spoke with indignation. "It is easy to be taken in, Rita, when you are all alone here. I'm sure if I were not protected by my sons," she went on uneasily, "who knows what pitfall I might stumble into. You must not blame yourself, do you hear? I forbid it!"

The thought crossed Elaine's mind that the music teacher might do harm to herself.

Elaine's eye caught sight on the table some volumes of Madame Blavatsky, Krishnamurti, Annie Besant, and a worn copy of *The Prophet.* In addition to her literary proclivities, her visits to New York City, Rita had always read widely in the occult and the supernatural, had attended seances in nearby cities. Elaine supposed now she would turn toward these dubious outlets more than ever.

"Don't worry," Rita said after a silence, "I'm not going to go off the deep end. I want to live to visit him behind bars. I want to see him in his prison outfit."

The two women parted both feeling closer to one another than ever before and also sensing a division between them they could not understand or describe in words. Perhaps it was the dizzy precipitousness of Rita's fall, together with its suddenness, that made Elaine draw back from her friend, for with all her own troubles, sorrows, and perplexities, the music teacher's ruin finally depressed her to an unbearable degree. In the past she had always looked up to Rita, despite their occasional differences. And though not so much older than herself, Rita was like a second mother to her at times. She would not think the less of her now, but her attitude toward her, she felt, would change. Elaine would see Rita, she feared, as broken, helpless, mercilessly bereft. She gave a kind of accusatory look at the books of mysticism as she was going out the door.

Rita Fitzsimmons had not made Elaine promise to keep silent on the subject of Kenneth Craig. After all, Rita herself had done nothing wrong. She was not an Adele Bevington at any rate. But she was about to be in the eyes of Fonthill something almost worse—a "fool," in the words of the judge in the trial Rita herself had made reference to, a fool whom no law, however paternal and solicitous, could have protected from herself, or insured in safety. She had loved a man who did not love her in return, and who had deliberately robbed her of her life's savings and inheritance.

Elaine vowed to herself all the next day she would keep her mouth shut on this particular subject if she had to bite her tongue out. But the very solicitude she felt for Rita, and her indignation that "the poor girl" had been fleeced by a hardened sharper and confidence man, would not permit her to be silent.

That evening Sally Edgeworth and Keith Gresham took supper at the boardinghouse. Sally was a nurse in a prominent doctor's office, and Keith, of course, was now a star boarder. The presence of Sally tonight somewhat annoyed Elaine. She could not let herself "go" when a woman was present at her evening meals, whereas when there were only men boarders present she was able to say all that was in her mind without fear of criticism. She much preferred, as a matter of fact, the company of men. It was nice, of course, to have a woman confidante, but for sparkling conversation, repartee, and wit, and indulging in a little harmless gossip, the company of men was to her preferable.

Elaine had gone to special trouble this evening to please Keith's taste in cooking, and both Alec and Ned noticed how shamelessly Elaine was flirting with the young veteran, piling his plate higher than the others', giving him a hand-painted salad plate, whereas the other diners had only chipped ironstone. She had a standing roast of beef tonight, and insisted on Keith carving it at a little side table. Sally Edgeworth, mild and inoffensive, with her bobbed and marcelled pale hair and cheap jade necklace, was also somewhat taken aback at the familiarity with which Keith treated Mrs. Cottrell. She saw him once pinch the widow's plump forearm, and Elaine giggled like a schoolgirl. He also, at the end of the main course, insisted on carrying from the dining room the remaining portion of the roast for her, and when she accompanied him back to the kitchen, he could be seen tightening her apron string and then letting his hand linger on her thigh.

At dessert, when the fuss and persnickety ceremony of serving such an elaborate meal had abated, Elaine put on her tragic face, as Ned once described his mother's expression in his own private book of reflections labeled merely *Ledger* (kept prudently enough in the chamber pot under his bed). While everyone paused, she began: "I have had such an unsettling exchange of confidences with Rita Fitzsimmons."

The name Rita Fitzsimmons needed no introduction to any-body who sat at table tonight. Keith, years before the war, had once been a pupil of hers, and Sally Edgeworth had known Rita and her family from the year one.

Having announced her topic, Elaine then shook her head, pursed her lips, and sighed to indicate that from now on her lips were sealed. Nothing more could be wrested from her on the subject of Rita.

"Is it an elopement, Mother?" Ned said, putting on a poker face.

Whether Elaine missed her son's sarcasm or merely welcomed his cueing her to her next speech, she went on with: "I am certain that whatever is said here tonight will be held in strict confidence and not go beyond the confines of this dining room."

A chorus of "You know we will not breathe it to a soul" and "You can count on our discretion" rose from all the boarders.

Elaine closed her eyes tightly, and a tear was forced from her left eye.

"I have felt of course for some time there was something wrong with Rita," Elaine began, then paused and looked hurriedly at each of her boarders. "But we are all out of coffee!" she cried. "Pardon my being so absorbed in my worry over poor Rita, which after all would probably be of no interest to you." She had begun to rise.

"No, no, Mrs. Cottrell!" Keith's booming baritone now rose over all other sounds. "Let me get the coffee for everyone." And he rushed out into the kitchen.

Elaine resumed her seat, and bowed her head with a certain stoic resignation, as if she would require all the strength she could muster to tell the story of the fall of Rita Fitzsimmons.

When second cups of coffee had been poured for everybody, and the last of the cake had been munched and swallowed with fervid delight, Elaine began again, her voice liquid with grief and bashful hesitation.

"Rita is a woman who has stored up unexpressed love for so

long, has been ready to shower the right man when he came along with all her pent-up generous feelings, that when a wolf in sheep's clothing did make his appearance, she was easily deceived. For all Rita's sophistication and her visits to New York City, she is pretty much a country girl. The man who swept her off her feet not only looked like the one she had been waiting for all her life, he promised her everything she had ever dreamed of since girlhood. And it is true he looked like Prince Charming. There is a noticeable resemblance, I believe you will all agree, between Kenneth Craig and the Prince of Wales."

A murmur of agreement came from nearly every throat except Ned's, who was staring at his mother with the narrow gaze of a prompter who sees that the leading lady in the repertory has confused the lines of one play with those of another, and is about to begin babbling.

"Mother," he interrupted her in a hoarse reproof, "remember . . . the confidence of a friend."

"What are you talking about!" Elaine's anger against Ned suddenly burst forth. He had cost her so much sorrow of late that his interruption at this juncture, together with her own feeling she was betraying someone's trust, caused her to give him a tongue-lashing that ended with: "I expect you had better go to bed."

"Oh, please, Elaine." Keith spoke up at that moment. "Don't send him away. I promise you I will have a talk with Ned after we have finished."

Elaine did not know whether to be pleased at this offer of guidance on the part of her favorite boarder or to be jealous of Keith's growing preference for her younger boy.

"Very well, Keith." Elaine tried to appear appeased. "We will let Puck's Bad Boy remain." She gave Ned a withering look. "But he should realize, I think, that we are not betraying a confidence here. We are speaking of a person dear to us all, whom we wish to help . . . indeed whom we wish to save!"

"But from what, Mother?" Ned's voice boomed in a manner reminiscent of Keith's, although it had the cracked tone of early adolescence.

"Ned." Elaine spoke in her pained, martyred manner, and asked in a whisper that could be heard to the apple orchard, "You haven't been taking anything, have you, in the cellar?"

"I am cold sober, dear lady," Ned replied in icy sarcasm, and Keith Gresham, against his will, broke out into a guffaw of appreciation.

"Ned always wants to hold center stage," Elaine informed the company with pained grandeur.

"But what *has* happened to dear Rita?" Sally Edgeworth's calm voice restored a kind of balance now to the table. "You are keeping us on tenterhooks, Elaine!" There was a trace of annoyance and irritability in Sally's manner that was not wasted on Elaine. Sally had become so flustered that she took Ned's napkin by mistake and wiped her mouth vigorously with it, staining it with her lipstick.

"I believe we can lower the center lights now," Elaine said to Alec, who immediately got up and doused all the lights but the little lamps that were giving out substantial illumination on the sideboard and on the wall.

Elaine nodded to Keith and gave Sally a frigid glance, then began: "Rita was starved for the one great love of her life, which she had been expecting since she was a girl. She never doubted Kenneth Craig was that love. After all, he went miles out of his regular route to see her. He showered her with gifts. . . . He brought her expensive cosmetics, some jewelry, perfume. He made her feel she was young, and if not beautiful, certainly stunning. She was growing into a beauty of a kind, I always said, when he courted her. And she looked years younger, no question about that. . . . They met every fall in New York also." She added this last bit of information with some hesitation. "She once told me that she walked on air for a week after one of his visits."

But Elaine's eyes strayed for a moment and then rested on Ned. The younger Cottrell was staring at Keith Gresham with a conspiratorial look of impudence and amusement that deserved a resounding slap across the mouth. Keith, she saw, to her chagrin, was sharing some of Ned's devilishness, but he hardly knew where to look, and there was a funny twist to the veteran's lips which Elaine did not appreciate at that moment.

"Yet Kenneth Craig did not turn out to be Prince Charming after all, one discovers," Elaine went on, again resembling an actress, Ned thought, who finds that the audience are not attentive during her big scene, but are fidgeting with their programs and shuffling their feet."

"No," the mother went on, "Prince Charming was actually another man altogether. For one thing, he was a married man—had been married twice before, in fact, and not divorced from his first wife. Not only was he not a hopeful bachelor but he turned out to be wanted for cashing bad checks, and forgery, not to mention bigamy."

Sally Edgeworth groaned faintly, but with a look of strained pleasure on her face, and shook her head several times.

"But while playing the part of Prince Charming he had persuaded our dear Rita to hand over to him, without one string attached, her life savings. Every cent she had inherited from her father and mother, every cent she has earned with her years of teaching backward and untalented pupils the pianoforte! All gone up in smoke in one stroke of the pen. . . . Mr. Craig is now in the city jail in Pontiac, Michigan, and he is to be tried on a charge of forgery. But how many other crimes can be laid at his door, who knows. How many other Rita Fitzsimmonses are there, do you suppose, in one little town after another?"

Elaine wiped a few tears away as she ended, and Sally touched her hand across the table. Her own eyes were red, though dry.

Ned leaped up, to everybody's incipient alarm, and turned on the overhead lights, and applauded his mother's narrative.

Clearing his throat, and making other initiatory sounds from his barrel chest, Keith Gresham spoke in a rather pontifical manner: "How on earth could a woman be so dreadfully mistaken in a man?" he exclaimed. "There must have been some clue!"

Whether it was this remark or the peculiar exchange of smiles and grins Keith Gresham had been making with Ned during her exposition of Rita's fall, Elaine shot out, addressing Sally Edgeworth, "Isn't that the man for you now! You obviously know nothing about love, Mr. Gresham!" She looked directly at the veteran as she said this.

"I am afraid you may be right there, Mrs. Cottrell," Keith replied in a manner that sounded more than vaguely hostile and bitter, so that all conversation ceased for a while.

"We will forgive Keith, however," Elaine said hastily to Sally, "won't we, Miss Edgeworth?"

"I suppose we will have to," Sally replied moodily. It was clear to everyone that Elaine's story of Rita Fitzsimmons's deception and betrayal had made its deepest impression on her. One of Sally's hands trembled as she drank from her water glass, and she kept shaking her head, and breathing in short little gasps.

"It's a terrible lesson," Sally finally said lamely, perhaps hoping by speaking to draw attention away from her shaking hands and heavy breathing. "We can't be too careful when we are dealing with strangers, can we?"

"But the men who betrayed Rita Fitzsimmons and Adele Bevington were not quite strangers." Ned offered his opinion, and he stared at Keith.

Everybody burst out in a kind of relieved laughter at the outrageousness of the remark, but when Ned went on to say, "Well, they *didn't* do what they did, I mean, with a perfect stranger, did they?" the laughter became quite vociferous, and lifted the atmosphere of sadness and tension that was threatening their digestive process. Mrs. Cottrell's feast of a standing rib roast, escalloped potatoes and garden peas, and fresh asparagus, with of course the banana cream pie as dessert, had received rather a setback by her saga of Rita and Kenneth Craig, and this final peal of laughter restored everybody to a better humor.

They all rose almost in unison and went into the front parlor for a game of cards, but Alec drew aside his brother and said under his breath: "You made Mother look like a prize idiot tonight, didn't you, you little simp?"

"Rita Fitzsimmons, though, isn't the only one who has been left high and dry, is she?" Ned retorted. Alec slapped his brother smartly and rushed out of the room.

About four o'clock in the afternoon a few days later, Elaine was bending over her ironing board, putting the last touches on the collars of her sons' shirts, when the front doorbell rang, somewhat apathetically, she thought. She called "Come in," but no one entered. The doorbell rang again, almost with less authority than the first time. She put down her iron and, stepping to the dining room called out, "Please come in!" and hastened back to her shirts.

Keith Gresham came in sheepishly.

"Why, Keith, why didn't you just come on in? Don't wait outside like the mailman or the bill collector!"

She made a gesture of helplessness in leaving her work.

He took off his brand-new Panama hat, which she eyed quickly, then finished the shirt collar she had spent so many pains on.

"Aren't you out of work early?" she wondered.

"Oh, yes, as a matter of fact I didn't feel too much like staying inside, and my boss said he thought I looked like I needed some sunshine and air. . . . He's a good man to work for. He was . . . *across*, too, you know."

Elaine looked up quickly and nodded. She had almost forgotten Keith was in the war—he looked too young and untouched to be a veteran!

"Oh, take that chair over there, Keith, dear," she said, pointing to a cushiony sprawling easy chair decorated with her own handmade slipcover.

He almost fell into the chair. He held a package in both hands.

"You remember when I took some snaps of the boys?" he inquired, watching her carefully as she began ironing another shirt.

"I do indeed, Keith," Elaine replied, without taking her eyes off her iron.

"Those lucky fellows, Alec and Ned . . . to get their shirts done with such loving care. I can smell the sun and air on them clear from here. My shirts always smell of chop suey I'm afraid, from the Chinese laundry!"

"Why, Keith, I'd be glad to launder your better shirts for you. You have only to ask."

"I wouldn't think of it, Mrs. Cottrell. . . ."

"Elaine . . . you must call me Elaine. . . . But I'm dying to see the photos. Let me turn off my iron, and we'll look, shall we?"

As she was turning off the iron she gave Keith a quick appraising glance. He was deathly pale, she thought.

She sat beside him on a high stool.

He took out the photos one by one.

Elaine almost seized them from him, and her wedding ring sparkled in the light. "What beautiful pictures!" she cried. "That is the best photo of our Ned I've ever seen." She smiled at him gratefully, but frowned at the look of what could only be pain in his eyes and on his mouth. "And of course that's Alec to a T!"

"Keep them, then, Mrs., ah, Elaine."

"You're positive I may have them?" She let out a cry of pleasure.

"I wanted you to have them. I have copies for myself, you see . . . and the negatives."

"Oh, won't they be delighted with them, too. Alec is always wanting photographs of himself, you know. He's stagestruck, I'm afraid."

"So he told me," Keith said in a low voice.

"I would give the whole world, Elaine, to have two boys like them! You are a lucky, lucky mother. Do you know how lucky?"

Elaine went on looking at the photos, not quite taking in his question until it echoed in her mind. She looked at him.

"I expect I am, Keith," she admitted. "But you'll surely be getting married any day now, I bet. . . . And you'll have sons, and daughters, too, I hope."

His pronounced silence caused her to laugh nervously.

"A young man like you, so personable, and attractive," she brought out. "You must have the girls at the office vying for you, now tell me if I'm not right."

"Well, as a matter of fact, my boss was saying the other day, a number have set their caps for me."

Something in the way he said this puzzled her. She looked back at the ironing board.

"I've interrupted your work, Elaine. . . . But I did want you to have the photos just as soon as possible."

"Keith," she said with strange abruptness. "Are you all right?"

"No," he replied with similar abruptness. "That is, not quite." He smiled in so winning a way she longed to take him in her arms. His mouth was the most beautifully formed of any man's she had ever seen. And his large gray eyes with the thick long lashes must have set many a heart beating faster.

"I have always wanted to tell someone outside of the army doctors, and . . . the boss," he began.

Elaine's throat went dry as sandpaper. She longed to tell him to say no more. She almost could have sworn she knew what was to come from those winning lips.

"You see, there won't be any boys or girls coming from my . . . fatherhood," he managed to get out.

"Oh, Keith," Elaine interrupted in a warning tone.

"Perhaps you don't want me to say more." He lifted up his face to hers. "Say so, and I won't add any more. You have your own troubles, I know."

His desperation and solitariness moved her deeply, and she bent her head forward, indicating he was to proceed.

"In France, you see," he started, but then stopped. "It was, they say, the bloodiest battle of the war. Maybe the bloodiest battle in the history of warfare. Oh, excuse me," he said, she knew not apropos of what. "I should count myself a lucky man to be alive. But you see, Elaine, in a way, the most important part of me . . . was left over there. . . . I mean I guess I look pretty fair, according to the boss and the way the girls take to me."

Elaine had gone as white as her visitor.

"But all that I had as a man"—he spoke like a witness bringing a long trial to its end—"was left behind. I won't never be a father now, or even a husband."

He picked up the photos suddenly and touched them.

"That's why your boys are precious to me."

He stood up.

Her own anguish at his story broke down any thought she might have of propriety. She took him hungrily in her arms and again and again kissed his face, which was soon wet with both their tears.

"Consider yourself one of my own, Keith," she said after they had tried and failed to get control of their feelings. "Consider yourself my boy," she added.

They held on to one another for a long time. Their joy at holding one another was as strong as their grief, and their tears were finally dried, first by their smiles of happiness at being so close, and then by their quiet subdued laughter.

Paul Ferrand had condescended to be Alec's voice teacher. Paul had earned a considerable amount of fame in Chicago in the opera and on the concert stage, and he claimed to be a close friend of Mary Garden's and on speaking terms with other famous divas. His career had been cut short by a nervous breakdown and an accompanying weakness of the chest. Much as Paul loathed Fonthill and its inhabitants, he was forced to return to his native soil, so he claimed, owing not only to illness but to the fact he could not trust any of his distant relations to manage the extensive holdings in oil and gas fields, lumber and livestock farms he had inherited from his grandparents. In fact Paul Ferrand was as rich perhaps as Widow Hughes. But while wanting to hold on to his wealth, he somewhat desperately wished to look back on his Chicago days and be recognized as an artist and celebrity, and not a real estate magnate. And as a teacher, he had had some success: one of his pupils, Stella McCloud, had gone on to a rather outstanding career in New York as an opera singer.

But Paul had resisted taking on Alec Cottrell as a pupil. The boy was poor, for one thing, and he was, Paul felt, too proud and bitter, and worst of all too cocksure of his own talent and "beautiful" voice.

"You respect nobody, you look up to nobody! How can I instruct you?" Paul had scolded the young man when he had finally begun teaching him.

Paul had also been Alec's Sunday school teacher in the first year of his "exile" from the Chicago opera, and Alec had misbehaved many times during the Bible lessons. It was clear Alec did not believe in Christ or feel there was indeed a God, and he claimed to find the costumes of Jesus and his disciples in the illustrated Scriptures "unconvincing." "They could not have worn nightgowns like that and done what they did," Alec once told the astonished Bible class. "All they probably had on was jockstraps made of goat hair."

Reluctantly, step by step, however, Paul had been persuaded to teach Alec. For one thing, Paul had been unprepared for the beauty and strength of Cottrell's voice. It was a kind of miracle of both sweetness and power. Of course Alec could pay his teacher very little, and usually asked to "owe" the little he was to pay.

But perhaps even more than the genuine endowment of the boy's voice there was the fascination for the teacher in hearing Alec run down everything in the world. No person, no institution, no idea, was spared. His pupil talked like a Bolshevik. And the teacher's long-suppressed bitterness at having failed to be an artist was enlivened and enriched by Alec's rages and rancor. In the end the teacher was instructed perhaps more than the pupil. And Alec brought back to Paul memories of his own wild youth and forgotten "radical" opinions, before he had given up and been satisfied with accumulating wealth and security.

Indeed Alec was very much like what Paul had been twenty-five years before, as Adele Bevington pointed out from time to time, but with one exception: Alec had a greater voice than Paul, and coming from a very poor family, he had the fire and fearlessness of true temperament, missing in the teacher.

The only drawback was that Alec would not "study," would not apply himself. Yet at times he would sing like a lark, and show that in certain songs and arias he was already nearing perfection.

At the same time, jealous and even resentful as Paul was of Alec's potential and the wayward brilliance of his mind, the singing teacher did not wish the boy to leave Fonthill or him. Paul always agreed in the end with Elaine that Alec was not yet "ready."

"But when will I be ready? When I am *your* age?" Alec had demanded one night shortly after his breakup with Enid.

"What will your poor mother do if you up and leave her and Ned?" Paul would usually end the "quarrel" with this refrain, and the mention of Elaine and Ned would work Alec up to a kind of demented fury.

"Yes, go ahead, take their part," Alec would say, and he would drink a little more of the whiskey Paul always gave him at the lesson's end. (He warned his pupil at the same time of the disastrous effect of even a little spirits on the human larynx, and pointed out the fall of John McCormack.)

"Well, since you forbid me to go to Chicago and try my luck, I don't see why you should care if I wet my whistle occasionally, since you always make a point of bringing out the bottle after one of our sessions."

"Alec, listen to me." The teacher went over the old arguments. "Now listen well." He would raise his right arm with his cigarette holder held aloft in his hand. "Eventually, you will go." He sang out the words as if he was about to favor Alec with an aria. "I see that very clearly. Some way will be found to provide for your mother and your brother. . . . But meanwhile, you must study! Do you hear me?" The arm descended from its arc and pointed downward. "You must buckle down to real work."

"While I work at the oil company as one of their slaves? How much energy do you think I have?"

"You have the supreme energy, Alec, if you only knew it," the teacher spoke with a kind of sullen admiration. "Learn not to waste it in rages, rantings, and vituperation."

"You can say that, can't you, you who have everything! Who have always had everything! You have never known what want and privation mean."

"Now, Alec, see here. You have never known real hunger or going without a roof over your head. Your mother has seen to that."

"My mother!" Alec stood up now, and frantically leafed through some sheet music on top of the grand piano. "My mother has been kept by me for years! I have been not only her son, but her . . . helpmeet!" He finally changed the word that was on his lips to this last milder one. "She has had all of me! If it weren't for her and that snot Ned, I would be on the train tonight for Chicago. Don't you see how she has held me back? And every time I even hint that one day I will leave, she weeps and carries on like a mad woman. She must manufacture tears by the gallon. She must weep in her sleep to keep me tied to her apron strings. And when she is dead and in her grave her tears will continue to flow, continue to beseech me to join her in the family plot at Poplar Grove, where she will hold me to her for all eternity! See where she has brought me!"

The teacher recoiled at this display of what he would like to have called bad temper, but that he knew was a passion that he was incapable of.

He waited until Alec had sipped some more whiskey.

"But look what you have," the teacher mumbled. "A wonderful home. A room you share now with nobody else. Fine meals— Elaine is a great cook, everybody knows that. She keeps your clothes immaculate." He stopped as if this last detail of Alec's good fortune sounded laughable even to himself. But going on: "Wait until you go to the city and live in some garret alive with vermin and filth, and eat stale bread and cheese at midnight. You'll find out what true poverty is. . . . Are you up to that?"

"I'm up to anything to leave her and Ned . . . to never see their faces again! To never see this damned town again. . . ."

"I think your love affair with Enid hurt you very deeply, Alec."

There was a long silence, during which both men stood motionless, silent.

Paul walked over to the piano, pulled back the sleeve of his silk dressing gown, and before he had sat down, began playing a few notes.

"I want to hear you sing Brahms's '*O liebliche Wangen*,' Alec."

"I don't feel like it."

"One of the characteristics of a true artist is he sings whether he feels like it or not. . . . You are so spoiled I wonder if you will ever be anything but what you are now."

Alec looked at Paul with pitying contempt. He was prepared to say something even more devastating about his teacher's personal life, information culled from Adele, when he thought better of it, and said: "Oh, very well, if you want to hear me sing '*O liebliche Wangen*,' sing it I will."

"Then don't hold your hands like a boxer's fists, Alec."

The pupil looked down at his hands, smiled, and nodded to his teacher.

Paul struck a few chords, and waited for the young man to sing a few notes in preparation. Then they began.

Paul was moved to tears at Alec's rendition. He held his hand over his eyes when it was over.

"Was I . . . good?" Alec inquired in a muffled voice when his teacher said nothing after the rendition.

"You've got it." Paul took his hand away from his eyes. "There's no doubt you have supreme talent. . . . But oh, Alec, the road ahead! My God, do you know what the path to true success in your field means?"

"I know what rotting in this backwater means. How can it be worse? If I go down, if I die in some garret alive with rats, isn't it better than staying here with Elaine and baby Ned? Answer me that."

"If you could learn to master your rage and turn it into your singing, God, where wouldn't you go, Alec. But you're so immature . . . you're more immature, I believe, than Ned."

"I should bloody your nose for saying that," the pupil responded after a pause, and then walked over to his accustomed seat, took up his glass of whiskey, and sipped a little more.

Then perhaps remembering his teacher's warning about strong drink, he rose and walked over to the fireplace and spat it out on the andirons.

"What a perfect savage," Paul whispered. "You'll turn everybody's head when you go to Chicago."

"Yes, but when?" Alec glared now at his teacher. "For that's the knot that keeps strangling me. *When?*"

Widow Hughes subscribed to many newspapers, magazines, church bulletins, Sunday school quarterlies, and real-estate fact finders. She often allowed the printed matter to accumulate unopened for weeks, months—sometimes certain issues lay about unread for years. Coming upon an old newspaper she would mistake it for a current one, and thence become confused as to what actual day of the month and year it was. (For instance she read of a ten-foot blizzard one evening when the temperature outside was well over 90 degrees Fahrenheit.) She would then call the courthouse and ask some harried clerk what day it was; or if she was on good terms for the moment with Elaine or her other neighbors, she would go inquire of them what day of the week, what month, they were now in.

"The poor dear lives everywhere but the present," Elaine once said of her after the widow had inquired what day it was.

But some few weeks after its publication, Widow Hughes read in *The Courier* of the proceedings of Judge Hitchmough's ousting of Adele Bevington from the Altrusa Club. Widow Hughes despised Adele Bevington, and had always suspected her of having been intimate with her late husband. (She had once spied Adele laughing immoderately with the pastor at a Ladies' Aid Society function.) But if she despised Adele, Rosa Hughes loathed and detested Judge Hitchmough. He had presided once over a case in which one of the widow's tenants had brought proceedings against her, and Judge Hitchmough had decided in the tenant's favor, a decision that had cost Rosa a small fortune. But beyond this there was the question of origins. Adele Bevington was, in the eyes of Mrs. Hughes, "one of us," whereas Hitchmough was a foreigner who still spoke English with a thick Scottish burr. Most important of all, perhaps, was the fact that Widow Hughes was the lifelong president of the Altrusa Club. Her grandmother had been one of the founders of the organization. No person or persons had the right to act in any capacity without her approval, consent, or knowledge, she was positive, and the action of ousting Adele Bevington went against all the widow's deepest convictions as to what was right and proper. She had been overruled, she saw at once, by a man who, like her late husband, was a member (in her mind) of a secret fornication society; but most intolerable of all to her was the fact he was an immigrant, and could only trace his citizenship back a mere generation, whereas she and Adele went back to before the founding of the republic.

The widow walked up and down the apple orchard for hours, planning her strategy, and every so often rereading the account of Adele's ouster in the newspaper.

Going upstairs, then, and putting on her party dress, and powdering her face with some imported talcum, she strode over to Elaine's and asked if Alec would drive her as soon as possible to Judge Hitchmough's residence.

"Judge Hitchmough?" Elaine acted surprised, for she was under the impression the old jurist had passed away.

"It is Judge Hitchmough I want to see, my dear. It's an emergency."

Elaine nodded. "Alec is at his work, Widow Hughes," the younger woman replied. She was seated on a little kitchen chair that Ned had recently varnished, sewing her boys' shirts, while she kept watch on a huge kettle of stew simmering on the stove.

Widow Hughes picked up a spoon from the table and tasted the stew, smacking her lips and nodding approvingly at Elaine.

"Wouldn't Neddy do just as well?" the mother wondered. "Or are you on the outs with him at present."

"I can't remember if we've buried the hatchet or not," the old woman replied, and took another spoonful of the stew.

"I have a soft spot in my heart for Ned, it is true," the old woman went on. "Probably because he is the handsomer of your two boys. But he is also the nastier ofttimes, so saucy and sarcastic. He often hurts my feelings. But Alec has his nose in the air too often for my taste. I think he looks down on me, whereas Ned, critical as he is of me, stands by me somehow."

"Oh, I do apologize for the boys," Elaine began in agitation, and bit the thread from her sewing. "I've tried to bring them up right, but—"

"Call Ned, then, why don't you," Rosa interrupted Elaine. "I'll make it right for him."

"You're always so generous, dear," Elaine began, and then stopped as she watched Rosa go and taste the stew again, and make even more enthusiastic smacking sounds over its deliciousness.

"I would offer you a plateful, my dear," Elaine said, "but it's really not properly finished cooking."

"You're so fastidious, darling girl." The old woman beamed at her. "And that fastidiousness has gone into the makeup of your boys. They're very fussy and hard to please, and I wonder if they will ever find a woman good enough, or even half so good as their wonderful mother."

Elaine smiled. Much as Rosa Hughes exasperated her, she sunned herself in the old lady's inexhaustible store of compliments and flattery. They almost made up for some of the terrible things the widow perpetrated.

"But while we stand here talking of stew and young men's upbringing," Rosa went on, "the culprit is over there not brought to the bar of justice."

"Who on earth are you speaking of, Widow Hughes?"

"Who but Judge Hitchmough! Do you think I'm up and dressed in my best frock and pumps to pay merely a social call on that old master of fornication?"

Elaine had put her fingers to her mouth urging circumspection.

"Neddy knows the way the wind blows, my dear." Rosa deprecated the younger woman's decorum. "Come on down, dear heart," Rosa shouted. "We have an important embassy to undertake this morning, my boy."

"Judge Hitchmough," Elaine muttered, and took up her sewing.

Ned had heard, of course, all the preceding conversation, and came downstairs now, as if on cue, looking soapy and polished and more than eager to earn a little spending money.

Elaine gazed anxiously at her second boy, but she could think to give him no word of caution or advice. At the same time the name itself of Judge Hitchmough, who had been not too long ago one of the pillars of Fonthill society, may have reduced her to this unaccustomed silence.

"Shall we be off then?" the old woman cried. "Take the evidence here," and she offered Ned a sheaf of old and yellowed papers.

"You will be my secretary when we talk to the gentleman," Rosa informed him.

Rosa and Elaine's son were soon off in the old woman's rattletrap of a Cadillac.

"At last and at long last he will be brought to the bar of my justice," Rosa kept saying all the way to the judge's house, and at every repetition of this phrase Ned would twist his mouth in an attempt to copy Alec's grimaces of cynical derision and bored disbelief.

At first the maid at the Hitchmough house told Ned, who had rung the bell, that the judge could not see anybody that morning. Rosa then presented her calling card, printed in gold embossed letters on thick material that resembled cloth. The maid retired with the card. In a very few moments, Judge Hitchmough himself appeared, his head shaking a little, an aftermath of a recent stroke, and his cheeks a decayed red color. He soon lost any presence of mind he might have had, on seeing Rosa and Ned with the enormous sheaf of legal documents. It was difficult, however, to know which of the two visitors facing him he despised more, the Cottrell brat, as he called him, or Rosa Hughes. He had always lived in a kind of irrational fear of the old woman. Perhaps she typified something unnerving about American life. At any rate she had always treated him as contemptuously over the past half century as if he were one of the tramps who afflicted the back streets of Fonthill with their ragged, superfluous presence.

"I regret I cannot give you as much of my time as you may require, Mrs. Hughes," the judge began once they were behind the closed doors of his front parlor. "I am in the midst of very pressing business."

"The relevant fact is, Judge Hitchmough," the old lady interrupted, "I happen to have unlimited time today, and unlimited time therefore will be taken until the matter under consideration is settled to the satisfaction of law and regulation."

"Sit over there, dearest"—Rosa Hughes addressed Ned—"and I will take this mohair-covered armchair, since there is nothing else in the room decent enough to sit in for our deliberations. Judge, do you sit over there, will you, by the large window so that Ned and I can both see and hear you clearly. He is to take down anything important bearing on the case. . . . I have provided the boy with notebook and indelible pencil.

Judge Hitchmough knit his brows, and turned ash-colored in his cheeks, and then stiffly took a chair, but without the poky slow-motion lowering of his body into position that had taken so many minutes when he had presided over his courtroom.

"This is all most unusual, if I may say so, Mrs. Hughes." The judge's anger began to break forth. He looked fiercely at Ned Cottrell.

"Crime is always unusual, Judge. You have taught us that," Rosa replied, and fished out from the papers Ned had carried for her the clipping from *The Courier* chronicling the expulsion of Adele Bevington from the Altrusa Club.

"Explain this," Rosa ordered as the judge grasped the clipping, then put on his reading glasses and gave a few glances at the article.

"Ah, yes, indeed . . . of course," he spoke in his old lofty manner now. "An unfortunate episode in the history of our little club."

"Little?" Rosa queried. "I would have used the epithet *venerable* possibly, Judge. Never *little*."

"You are quite right." Judge Hitchmough thought better of his statement. "The Altrusa Club is a very distinguished organization. That is why we cannot be too careful, true?"

"And *who* is the president of the Altrusa Club, Judge Hitchmough?" Rosa asked in icy menace.

Ned was gazing at the old woman with wonder. One would never know from her behavior now how crazy and dipsy she acted most of the time. Today Widow Hughes resembled some distinguished female jurist who has consented to try a notorious and long-at-large malefactor, and who is conducting her cross-examination with all the calm vigor and ease of her long professional career.

Judge Hitchmough gasped. He had forgotten for years that

Rosa Hughes was the president of the Altrusa Club. Indeed, Judge Hitchmough, like everybody else, had almost forgotten Rosa Hughes was still among the living, for she never attended the club meetings or answered their communications and bulletins.

"And what is the tenure of my presidency?" Rosa raised her voice to such a volume that the beaded curtains at the far corner of the room jingled slightly.

Hitchmough now turned beet-red in his cheeks. He removed his glasses, and twisted his lips.

"My tenure is for life, Judge Hitchmough," Rosa informed him. "Life!"

"I recall that now, Mrs. Hughes," he mumbled.

"He recalls it now," she cried, turning to Ned, as if to impress on him to copy down this important admission.

Judge Hitchmough nodded several times, or perhaps more exactly his head shook tremulously, counterfeiting agreement.

"Adele Bevington's father," Rosa swept on, "along with my mother, was one of the founders of the Altrusa Club. It was a club intended for Americans of very old lineage." She stared with such malice that Ned was made almost as uneasy as Hitchmough.

"Americans of the oldest lineage," she repeated with a final whistling sound.

"Adele Bevington must be reinstated," the old woman flashed. "At once! With one stroke of a pen!"

"But my dear Mrs. Hughes"—the old man now rallied—"all the members of the club voted to remove her!"

"Under your baleful and foreign influence, no doubt. And without my knowledge or permission. Without the slenderest piece of say-so from the supreme power of the Altrusa Club, the president whose office is for life! . . . If you will consult the constitution of the club," Rosa said, drawing from her handbag a battered, stained rules-of-order book, and commanding with a glance that Ned hand it to the judge.

Trembling now spasmodically, Hitchmough was almost unable to adjust his glasses, but after a struggle he read the paragraph that his examiner had underlined expressly for him.

"Read the section aloud, if you will be so kind, Judge," she said, and then closed her eyes, smiled, and waited.

The old man began to read the paragraph, but one would have

thought he had only recently begun to study English. He mispronounced almost every syllable, faltered over every phrase, was muffled in incoherence as he finished: "No business of any importance shall be transacted or brought to conclusion without the knowledge and approval of the president, who always holds life tenure."

"*Life tenure*," repeated Rosa solemnly, and exchanged a look of triumph with Ned Cottrell.

Handing back the document to Rosa, Judge Hitchmough got out: "But do you approve of Adele Bevington's behavior, my dear lady?"

"We are confronting a matter of law at this moment, Judge." Rosa spoke loftily. "We will come to moral questions in a moment. First, the law! Have you or have you not conducted the affairs of the Altrusa Club correctly and in consonance with the constitution? The answer, Judge Hitchmough, is a sorry no. You have acted illegally and without authorization and you have willfully and deliberately usurped my authority."

Rosa Hughes put down her sheaf of papers, her large velvet reticule handbag, her gloves, and walked to the center of the room, her rope of pearls swinging about her throat in so violent and rhythmic a way that her two auditors gazed like men being put under a spell.

"Authority, authority," she began then in her decayed contralto. She gave Hitchmough her most terrible look; then her body was still and the pearls fell to the side of her silk dress decorated with gold sequins. "My husband was a debauched and indeed a criminal lecher!" Rosa now spoke in a manner more consonant with the Rosa Hughes Ned knew in the apple orchard and in the countless vacant rooms of her mansion. "He has doubtless gone to hell, where other parties doubtless shall soon join him in companionship. No question about where he is at this very moment! Burning in the immortal lake. . . . But hypocrisy was not one of Pastor Hughes's shortcomings. Vile and impure as he was, and no lake in hell will purify him, he did not pretend to censure other people's weaknesses and foibles. He knew the flesh was weak, and he forgave sinners freely. . . . You, on the other hand, Judge Hitchmough"—and Rosa rushed now to where the old man was watching her least movement with frozen concentration—"you, in your black robes, my fine jurist . . ."

"Not in front of this young man, Mrs. Hughes, I implore you." Hitchmough managed to interrupt her, and as he did so a great froth of saliva came out of his mouth and fell about his collar and the buttons of his vest. He dared not reach for a handkerchief to wipe the effluvium away.

Staring at the string of his spittle, Rosa continued: "This young man, as you call him, Judge, knows everything about life! I have observed him from infancy. Indeed I am as good as his godmother. He knows everything about life because his poor mother is required to keep a boardinghouse. Nothing has been spared him. I can therefore talk freely, for he has never had the luxury of knowing innocence. But even had he retained his innocence, he should be introduced to hypocrisy at this time, especially if he is going to be a writer."

"No, no, no!" Hitchmough almost screamed now, and managed to scramble to his feet. "I will not allow this common vaudeville to continue under my own roof! You are a mad-woman!"

Rosa Hughes's eyes had for some time been roving to a great farmer's parasol standing in the corner of the room. She seized it in a motion as quick as that of a young athlete and brought it down on the head of the judge, who, acting indeed as if he had expected this "business," merely seated himself again and turned his attention to her as conscientiously as if he were back in his own courtroom listening to an important witness.

"I hold before me, Your Honor, a list of the women you have fornicated with over the years, together with the date and place of your assignation and the number of times you enjoyed the parties in question."

"Ned Cottrell!" The old man appealed to Elaine's son. "For God's sake!"

A smart blow from the farmer's parasol silenced Rosa's "wit-ness."

"Are you ready to hear the names of the women you ruined?" Rosa inquired, waving the sheets of paper before him. "Very well." She spoke with grieved concession when there was no more word from the judge.

Hitchmough suddenly held his left side, and turning to Ned again complained of severe pain there.

"Pain, my eye!" Rosa interrupted, and in a firm voice began reading off the names of the women the judge had been intimate with: "Irma Johnstone, in the choir loft of the Pentecostal People's Church. Effie Builderbach, in the maid's sitting room of Mother Benton's nursing home. Minnie Ridenower, in the emergency kitchen of the Elks Lodge. Camilla Rogers McCloud, in the Hotchkiss Mausoleum of the Poplar Grove Cemetery."

Judge Hitchmough had put his hands over his ears, but Rosa Hughes merely raised her voice to a higher pitch and continued: "Carlotta Abbot, Lily Buitone, Margarita Mason George, Cynthia Gracebridge, Laetitia Overholt, Mamie Simpkins Thornton, the former Mamie Hopkins, Amelia Tuttle, Daisy Tuttle—mother and daughter," she explained to Ned.

The reading of the list, which appeared endless, was stopped by a crash almost as deafening as a thunderclap. Judge Hitchmough had risen, overturned several chairs, broken a huge porcelain vase of supposed antiquity, and made an attempt to seize the papers from Widow Hughes.

She eluded his grasp and continued to read out: "Cora Bayliss, Maude Badger McCain, Nettie Simpkins Grant—"

"Can't you stop her, my boy," the judge cried over the renewed roll call of women, who, for the most part, had long since been carted off to Poplar Grove Cemetery. "Can't you *help* me?"

"Stop, stop her, in God's name." The old man went over to Ned and, losing his balance, fell on his knees before the boy who had never known innocence.

"Elsie Maynard Jocelyn, Julia Shrove Cramer."

Whimpering and crying out like a devout Catholic hearing the names of the saints, the old man began driveling again, so that his entire vest and coat was covered with froth, spittle, and tears of rage.

But all at once both the accused and the prosecutor became silent, as abruptly as if a reel at the Royal Theater had broken. They heard a sound that could be counted on to break up almost any trial, conference, or gathering. It was the sound of wild, boisterous, unrestrained laughter, first coming from the upper register and then descending into the rumble of a belly laugh. Ned Cottrell had broken into one of his catching guffaws, which so often disrupted his mother's supper table.

Both the older parties listened as carefully as if they were hearing music, or a radio announcer advising them of a calamity. Widow Hughes put down her sheaf of papers, Judge Hitchmough took his seat again, and put on his glasses, which were partially broken in his flailing about the room and upsetting the furniture, but he scarcely noticed they were broken.

It was the laughter of youth, one might suppose, routing the follies of age. At any rate the sound was clean, clear, boisterous, unashamed, and had a pure and animal gaiety even Judge Hitchmough perhaps admired; at any rate he gave every indication of listening in a kind of frozen attention.

Straightening out her rope of pearls, then, and putting down the roster of names, Widow Hughes began to laugh also, at first a quiet little ladylike laugh, and then a heartier laugh, ending in a cackle of a guffaw almost as hearty as Ned's.

And slowly, from deep down, and from as far away, it must have appeared to him, as his native Scotland, came a sound that would be difficult to describe, but that the Widow later described as the sobs of remorse of a hardened lecher.

"For we have, after all, in Judge Hitchmough, what the Good Book calls a whoremonger," Rosa informed Ned as he drove her home late that afternoon. "And you may tell Adele Bevington now," she went on, after a pause to allow the biblical term for the judge to settle into Ned's mind, "you may tell that abandoned woman," she went on as the car braked to the front of her garage, "tell her that she has been reinstated by the Mrs. Reverend Rosa Hughes, widow of the late Pastor Hughes. Reinstated for one and only one reason. Because she comes from a prominent family, whose roots go back to the founding of this nation. That and that alone has saved her. For Adele was born to be a whore, and there is nothing we can do about that. It is out of her hands. She will spread her legs until the last trumpet sounds. . . . But she is from a distinguished American family, and Judge Hitchmough, though he sat on the bench in his black robes for half a century or more, is, compared with her, nothing but a common upstart whose mother took in washings and whose father was so rotten with syphilis they had to carry his body out in bushel baskets to the cemetery. . . . Be sure to tell Adele then the good news when you wait on her next."

"It comes too late, much too late," Adele remarked a few days later after Ned Cottrell spilled out the results of Widow Hughes's session with Judge Hitchmough. She laughed, however, as much as Ned had laughed at the time, over the discomfiture of the old jurist, and she found the reading of the roster of names of the women the judge had "ravished" too delectable to be true.

"I would give anything in the world to see the judge listening to the names of his lady loves!"

Adele became pensive, then, reading and rereading the document of her reinstatement, signed by Mrs. Rosa Hughes and countersigned by the deposed head of the Altrusa Club, Judge Hitchmough.

"No, no, Ned," she said after a long silence, "I cannot accept reinstatement. You will have to go to Rosa and tell her so." She stared at him, finding it incredible that so young a man should be an intermediary for her with the widow and the judge. "As I say," she went on, "it comes too late. Judge Hitchmough was actually right in having me dropped from the Altrusa. Right for all the wrong reasons. And Rosa was right in having me reinstated— for all the wrong reasons. She wanted to punish Hitchmough because he cannot claim American ancestry for as far back as she and for having usurped her chair as president. But Rosa has always loathed me even more than she has Hitchmough. She gloried in my being punished for my illegitimate son. She noised it about the town more than anyone else, making my sin public. But Rosa Hughes hates all women. For years she had to put up with Pastor Hughes's incessant unfaithfulness to her. He is said to have been engaged in intercourse with a young woman right against the pulpit one afternoon when Rosa, using her own key to the church, walked in and caught them. 'Finish the sermon, Pastor!' she is said to have called to them, while advancing up the carpet which led to the pulpit. 'Don't let your legally married wife stop you in your pastoral duties!' Pastor Hughes," Adele shook her head. "So long ago! A red-faced hirsute bull of a man. He pinched my leg once shortly after my disgrace—I was in a dry-goods store and he spotted me from outside through the show window. He came in and pretended to be making a purchase. Then, sidling up to me, he all at once put his hand up my dress. In retribution I tore off the cheap J. C. Penny tie clasp he was wearing, which tore his shirt loose at the same time. The clerks saw only my gesture, not his. It added to my notoriety at the time, as they thought my action was a pass at him. Well, he was, I suppose, a handsome man, appealing to ordinary tastes."

She handed back the "document" of her reinstatement to Ned.

"But won't your refusal to go back to the Altrusas hurt Melissa terribly. . . . She has fought for you so hard," Ned pointed out.

Adele frowned deeply, and shook her head. "Poor Melissa," she muttered. "I suppose you are right."

"Perhaps you could go through the formality of being reinstated for Melissa's sake," he suggested, "and then you never need go back, if you don't want to."

Adele laughed. It was a kind of laugh Ned had not heard come from her before. It reminded him a bit of the sound the ice tongs make when they grasp a large keg of ice.

"Melissa has only one love," Adele said absentmindedly. "Her younger brother." She looked straight in Ned's direction but without seeing him.

Ned fidgeted and looked away. No matter how many of the books she had given him to "extend his education," books Elaine had said were scandalous, none of them had reached him with their "message" quite as directly as this offhand remark of Adele's. The fact was Ned was shocked.

"I'm not exactly sure what you mean," he said finally.

"You're not sure!" She sounded as angry as Elaine. "My dear young man, if I say to you the clock has struck twelve, do I have to explain my statement! Really and truly, Ned. I sometimes despair of you!"

"But how does her love . . . express itself?" Ned went on doggedly.

Adele laughed again, this time in her accustomed way.

"You are a caution, I declare, Neddy . . . but I wouldn't change you for the world. No wonder your mother and brother are so fond of you, though you exasperate them to the point of murder. You are like a pool of water one can see clear to the bottom of, but which is nonetheless very deep for all its clarity."

"You don't mean Melissa has stepped over the boundary?" He pursued the matter.

"Oh, come, come, Ned . . . that's the whole point of it. I doubt her brother Farley is even faintly aware of his sister's proclivities, though of course he encourages her to love him by every breath he draws. And why has he never married? Big strapping football player, a college wrestler, always going hunting, and so on. True, he injured his back playing quarterback, and was slightly wounded in France. . . . But he sees his sun rise and set in his sister's eyes. And how does she love him, Neddy? Have you never seen them together? She all but drools at the mouth in his presence. Once I was invited to their home for dinner. Farley was upstairs taking a bath. I believe he bathes four or five times daily. A telegram arrived for him from one of his legal clients. He came downstairs in his bathrobe, dripping on every step and all over the carpet. Melissa handed the telegram to him. She was unaware, I am sure, of the expression on her face. But it told everything. It was a look, well, giddy, hopeless, helpless, swooning, idiotic. She oh so faintly touched his wet forearm, which had emerged from the bathrobe sleeve. She flushed to the roots of her hair. . . . I had known it before, of course. And I have observed it many times afterwards. She worships the ground he walks on, and he lives and requires that worship. That is her life, *their* life. I doubt he marries. What wife could worship him twenty-four hours of the day like Melissa. He will blame his football injury, his wound in France, for staying at home, as her secret husband."

Ned's mouth was half-opened, a mannerism of his that always drew criticism from both Elaine and Alec, who warned him about looking like a mouthbreather. But Adele was too absorbed in her recounting of Melissa's story to be completely aware of the effect it had on her listener.

"No, I see now," Ned told her, "that you can't go back to the Altrusas."

"I don't know what to do though about Rosa Hughes," Adele grumbled. She looked out in the direction of Main Street. One would have thought Ned had gone home and she was talking to herself. "If I write her a thank-you note," she went on in her absentminded ramble, "I will be treated to her endless telephone calls or epistles. And if I visit her in her mausoleum of a house, I will have an attack of asthma from inhaling the dust of the last century. That house of hers has not been properly cleaned since McKinley was shot. I am positive she has not shampooed her hair since Pastor Hughes was found dead in the bathtub. . . . Oh, I may phone the old thing, but she is so deaf, I wonder whether she will recognize my voice, let alone hear what I say in way of thanks. . . . I am *not* grateful to her. Hitchmough, though, will never get over this." Adele grinned. "You say she hit him several times with the county fair umbrella? And she ordered him to resign from the club? The idea crosses my mind also that I would allow them to reinstate me if he were barred from the Altrusas. But that type of vengeance is too obvious for my taste. It would make the old man have a cause. But the club will never be the same. People who have any taste at all will stop going, I'm certain. And Rosa will now go all over town and tell people of the buried scandals of Judge Hitchmough's life some fifty years ago! No, I will leave everything just the way it is. . . . I will refuse reinstatement."

"You *are* strong, aren't you?" Ned observed.

She came back from her reverie with a start and stared straight at his mouth.

"You must not breathe with your lips wide open, Ned. . . . It's not good for your health. Try to keep your mouth closed, dear."

She sat thinking a while longer. "I am very grieved and hurt your brother, Alec, never comes to see me anymore, Ned. . . . He blames me, of course, for breaking up his crush on Enid. Actually I had very little to do with all that. Enid was going to New Orleans. She could have been his sweetheart only a short time longer in any case. I suppose Alec gives all his time now to that faded old morning glory Paul Ferrand."

Ned colored a little and kept his mouth tightly closed.

Adele had told everybody that Widow Hughes would summon her, and that she would not obey the summons. "I will never go there!" She had even stopped "wretched" Rita Fitzsimmons to impress upon the music teacher her determination. "Let the old crone come here, if she must speak to me of her beneficence. Let one of her many factotums bear her to my house. I will not darken the door of her mausoleum. And gratitude to her! For what? For destroying old Judge Hitchmough?"

But Adele was grateful, and of course Adele *would* go. It had always been hard for Adele to admit she owed anything to anybody. She had enjoyed her years of martyrdom. And she knew as she sipped her brandy in the late hours, looking over at the Royal Theater, that only Rosa could have reinstated her, and her reinstatement was a victory.

So she went.

But Adele had been quite unprepared for the condition of Rosa's drawing room, and for the first glimpse of Rosa herself. The pastor's wife had aged shockingly—she was no longer merely old, she was a true ancient—and only the silk dress she wore looked familiar. Adele must have seen her wearing that dress at least thirty years ago! From under the hem of her decayed garment hung the fringe of her satin petticoat, hopelessly ripped and pieced together with gold safety pins. The curtains hanging from the eight-foot windows were black with grime, their pattern no longer decipherable. Through the open back door countless horseflies flew in and out, like creatures bearing more tidings of wrongdoing to feed Rosa's unappeasable appetite for gossip.

"They come from the orchard, and are not carrying disease, my dear Adele," Rosa said, describing the flies. "They're a kind of company for me, too."

"I did not come here today, Mrs. Hughes, to tell you I am grateful," Adele stopped her.

The old woman snorted. "Of course you didn't, petty." The old woman smiled. "You forget I was present at your christening. There was talk of my being your godmother. But at the christening itself you spat into the face of Reverend Dundee or whatever his name was. . . . You have been spitting ever since. Gratitude from you? Do you think I have lost all my faculties, you simpleton?"

Rosa had picked up a Japanese fan as she scolded, and now almost smote herself with it, though the flies paid no attention to her motion, and lit on her dusty pile of hair held in the back with a Spanish comb.

"These flies know me," the old woman went on again. "They

are faithful companions right on up to the first killing frost. Then they vanish to appear again with the warm April sun."

"I came here today"—Adele raised her voice—"because I have some manners left, and I have always respected you. I know you think what you did was a kind act. I refer to my reinstatement. I acknowledge the thought, if not the kindness. Gratitude, I am afraid, I have none."

"Fiddlesticks, or as my late pastor might have said, rot!" Rosa retorted. "I know why you have come, and you know it, too, if you would get your mind out of the gutter for a half hour at a time."

"Now, Rosa, I will not sit here and hear one of your warmed-over sermons on sin and perdition. . . . I am beholden to no one and nobody."

"Yes, and look at you," the old woman scoffed, and swept the Japanese fan across her great bosom. "What have you to show for your many decades of vice and intemperance, your flouting the moral order, your late hours and fine New York gowns, and enough cosmetics on your old weather-beaten face to make Jezebel herself blush? What have you today that can give you the slightest modicum of happiness or peace or a good night's sleep?"

Adele's mouth hung open as wide as Ned Cottrell's for a moment; then, coming to herself, she said: "What happiness does anybody have, Rosa, will you answer me that?"

"You have disgraced the name of Bevington." The old woman kept her eyes riveted on Adele. "But I could not let you go down any further, to be burned at the stake by a latecomer to these shores, and with no antecedents himself but the fact his dad was an ironmonger and not far short of a rag-picker. . . . Hitchmough to drive out a Bevington from the Altrusas! He had another think a-coming, that begrimed whoremonger! . . . No, my dear Adele, whether you wish to admit it or not after your years of prostituting your body in Chicago, you and I—we are the last of the quality and the aristocrats in this town. Everybody else is dirt compared with our ancestry, some of them clean dirt, it is true, but most of them dirty dirt, like Hitchmough."

Considering the widow's appearance, Adele could not restrain a wry smile.

"Smile, giggle, laugh, Adele . . . but the truth is the truth. We are the last of the well bred, you and I. The last of those with antecedents. From now on there will be naught but bilge water and garbage, half breeds and mongrels. They will inherit the earth. We will be a forgotten whisper."

"Oh, well, what did the world offer when we aristocrats—as you call us—ruled? Very little. . . . They offered *me* very little."

"That's because you never appreciated how lucky you were. You were always spoiled. So you became a whore. Your daddy couldn't say no to you. Had you asked him to tear out one of his eyes and give it to you, he'd have done so. He protected you in your fornications and adultery because he loved you most unwisely. Your mother, who worshipped your daddy, joined him in overlooking your terrible sins."

Adele pulled out a cigarette from a jewel-studded holder and, without asking permission, lit it. Then, when Rosa said nothing, she began to inhale and exhale loudly the thick Turkish smoke.

"I could not let your daddy look down from heaven and see you ousted by some little cattle-boat immigrant turned jurist, now could I? Much as I disapprove of you, and let me digress here for a moment. Cigarette-smoking I believe is right for you because you have spread your legs on the highways and byways so often I will not quibble with you over the tobacco habit. Better smoke at your age than open your lips to even fouler practice. . . . But to come to the point. I could not allow old Hitchmough to best us. He called me on the phone today, come to think of it, and told me in that bleating voice of his he was resigning from the club. I replied, 'Judge Hitchmough, resignation is not quite the ticket here. What I am about to say I say regretfully, as a Christian, but since you are not a Christian but a lawyer, God will overlook what I advise here. Suicide is your only path to honor. No, you heard me aright, Judge. Resign, of course, but kill yourself immediately after. Your name will then regain perhaps some of its luster if not its complete honor.' "

Adele dropped her cigarette. She looked about her. As she would say to Ned and Alec some time later, she felt she had met her match, or at least met someone who put her in the shade temporarily. Not that she would want to be like Rosa Hughes. Never. But someone who could excel her in outrageous individuality and indomitable perseverance.

"And do you expect Judge Hitchmough to oblige you by cutting his throat?" Adele inquired, and picked up her cigarette from the carpet, blew off the thick accumulation of dust on its burning end, and then inhaled loudly.

"It's Hitchmough's only recourse, Adele." The old woman considered her visitor's sarcasm. "But to return to the subject of your lack of gratitude," she went on. "I expected that of you. I did not have you, however, reinstated for yourself, but for your mother and daddy, God rest their white souls. They did not deserve a blackguard daughter like you, but they bore their disgrace and burden like true soldiers of Christ. You were their cross, and their punishment. Because of your sins I am sure they went straight through the Gates of Glory without one vote against them."

Somehow the diatribes and imprecations of Rosa had calmed Adele. She was reminded of her early youth, of the idyllic days of sunshine and peace in the closing years of the last century.

Yes, Rosa's utterances were in their way, terrible as they were, also soothing as a lullaby.

Adele smiled and nodded.

"No, I could not let you go down to infamy by expulsion without raising a hand, Adele Bevington. I have only done my duty where you are concerned, and I expect no gratitude from you. . . . I do not suppose you are even grateful for the caresses of the young men who lie naked with you . . . the ones you cull and drag home with you from the Royal—I have reference to those."

"Ah, Rosa, Rosa." Adele only smiled and lit another Turkish cigarette.

"Thank God, Pastor Hughes is not here, Adele, for you would fire his passions to setting fire to the house, old as you are. . . . But I did not bring you here to tell you how vile you are. After all, you rehearse *that* day and night and are better acquainted with your sins than I could be if I watched you from the alley facing your bedroom. . . . I want to give you something, my dear. Where is it?"

She walked over to the mantelpiece and took down a box wrapped in thick gold paper.

"Here, take this, Adele. I don't want my daughter-in-law to have it."

"But what is it?"

"Go ahead, open it, and *mum*." Rosa put both her index fingers to her lips.

"Not your ruby and seed pearl necklace!" Adele cried on opening the box.

"It will only get lost here," Rosa said. "I don't think I'll last the winter, and I won't have that harridan of a daughter-in-law of mine wear it around her brown old throat. . . . You at least are beautiful, though past your prime."

Adele began to weep a little.

"Stop that bawling now," Rosa commanded. "It's not sincere anyhow. You don't appreciate the gift, and I didn't give it to you to make you feel grateful. You are incapable of true emotion. I gave the ruby and seed pearl to you, I suppose, because in a way I'm happy you've been bad all your life. I respect energy, though God will damn me for saying so. You had the courage to be bad as some saints have the courage to be only good. It's all vim and vigor, when you come down to it. . . . Who knows, maybe there is no God and no Jesus, in which case, Adele, you have lived life the way it should be lived. Pastor Hughes, of course, has gone to hell. I'm sure of that, and because I lay next to him in bed all those years after he had fornicated earlier in the day from noon to twilight, I will have to join him in the blackest river in Hades. I was his confederate in sin by sleeping with a man who was an accredited lecher."

Hardly listening to the widow, Adele went on admiring her gift. She felt she was a young girl again, back home, being scolded, being loved, then presented with a gift, a priceless gift such as her own father could not have given her, though later, her seducer, George Etheredge, would be able to.

"You won't begrudge me this gift then later on, dear Rosa?" Adele wondered.

"You sound like the goose girl next door now!"

"Who is the goose girl, Rosa?"

"Elaine, the mother of sons," the old woman mused.

"Oh, yes, of course."

Adele studied her benefactress. Her eyes were no longer so lively, the lids closed somewhat spasmodically. Then her cane fell from her outstretched bejeweled hand.

"Rosa?"

"Go along, now, my dear." She started from her doze. "Don't kiss me, though, on your way out. I don't know where your mouth has been last, and Dr. What's-His-Name recently told me half the town has syphilis in the catching phase. . . . You're welcome to those jewels, but don't thank me. I know you're incapable of gratitude, but we are the last of the aristocrats. The river of hoi polloi is waiting for us to step down. Our mansions and fields and farms and rivers will be overrun with their off-spring. They will tear everything beautiful and starlit to smithereens. . . . Go on, now, leave, Adele. I want to nap for a while. . . . But Judge Hitchmough must kill himself. He has no right to live. . . . Goodbye, my dear, and enjoy your jewels, and your young men."

Both Elaine and Ned were bedazzled by Alec's secret diary and the additional loose sheaf of notes that adhered to it. Mother and son were like children perhaps who have been forbidden to open expensive confections, jellies and jams hidden high on the pantry shelf. The parents know the children will climb up and open the sealed containers and partake of them. Alec, too, must have realized that both his mother and Ned would open the unlocked drawer and read what he had written. Why else would he leave such incriminating documents where they could be so easily found and certainly perused?

But these confections and candies contained poison.

Elaine, opening the diary, one morning late read:

It is all settled. I will be leaving about Thanksgiving for Chicago, and begin my career there if it kills me. I must escape this she-tiger Elaine and her equally vicious cub Ned. I will never be a man, never even learn to breathe properly unless I am free of them both. Let them both starve to death. They are both in good health, and can earn their own way without my being their Dad-husband and star lodger and boarder. Or let Elaine prostitute herself. She's still good-looking enough and voluptuous for all the extra pounds she has put on over the years. If I stay here another six months I will either cut my own throat or kill both of them, as God is my witness.

For a while Elaine felt nothing after reading the latest entry. She recalled out of the blue one of Keith's stories about a battle he had lived through in France where he had been grievously wounded but at the time had felt nothing. Only a gradual feeling of drowsiness and a clouding of the brain, followed by the gradual glimpse of his own blood gushing forth from his breast, gave him the evidence he was shot. She, too, was mortally wounded. Only, unlike Keith, she would never be well again, she told herself, for bitter as his scar was, her wound, she felt, would never heal.

She waited until Ned had also read the entry, which she hoped he would do sometime before Alec came home from the oil company. (Alec seldom came home at all anymore, although the whore Enid was no longer in town.)

She was gratified to see that Ned was almost as upset over what he had read in the diary as she was. He came downstairs red-eyed and pale. They fell into one another's arms and sobbed out their grief.

Gathering up her strength a bit, Elaine made a fresh pot of coffee from the beans she had purchased from a Syrian only a day or so before. Its diabolical strength allowed her and Ned to speak a little more freely.

"I could have had a career as a singer, too, Ned," she began. She was calm, composed, her eyes now dry as sawdust. "I had a wonderful voice, everybody said, and a young man who had been a great success in musical comedy, Perry Lindquist, wanted me to elope with him, and join him on stage. . . . I was sixteen, just think of it. But my father would not hear of it. He had in mind your dad for *my* career. And my mother, though she wanted me to go with Perry and pursue a stage career, could not stand up to my father. There were scenes, explosions, even threats of disinheriting me, and like a fool I obeyed my family and did not go off with Perry. . . . I married your father!"

Ned winced, for no matter how many times Elaine had told him the story of her ruined hopes and sacrifice, this chronicle always made him completely wretched.

"Of course," she went on, "your father was as handsome as an Arrow collar ad, indeed he looked like he was made out of porcelain-covered steel. His teeth were so shining and white that once a man seized his jaw to see if his teeth were false. But he should never have married, Marius shouldn't, just as I should have run off and been an actress and singer. After the first weeks, both your dad and I knew we had made a terrible mistake, but I was already pregnant with Alec. . . . Your father was always gone from the first days of our marriage. It was as though even then you boys had no father. . . . The report of his death still seems implausible to me, for our marriage was hardly, to tell the truth, real. All that was real was you boys. I poured all my love and hopes into bringing up you and Alec. I was your mother and your father, and your sweetheart, too, I guess. See where it has got me! You're both ready to leave me, and what will I have to show for my life?"

"Mother, I will not leave you." Ned spoke huskily. "I will stay . . . till you swear on bended knee you don't need me no more."

"Oh, Ned, Ned. Thank God for those words." They held one another in bitter, painful embrace.

"We must let him go, Ned." Elaine spoke after a while. "We cannot hold anyone that set on leaving. The bird must fly out of its nest. . . . Yes, he's stayed too long. I see it all now. He must go, go forever. I will open the door of his cage. He will find out, though, how loving the world is, Neddy. He has no idea of what is in store for him. Has no idea what people are. No knowledge of the snares and pitfalls, the deceit and wickedness and double-dealing. But I won't stand in his way. I won't be like my father was to me. I've kept him too long as it is. But he's more immature than most boys. Always was, probably always will be. He barely shaves twice a week, his cheeks are still peach fuzz. But go he must, go he will. I'll not say a word, if the ventricles of my heart burst in my breast, go he shall, go he must. He will never say to the world his mother kept him from a career."

She extricated herself from Ned's embrace. How fierce but calm she looked, how determined, and yes, how beautiful. She was too beautiful, he saw, to have been just a mother. She should have indeed gone with that man to be on the stage, and then, he thought with consternation, there would have been no Alec, no Ned. . . . How strange, his very existence depended on her having obeyed her father, and here they all were plunged into a misery which would end only in death and the grave. And even in death, who knows? As Widow Hughes warned of her own punishment by a river in hell, they might meet in the afterlife also on some black shore, there to bewail and weep over the sorrow of this life.

Elaine had forbidden Ned to see Val Dougherty, but she must have been perfectly aware where her second son went on his frequent absences from home at night, and she feared to make an issue of these visits to the iceman for fear the boy would spend even more time with the "fugitive," as Elaine now called him.

It was Alec who told her of Ned's almost nightly visits.

"He is learning to ride, you know," the older boy informed his mother. "And the next thing we hear, I suppose, is he will have broken his neck."

"You would say that!" Elaine flared up. She was very bitter now, after having read the latest installment in his diary, and she treated Alec with the cold propriety she displayed toward one of her poor-paying boarders.

Ned was not exactly welcome at Dougherty's Star-Lite Stables. Since his wife and foster daughter had left him, Val saw almost nobody. A few old army buddies would show up sometimes in the evening and they would play Black Jack or merely sit and drink and stare at one another. Val was sick of hearing about their questionable heroism in the war, how they had cleaned out machine gun nests, rescued innumerable Yank prisoners, intercepted codes, and so on. He wanted to forget the war. He wanted to forget his marriage. He wanted to forget everything. Except his horses. Sometimes he even wanted to forget them.

When Ned would first appear in the gathering dusk he always hated him. Then something about the boy's trust made him relent. Gradually he found himself teaching Ned.

"You don't ride too bad, matter of fact," Val said to him late one evening after Ned had ridden around the track a few times on one of the more spirited horses.

Having given his grudging compliment, Val went on staring at Ned for a full minute until the boy looked away in confusion.

"By the way, I got something to tell you." Val scowled and began leading the horse Ned had been riding to the stable. "You got a minute? Or do you have to get home to your ma right away."

"Sure I got a minute."

They went into the house by the rickety kitchen entrance.

Inside Val lit a kerosene lamp, and then sat down heavily in the wooden armchair. On the table facing him lay a letter. Ned's pulse quickened.

Ned no longer smelled horse around Val, for the reason that he had begun, he was sure, to smell of it too. His mother complained bitterly about his "bad odor" from time to time when he returned from one of his afternoons or evenings with Val, but she did not seem to have connected his bad odor with riding lessons.

"Shall I read it to you?" Val had picked up the letter.

"But who is it from, do you mind tellin' me?"

"Oh." Val spoke between yawns and looked hard at the envelope now as if he wasn't positive who it was from.

"It's from my ex." Val eyed Ned from the side. "My former little woman." He laughed nastily.

Ned colored a little and cleared his throat.

Val awkwardly took the thin piece of stationery out of the envelope and studied it. The boy realized then all of a sudden that Val could read only with difficulty. But he was not prepared for what the Star-Lite Stables' owner was going to read to him. Both the sound of the words and the sense of the words he was hearing read became unclear to him, as when one is trying to decipher a road sign at night in a sudden downpour of sleet and rain.

Folding the letter after his halting delivery of its message, Val said: "So the baby's dead, and you ain't no father at all."

"What's a miscarriage?" Ned wondered abruptly.

Val looked at him cautiously, but did not reply for a lengthy while.

"You can get their pants off, can't you, but you don't know what miscarriage means." Val did not say this in a critical way, Ned felt, but only with some sense of bewilderment, if not confusion, at the way the world runs.

"It means," he said aggrievedly, "the kid come out too early from inside her, and was dead when it come out."

Ned gagged slightly, and to cover up his nausea he coughed violently.

"So," the stables' owner said, still eyeing his visitor, "you are scot-free now, you can tell your ma. . . . They didn't even have to shell out the money for an abortion, if you know what that is. . ." Val went on studying the envelope as if it might contain some additional bit of information.

"My wife, by the way, ain't comin' back neither. That's the real good news for me in this note." He tapped the envelope.

Still eyeing Ned, Val began to say something several times, changed his mind, but finally got out: "What's wrong with you? Your're practically green-colored."

They both stood up then at the same moment.

Unaccountably, Ned seized both the older man's hands in his, and the horse trainer looked down at them, now imprisoned by Ned, a curious questioning look in his eyes.

"Please, please," Ned began, "will you teach me to ride good, Val? Not so good as you maybe, I don't expect that, but *good*. . . . Teach me to ride good. I don't know how to do anything good. Will you? I'll obey you in all things."

Val Dougherty slowly pulled his hands out of the boy's grasp, but Ned took his hands again and held them, and again the horse trainer looked down at his hands, caught in this callow youngster's grasp.

"I'll pay you, I'll pay you good," the boy was going on.

Suddenly Ned let loose of the trainer's hands.

"I don't know how to teach nobody," Val said after a little while, moistening his lips fiercely with his tongue.

He picked up the letter from the table, folded it several times, and put it away in a little drawer in the kitchen cabinet.

"I learned to ride by myself, without nobody. . . ."

"If you could just watch me ride, then, Val, and give me a suggestion or a hint, you know, so as how I should do this, do that."

Val picked up an old toothpick and stuck it in the corner of his mouth. Slowly a smile came over his weathered lips. He shook his head.

"But ain't that what we're doing now, Ned?" he wondered. "Ain't you ridin' and I'm watchin' you ride round the track? I don't want no money from you for that. . . . But I'll tell you somethin'. I feel a whole lot better about you now that you ain't a father. You ought not ever be a father . . . at least not for ten, twenty years. . . . It'll be a load off your ma's mind, too."

"And I can ride in front of you around the track, then, Val . . . every day?"

"Ain't that what we're doin' already?" The older man sniggered. "God damn it, ain't we been havin' lessons all along without our knowin' it? You tell me!"

He took Ned by the scruff of the neck and shook him hard, and then, letting him go, he stared at him, and burst out laughing boisterously. It was the first time Ned had ever heard Val laugh a real open good laugh. He tried to take the horse trainer's hand then to say good night, but the latter kept both his hands now behind his back, so that Ned merely touched him on the shoulder by way of saying good night, and then hurried out the kitchen door into the dark of the evening on his way home.

Keith Gresham eyed Ned with almost hungry curiosity as the boy arrived late for dinner. Elaine was so flustered over the sauce she had made for the spareribs and the failure of a casserole of rice and cheese to brown perfectly that she scarcely noticed her younger son was late and had not combed his hair or put on a necktie. They were all beginning to take it for granted that he usually smelled of the stables when he came home. Except possibly Alec, who scowled malignly at him and called him a terrible word, which caused Keith to giggle in spite of himself.

"My sons will corrupt you, Keith, if you don't watch out," Elaine joked, as she brought in the huge array of spareribs, still sizzling on the turkey platter.

"They are both incorrigible, I declare," she went on. "But of the two"—and here she looked over at Ned—"the younger, I fear, takes the cake."

Ned had observed for some time now how much his mother flirted with Keith, and how without the ex-soldier's probably being aware of it, he flirted (or so Ned felt) with Ned.

At any rate Keith watched Ned all during the meal, with unfailing amusement, one supposed. One night, after dinner, Ned had said to Gresham in a whisper in the hallway, "What do you find so amusing about me, Lieutenant?" Keith had laughed and poked him in the ribs.

Elaine had of course "tattled" as usual the day before yesterday and told Ned that Mr. Gresham had had nearly all his insides blown out in France in one of the greatest battles of this or any other war. "It is nothing but a miracle he is here today," she had said, while mysteriously suggesting she knew even more about his injuries and his heroism.

She won't marry him, then, Ned said to himself, unless she's really desperate later on for a husband.

In the hallway that same evening when Keith had poked him in the ribs, Ned had told the veteran he was learning to ride all of Val Dougherty's horses.

This evening, though, Ned realized that Keith suspected something had "happened" at the Star-Lite Stables.

After doing a few chores for Elaine, Ned walked out to join Keith Gresham on the front porch, where he found the lieutenant smoking a Camel on the swing. Alec had gone off to his singing teacher, and the ladies who had taken dinner with them that evening had volunteered to help Elaine in the kitchen with the dishes.

"You hardly ate a bite of dinner," Keith began. Then when there was no reply, he asked, "Want a smoke?"

"Oh, well." Ned avoided looking at Keith directly and took a cigarette from the extended pack.

Keith helped him light the cigarette with a very fancy lighter.

"I think I can read you like a book, Ned." The lieutenant spoke almost inaudibly.

There was a strong smell of something chemical coming from Keith's hands, almost as if they had been dipped in ether, or some other hospital odor, and this all at once brought to Ned's nostrils his own smell, which came from the horses, he supposed, and was at this moment as noticeable to himself as it must be to other people.

Ned took in, too, for the first time what long black lashes Keith had, almost like those of a movie star. He moved away a little from the veteran on the swing.

"What is troubling you?" Keith said. His voice, more vibrant in the dark of the ill-lighted porch for some reason, was almost bass. The Germans had missed his Adam's apple, all right, Ned thought to himself, and then decided what a terrible thing this was even to think about a young man who had given everything for his country except his actual life.

"You can tell me, if you like, Ned."

"Then you'll go and tell Elaine."

"Not if you tell me not to."

"Or maybe you should be the one to tell her. I certainly don't know how to tell her." Ned smiled as he thought of how Keith would tell her about the miscarriage. Then they would probably kiss. The thought made him both angry and pleased. But if anybody was to kiss his mother, it would be best, he supposed, if Keith did.

Ned, trying to avoid looking into Keith's face, as he got himself ready to tell his news, noticed the boarder had a large sparkling ring of some kind on his left hand, the third finger. It reminded him of Adele. He wished Keith did not wear that ring. It did not look right for a man, he thought, and he recalled Val Dougherty's sinewy unadorned hands, with the many cuts and bruises and blackened nails. But, he looked quickly again, Keith's hands were strong, too. And whereas Val had never killed anybody, he remembered now hearing at the barbershop once that Keith had killed over a score of Germans, many of them with his bayonet.

Ned stirred uneasily again on the porch swing.

"I'm waiting, Ned." He heard that deep bass voice then, deeper than that of the horse trainer. The night outside had settled in, without stars or moon.

"You've heard I was to be a father, Keith," Ned began.

"Yes," the boarder said in a kind of annoyed manner, from behind the many little circles of tobacco smoke. The "yes" also sounded hostile, even angry.

"Go on," Keith spoke in a more matter-of-fact voice.

"Well, I got this young lady in trouble. Elaine must have told you."

Keith was lighting another cigarette, and that was when Ned noticed how badly the older man's right hand trembled. But then he remembered it always trembled when he tried to hold something for more than a brief period. He tried to think of Keith holding the bayonet and plunging it into an enemy soldier's bowels. He wanted to ask Keith outright just how he had done it, just as he was always on the point of asking Val how he got his cock into a mare's cunt, if indeed Val did that. The vision of the bayonet and then the penis of Val plunging, these two upraised objects in his mind, made him suddenly sick. He had eaten too much of the rich meal. He excused himself hastily, went down the alley and retched painfully, but nothing would come up. He felt he must be deathly pale. Perhaps it had been the cigarette. He dropped it and stomped it out.

Keith was standing right beside him.

"What is it, Ned?" He felt the boarder holding him to him. "Tell me what it is." This was an embrace Ned could not quite understand, but it loosened his tongue.

"That baby I was to be the father of, you know, Keith?"

Keith let go of him but held his hand. "Go on," the boarder urged him.

"That baby has miscarried."

"I got an Alsatian girl in trouble *over there*," Keith said in a faraway voice.

"Did you now?" Ned said, more comfortably.

"I still send her money because she had the baby . . ."

"You're then a . . ."

". . . father," Keith finished for him.

Keith suddenly drew the boy to him and kissed him coldly on the lips. Ned was too puzzled to resist. He felt it was very peculiar, yet he understood the kiss, and he was glad Keith was close to him now after the "terrible news."

"Will you let Elaine know all about it?" Ned was saying.

But he saw the veteran was barely listening to him, indeed was barely aware perhaps he was standing beside him. He heard the veteran's deep tones, saying: "It's all so painfully empty and lonesome. . . . I don't think I can stand any more of it . . . the whole dreadful way we are born, die, and are never missed. The fact there is *nobody* . . . nobody really. . . . We come out of a yawning tomb of flesh and sink back finally into another tomb. What is the point of it all? Who thought up this sickening circle of flesh and blood? We come into the world bleeding and cut and our bones half-crushed only to emerge and suffer more torment, mutilation, and then at the last lie down in some hole in the ground forever. Who could have thought it up, I wonder?"

Then, as if coming to himself, and pushing Ned roughly away from him, he said, "Yes, sir, I will tell your mother . . . later. . . . But if there are any details, tell her yourself. Good night, sir."

He watched the veteran disappearing into the darkness. Ned

stared after him incredulously, and though frightened, he felt even closer to Keith at that moment than he did to Val. . . . That was because Val, he supposed, was better able to go about his business. And he had his horses, then, too. Keith had nothing.

An hour or so later one of the lady boarders was performing on the out-of-tune Knabe piano in the front parlor, so that Elaine was not aware that Keith had come into the kitchen, where she was putting away the last of tonight's dishes. She turned in his direction when he said "Mrs. Cottrell," and then, correcting himself, he said: "Elaine."

She was more startled by his white, drawn face than by his sudden appearance in the kitchen, and she let out a little cry.

"I'm sorry if I surprised you," he mumbled in apology.

"What is it, Keith? And where is Ned?"

"Ned's gone off on his wheel," he mumbled, and shook his head as if in disapprobation.

"At this hour?" She gave him a kind of reproachful look. "I'll be through here in a minute," she informed him, turning now to some large cooking spoons and forks, which she put away in a cupboard drawer. "We can sit out on the back lawn, if you like," she added in a less worried manner.

"I was just looking at all the fireflies out there," he told her. "It should be nice out in back, I'm sure."

"What is wrong, Keith?" She spoke as severely now as when she gave a dressing down to Alec or Ned. She bestowed upon his face a searching examination, as if to decipher what he had come back so expressly to tell her. Perhaps he was going to leave her! Just when she needed the money so badly, and had come to depend on him as her "star boarder."

"You look quite ill, Keith." She tried to catch his eye as she spoke but he stared out the back window, looking upon the garden.

"No, no, I'm all right."

"Sit over here." She motioned toward a large wood bench. She lit one of the lamps Alec had installed a year or so ago for a garden party he had given for his "musical" friends.

"Just tell me what it is, Keith. I don't think it had better keep," she advised him. She hovered over him, her hands both slightly raised.

He swallowed audibly, and the color drained from his face again. His lips, usually so red, so kissable in their perfect formation, were almost white, and drawn against his teeth.

"My news is not exactly bad," he hastened to assure her.

"Not exactly!"

"Mrs. Cottrell"—the last name slipped out again—"that girl your son was so close to . . ."

"You don't mean that Enid creature?"

"Oh, no, not her . . . I'm talking about Ned's girl."

"Well, go on."

"That baby miscarried."

She had begun to put the last of the tea towels over a makeshift clothes drier that Alec had made for her in his manual-training class. She wheeled about when she heard his statement.

"Then there is *no* baby? There will be *no* baby!"

"A miscarriage, yes," he repeated, thinking she must surely know what that was better than he ever would.

She fell heavily into the chair by the large white-pine kitchen table.

"Mrs. Cottrell! Elaine." He sprang up to help her. She was a good deal more pale now than he.

"In that top drawer of the little cupboard over there you'll find some red medicine in a medium-size bottle. Please get it, and bring a glass of water."

His hand went to the cupboard and the medicine with the alacrity and ease of one who performed this action several times a day. He took off the tiny rubber stopper from the bottle and handed it to her. There did not seem time for a spoon or the water. She took a swallow. He had meanwhile hurried to the sink to draw a glass of water, and he now handed this to her, but she refused it.

"Then he's not to be a father?" she beseeched him, and took his hand. "He's free?"

"There is no baby." He repeated his news to her. "Yes, he's . . . free."

"Who told you?" she wondered dubiously.

"Ned, of course . . . and he learned it through Val Dougherty."

"Oh, God, *him*. Then how can we be sure the news is true?"

Keith watched a tiny red trickle of the red liquid coming from Elaine's lips.

"The color is coming back into your face," Keith said softly.

"Why didn't Ned tell me," she complained. Then she began to laugh all at once, a laugh of the kind he remembered from soldiers coming out from an anesthetic.

"Why didn't Ned tell her!" he repeated almost savagely to himself, but aloud. He felt so ill himself he picked up her bottle of medicine and took a swallow. "I hope it does me some good, too," he said, sheepishly looking at her.

"I don't even know what it is, Keith. . . . You have been looking so haggard, dear boy, I'm sure a sip won't hurt."

He tilted the bottle and drank some more.

"I believe it's only cordial, Elaine."

She had ceased her strange laughing.

"He could never have been a father," she began. "You don't know what a weight has been removed from my heart. And that awful wife and daughter of Dougherty. Will they return, do you suppose?"

"Not if Val has anything to do with it." Keith spoke with positive assurance.

"Why can't my boys meet decent girls?" She took the medicine bottle now and drank more generously from it.

"Thank God, thank God, Keith. . . ." She wiped her lips with a dinner napkin. "Yes, you are the bearer of good news. . . . We'll go out in the back now, if you like, and watch the fireflies. When there are so many of them, it means summer is coming to an end."

The piano had stopped now in the front parlor, and one could hear the various sounds from outside, the tree toads and the katydids, and nearer to the house the crickets in the rock garden.

"You're sure it is true, Keith?" she asked again as they started to go out the door, but without warning he bent down and kissed her. Her lips moved in a queer but pleased smile.

"I'm as relieved as you are, believe you me," he told her. "He's much too young to be a father, isn't he?"

In the dead of night the entire neighborhood was awakened by the scream of the ambulance, a police siren, the hoarse voices of men, doors being opened, and then left to bang in the wind.

The uproar all came from the house of Widow Hughes. Elaine rushed to the front door only in time to see the widow being taken out on a stretcher, followed by her cursing son, Barney, wearing only his B.V.D.s.

Alec had to restrain his mother from running after the ambulance. Groaning, Elaine sat down on the edge of the staircase. For a long time she refused to budge, although Alec and Ned, who had got up almost at the same time as their mother, urged her to be "sensible" and come back to bed.

"I have lost a good and true friend," she kept repeating. "I don't know what I will do without her."

"I thought you hated her, the way you always talked about her," Ned retorted.

"Look who's talking!" Elaine rebuked him bitterly. "And remember all she did for you, too!"

Suddenly they were all silent as they felt the loss of Widow Hughes.

"But you don't know she is dead," Alec finally observed.

"Oh, Alec, at her age! I doubt we ever see her again! What will become of her wonderful house, and all her property in the country, do you suppose. It will all go to that drunken son of hers, Barney."

"Come to bed now, Mother," Alec insisted. "You don't even have your bathrobe on, and are sitting with bare feet on the bare floor!"

Elaine allowed herself to be helped up and guided back to her room, where she lay the rest of the night open-eyed, frightened and chilled by the thought of death and the precariousness of all things human. "Everything is eggshell-thin when you think of it," she muttered as the first streaks of dawn appeared at the window. "Nothing durable, nothing lasting."

She called the Home and Hospital the next morning and learned that Rosa Hughes had suffered a mild heart attack, but was rallying and would be able to see a few visitors the next day.

A feeling of such blessed relief came over Elaine on learning that Rosa might live after all, she came close to fainting. She was unable to explain her own feeling of gratitude and joy. She felt she herself had been rescued from death. Maddening as the old widow was, Elaine now saw that she was an integral part of her life. Without Rosa some very basic support would be removed from her world. She prayed constantly that day that the widow would be spared, and she lighted a little candle in the hallway, usually lit only at Christmas, for her recovery.

The next day the two boys and their mother drove to the somewhat fashionable Home and Hospital, with its endless stretch of green lawn and its many surrounding hills. They were informed by a guard that Rosa Hughes would be able to see them in the first-floor suite.

They entered the spacious clean-smelling room, which had only just been scrubbed down, to judge by the biting smell of lye and yellow soap, but saw ahead of them, in an adjoining room, propped up in a queen-size bed, a handsome woman whom they did not recognize.

"We have made a mistake, madam." Elaine apologized to the unknown woman.

Elaine urged her sons to follow her on out, but as they were leaving they heard the familiar contralto: "You don't know your own next-door neighbor, dear hearts? Shame on all of you!"

Elaine and her sons turned around, and then recognized in the "beautiful" stranger Rosa Hughes herself.

For the first time in twenty-five years, perhaps since the death of Pastor Hughes, the widow's hair had been carefully shampooed and "set," her face and throat bathed and softened with creams, and she was wearing a clean gown, which fit her perfectly. A pearl choker completed her metamorphosis.

Rosa accepted with delight Elaine's contrite acknowledgment of her mistake in not recognizing her.

"Not to know your own neighbor of so many years!" the old lady repeated again and again. "Think of it. And even Ned here stared at me ablank!"

"You don't know how wonderful you look, Rosa," Elaine told her, taking a seat at her bedside, and holding one of the old woman's hands in hers. "So beautiful and so young."

"That's enough of compliments, my precious." Rosa smiled. "My son was hoping this would be the end," she reflected, looking down at her nails, which, carefully manicured as they now were, appeared unlike her own, as her face had appeared to the Cottrells as that of a beautiful stranger.

"I cannot, I will not, give Barney the satisfaction of dying at this time. I must live to spite him and that strumpet wife of his. . . . He doesn't deserve the happiness my death would give him. No, Barney must precede me, my dear, on Charon's bark. No question about it. I can give him a better funeral in any case than he can give me. He'd send me to a pauper's grave and pocket the difference. But you are wondering how I landed up in this expensive hotel for the fancifully ill. I'll tell you. Barney and I were quarreling over my country properties. I slapped the ungrateful pup for an insolent remark he made to me, and was about to hit him really hard when I lost my balance and fell over a footstool and cut my head. . . . I did *not* have a stroke, as that fool night nurse claims." She jeered at this description's having been applied to her. "The doctor here is an idiot, and is attempting to hold me prisoner as long as possible so he can get his full fee. He's put up to it, I'm sure, by Barney's wife. She was the late Dr. Crawford's daughter, remember, the one who prescribed opium to all his women patients. She had the gall to come here a few minutes ago, Barney's spouse that is, and like you, did not recognize me and asked where Widow Hughes was, and I told her that Widow Hughes had passed on. A smile of such happiness you'd never believe began to light up her hard-boiled old puss until the truth dawned on her, and then she came on in and nearly suffocated me with her Woolworth lipstick kisses. Yes, you can go back to the neighborhood, Elaine dearest, and tell everybody I will be home any time now! I will contest the hospital bill, as I should never have been brought here at all merely for losing my balance over a footstool!"

Elaine gave the signal then for Ned to present the old woman with two dozen yellow roses, which Rosa seized and held tight to her bosom.

"You are my only loves," the widow said softly, and began kissing each of the roses. "As of this moment I disinherit all other parties! All of them. . . . You shall from this time forth be my family!" And she urged each of the Cottrells to advance and kiss her not once but, in the old woman's words, *again and again and again*.

After several other tumultuous expressions of affection and abiding love on everybody's part, the trained nurse managed to usher the Cottrells out of the room, and as the door closed on them Elaine could hear the woman scolding Widow Hughes for "frittering away your energy on visitors when you know perfectly well how ill you have been!"

"What do you mean by visitors"—the widow's voice easily reached them—"when they are my nearest of kin. How dare you boss me when you must know who I am and what my antecedents are! Leave my room at once, damn you for the snoop and a troublemaker that you are, and bring my release papers instantly before I call the sheriff."

Adele's reinstatement among the members of the Altrusa Club meant nothing to her. She thought, as she walked the spacious rooms of her house, that she would have preferred to have remained "ousted," "dropped," "banished." What satisfaction was there now even in having old Dr. Hitchmough eat humble pie. And she thought back, like Widow Hughes, to the old man's "antecedents"—his father (or was it his grandfather?) had been a dealer in old iron, discarded paper, and rags, was indeed nothing but a ragpicker. She had seen the old man going about in the early morning, when she was a girl, with his wheelbarrow loaded with what he had salvaged at midnight from the public dump.

And her reinstatement would not bring back her lost son, or make her forget the shame and humiliation of her youth.

She felt she had nobody now. Both Alex and Ned had less and less time for her. Though she continued to read voraciously, she could not after all read twenty-four hours out of the day. Nor could she spend all her evenings drinking her medicine and listening to her phonograph and occasionally her radio. She found herself sometimes for hours lost in a kind of reverie, whose tenuous content faded quickly as she was roused from it.

Her chief entertainment came always at night, when she would stand at her high front window and watch the young people file in and out of the Royal Theater.

One night, having taken too many sips of her medicine, she decided to put on all her diamonds. First, however, she spent a good hour on her coiffure, and having donned her finest silk dress (she did not recall it was George Etheredge's last gift to her) and ballroom pumps, she took her post at the window, her jewels the only illumination in the room. But nobody looked up at her, though she almost pressed her face and body against the glass. She was, in fact, about to leave the window when she recognized below Keith Gresham, whom she barely knew except to say how-do-you-do to on the street. She had met him once at the Cottrells', and she remembered he had been in the war.

All at once Keith drew nearer to her front window and looked up at her. As he did so she smiled and nodded to him as one would to a familiar friend. He came closer, still gazing upward at her. His eyes had misted over, and his mouth looked as if it had been crushed against a paving stone. His strong, heavily veined hands rose slowly and were clasped over his heart. His gaze never left hers. They stood there for what seemed minutes, never taking their eyes off one another. Adele's right hand then moved deliberately, ever so slowly, in a beckoning, welcoming arc. Without taking his eyes off her, he moved across the street to the front entrance of her house. Soon she heard his footsteps coming up the long succession of steps. She heard her door open—she had, she realized, left it unlocked.

She was at a loss what to say or do when she saw him standing at her open door. She was reminded of the time when she had been persuaded against her will to take part in some amateur theatricals of the Fonthill Thespian Society. On the opening night of the play, one of the male actors became confused, and came on stage some half hour before his cue, and began a long speech entirely out of context and order with the speech she was to deliver. She had longed for the prompter to advise her what to do at that moment. She longed now for a prompter to intervene and tell her now what to say, what to do.

But her medicine gave her the strength to smile and welcome this stranger off the street.

"You will be more comfortable, I believe, in this chair right here." She heard her own words with surprise. "Mr. Gresham, isn't it?"

"Why should I sit?" His voice was sulky, almost menacing.

She saw that he had been drinking heavily. He moved a few steps closer to her.

"Did you go to the movie tonight?" she wondered. She moved a few steps away from him. He closed the distance between them, coming almost directly up to her.

"No, I did not go to any movie," he replied, breathing heavily. "Did you?"

"I usually go only in the afternoon," she told him. She sat down rather heavily on a large green settee. He swiftly and without making any sound sat down beside her. He immediately took her hand in his and pressed it.

"You're ablaze . . . with stones," he said thickly.

"Ah, yes, so I am." She looked down at herself, as if in surprise also. She had actually forgotten how extravagantly she had attired herself.

"You lit up the entire street out there," he went on. "Yes, you're ablaze." He took her hand to his mouth but merely kept it there for what seemed a long time until he kissed it wetly again and again.

"Don't look at me like that," he warned her.

"Like how?" she said, staring at his mouth on her hand.

"Adele," he said. "You are Adele, ain't you. Of course you are. Don't lie to me, looking at me that way. I know you. Adele, I know you." He kissed her hand painfully again.

"Yes, I am Adele," she said, and she took his free hand now in hers and pressed it.

"That's better," he said. "That's much better."

Hardly knowing what she was doing either, she kissed his hand gently, and then released it.

"Thank you, Adele," he muttered. "Thank you."

"You have been taking 'medicine' I see also," she said rather piteously.

"Heart medicine." He raised his voice. "Yes, I have."

"Is that what you call it?" she laughed her sad little laugh.

"I don't call it nothin'," he replied. "Do I?"

"Yes, you said it was heart medicine."

He shook his head.

"No, Adele," he went on, still occasionally kissing her hand, "I have not been to the movie like you. The screen blurs when I go, anyhow. . . . I have not been to the movie. . . . I only like to watch live people. I have been to the Hole-in-the-Wall behind the Mecca."

She knew he meant an illegal saloon even she had barely heard of.

"But the movie I have always wanted to attend the most is the Adele Bevington movie. You know that. I have always wanted to visit Adele Bevington. And tonight . . . she has given me the nod and the invite."

He took both her hands in his now and covered them with immoderate kisses.

"Would you like something more to drink?" she inquired, although she realized he had had too much already. "You have only to ask," she said, and realized at once these words were no more hers than a line from some idiotic amateur theatrical read from a script. She felt desperate.

"I would like whatever has made you ablaze, Adele."

"If you let go of my hand then, Mr. Gresham."

"Never," he answered back, then smiled slowly and very slowly released her. "Go." He imitated a military command. "On the double. Run! Run away from me like all the others. Everybody runs away from me. I have only to appear, they all skiddoo. They never come back neither."

She went unsteadily out of the room, leaving him muttering. She stood for a while before her little cabinet, as if again she had lost all her cues and stage directions. She opened the little door, and stared at the inevitable brandy. She took off the cork, picked up one of the tiny cut-glass glasses, and poured hardly more than a tablespoon, and brought it back to her guest. He had laid his head down on the arm of the chair. His thick chestnut hair full of tangles had become disarranged and fell in surprising length over the worn velvet of the chair.

"Mr. Gresham . . . have a sip."

"Lieutenant Gresham," he said, rising up and saluting her. He stared at the glass suspiciously, took it from her, drank it off, and then fell back against the elegant cloth of the chair. His teeth protruded from his mouth with wonderful ferocious whiteness.

"I want to sleep in clean white embroidered sheets tonight," he said. "Not in the trenches with the scurrying rats."

"That was long ago, Mr. Gresham."

"What do you know about *long ago?*" he snapped. "Aren't you ablaze? Weren't you ablaze when I was in the mud with the rats? What do you know about *ago?*" He got up with surprising steadiness. She felt he was about to hit her, perhaps indeed he was, but instead he lost his balance and fell, thrashing, to the carpet.

"No, no, no!" she cried, and he echoed her cry, but his voice seemed a city block away.

"You must get up, Mr. Gresham," she begged him. "I can't carry you."

He rolled his eyes, then closed them.

She knelt down beside him, foolishly, wondering what she should do.

"Mr. Gresham, you will catch cold," she would say, or, "You can't just lie there, you know," or other useless admonitions. The lights on Main Street had all gone out. But she felt there was no hour now anywhere. She did not want to look at a clock.

When she turned to him again she saw that he had urinated copiously all over himself and his water was flowing over the rug.

Then slowly, laboriously she began dragging him toward the guest bedroom. "You can't sleep in your clothes," she kept saying to him. "I will have to take things into my own hands."

She talked on in the hackneyed phrasing of a dramatic script that did not exist. Everything she said sounded copied, implausible, boring, unlike anything she had ever thought, let alone pronounced.

Finally, anger took over, and she was able to get him on top of the bed. Disgust and nausea followed at the fact he had both urinated and defecated. She was able somehow to remove his jacket and trousers, and then, taking off her own dress and most of her jewels, she began the more difficult task of removing his underthings. She was not aware at first of what she had uncovered. She was still worrying fastidiously about his having "soiled" his clothes, but when she had him stretched out before her, stark naked except for his socks and garters, she saw what she later described to her own terror as the root of his sorrow. The scars, the fearful wounds, the mutilation, the pieces of black-and-blue filings under his skin, which she supposed must be the remains of bullets or shrapnel—she had no idea what. And yet, she reflected, he was beautiful in his ruin, too. She feared he was dead. She touched his chest, which had been spared the damage and atrocity of the rest of his body. His heart was beating. She looked at his white throat, flecked with the natural rose color the cool air of the night had brought to his skin. Her head fell over his breast. She pressed her lips there again and again. Then she would raise her head and look at all of him again. She went on kissing him desperately, yet almost methodically, as if kisses were a prescribed medical procedure here.

She had the urge to cover his nakedness with something at that moment in tribute both to his handsomeness and to the mutilating wounds he had earned as a soldier-hero. She took off her finest diamond necklace and with difficulty put it round his neck. He groaned when he felt the cold stones against him. She hurried to her bureau drawer and drew out one diamond necklace after another. She draped his neck with these, as if they were the supreme, the only, medals of honor. Then she kissed his red mouth and his ashen cheeks and his white brow. In a surge of something, she had no idea what or from whence, she devoured his entire body with kisses, even those ruined parts of him which would have made a common woman, she felt, run from the house. She took off his garters and socks and kissed his badly scarred feet. Her saliva bathed the toes and the nails. Then, feeling somewhat dizzy, she brought herself up to his chest again and fell against his beating heart.

He began to talk and "tell" under the throb and pressure of her countless kisses. She called it Keith's chronicle. Except it would never be recorded. It was told, in fact, she understood, to be blotted out forever once it was uttered. The truth, he muttered, is only whispered and muttered from one soldier to another, then expunged forever.

He had begun then his talk, but only after countless words unconnected with sense, or single names like "Kaiser," "Soissons."

"Keith," she asked once, "you said 'Soissons.' "

He stared at her in outrage, his eyes rolling. He pushed her away from him.

"People are the depth of mud puddles," he began then, talking in sentences instead of single syllables and names. "The depth of a rain puddle when they should be deep like the sea! Where are the sea-deep people?''

"You did mention Soissons," she persisted.

The name appeared to clear his brain. He nodded.

"I was shot in or around there in what you folk call the Great War. . . . Does that answer your question." He spoke rapidly now, his eyes on the ceiling as if reading the words there. "Wounded in a great forest inhabited by owls."

He touched the diamond necklaces about his neck and throat with the perfect equanimity of someone who had worn these every day of his life.

"Owls?" she repeated, but this interruption annoyed him, and he moved away from her.

"They watched me by day, by night, as I went walking through the knee-deep mud looking for—what? Water. Looking for water. . . . Then somebody, a witch like yourself, flew right at me. But it wasn't someone, it was owls calling to me. Like women, they had snow-white breasts and coral nipples. I feared and loved them. Dreaded their touch and wanted them, I guess, to swoop down and take all that was left of me. . . . Then I woke up like I had new eyes to see with. I seen a woman in a starched stiff white hat watching me instead of the owls. I knowed though she had once been a owl herself. . . .

"Now"—he raised himself up in the bed and stared at her— "remember, Adele, to forget as soon as I tell you. When soldiers tell one another these things, they forget them forever. Be a soldier for once. Forget Soissons."

He grinned, perhaps tried to laugh.

"The depth of a mud puddle," she repeated. "Yes, that's all we know back here. What do we know about the forests in Soissons or for that matter their owls."

Dr. Radwell had been out on two calls that night: the first one, at which he had arrived too late, the sick man having already died in the arms of his wife; and the second, the delivery of a baby— the doctor's chief province in the practice of medicine. It was on the whole an easy delivery, but even the easiest taxed his strength almost beyond endurance at his stage of life. Returning from the delivery (in those days more babies were delivered at home than in the hospital, at least in Fonthill), he and his companion, Eddie, had for some reason or other driven down Main Street on their way home, though this route was a mile or so out of their way. As they approached the Royal Theater Dr. Radwell, who was not driving, glanced up at Adele's front window and saw not only the whole floor lavishly illuminated, but fancied he caught a glimpse of Adele herself hurrying past the window. It was nearly three o'clock in the morning.

"Let's go up to Miss Bevington's." The doctor touched his companion on the sleeve.

"No!" Eddie cried. "I'm dead beat. I can hardly manage this vehicle, let alone be treated to one of her performances."

"But she may be ill," the doctor pleaded. "Eddie, please. We must go up. . . . Something must be wrong there. . . . Besides, I could stand a cup of her French drip coffee."

"A glass of her liquor is more like it," Eddie snapped, but he was relenting a little as he considered the idea a second time. "All right, since you're worn pretty well to a frazzle, Doc, why don't we go up?" He turned the car into a side street for parking.

Eddie and Dr. Radwell found the front door wide open, and from the bottom of the staircase, they could see that the door to her flat was half-ajar.

Apprehensive, Dr. Radwell hurried on ahead. Inside the front parlor he could see nobody, but heard from the guest bedroom the deep voice of a man murmuring something unintelligible.

He walked toward the room. The door was wide open. He walked on in. Keith Gresham was lying stark naked save for several necklaces thrown haphazardly across his smooth white chest. The sight of his angry wounds, which looked only half-healed, the jagged marks and discoloration left by shrapnel, bullets, botched in-the-field surgery, gave even the doctor, hardened to every one of life's horrors, pause. But the cruel mutilation of the young man's groin brought a cry of pure grief from the physician. Then recovering from the sight he had stumbled in upon, he stood dumbfounded, remembering in a flash, as people are said to remember when dying, all their past life, the story of Adele Bevington. This comely young man, who looked like someone rescued from the hands of an executioner, became for the doctor at that moment the confirmation and proof of all that people had said over the years concerning Miss Bevington. But instead of joining the chorus of tongues who decried and condemned her life, the doctor found himself glorying in it. He had never dared live fully except in the ceaseless round of his duties to prolong the life of his patients or help them in their departure from this life. The naked stranger, lying with his scars and scattered sex and adorned with precious jewels, made the old physician hope Adele had been as bad as everyone had always said, made him pray indeed she had been worse than any whore whose annals he had pored over in old books.

As he stood there in a kind of stupefaction of happiness, Adele and Eddie came into the room together.

Adele brought with her a man's dressing gown. Dr. Radwell gave her a sidelong look in which all his wonder and admiration conveyed themselves to her, and he nodded in solemn approbation.

"He's been quite ill, Charles." She spoke coolly.

They stood exchanging looks of complicity, like two confederates who have broken the law together from time out of mind.

At that moment Keith opened his eyes. He looked about him, then down at himself, tried to cover his lower body with a cushion lying near him, and then turned a gaze of baleful hatred and rage at the three people watching him.

"Haven't you God-damned scarecrows standing there ever seen a man before? Stare with your fucking mouths open, will you?" He took away the cushion that he had put before him, and pointed now to the cicatrix of his groin. "Take a good look while you're at it. There's still more left of me than I bet either of you two sit-down-to-pee prisses ever had! Go on, stare away! Ain't you brought your operating kit, Doc? Well, then go and operate instead on your little friend and companion there, why don't you! You'll never get me under the knife again."

Keith rose from the bed. He tore the dressing gown out of Adele's hands and put his arms through the sleeves, tearing the fabric in several places as he did so.

He rushed out of the bedroom and into the parlor, from where they could hear him upsetting tables and chairs. A great resounding crash then sounded, so that one would have thought a shell had burst there.

The three onlookers hurried out into the parlor. Keith had thrown a chair at the heirloom pier mirror, and he stood carefully staring at himself in the cracked residue of the glass, with intense concentration.

"Yes, she's amused herself studying my fifty or sixty operations, and the countless scars, adhesions, stitches, and catgut from butcher surgeons. . . . She only takes in us ruined young men. The whole and the hale get loose from her grasp."

He pointed to Adele. He screamed in glee as the three watched him. Then without warning he fell to the carpet, and a kind of foam came out of his mouth. He screamed again and kicked his bare feet into the air.

"Keith, oh, Keith!" Adele cried and bent over him. She cradled his head in her arms.

He had opened his eyes wide and was looking now for the first time at the diamonds hung round his neck. Then a kind of fit of trembling and frothing and more screams followed.

Dr. Radwell had knelt down, and was listening to his heart, taking his pulse, looking into his eyes with a lighted instrument, and doing all the other things doctors do in a crisis.

"You're too late, Doc," the patient scoffed. "The damage is all done, they've sewed me up for the last time, and all there's left to do is put me in the ground, but you medical men are too chickenhearted to finish a job. You can cut and saw and sew and stitch and mend and dope and sever, but you're too damned ballless to put us in the ground. You leave that to the buzzards. If I could only put the knife in you the crooked hundreds of times they have stuck it in my guts. . . ."

Keith laughed as he saw the doctor producing the hypodermic needle. He giggled, and grinned grotesquely at Adele, and flecks of blood came out of one corner of his lips.

When he had subsided under the injection, the doctor and Eddie carried the ex-soldier to the bed where they had discovered his shame and brought on the attack.

The two men sat for a while by his bedside, the doctor holding his hand and counting the beatings of his heart.

Adele stood by the door, still adorned with her jewels. Her

white hair had come down, her face was drawn, pale, and old. She never took her eyes off the sick man.

"You'll be having him as a patient for some days at least, Adele," Dr. Radwell told her. The look of admiration, even pride, was still in his eyes. She looked away from the patient now to the doctor. She was happy the doctor was so pleased with her, and a faint smile ruffled her lips.

What Dr. Radwell often warned his patients about was the danger of "delayed reaction" after an emotional crisis, and he had often counseled Adele Bevington about this phenomenon, which defied medical knowledge. And Dr. Radwell, had he been in touch with young Ned Cottrell at this moment, might have diagnosed the boy's state of mind in the same way.

At first Ned had experienced nothing but a faint bewilderment on learning that his "child" had perished by a miscarriage. The whole series of events—his loving Marilyn in the high grass, his learning she was pregnant, her sudden departure for the West with her mother, the lack of any further communication from her since then, and finally the "letter," read beside a smoking lamp at the horse tender's house, to the effect that his "son" had died, that he who was to be a father therefore was not a father, and so on—all these things had left him stupefied.

Ned had lost his appetite, and, in Elaine's phrase, "only picked at his food." But what seemed to cause her second son even more anguish than what had happened to Marilyn was the mention of the name of Keith Gresham. When Ned heard the veteran's name he would look away and turn scarlet.

Of course all Fonthill soon knew of the young ex-infantryman's having gone to Adele's house uninvited, dead drunk, of his menacing her, then smashing all of her heirloom furniture, including a priceless mirror, and finally having to be given an injection by Dr. Radwell, who had been summoned by Miss Bevington when all else had failed.

Studying her boy, Elaine was not sure which of these recent events lay behind Ned's sickness, his "losing his baby" (actually Elaine never had believed he was the father of the child, for to her Ned was a child himself), or his disappointment in Keith. She had been convinced that Ned looked up to the "young hero" as a second father, and she supposed the gossip about the soldier's running amok at Adele's had depressed and dispirited her son.

"You have found out your idol has feet of clay," Elaine said abruptly to Ned one evening when he was helping her do the dishes.

Ned stared at her with wonder. She seemed to understand everything and yet nothing.

"Perhaps, dear," she went on, oblivious of the effect her words had made on her son, "if you were to go pay a visit on Keith . . . they say he never goes out of the house now. I suppose he is too shamed to come to dinner here anymore. Why don't you go to see him, Ned. He would admit you because you're a boy and a friend. You could tell him we think nothing of what has occurred, and to come back here where he belongs. Everything is forgiven someone who has given as much as Keith has. . . . I believe I will send him a little something to eat, and you can take it to him. The poor fellow may be just sitting there in his grandfather's old ramshackle barn of a house gnawing his heart out. I don't know why he has never married, a handsome strapping boy like that."

Ned did not particularly want to see Keith. He did not know why. Perhaps it was the strange kiss the veteran had bestowed upon him that night in the alley. Perhaps it was from looking at Keith's powerful hands, the bulging veins, which made him always think of the soldier bayoneting Germans. He did not know what it was. But then he decided he *could* talk to Keith about what had happened between him and Marilyn. He had to talk to someone.

Meanwhile Elaine had prepared some fancy sandwiches, a flask of her own homemade dandelion wine, some strong coffee, placed in a thermos bottle, a fresh apple pie, and all of this was covered with pure linen napkins. Ned shook his head at such extravagance. "All it needs now, Mother, is a few gold pieces sprinkled on the top," he muttered. But it pleased him to have so generous a mother, though he was a bit hurt that she was so "soft" on Keith. But better Keith, he supposed, than some of the other "fellows" she went out with.

So he went to Keith's house with the late supper.

Keith lived all by himself in a twenty-room frame house down near the river. He had few, if any, neighbors. There was no doorbell, so that Ned had to pound on the heavy frosted glass of the door. He was about to leave and take back the late supper when the door was swung open almost violently. There stood Keith all right, with an assortment of bruises and cuts on his face, court plaster over his temple, a split lip. He grinned faintly when he recognized Ned, and stared keenly at the big package the boy was holding.

"Come to inspect the damage, I suppose?" Keith quipped. His voice was even lower in register, heavier, more menacing, and carried for blocks around.

Ned merely handed him the "supper," took off his little skull cap, and wiped his feet on the Welcome mat.

Inside, Keith was busy unwrapping the box, and he let out cries of surprise and delight when he saw what it contained.

"Your mother knows how to win hearts, that's all I can say," he sighed. "I tell you I am famished, Ned. I've been sitting here too beside myself to cook or go out to get any grub. Nobody has peeked in to see how I am. . . . I half expected the sheriff, but even he has given up on me, I suppose. I am in disgrace, you know."

"No, you're not," Ned said in the thick manner he was accustomed to use when embarrassed. "They excuse you, Keith."

"Oh, I bet they do now!" Keith scoffed and began on one of the chicken sandwiches, chewing loudly enough to be heard out to the highway.

"It's Adele they blame." Ned's voice was soft as satin. He had invented the remark on the spot.

"Oh, Adele." Keith shook his head and stopped chewing for a moment.

"They always blame the woman, I guess." Ned quoted his mother.

Keith gave the boy a long searching stare.

"Help me drink some of this wine, why don't you? I'm not going to let you have any of my supper, though, unless you insist. On account of I've been marooned here for days without a bite to eat."

Suddenly the veteran grinned and said, "So they always blame the woman, do they?" He laughed, and as he did so Ned studied the "battering" Keith had taken. One of his hands was very badly cut and bruised. And Ned noticed a nasty scratch around his hairline, which made him think of a "scalping."

"Oh, don't act so surprised at the damage to my puss now, Ned, come on. Ain't you ever seen a prizefight by now? It's nothing. . . . What worries me is my boss may fire me when he learns about it."

"Why did you go to Adele's?" Ned wondered.

Keith chewed in a serious fashion now—pieces of saliva and food came out on his lips, and his tongue was visible thrashing about in furious propulsion. He had worse table manners at this moment than Val, Ned decided. Yet at his mother's table he had always eaten rather daintily, wiping his lips fastidiously, and chewing his food like a gentleman.

All at once Ned drank thirstily of his mother's wine.

"I don't know what got into me exactly," Keith reflected, after he had eaten everything in the picnic basket and was brushing the crumbs off his shirt. He picked up the thermos bottle and drank the coffee directly out of it.

"Did you down half that bottle of wine?" Keith inquired after a pause, fixing Ned with a look of amazement.

"So what if I did. Don't I have the right to numb my disappointments, too?"

Keith sighed disgustedly, and began picking his teeth with his pen knife.

"What are you disappointed about, dare I ask?" Keith's eyes narrowed and he looked somewhat savagely at the boy.

"The fact I was going to be a father, and then I'm not. The fact she lost . . . our little boy."

"See here," Keith began, as if some personal outrage of his own had been mentioned.

Some wine came out of the corner of Ned's mouth. Keith clicked his tongue. He picked up one of Elaine's linen napkins and walked over to the boy and wiped his mouth in a kind of deliberate, ceremonial way.

"Thanks." Ned tried to sound as nasty as Val Dougherty might have under the circumstances.

"I suppose trouble is trouble," Keith muttered, "even when it's having your girl lose her baby."

"So you're the only guy in the world ever had any bad luck," Ned shot back.

Keith's hands were clenched, and his eyes, usually a soft gray, darkened, and flashed queerly.

"Where's your pee parlor?" Ned shouted in a cracked voice.

Keith pointed to a little room at the far end of the hall. When Ned had sauntered off, Keith picked up the wine flask and stared at its contents.

"I can't send him home drunk, can I?" he muttered, taking a deep draught.

"Where's the light in this God-damned privy of yours?" Ned's voice came muffled and distant, almost as far away, it seemed, as Soissons. Keith shook his head and kept the wine bottle tight against his lips, drinking slowly, industriously, with intense concentration.

"I can't see a damned thing in this sink hole!" Ned's voice came even fainter, as if he were vanishing.

Keith put the bottle of wine down. "Who needs a light to piss?" he said thickly, and rose unsteadily. He touched a finger to one of the cuts on his face, and felt the pressure open it again.

He walked in zigzags down the hall to the water closet, and every so often he would stop and hold one hand against the faded wallpaper with its design of bluebirds and honeysuckle.

He flung open the door and stared at Ned, who had his cock out, but was not pointing it in the direction of the bowl.

Keith pulled a long string, which turned the light on.

"What's that you're holding in your hand?" Keith stared at him.

"Now you've turned the light on, why don't you go back there and finish your supper?" Ned said very quietly.

"On account of I've finished it, that's why." Keith went on staring at Ned.

"You ought to praise God morning, noon, and night you have a cock like that," Keith told him. "Do you know what I mean?"

"Will you get out of here and let me pee?" Ned was laughing in spite of himself. "I can't pee with you watching me, Keith." He tittered and almost screamed. He was fearfully plastered.

"You'll learn to piss in front of a whole regiment when you're in the army." Keith spoke, however, in an almost savage tone of voice.

All at once the veteran knelt down on the tile floor and looked up at Ned holding his prick as he tried to pee.

"It's a beaut, a beaut! You lucky son of a bitch. With a thing like that between your legs you shouldn't have a care in the world!"

But then, without warning, Keith leaped up, and with a kind of war whoop ran out of the room.

A few minutes later, when he came out of the lavatory, Ned could not find Keith anywhere. He called him by name, first and last, would have called out his middle name too had he known it. No answer. He swore. He noticed the bottle of wine then was empty.

He went up the long, rather circular staircase, calling out dispiritedly.

He opened each of the bedroom doors. Then, hearing a noise from a room at the very end of the hall which he had overlooked, he went to that door. Opening it, he took in Keith lying down on a four-poster, his right arm over his eyes.

After a very long while the veteran took his arm from off his brow.

"Get out, or I will kill you," Keith said, and he drew out a gun from under his pillow. "I mean what I say!"

Ned was too frightened to move. He stood rooted there, and then, finally, he managed: "Oh, Keith."

"Oh, Keith, yes," the older man said in a whisper. He laid the gun down on a night table beside him.

"Go home, Ned," he said after a while. "I don't never want to see you again."

"But Keith . . ."

Then, chilled by the strange silence that followed, the boy turned to leave. His anger mounting, he slammed the door behind him and raced down the steps.

Keith leaped up and pursued his visitor, but he had to run a block before he was close enough to catch up with him.

"Ned, Ned," he began, and seized the boy's arm. "You have to overlook anything I done or said," he cried out. "Ned . . . don't leave me."

Waiting for the boy to respond, he said, "Look at me, Ned."

He reluctantly faced the ex-soldier.

"Thank your mother when you go home, Ned . . . thank her."

Without warning Keith had kissed Ned, as he had done that past time in the alley. It was a strange kiss, the boy reflected later. It was a little like the last time he had ever seen his father alive. He, too, had taken him in his arms and kissed him. A kiss not easy to understand but one that a person remembers. Ned put his hand on his lips where Keith had touched him.

"You and Elaine are all I have. . . . Don't tell her that, though. . . . I will get to be myself one day again. . . . Don't tell her that either. . . . You must bear with me, Ned. . . . You're too young to know what this life is all about . . . . but if you could bear with me . . ."

"All right, Keith," Ned said huffily. His intoxication had passed, and he had a fearful headache.

He stretched out his hand to shake with Keith, but instead Keith pressed his lips to his hand and then giving out a cry like a wild Indian, lit out toward his ramshackle, dilapidated house.

Alec barely took in, certainly paid no attention to, the new scandal that was going the rounds concerning Adele and his mother's star boarder, Keith Gresham. His mind was entirely on his departure and his escape from Fonthill. Had the nitroglycerine factory on the edge of town blown up, it would not have diverted him from his single thought now—flight.

But the town gossip reached him, of course, and the name of the woman he had once paid so much worship to, Adele. So he listened finally haphazardly to the story. They did not blame Keith, of course—he smiled bitterly—for if the veteran was not a popular young man in town, he was, witness the Congressional Medal of Honor he had received, a war hero, though he never mentioned his various medals and citations, and kept them locked away in a safety deposit box.

But, wouldn't you know, Alec reflected, poor Adele was the one who was condemned in this latest scandal. Undoubtedly, so went the talk, she had made the soldier drunk, and then seduced him. They had forgotten their own gossip, which had it that

Keith's sexual organs had been nearly entirely shot off in the late war, and that he would never function again as a man. Now, in contradiction to their own story, they were equally positive that Adele Bevington had engaged in an orgy with the war hero, which, together with the strong illegal liquor she forced down his throat, had made him run amok and destroy most of her front parlor.

It was the "story" that perhaps gave Alec the courage to call on her. He needed her counsel, and her blessing for him to leave Fonthill.

When the older Cottrell, then, appeared unexpectedly one evening at her home, after he had slighted and avoided her for so many weeks, Adele naturally thought his presence was to be explained by her new disgrace.

She had put on an unusually stunning evening dress for no particular reason, wore no jewelry of any kind, and her white hair was fastidiously marcelled. He barely noticed what she had on, and had she come to the door in sackcloth and ashes, he would hardly have looked at her twice.

For her own part, she was too surprised by his unexpected arrival to reproach him for his unfaithfulness and neglect. She greeted him warmly, though not with the effusiveness of old times. Those wonderful days were, she reflected, forever over.

The minutes passed and he made no reference to Keith or what people were saying. And gradually his eyes took in her dress and her hair, and he smiled, and said something flattering, as he might have when they were such close friends. He stared then briefly at the cracks in the heirloom mirror, which had been repaired at such expense, but which would always show the marks of Keith's destructive rage.

"The tea kettle is already boiling, Alec," she told him. "Won't you have a dish now you are here."

He turned his eyes away from the mirror, smiled, and nodded.

The tea had never tasted better. Alec had often complained at home that Elaine did not know how to brew tea like Adele. Elaine insisted on serving something as plebeian as coffee, and a common Atlantic and Pacific brand at that. This delicious if slightly heady brew, with its faint suggestion of the petals of flowers, loosened his tongue at last. His sparkling blue eyes shone with something of their old admiration and affection for her.

"I have made my final decision, Adele." He began now on the business that had brought him here, and he moved his chair so that he no longer faced the mirror.

"Don't tell me, Alex, you are going to be married?" she said lightly, but then regretted the remark in fear he might think she was referring to his unhappy affair with Enid.

"No, nothing that ordinary," he replied in imitation of her own kind of banter from times gone by.

She laughed her old carefree laugh, a laugh that George Etheredge had once told her was like the sound of silver bells.

"Adele," he said solemnly. "You have been my most wonderful friend. I have shamefully neglected you. Yes, I have," he insisted as she raised a hand of denial. "I have been selfish, mean-spirited . . . I wasted myself on that fly-by-night girl." He stopped at a glance of impatience from her. "But it's you," he continued, "even more than my voice teacher who has given me the courage to decide to do what I am about do. . . . For I cannot go on"—his old hysteria rose for a second—"as I have been going on," and his voice fell and he shook his head.

"Tell, me, Alec."

"I am leaving for Chicago a day or so before Thanksgiving, Adele."

"You're going on a visit?" She stirred her tea.

"No. I'm going for good. I'm making the break, as you used to call it."

"But then you have prospects?" She spoke with hollow gladness. "Someone has removed the first barrier for you!"

She was as unprepared for Alec's going away as his mother. Her voice betrayed her. She considered his leaving folly, and his plans destined for immediate failure.

He was intensely irritated by her caution, by her obvious lack of belief in him—all of which he read in her lips and eyes and voice.

"If I don't go now, I will never go!" He spoke these words with the desperate and frantic urgency with which he uttered the same words alone in his room.

Then looking at her with a kind of surprised wonder, as if she had appeared before him just now out of nowhere, he cried: "Surely you of all people should know that! That it's now or never!"

But she did not bend under his fury as Elaine and Ned did.

"I haven't the faintest doubt that you will go, Alec," she began, and her voice drowned out the last syllables of his words. "And I have no doubt that you will be successful. It stands to reason, with your determination and your talent. But one can't just go out into the void without preparation, without a foothold of some kind!"

"Foothold?" He struggled with his anger. Perhaps he even thought of wild Keith Gresham at that moment, rising and smashing everything in sight. "What do you mean by such a word?" He held himself down. "Do you think I have a *foothold* here? What on earth do you think I am doing with my life here?"

"You are studying, Alec." Her voice was not steady but it was strong. "You are preparing for your future career. You know it."

"Ah, am I?" He spoke now in tones that greatly resembled her own when she lashed out at all those who had attempted to destroy her in her youth. "Preparing! And I suppose I should go on preparing until I am an old man! Is that what you mean?"

"Alec, you are shouting, my dear."

"Am I, Adele? Then allow me to do so, if you are going to be so obstinate and unfeeling." He stood up.

"For God's sake, dear boy, take your seat again. . . . You cannot go until we have talked it all out. We need not lose our heads. Who else wants you to succeed more than I, answer me that."

He compressed his lips to a line, and sat down stiffly.

"I am going in a few weeks, Adele, and I am going for good. I will never come back to this cinder heap again. I am sick of *preparing*! Sick of waiting. Let Ned take care of his mother. Or Keith Gresham!" He shot this last name at her with deliberate malice.

Her lips moved convulsively, then compressed into a thin line.

"I thought that you of all people," he went on, "would encourage me, wish me Godspeed, urge me, command me to go! But you are, when the chips are down, as cautious and as careful, as timid and as deliberate, as any old-maid schoolteacher. After all, *your* mistakes were always supported by a fat bankroll!"

He watched her head lower. He expected tears to flow, as in the case of Elaine.

"What does your singing teacher think of your plans?" came her rejoinder.

He could not believe she would say something so irrelevant and meaningless after his barb. Perhaps she had not heard what he said.

Without warning, Alec's voice broke, and he came near to letting out a sob, but he bit his lips and replied with a vehemence that brought back to her own astonished consciousness her quarrel with her father when he had discovered she was pregnant by George Etheredge.

"Paul Ferrand is afraid as you are, Adele. . . . After all, he has stayed here all his life. He is jealous I am leaving!"

He stopped short. She was already on her way to her little cabinet. She opened it and took out her medicine.

"Can't you leave that stuff alone even for one evening?" he cried.

She merely took a swallow in reply. He was frightened for her. Her attention had lapsed, certainly. What he did not know was that her mind had gone back a quarter of a century, back to her father, back to George Etheredge, back to running away, coming home, waiting, giving up, surrendering.

"Adele, forgive me." He was standing by her, but she was still far away.

"You said your singing teacher was jealous." She spoke dryly. As on some of her visits to the Royal Theater, the film had broken, there was a wait, and then the picture began again at the place it had broken off.

"Adele," he said, frightened at her behavior, "are you all right?" He reached for her hand.

"I have not been all right for a long time, Alec." She broke away from him and started toward her chair. He was astonished at her gait. One felt she had on a crown, the way she walked away from him. She sat down and smoothed out the folds of her sumptuous dress, which had suddenly changed color in the deepening shadows, so that it resembled purple.

"Jealous." She went back to his charge against his singing

teacher. "I suppose we are all jealous of you. After all, you have your whole life before you. We have only days before us. Evenings, rather. A few evenings in winter."

"Yes." He smiled, thinking, perhaps not having heard what she had just said. "He wants me to stay here forever and keep him company in his afterglow of failed ambition."

"I do admire your courage, Alec." She gave her testimony now. "I was only thinking perhaps of your welfare. Ambition doesn't recognize welfare. If you must go, you must. Even if you have no prospects there."

He glared at her.

"I will make my own prospects! It is you, in fact, who taught me that. It's you, after all, who fired me with ambition, urged me on to make something of myself. Then when I am ready to follow the teachings of my mentor, you pull the rug from under me, and take another drink!"

She stared out the great window into the street.

"I was only thinking of that great empty city, I suppose. That was where everything went wrong for me. But you are, after all, a man. You can make your own way. They can't catch you, hold you as they did me. Don't be angry with me, Alec, because I love you. Love is selfish, jealous, wants to hold. Forgive me. Go, Alec, go. You're right to leave me. You're right to leave all of us."

She got to her feet and went to the window. Some workmen were changing the words on the marquee at the Royal Theater. Her eyes were too wet to see what the letters were.

He went over to where she stood staring out at the street.

"Do you mean that, Adele? You are ordering me to go?"

"On one condition, Alec." She turned to look him straight in the face. "That you will let me give you something. Money. No, don't look at me that way. I insist on giving you something. Alec, I have a lot, and what do I need it for? The only expense I foresee in my own future is the undertaker's bill, and that will be the cheapest one they can provide." She laughed. "If you won't take it, I will burn it in front of you. So it's settled."

He struggled with a tumult he had never known before, and which kept him speechless.

He held both her hands. "If I don't go now, Adele, Elaine and Ned will hold me forever. I have just enough strength at this moment to break the bonds and leave. They have me in a straitjacket. I can't breathe without their say-so. Don't you understand? I know I am doing wrong to leave them, to clear out. But if I stay I will die, or be like those ex-soldiers in the vets' hospital. Maybe I won't die in a year or in ten. Maybe I'd last for fifteen, but not as me, not as a man. But as a wraith. That's one of your favorite words. Don't you see?" He brought her white hands up to his lips.

"More than anybody you could tell this all to, Alec, I do see." She took her hands away from his mouth. "My whole life has been that of a wraith. Evening came to me early. My whole life has been evening. I died, Alec, long ago. No, no, I am not asking for your sympathy or pity. I have none for myself. I don't want sympathy from anybody. I am telling you what my life is. I ask only one thing from you. That you take my money. And when you run out that you ask me for more. You don't need to write me letters. I don't need them anymore. I don't need anything, except to give you what you need. You will succeed. It is a great and terrible city, Alec, so be careful. Treasure only your gift. Don't give anything to anybody. Don't trust anybody but those who can help you with your gift. Don't give love, or receive it. Just your gift, Alec. Do you hear me?"

He took her in his arms and kissed her mouth, her cheeks; then looking down from his height on her crown of hair he kissed her there.

But she barely returned any pressure or affection. Perhaps, if she had let herself then, she would have smothered him with her strong love, and like Elaine, would have closed the door forever against his leaving.

"Don't ever look back, Alec, once you're gone."

Those were her last words to him that night.

Adele had been contemplating going to see Dr. Radwell for a "consultation" even before Keith Gresham's fearful descent on her. But after Alec's visit, and his informing her he was leaving forever, she realized she must see the doctor at once. Her left hand trembled so badly now that she could grasp objects only with the utmost pain and difficulty. Her mouth too sometimes would go into a kind of spasm while she was speaking. No other doctor could be considered in her case, she reflected. At least Charles knew who she was, and what she had been. And she felt at last she knew who he was. One castoff cannot very easily look down upon another.

With this thought held firmly in mind, she got up her courage, hired a livery cab, and drove to the doctor's house without a prior appointment.

Charles Radwell still lived in his mother's wood-frame Victorian house with the porch of intricate workmanship enfolding it on all sides, and atop the whole edifice a kind of turret, from which she fancied the doctor often looked down on the world with a mixture of pity and scorn. Near the decaying old house was a little brook, and immense elm trees, which made the house itself invisible until one entered the sloping yard. Nearby a small church of obscure denomination pealed out the time every quarter hour, and over all this was the sky, free of obstructions, of a blue not known to towns, and filled with countless soaring birds of every description.

The doctor, seated over a book, with a French cigarette in his hand, barely looked up to greet her. He had never been to France, but a huge map of Paris hung over his desk, and he read almost nothing outside of medical works except French nineteenth-century novels. But the pity was, as she often told him, he read them in English!

"I was expecting you, Adele." He smiled derisively and watched her take off her big-brimmed hat, with one large flower attached to it.

She sat down as near him as she could, on a little leather hassock.

"What is that scent you are wearing?" he wondered abruptly.

Confused for the moment, she looked about her, as if absentmindedly she had brought in a spray of flowers of some kind.

"Oh," she laughed. "White rose," she told him. "My mother always used it." She picked up one of the novels he was reading.

"Charles, I cannot sleep."

"I don't wonder." He smiled again his faint, sad, tenuous smile.

"If some crazy doughboy paid me a visit like he did you, I might have difficulty closing my eyes too."

She shrugged her shoulders.

"But it's very bad this time," she began in a low whisper, as if perhaps Keith Gresham himself might be outside listening to her.

"And splitting headaches," she complained. "Don't you have some very old remedy for that, which people took long ago? Something that will relieve it better than those little purple pills you gave me last time?"

"Everything which I dispense, Adele, is what people took long ago." He took her hand and pressed it.

"But if you're going to have these fracases and free-for-alls with young soldiers, my dear, and with soldiers young enough to be your grandsons, I'm afraid no medicine or elixir known will be much of a palliative."

"My grandsons! Really, Charles." She laughed in spite of herself.

She was tempted to say, "And of course you don't sleep with your groom, who is only one-third your age."

She felt he divined what she was thinking for he said immediately: "What I do wrong, Adele, nobody hears of."

"I don't know that I agree with you." She considered his remark. "I find that we tell everybody the truth at last, no matter how secret we think we are."

"But you have always managed to make your fallings-by-the-wayside public knowledge, dear Adele."

"Except this time I am not going to have a child, Charles."

"Certainly not from Keith Gresham." He said this with a kind of cruel directness she found offensive.

"The other matter which has distressed me is that Alec Cottrell is leaving home."

She felt that the doctor changed color as she said this.

"You're certain?" He drew in on the cigarette.

"*He's* certain. He's told me he's going for good, Thanksgiving."

"But what will his mother do if he goes?"

Adele smiled. She recalled Charles's long, *slavish*, she supposed was the word, devotion to his own mother. A devotion that had made him capable, she had often confided to her own diary, a diary no one spied on, capable finally of sleeping only with a groom.

Charles got up, upsetting the ashtray, which Adele picked up for him.

"Won't you try one of these, Adele?" He offered her one of his French cigarettes.

She took one, and he lit it from a gleaming gold lighter.

"Didn't you try to stop him, Adele?"

"Alec?"

"Of course, Alec! You don't think I meant the doughboy, do you?"

"Oh, Charles . . . you doctors are so horrid always. . . . But you're the only man I can turn to. You know everything, I suppose, and you care for nobody. You've exhausted any source of love you ever had."

"When did I do that? You only mean when I ceased to care for you, Adele. There are other loves, too, but you would only understand them in some French novel, never in life."

He got up and raised the blind so that the sunset was visible.

"Adele"—he turned to her with so eloquent a look he appeared young again—"stop him from going! Alec! Don't let him go to Chicago."

She put her cigarette out, half-consumed, but he almost fiercely put another in her mouth and lit it for her.

"You are the only one who can stop him." He pursued his thought. "Chicago! That boy? He can't go."

"But he will," she told him mysteriously. It was the doctor's eagerness for her to stop Alec that allowed her to see that he really was leaving, that he would go.

"If you could only see how determined he is to leave." She thought back to her session with him. "How he hates Fonthill. And how he chafes under his mother's and his brother's domination of him."

"How could poor Ned dominate him."

"You'd be surprised, Charles." Adele broke into a derisive grin.

He looked at her sharply.

"I must tell you that I have not been able to erase from my memory the picture of your veteran lying without a stitch on. I was as unprepared for that as when I first began practicing medicine, and my first case was a young boy who . . . blew his brains out. . . . I thought I was hardened, Adele, to everything by now. You spoke of my 'exhausted' love. My sense of the terror of life isn't consumed, at any rate."

She gazed at him admiringly.

"Try to get Alec to see the light of reason," he begged her.

"You never left your mother. Other men do," she said at last.

Looking out at the sun he did not appear to have heard her.

"I will see him again, of course, Charles," she promised. He nodded, still looking outdoors.

"But only on the condition you give me something properly strong for my nerves. After all, why should Adele Bevington be the only woman in the world who is not allowed to sleep."

"Yes, I wonder why." He turned to face her, smiling.

"You strong, dreadful American women," he muttered and hurried out of the room.

She opened the novel he was reading and read a paragraph. She shook her head. She laughed.

"What did those old French boys know about a woman either!" she scoffed aloud just as Radwell was reentering the room.

"What are you muttering, a curse?" he asked her. He had brightened considerably.

She looked at the little box he was carrying in his hand, and rose and took the medicine from him.

"Will this really help, Charles?"

"Not at all," he replied. "Not in the most minimal way." He kissed her on the mouth.

"You men who don't like women, or like women perhaps too well," she reflected. "Like him you call the doughboy. Keith Gresham. You all kiss so well. Rough male men kiss so badly. Often don't kiss at all. They kiss like a dog bites. There! I bet you won't find that observation in one of your French novels."

He laughed in spite of himself, then looked at her searchingly.

"I will speak to Alec. I will ask him again not to go away," she said.

"But you won't mean it if you ask him," he said with a queer sadness. "No, I see, I guess, now, that he will go."

"Charles, you must remember something. You never left home."

He looked away, then smiled and took her hand.

"Even if Alec goes to Chicago, and stays, Adele, he won't ever have left either. Home is all he will ever have had, if he goes to the ends of the earth. I guess I didn't need to leave home to find that out."

She waited a long time before speaking again.

"You're sure then you've given me real medicine, Charles, and not some little concoction of sugar and salt here."

"I'd be the last man on earth ever to try to deceive you, Adele," he told her, and opened the door to the street. The livery cab was waiting there, with the driver inside, dozing.

"After the medicine calms you down, I'd like to talk to you also one day about that young ex-soldier of yours. He has come home to stay."

She waved goodbye and thanked him for the medicine by kissing the little box it was contained in.

National events turned ugly, in Elaine's phrase, but she barely read the newspapers now. And she no longer read Alec's diary. She had only to look at his face to know he was leaving, was, in a sense, already far away.

The "ugly" national events became local. Angry farmers who had lost their savings in the Fonthill First National Bank gathered one day round the closed doors, demanding their money. A plate-glass window was broken, then the door was forced by the crowd, beaten down by sheer weight of numbers. Soon the farmers, the unemployed young men, the drifters and wastrels who lived around the courthouse, had charged into the bank itself, over-turning furniture, potted palms, cuspidors, green lamps, and ripping down all the calendars, as if time and money were no more. Unable to control them, the local police had summoned the state militia. There were several persons killed, many injured seriously. The town of Fonthill was cited throughout the national press, and the riot described as a "straw in the wind."

But Elaine barely finished reading the account of the insurrection. The last entry in Alec's diary was more vivid to her, written so far as she was concerned in true blood.

She had already relinquished him, had already let him go!

One ray of hope entered her dark house. Keith Gresham, looking emaciated but somehow more handsome, his hair cut severely short, his gray eyes larger, more hollow and accentuated by the long curling lashes, more winning than ever. Her open arms caught the veteran off guard. He turned away from her, choking spasmodically.

"I thought you would turn me away, Elaine," he kept sputtering. "My own mother would have."

While the other boarders were gathering in the front parlor prior to sitting down at the supper table, Elaine conferred with Keith in the pantry, a room almost as large as the dining hall.

"It was all Adele's fault, Keith," she repeated countless times. He shook his head dispiritedly.

"Adele should have been in the films," Elaine went on, "where she could have acted out all these roles of hers without fear of arrest or censure. After all, they show everything now, ancient Rome and its orgies. She has missed her calling."

She tried to give Keith to understand that anything he had done was forgiven, but her forgiveness and absolution only made him more miserable. He wondered now—not only what he had done at Adele's, but what people thought he had done. And Elaine's blanket forgiveness of him tonight made him think he must have done everything.

Keith was placed that night at the head of the table.

Under the strong center light, a kind of flashy, ornate chandelier of elaborate workmanship, ostentatious enough to have graced a sporting house of the era, all the other boarders could see that Keith had received considerable damage from having smashed the mirror, lamps, chairs, and imported vases at Adele's on the night of his fracas. His face was still badly cut up (at least fourteen stitches had been taken on his mouth alone), and he had lost some teeth. As all looked at him furtively from time to time, it was inevitably brought home to them that sitting facing the boarders was a man who had time and again used the bayonet against living soldiers, who had thrown grenades, killing many, who had, it was said, blown out the brains of twenty German officers in a night foray. And despite his heroism, so went the story, he had misbehaved so violently after the armistice, he was, despite his many citations and medals, brought home in irons.

"Keith?" Elaine's troubled voice came to him, and he raised his head, smiling painfully with his injured lips.

Speaking directly to her as if they were alone together in the dining room, he said loudly: "You have not turned me from the door. Beautiful—beautiful—" but he stopped, sensing now there were others present. Then, rising awkwardly, and the linen napkin, larger than those that had been given to the other boarders, falling from his hand, he made his way straight to Elaine. She rose questioningly, and almost fell into his outstretched arms. He kissed her again and again, while a faint cry came from some of the women present.

"I will be worthy of her after all." He turned with a note of fury in his tone to the other boarders, who, it seemed to him, had all at once appeared uninvited. "I will show everybody that Lieutenant Keith Gresham is, after all, a gentleman."

With shaking hand, he pulled from his pocket some kind of medal, and with savage methodical certitude pinned it on his breast.

Then saluting again and again, with a cry that sounded like terror, he stumbled back to his seat of honor and spread the napkin across his chest.

But Elaine remained unaware of the impression Keith had made on her sons and the other boarders. She only knew the happiness of having found a new son to take the place of the one who, as surely as dawn and darkness rise and fall, was about to leave her house forever.

Elaine noticed, despite her own preoccupation, that Ned watched Alec with constant worried stares. When Alec had been considered a permanent part of the household, someone who would always be present, never absent for too long, Ned had wrangled and quarreled with him, was ever ready to pick a fight—but if the antagonist was to leave and never to return, what then?

In this Elaine understood her younger son very well.

So Ned would gaze at Alec, until the older brother one night, throwing down his napkin at table, shouted: "What is so absorbing in my countenance that you sit staring holes in me?" (Alec had been reading an old novel with faded paper and broken spine, which Adele had lent him ages ago, and which somehow he had never got round to reading until now, and he spoke like the abandoned hero of the yarn.)

"I was admiring your snappy haircut, Alec," Ned replied with his old sarcasm, but the remark lacked the usual bite and sting. He spoke almost as if he had said, "I was only hoping, Alec, you would change your mind and not jump ship."

"Then keep your damned prying eyes to your dinner plate," Alec snapped. "You ought to know what I look like by now without acting like a photographer."

"Will you two stop your confounded arguing!" Elaine intervened, but without the forcefulness or the authority she had exercised in days past. For she knew her role as "umpire" or "referee" in their constant skirmishes with one another already belonged to days soon to be relegated to "past time." Only she would remember them forever, if everybody else lost track of them.

Elaine had also observed that almost in spite of himself, Ned was becoming closer to their star boarder, Keith. She thought she knew why. She knew that the man he had always tried to look up to was Val Dougherty, but when the real trouble came, when their house appeared about to tumble and fall, Ned sought out the companionship and trust of a man who had known more sorrow than the whole town put together. For what did Val know but horses and pride in his own self-sufficiency. On the other hand, Keith must understand or at least accept all human shortcomings, griefs, failures, heartbreak.

At first, it is true, she had tried to keep the two apart. She had felt that Keith might say or do something that would propel Ned still farther on his truant path. But from the time she had learned from Alec's diaries that their "mainstay" was about to leave them and remove his protection from them forever, she almost pushed her younger son into Keith's protective custody. And the ex-lieutenant, shattered by his latest "outrage" at Adele's, had the impression at times that he was being put in the stockade again, and his only other fellow prisoner was Ned, who, too young to understand, was still a gentle listener, incapable of passing censorious judgments on the veteran.

One evening at work in the kitchen Elaine let her eyes stray out to the grape arbor. There the two sat, Keith and Ned. Their calm and peaceableness in one another's company caused her to marvel. They looked, at that moment, inseparable, and she felt that something of the spirit of both Marius Cottrell and his son Alec had come to rest in the person of the star boarder.

"All the same, Val Dougherty must wonder what has become of you," Elaine said a few days later as the last of the dishes were being put away after the evening meal. "Don't tell me you have given up your riding lessons."

"Keith has promised he will show me how to shoot," Ned told her.

Her first inclination was to forbid him to handle a gun, but then she knew she must say and do nothing to drive Keith from their company and their evening meal. He must remain now as their mainstay.

"Very well," she began, picking her words carefully, "try to remember to be careful when you handle firearms. Pay attention to his instructions."

She was combing his hair as she talked to him, for its natural curliness had got in such a snarl he found he could not get his own comb through it properly, and Keith was coming in a few minutes to take him to a picture show.

"Now let me look at you," Elaine said when she had combed out all the snarls.

He stood up and exchanged a troubled look with her.

"That will have to do until we can get you to the barber," she said, putting down the comb. "Hurry on now or you'll miss the beginning of the movie."

The late autumn thunderstorm had kept Ned fitfully awake, partly because he liked to see the lightning so much, and perhaps even more to hear the thunder. He was always sorry he could not climb one of the big elms during one of these electrical storms so he could get closer to the different-colored lightning flashes and hear even closer the ear-splitting thunderbolt. "Thor is driving his war chariot," he whispered under the covers.

Ned heard the door to his room open, and bare feet on the threshold.

Peeking out from the covers of the quilt, made by his grandmother long ago, he saw Alec, hair ruffled, no top to his pajamas.

"Neddy?"

That was the first time in maybe two years Alec had called him that.

"Can I come in, Neddy?"

"You're in, ain't you?" Ned spoke with the quilt still covering his face and head. Alec came over and sat down on the edge of the bed. Something must be up, Ned knew, and he brought his head out from the quilt.

"Well?"

"I've had a terrible dream. Nightmare. Can I get in under the covers with you?"

Alec was shivering as if he was about to have a chill.

"Oh, all right. But only for a while." Ned remembered too well how Alec insisted that he sleep alone.

"I know I haven't always been good to you, as a brother should," Alec began when he was nestling close to the younger boy. Alec smelled of liquor.

"That's gospel all right," Ned scoffed.

"My dream was so God-damn awful, Neddy. I'm still all goosepimples."

"Oh, you heard the thunder in your sleep probably."

"Heard hell, if you ask me."

"Well, let's have it then," Ned snapped, turning his face away from Alec. But the older boy held him tight.

"I was walkin' in this woods, Ned, only the trees were all flags, you understand?"

"You mean like the Stars and Stripes, or like flowers?"

"Like the Stars and Stripes, yes, only they wasn't like Old Glory either. They were more like banners and pennants. They kept waving like they were alive."

"What's so scary about that?"

"You wait." Alec raised himself up in bed so that he could look down on Ned's face and lips.

"The flags begun to sort of rise up then like plants, you know, that grow a thousand times faster than they do in nature. They

rose and rose and unfurled like plants, too. They wrapped theirselves about me, first my little toe, then the rest of my toes, then
my ankles. They made sounds like a woman's long dress rustling,
you know, at fancy balls. They kept furling, furling, furling until
they covered me tight as bandages . . . head to foot. Oh, Neddy,
Neddy." His brother was sobbing as he told his dream. Ned took
his hand in his, though he was not so much sympathetic perhaps
as scared.

"Then when the flags had entirely wound themselves around
me," the narrator went on, "around me so I couldn't move nor
breathe, there was this terrible crash."

"The thunder of course."

"This crash in the dream was not thunder, and when it sounded the whole field of flags begun to take me down into the black
earth with them . . . down, down . . . oh, Neddy, Neddy."

Ned let Alec hold him and thought it over.

Outside the thunder was getting more distant, but the lightning came even more frequently, and many of its flashes looked
pink, almost green at times. Ned had never seen so much
lightning for as far back as he could remember.

"I wonder what it all means," Alec said after he had quieted
down a bit. He too stared out at the sky.

"Search me."

"But scared as I am, Neddy, terrified maybe out of my wits as
this dream has made me, I got to tell you something. You are,
after all, my brother."

"Nothing we can do will change that, all right."

"And I care for you and love you, Neddy. Don't always show it
maybe. You know how brothers are. . . . But if I don't leave
Elaine, I'll perish. . . . Like the flags that wrapped theirselves
about me and took me down into the black earth. I got to leave
home and become a man. I can't be her helpmeet in a boardinghouse! Neddy, look at me!"

"I've looked at you all my life, Alec. . . . I'm lookin'. I'm
lookin'."

All at once Alec kissed him on the mouth.

"I have to leave," he repeated. "I can't stay or I'll perish."

"We knowed you were leavin' anyhow, Alec . . . so go. Elaine
knows it too."

"How?"

"All I know," he lied, not wanting to raise the issue of the diary, "all I can tell you is she said she was resigned to your lightin' out. She's expectin' you to leave."

"And she feels she can get on without me being the head of the household?"

"Christ, Elaine is the head of the household. She'd get on if she lost a thousand sons, and you know it."

"I could hug you for that for as long as I live. . . . She is a strong woman, ain't she?"

"Oh, yes. . . . Elaine is that."

"But it won't cut her to bits to lose me?"

"Not forever," Ned said cautiously. He was beginning to feel the need for sleep.

"I know I will miss you both desperately when I pull up stakes. . . . It will half kill me to go. But if I don't go now, Ned, I'll never go. I'll just stay here forever and be like Elaine's husband and main support. That's what I can't take. . . . She thinks I'm to stay forever."

"No, she don't, Alec. She don't anymore, anyhow." He thought again of the diary. "She's prepared to lose you, Alec. She wants you to go. Then her and me will get on some way or other. She has her gentlemen friends, too, after all."

"Yes, God damn it, she does." Alec was all at once indignant and bitter.

"And there's Keith Gresham now, too," Ned added with sleepy belligerence.

"So there is," Alec muttered between clenched teeth.

"If worst comes to worst, I can always go work for Val Dougherty. He's rich as Croesus. . . ."

"Oh, Christ, you don't want to work for that man, do you?"

"We'll see . . . we'll see." All at once Ned appeared the older of the two, the calmer, and out of his barely fifteen years, he was in possession of all the advice and counsel.

"If only I had not had that dream, Neddy. . . . If only I hadn't seen those flags and that black earth they came up out of. I'm telling you, I'll never be the same fellow again."

"You'll go to Chicago, Alec, and you'll make good. Mark my words."

"Amen."

Alec leaned over then and stared at his younger brother. Then he lowered his head and kissed him as he used to do when Ned was a baby. He kissed him softly, but the tears from his eyes spattered against Ned's face as smartly as hard rain or small pieces of hail.

"You go back to sleep now, Neddy, and thank you. . . . I'll always be grateful for this little talk if I live to be a hundred. . . . Good night."

Even when his wife and foster daughter had lived with him, Valentine Dougherty often walked about his considerable property stark naked. Few, if any, cars drove near this section of his holdings, but even if people had come close enough to see him unclothed, it is doubtful he would have cared by now. His walking mother-naked took place usually at night. On almost every tree and post he had affixed signs:

NO TRESPASSING
VIOLATERS WILL BE PERSECUTED
OR SHOT!

Now that his wife and "brat" had left he felt free at last from violators of all kind. For he regarded, finally, humanity itself as a trespasser where he was concerned, and had the world ended in conflagration and he remained its last and sole inhabitant, he would have felt no regret but would have breathed a sigh of relief. He had felt this way even before he had been an infantryman in the war. But his experiences in battle, which he had never communicated to another human being, must have reinforced his deep-seated anger and his loathing of the human race, which came out in garbled curses and imprecations when he was drunk.

Despite the fact it was now late October and the nights had a touch of frost, Val took his evening walk in the raw. He had never liked clothes. Nothing he could buy or ask his wife to buy for him at the Army Surplus or J. C. Penney or other ready-to-wear clothing stores suited his gigantic frame. Once at the age of fifteen he had shot a bear, and had crudely cleaned and dressed the skin to fit his body. It was the only garment he had ever liked, but he tired of it also, and had it made into a rug.

Striding naked, then, toward the stone quarry tonight, he became aware of the sound of footsteps, then of sighs, groans, muttered words. He stopped in his tracks and sniffed like an animal that is aware of a hunter. His breath came from him in large white clouds; a sweat, stemming probably from rage or permanent disappointment, began to break out over his body, making him feel the chill of the night. His tongue, pressed against his large upper teeth, made menacing sounds that recalled some sort of reptile about to strike. Then a kind of gurgling came from deep in his throat.

The figure of a man crossed his path and rushed frantically toward the dark mass where the stone quarry waters were situated.

"Stop!" Val commanded in a voice that seemed to echo for miles around, but the one word coming from his throat sounded barely human and made the figure hurry on faster toward the quarry's edge.

Val ran then like one of his own half-tamed horses. He was none too quick in pursuit, for the figure he followed was now poised above the quarry, ready to plunge below. The horse trainer lunged, caught the trespasser by the throat, and dragged him back; and then, in astonishment at the identity of his prey, he threw the man to the earth, from which hundreds of wild thistles had been growing.

"Judge Hitchmough!" Val cried, and there was some trace of awe, if not respect, in his tone, but then, a wave of his incorrigible misanthropy coming over him, he kicked the prostrate figure, and demanded: "What are you doin' on my land? Didn't you see my signs, you!"

"Let me alone, why can't you . . . oh let me alone," came the muffled response.

Val Dougherty began to laugh. Then, feeling the chill of the night, he rubbed his huge arms and clasped them over his chest.

"So what do we have here, ladies and gentlemen?" He spat out the words, strings of saliva following his question. "The great Judge Hitchmough himself, trespassing on private property. And about to exit from this world as a suicide to boot!"

He kicked the prostrate figure and screamed: "What are you doing on my land. Hey? Have you read so much law by day you can't see a No Trespassing sign by night?"

Val kicked the old man again, and the judge let out a cry that sounded almost like one of relief rather than pain. Perhaps to be kicked was of such little consequence after what he had already suffered that night.

"Get up on your feet, you old bag of bones, or do you want me to call the state police?" Val said with quiet loathing, still kicking the judge, and then, when there was no response, he bent over, picked the old man up bodily and slung him over his shoulder, and headed indifferently toward the back of his house with his burden carried as nonchalantly as a sack of weeds.

In the kitchen where he bore him, Val was further disgusted somehow to see the judge had no shoes on.

He almost threw the half-conscious jurist into a chair.

Studying his guest for a moment, Val shouted: "Since you've broke the law on so many counts tonight, Your Honor, shall I offer you a drink of homemade moonshine and we can break the law together?"

"Serve anything you wish," the old man replied. He took off his glasses and peered through them. They were broken.

"And Your Honor won't have me arrested then tomorrow morning for violating the Volstead Act, as you did years ago with the whores at the Carlyle House after you had enjoyed their bodies the night before?"

"Insolence, insolence! Everything, everywhere, nothing but insolence." The old man spoke with expressionless fatigue. He looked at the dreadful drink his host banged down on the table before him.

"Insolence, maybe. But the truth, absolutely! Which you ain't familiar with, Judge."

The old man drank almost all the liquor down at one gulp.

"That harridan has brought me to this," the judge said after a pause.

In reply, Val poured him another drink from the huge jar that held the spirits.

"You were a fool to have rescued me," the old man babbled on. He glared at his rescuer with resentment.

Val spat on the floor. "I wouldn't allow your whited sepulcher of a body to befoul my quarry waters, Judge. What if next summer some housewife was to begin chipping a piece of ice and seen your eyes or teeth or one of your fingers sticking out from what should be pure congealed water, huh? Did you ever think of the consequence of your wanting to kill yourself in my quarry water, you hideous old goblin? No, you're damned tootin' you didn't. Besides it's too easy a death for the likes of you. You who've sent the poor and the hungry and the jobless to jail these thousand times. You should rot in a dungeon until you recognize you're a man, if man you are. But you never admitted you were a man, did you, as you sat on your hairy old balls in your holy black robes, did you?"

"Ha!" the judge snorted, and when his mouth opened Val saw he had no teeth at all.

"If I did not relish my freedom so much, you old worm"—Val went up directly now to the empty hole of a mouth of his visitor—"I would dash your rotten brains out here and now with this hammer," and he raised a fearful-looking piece of iron over the judge's head. The old man turned away, but soon took up the drink again and swallowed more of the corrosive draft.

"So a harridan, you say, drove you to your suicide," Val sneered, still studying his guest with savage scrutiny. He downed another drink. "And who is this harridan, may I inquire? And where does she reside?"

"You gloat, don't you"—the old man edged toward the tone of eloquence that had made his court famous—"now I have no power, and my court is no longer in session."

Some of the judge's authority and therefore menace came out in those words and the glance from his half-blind eyes, so that Val paused for a moment.

Then, slapping the old man smartly across the mouth, he cried, "You are in my court, and I asked you a question. The name of the harridan!" At the same moment he snatched away the jug of moonshine that the old man was reaching for.

Laughing, he himself drank for a long while, then belched with rich satisfaction.

"I will never tell you," the judge said.

"You'll do as you're told in this house, and you'll drink only when I tell you to drink." He laughed again as he saw the old man's eyes stare at the jug of liquor with such longing.

"So my illegal booze titillates your old palate, does it? By Christ, I wish it had rat lye in it."

He pushed the jug toward his visitor, and the judge picked it up and, like his host, drank from the lip of the vessel.

"Rotten to the core," Val observed while he watched the old man narrowly.

Neither Val nor his visitor heard the door to the kitchen open and could not see Ned Cottrell, fresh from his long confab with Alec, too disturbed for sleep, standing on the threshold. But finally the judge turned and saw him, recognizing the boy even without his glasses, and wincing as he saw this new witness to his shame. Val then turned about and recognized his pupil.

"You would come at such a time. And what are you doin' out of bed at an hour like this."

Ned did not reply. He was too thunderstruck to speak as he took in the sight of these two men together, drinking in the dead of night, Val stark naked, the judge drunk, covered with mire, and without his glasses.

"Well, you can drive the judge home then, when he's drunk enough," Val sneered. "Come in and park your ass on a chair and keep your lip buttoned shut." "Now tell this court"—Val raised his voice to deafening volume—"for this court is in session, by Christ, tell us the name of your persecutor!"

When the old man looked blank, Val shouted: "The name of the harridan who drove you to suicide!"

"Ah, *her*," the accused replied, and passed his hand over his face.

The judge turned momentarily to Ned as if the boy might prod his memory.

Val Dougherty let out a laugh so demoniacal and boisterous that, used as he was to the sound, Ned shivered, then getting up his courage, said: "Val, shouldn't you put something on?"

Val cuffed the boy across the mouth. "Don't interrupt the witness." He turned his baleful look again toward the judge.

"Her name!" he repeated.

"Who would it be, do you suppose, but Widow Hughes," the old man replied, and he raised his eyes to the rafters as if he had committed perjury or perhaps blasphemy. "Rosa Hughes," the old man testified again.

"Don't repeat answers to questions without permission of the court," Val warned him. Then, turning to both his visitors, he roared: "Mind whose roof you are under here! Both of you! You are under my domain and my right of property. One of you has committed a criminal act tonight, and the other," he said, looking at Ned, "is a spoiled, incorrigible stuckup underhanded little snot. . . . Drink!" he commanded Ned, whom the judge was eyeing with a kind of amazed admiration, for the young man was as calm and unmoved by the carrying-on of the horse trainer as if they were rehearsing the scene before the picture-show camera.

Ned took the glass proffered him and drank off a mouthful.

"Well?" Val demanded the boy's verdict on the drink.

"It's a scorcher all right," Ned told him, and both the judge and Val snickered in spite of themselves.

"But returning to this case"—Val came back to the proceedings in progress—"how did that bewigged old hellion Rosa Hughes push you to drown yourself on my land? . . . The boy here should hear it from your own lips, shouldn't he, especially since he is going to drive you home once you are plastered enough, and since, living next door to the hag, he knows her to a T."

The judge shook his head and tasted more of the moonshine.

"I have this day been expelled from the Altrusa Club," the old man began. "By her hand. I had forgotten she was lifetime president." He took out a piece of crumpled newspaper from his coat pocket. "But instead of informing me by letter, though I suppose a letter eventually will come to me, she had it printed in the daily newspaper, in *The Courier*." He waved the clipping now about. "On the front page! Of course she paid the editor to have it placed in that spot, no question about it. So that I saw myself in headlines as if I had committed a crime, as if I were an outcast!"

Val had taken the clipping and was reading it, Ned saw, with difficulty, moving his lips, and going from syllable to syllable.

Banging down his two fists finally on the table, Val cried out: "But what is this little dismissal from an old ladies' club compared to the sentences you've handed down over the years? Answer me that! Answer the court that! For this court is in session, are you aware of that, you old molted baboon. In session! And you have been found guilty!"

"Guilty of what?" the old man inquired in a kind of childlike way.

Val turned to Ned. "He asks, the old crud, what he's guilty of."

The judge winced and held his head in his hands.

"You are on trial," Val thundered on. "But with a different proviso, do you hear, than in your beshitted courtroom. In my court," Val went on with rising volume, "you shall be found guilty before the trial begins, during the trial's proceeding, and after the trial ends. Guilty, guilty, guilty! . . . No, no, don't sputter so. You know you always found anybody but the rich and powerful guilty even before the proceedings got under way in your court. For the first time in your life, Hitchmough, you are free to admit the truth: that you never allowed justice to be done or heard or pronounced once you put on your black robes and called your court in session."

"Stop it," the old man rang out, then lowering his voice till it was almost a thin whisper, uttered for his own ears: "Stop this fanfaronade. I will not be persecuted in this fashion a moment longer." He rose and turned to Ned with a look of pleading.

"Sit down," Val ordered him. "No witness has the right to rise without the permission of the court. And don't look to that little pissant for help, Judge. I am the man you have trespassed against, and as the sign says in plain English, Violators will be persecuted. Therefore put your bony ass back on the wood of the chair, and don't open your mouth again until the court tells you to."

"Put on some clothes, why don't you, if you're to hold a trial." Ned repeated his objurgation.

Instead of flying into a new rage at the boy's statement, Val only snorted, and went to a corner of the room, where an old unmended bathrobe was hanging over a stepladder, seized it, and flung it over his shoulders without bothering to put his arms through the sleeves.

Clearing his throat, wiping his mouth of spittle and moonshine, he continued: "By Christ, I'll teach an old night-prowling possum like yourself to come invading my property, and with the prior intent and purpose of drowning yourself in my quarry waters!"

Whether Val was "acting" or not Ned could not be sure, but the horse trainer rolled his eyes and twisted his mouth until his contortions were enough to put the fear of God into the most hardened criminal, not to mention trespasser.

"You will answer my questions and you shall tell the truth, or by God, I will issue the order here and now for you to be hanged."

Ned at this point laid his head down on the wood of the dining table.

"Sit up and keep your face turned toward the accused," Val ordered the boy. "Or by Jesus I will break your neck in the bargain."

"Let me take the judge home," Ned begged him, and sat up straight in his chair. "You've played prosecutor enough. You've said enough. Can't you see he's half-dead with fright?"

"I can take it, Ned," the old man intervened. "Let him have his say. . . . I have deserved this. I take cognizance I have not been the man I thought I was."

"That's a mealymouthed understatement to take the cake, if I ever heard one," Dougherty shouted. "Not the man you thought you was! When all the world knows you have been throughout every night and day of your life a damned bully, crook, cheat, and hypocrite! And had it been some other bloke's quarry you chose to drown yourself in, I'd not have lifted a finger to save you. But not in my waters will your corpse be allowed to float and rot. . . . The next time you feel like doing away with yourself go to Widow Hughes still, which she keeps in the bowels of her mansion, and drown yourself in her illegal rotgut. . . . Ha, our little jurist here didn't know the widow made illegal booze, did he? Why, she's been drunk ever since her husband's funeral."

"No, that's no so, Val," Ned interposed. "She don't touch a drop, and you know it. She don't need a drink to be crazy."

The judge studied Ned with a kind of rekindled curiosity and perhaps admiration.

"You will speak in this court only when spoken to, is that clear, Cottrell? Just because you've managed to fool your teachers enough to reach junior high school, don't pretend to Val Dougherty you're anything but a half-witted baboon and know-nothing and can't even keep your ass straight on a horse going at a amble."

Val pulled out now an old ledger from a little partition under the kitchen table, and pretended to leaf through it in search of "evidence."

"Years ago," the horse trainer proceeded, "Your Honor sentenced to the workhouse a girl friend of mine on the trumped-up charge she was a streetwalker. . . . Name of Nettie Howard. That girl," the horse trainer went on, "should have been my wife."

"I have no recollection of her. You must remember, Dougherty, I have not been on the bench for ten to fifteen sessions."

"No recollection of Nettie Howard! Then how old in creation are you?" Val wondered.

"Eighty-five this past June."

"That's too old to be yet alive, then, but by God this court will try you anyhow, and would try you if they had to dig you up from your grave."

"Dougherty, Dougherty," the old man beseeched him. "Let us have no more of this farce. Think of the example you are setting for this young man!"

"That *I* am setting, Your Honor. . . . Do you not recall you have attempted to do away with yourself tonight! By God, you have your nerve to talk about examples."

Val Dougherty hurried over to a cabinet cupboard nearby, unlocked it, and brought out a fifth of whiskey imported from Canada.

"Enough of rat poison," he mumbled, and broke the seal of the bottle with his teeth, and drank thirstily for at least a minute. Then, wiping his mouth against the back of his hand, he slammed the bottle down on the table and roared, "Drink, and be damned, the both of you."

The two men silently obeyed him, as Val went on leafing through the pages of his ledger.

"Why"—he began reading his own writing with as much difficulty as if he were consulting Blackstone—"why are you against Adele Bevington in the first place, and why have you borne false witness against her over the years?" He slammed the ledger shut.

"Adele Bevington?" the old man reflected, as if searching his mind for the identity of one long claimed by the oblivion of history.

"Adele Bevington." Dougherty repeated the name.

"Why, yes," the old man came to. "She was a harlot from her early youth, I recall." He sounded like someone talking in his sleep now.

"But did this harlot, as you call her, accept money for her services?" Val inquired, staring stonily at his ledger.

"She did the act of darkness gratis," the old man said, his eyes closed, his mouth almost sealed as he spoke. "For pure pleasure," he added.

"Where did you get the words 'act of darkness,' " Val said, not taking his eyes off the ledger.

"From an immortal bard," the old man muttered.

"Immortal bard, my ass!" The horse trainer turned to Ned, and then, seeing the boy was about to come up with an answer, he cried: "Button your lip, and keep it buttoned if you know what's good for you."

Whether it was the strong drink or his weariness and age, Judge Hitchmough began to fall into the spirit of this courtroom, and as if a real trial were in progress, faithfully and conscientiously answered one absurd question after another put to him by the owner of the Star-Lite Stables, as Ned, overcome by sleep, let his head fall over on the table, and began to snore. When he wakened with a start a few minutes later, the trial was still in progress.

"And to the best of your knowledge, then, was Widow Hughes herself a harlot?"

"Yes, to my best memory, sir, she was," came the old man's reply. "I believe she met men behind the Green Gables Dance Hall heavily disguised during the first year of her marriage. She had four abortions, according to Dr. What's-His-Name. Yes, four."

He held up four fingers.

"No, no, there you've made a terrible mistake, Judge." Ned rallied to the defense of the old woman. "She may be wicked in other ways, but she is down on fornication."

Both Val and the judge gazed at him with uncomprehending, dazed eyes, as if he had come out of the hard wood of the floor.

Looking at them closely, Ned saw they were both far gone in their cups.

"All women, my boy, are harlots," the old man mumbled, and

thin trickles of sweat fell from his brow to his cheeks and chin and to the table.

"And what are men then?" the boy wondered almost too softly to be heard.

"Why the jackasses women make of them," the judge answered in his old majesterial tone.

"Shall I drive him home in your car, Val?" Ned inquired, and stood up.

Putting on his broad-brimmed Borsolino hat, which he had bought in Chicago years ago, Val rose with difficulty and got out: "The verdict of this court is the defendant is guilty on all forty counts, and can go home and hang himself at his early convenience, provided he does the act of hanging in his own attic and with his own rope."

Having said this, the speaker of these words fell back in his chair, slipped out of the chair to the floor, and rolled over, openeyed but unconscious.

"Come on, my boy." The old man stood up and appeared absolutely cold sober. "We must get out of here before the dog comes to. Come on, this is no place for either of us."

Ned gave his friend stretched out on the floor a long look, and then, taking the judge's hand, he led him out to Val's truck, whose headlights were on, blazing into the country darkness.

It was the Sabbath, and Keith Gresham had started on his second quart of corn liquor, cleverly disguised in a jug of his own brewed black coffee, when, looking up from his meditations on how good it was his grandpa had left him such a big house to die in, he caught sight of (or spied, as he would have said) a small marching procession of very old men bearing banners, and waving a huge Old Glory. It was the last of the Grand Army of the Republic, those Civil War veterans who went round the town and county distributing leaflets about God and America, and visiting any and all veterns from whatever war, bestowing on them advice, and prayers, but not money. The leader of the procession was Captain Silas Cracknell, who had already prayed over Keith's head several times in the past month.

"By Christ, I am too drunk to get up and hide from them," Keith muttered.

Before Keith could bring another drop to his lips, Captain Cracknell, who at the time of this story was well over ninety, a veteran of the battle of Chickamauga and many others of similar fame, was standing over him. In his right hand he held the Bible, and in his left a small silk flag. The other ancients waited patiently on the uncut grass.

"Son, how are you this blessed morning?" Captain Cracknell began. "May I rest my bones on a chair, if you don't mind, as we have our little talk? . . . These walks uphill tell me I am no longer a young infantryman."

"Have a sip of coffee as you sit."

"Never touch the stuff."

"Brewed it myself, Captain Cracknell."

The old man had found a discarded rocker to sit in, and he rocked now a few times, but perhaps feeling the gentle motion was not consonant with his serious purpose, he rose and sat down on a plain wood chair.

"I come to talk of higher matters, my boy." He peered at Keith now, and shook his head. "Pressing matters, son. . . . Even as we sit here, the Kingdom may have come, and we know it not."

Perhaps hardly knowing he was doing so, Captain Cracknell picked up Keith's cup and sipped from it.

His tongue, afterwards, went rapidly over his lips several times.

"What brand of coffee is that, son?"

"Bourbon creole, Captain."

"I see. Strong as the bark on a pine tree." But the captain sipped some more, and Keith grinned like one of the wild lynxes that lived behind his house.

"Did you attend church today, Keith?" the old soldier wondered, but without the severe interrogatory tone he usually put into his words.

"Yes, sir, and Sunday school to boot, Captain Cracknell."

"Good, good."

Keith began pouring his guest a little more of the bourbon creole.

"Whoa, whoa there!" the captain warned him. "This is a powerful morning drink."

"I read my Sunday school lesson last night before I went to bed, Captain," Keith told him.

"Now you're pulling my leg, my boy." The old man grinned a little. "Those old soldiers waiting out there on the grass were barely able to pull their limbs one after the other to get here. . . . You live on a horrible incline, Keith."

Keith raised his eyes to take in the scattered file of the ancient G.A.R.s. He trembled all at once.

"My grandpa did not like people," he explained dreamily. "And he built his house as far from other folks as he could, up the steep side. . . . I take after him."

"No, you don't, Keith. I knowed your grandpa better than you. . . . Besides you're a hero."

"I take after him, I say. But I'll tell you something. I feel I will never leave this house. That's how bad off I feel I am sometimes . . . especially after Sunday school."

"What reason would you have for leaving?" the old man chided. "It's your home, for heaven's sake. That's all life is, a home." Captain Cracknell looked admiringly at the property. "Twenty rooms at least! Big roof, wonderful beams, fine new eaves you just installed. But the windows ain't washed, and many of the windows has no blinds. Neglect shows itself, Keith, in those little things. You must tidy up. Tidy up."

A long lapse of quiet ensued.

"Kiss the Good Book." The old man came to attention, and he pushed the Bible toward Keith's lips. The veteran kissed it.

"We worry about you, my boy . . . we worry." He waved his hand encouragingly toward the little army waiting on the grass.

"I hope it helps, your worryin'," Keith mumbled, grinning. "Say, you drank that off all right, Captain." He pointed to the cup in which the bourbon creole had been. "Want another? . . . I'll go get you a cup of your own. A guest shouldn't have to drink out of his host's cup."

"No, no, Keith, don't fret now. It's too strong, that brand . . . too strong my boy."

Keith bent down and tightened his shoelaces.

"Do you want me to tell you what our Sunday school lesson

was for today, Captain?" he asked straightening up in his chair.

"Now, Keith, you're pulling my leg again, by golly. It ain't right to make a fool of me, and you know it." Captain Cracknell laughed; then his countenance changed quickly, and he looked sad and frowned.

Keith was staring at the old man's medals, which tinkled like dime-store bells whenever he moved.

"I don't think the Master and his apostles dressed theirselves the way the Sunday school lesson pictures make out, Captain Cracknell—if you will allow me to speak of sacred things. They're not covered with dust and sweat from their journeys in the Holy Land. They look bandbox fresh."

"You will pull my leg, Keith. . . . And I'm sweating like a dray horse from that drink of yours. Should never touch nothing but water, that's my motto."

Keith's eyes strayed back to the Civil War soldiers standing in his yard. They looked like some dead Belgians he had seen propped up against a wall in a courtyard once. He groaned.

"I have come not to preach to you, but to give you a helping hand," the captain was saying.

Very abruptly the captain began to shiver a little. Well, it was getting on to winter, of course.

"You wait right here, Captain Cracknell," Keith urged him, and jumped up and went inside.

"Just a few more minutes, boys," the old soldier encouraged his troops. "Then, we'll be marching on." He stood up to address his buddies. "I have to set this young man straight, you understand. He's bad off . . . bad off . . . never seen a young chap in worse shape."

Keith came out on the porch carrying a thick wool sweater.

"Put this on, Captain, for you're shakin' like a oak leaf in winter."

Keith helped him into the sweater, but as the garment hid his medals, the old man began to whimper and complain and fidgeted with the neck of the sweater. Then he sat back and thought of the speech he wanted to deliver.

"The news is bad," Captain Cracknell began when Keith had seated himself and was sipping indifferently out of the cup he had shared with the old soldier.

"The talk I hear, the tales that circulate! You see, Keith, we fought in different wars, that's part of it. And though my generation freed the nigger and had to see they was helped out of bondage, still even the niggers spoke some kind of English, whilst, you see, you was sent to where the heathens and infidels didn't know our own tongue or our ways. That's what has ruined you, Keith, not the shrapnel and the bayonet wounds, and the bombs."

"What, Captain?"

Holding his hand to the side of his mouth, the captain whispered: "The bad disease you got from those French women."

"Oh, that," Keith reflected, and picked up his pack of cigarettes, opened it, looked into the rows of neatly packed tobacco, then put the pack down, and blew out air from his lungs. "Yes, I get your drift."

"But there is a greater Jezebel than the French harlots. She is among us," the old man droned on, and Keith could see he had come to the heart of his discourse and the purport of his visit.

"She has waited all these years for just such a one as you, Keith."

"The devil you say." He spoke in boyish surprise, and reached now for a cigarette, put it in his mouth, and puffed on it unlit.

Then coming out of his haze he asked, "Which one, Captain?"

"You mean there is more than one of them in your life?" The old man paused as if he had forgotten the rest of his prepared speech. He studied Keith almost fearfully. "No," he said quietly. "Couldn't be."

"There is Mrs. Cottrell. Elaine," Keith spoke as he might have in Sunday school class. "And there is Miss Fitzsimmons, and Widow Hughes, and of course Adele Bevington."

"Miss Bevington," the captain chided. "You mention the queen harlot as an afterthought. You do not deceive me, Keith."

The old man got to his feet, shaking.

"Sell it!" He pointed to the soldier's house. He especially pointed for a long while to its roof. "Sell it, and be gone. Flee while there is time. Run. Run for your life. And you mentioned her last. As an afterthought. When she holds you body and soul in her toils! Oh, Keith, Keith, Keith." He sat down.

Stamping out his cigarette, from which he had hardly taken

two puffs, and gazing out toward the row of catalpa trees that hid the bend of the river, Keith said: "What have you got against Adele Bevington?"

Captain Cracknell stared at Keith with stupefaction, incredulity, sleepy horror. Keith noted with satisfaction that the bourbon creole had made the Civil War hero more than a little muddled.

"In a minute, boys," the old man called out now to his troops, who were beginning to raise a murmur of impatience and dissatisfaction. One or two of them, in fact, were moving away down the hill to the road. "I'm about through here. . . . Keep your formation, there, men." He raised his voice when he saw two or three of them beginning to break ranks and move toward the porch. "Stop right there, boys. . . . This is a very crucial conversation I am having here. It can't wait."

There was a sudden severe break then in the old captain's line of thought, similar to those breaks in the film at the Royal Theater when the audience must sit back and wait for the man in the projection booth to put the broken ends of the film together and resume the showing.

The captain's mouth opened and closed. He passed his hand over his brow and eyes.

"The poison of the women of France," Captain Cracknell was continuing when he heard a sound coming from Fonthill's most recent hero, who would bear even more medals and citations than Captain Cracknell, could he but remember where most of them were hidden or locked up. It was a sound such as the captain might have heard at Chickamauga. It was a little like a child being strangled, or the cry of an infantryman whose gangrenous leg was being removed with the help of only third-rate whiskey as a painkiller, or indeed the sound a man makes when a bayonet goes through his windpipe. Yet the sound was unlike any of these.

Falling down on his knees before the captain, and holding the old man tightly with both his hands, pressing the old man's legs together as in a vise, Keith Gresham was, it might be said, choking to death on his own words: "Captain, they were not women, but owls, let me assure you. Pay no attention to what anybody else may say. I was there! Do you hear? They were owls. Owls, owls! A whole forest of owls as I lay with my guts rolling out so easily onto the mud of Argonne Forest. These white owls rested in my groin for so many days, and yet, who knows? But"—he held up his face to the captain—"weren't they maybe, as you say, perhaps, after all, the women of France, too? Weren't we all hiding from the Germans?"

Getting up from his knees, Lieutenant Gresham then took out his service revolver, which he had kept hidden under his jacket, in his heavy belt with the fiercely scintillating gold buckle.

He walked out to the flagstones, which stopped at the greensward of the uncut grass.

He raised the gun toward the roof of his house. There was a deathly quiet on all sides. One could have believed that even the sound of the river had ceased its gurgling, as it did when winter froze it to its bed.

Lieutenant Gresham shot once, twice, thrice, who knows how many times? He emptied his gun of all its bullets, all aimed at his roof, and chimney, or rather at heaven.

When he had finished shooting there was deathly quiet again, just as when he had raised the mouth of the gun toward the roof. He replaced the gun in his belt, and covered it with his jacket.

The small platoon of the Civil War veterans moved back slightly, disobeying orders from their captain. But they made no sound, engaged in no forbidden talk or murmurs.

Only when the captain himself rose from his chair and walked down the front steps of the house did they begin to whisper and mumble among themselves.

Captain Cracknell stopped on the flagstones at the base of the steps leading to the house. He had caught sight of some of the spilled bourbon creole on his jacket (he had removed the present of the sweater bestowed on him by Keith Gresham).

Turning back, the captain caught sight of Keith staring at him. From the younger man's lips two cigarettes were lit in conflagration.

"I cannot save you!" the captain called. "There is a power here greater than mine," he went on. "What it is I do not know, but it is beyond me."

He held up the Bible now and the flag, but without the strength and the motion he had possessed when he first paid his visit today.

"Men"—he turned to his platoon now—"we must be off to our next confabulation. There is no more work to be done here. . . .

Lady Conway, whose husband was our commander-in-chief, you recall, is on her death bed. We must go to her at once. . . . Forward, march.''

But the captain did not follow the old men who were marching off. He turned back again to look at Keith.

"My boy, my boy," the old man cried brokenly.

Keith was drinking now thirstily from the jug of bourbon creole, stopping only long enough to shake his head.

He could not remember, he knew, what it was the captain had said to him here today, could not recall indeed what *he* had said, certainly did not know he had emptied his service revolver, pointing it at the roof of his house or at the yellow sky.

"Corn liquor is a treacherous mother," he said at last to the captain. "Remember that when you go now to save the Indians. I reckon it's the Indians who are next on your list. You'll find them out yonder''—he pointed toward the river—"out there with the owls and possums and the lynxes. They will listen to you, Captain Cracknell. . . . I'm already converted."

He followed, almost running now, after the old veteran, who in turn, hurried as fast as his feet could carry him in the direction of his platoon. "Go out into the woods, Captain, to find your pulpit. But when you get to the Indians, tell them I'm converted. Converted to Adele, tell them. Hear? I'm Adele's, body and soul. Converted! Converted!"

It was then that Captain Cracknell stopped and turned around. There was a terrible look on his old, withered face. The look stopped Keith's mouth and lips, froze his advancing step. It was not a look of indignation or reproach or disapproval or moral righteousness. It was a look of horror, and *memory*. Captain Cracknell, for a brief moment anyhow, before he would go perhaps out to save the Indians, had seen, out of all those who had known about it, what had happened to Lieutenant Gresham in the mud of Picardy or the Forest of Argonne, or wherever it had happened, and for a brief flash, had also known that no words or expression of love or hope could bestow the syrup of healing and peace on the young man in this life or perhaps the next.

When the words about Adele escaped his lips as old Captain Cracknell was leaving him, it was the first time Keith was fully aware what had happened to him. He was in love with Adele Bevington. In some "unholy" way, he supposed. But isn't all real love unholy, he wondered. He had always found it so. The trouble was, he decided, he was in love sometimes with everybody. As a boy he could never choose which girl, or even young boy, he loved the most. All human flesh sometimes seemed so appetizing, so irresistible, he had wanted sometimes to kiss everybody he met on the street. Until maybe the Forest of Argonne and the owls. No, they had made no difference. He loved just the same now. Only he was a dead man loving now. He loved as from beyond the grave.

He went to the Royal Theater every evening now. He slept through most of the reels. Both the women and the men in the photoplays had on lipstick. That was the only thing he remembered clearly. And the long movies about the Great War were so ridiculous he found himself laughing uproariously throughout, while the middle-aged women around him were weeping buckets.

He only attended the Royal because he knew that when the movie house closed, and he would come out with the young lovers and the soul-sick housewives, *she* would be at her window.

He was never wrong. But when Adele saw him now she retreated within her spacious room.

"You damned queen up there," he would mutter when the crowd had disappeared and the streetlights were beginning to go off on Main Street. "Monopolizing moonshine."

He was shivering in the late fall cold wearing only a pongee shirt that his mother had given him for high school graduation and that he could still wear: same neck size, sleeve length, nothing had changed. The war and his wounds had kept him young.

Then he would walk up the steps to her front door. It was open, but they both pretended she had locked it and he had broken the lock. Then she would say, just as in the picture show, "Who is there?"

"The man of your dreams," he usually said when she opened the door to her parlor, in tears.

"This has got to stop," she said this evening after she had swung the door open on him. "I can't have it!"

"Why don't you put on your jewels, Adele," he suggested, sitting down in her favorite big chair.

"Oh for pity's sake," she said, but he knew she would go in her bedroom and put on at least some of the diamonds.

"I wish you'd put on the whole assortment like you did for me the first night." Keith spoke in an undertone.

She was already preparing his "medicine" from a big decanter.

"I want you to be sparing with this," she advised him as she handed him a large glass of the drink. "I am running out. . . . None is coming from Canada lately." He fingered the cut-glass of the tumbler appreciatively.

"Please put on your diamonds. Pretty please." There was a kind of urgency in his voice. She saw he needed to see her in the jewels almost as much as, perhaps more than, she needed to put them on.

"Just for you, Keith, I will," she conceded.

He lay back in the chair, barely testing the medicine, grinning happily.

She was gone a long time but when she returned he saw the wait had been worth it.

For there she was, with her crown of white hair so immaculate in its coiffure, her alabaster skin, her sky-blue eyes, and the sparkling gems covering almost every inch of her, and setting off her almost invisible satin gown.

"You should wear diamond slippers, Adele," he said through his short, irregular gasping for breath.

"Oh, but the donor who gave me these has no more."

"And you should also wear a crown of jewels on your beautiful hair."

"I'm afraid you are making fun of an old woman."

"I wouldn't have you an hour younger, Adele."

"Drunk as a lord." She shook her head.

"Wrong. I'm cold sober."

She seated herself, as was the custom now of their evenings together, in a little chair near him, but tonight he rose and came over and knelt on the carpet by her feet. He kissed her silk stockings and she would warn him not to pull the hose awry, and he would put his hand under her dress, and she would slap him.

"You're making fun of love, Keith. I know you."

"I love you."

"Oh, will you cut it out!"

"I can't help myself." He kept kissing her legs, then he took off her shoes, and kissed her feet. "Imagine me," he said, "going to movies every night." He spoke as if reproaching another person who was present in the room. "I can't believe it." He looked all at once at his massive hands. "Can't get it straight in my head."

"Those women in the ticket booth and the ushers think we are crazy," she said. "We go to the same film two and three times a week."

"Wasting our time, wasting our money," he mumbled between his kisses. He had put aside his drink on a little side table, and laid his head in her lap.

She smoothed the thick auburn curls. Whatever else had happened to him, his head and hair and eyes and lips and chin, the long velvet lashes about his gray eyes, they were whole, they were spared—for her. She kissed him fervently again and again.

Deep night had overtaken the street outside. Her breast shining with the jewels appeared to give light in the darkness like a distant row of planets in some rare astronomical phenomenon.

"I have told everybody I am in love with you," he said, raising his head from her lap and staring at her accusingly.

"And I wonder what everybody had to say to that," she replied, and kissed him on the mouth.

Adele Bevington had disturbed the moral order and tranquillity of Fonthill twice in a generation. But whereas her first infraction of decency had occurred when she was too young to be held fully responsible (her seducer being a man of such eminence and wealth, the sin was regarded as more his than Adele's), her second disruption of social decorum was held to be more serious. Few people remembered any longer her first assault upon respectability: her illegitimate son was not here to remind them of it, for one thing. But whereas when she had been pregnant without having a husband to support and protect her name in 1900, and when she had no way of even surviving except by living under the roof of her father, whose wealth and respectable position in the community helped silence some of the gossip and scandal, today she was alone against all that rumor and talebearing had to bring against her; but today, instead of being defenseless, she was strong, and instead of being dependent on others, she was self-sufficient, even wealthy, at least for that time and place.

But she still could not stop the crowds of young men and women and idlers from congregating in front of her window facing the Royal Theater, hoping for a glimpse of the abandoned woman.

And one night a vandal had written in pitch across the front of her house the words:

HARLOT THEN,
WHORE NOW.

Adele refused to have the words expunged.

Knots of curiosity-seekers constantly stood in front of her house, sometimes reading the words out loud.

The mayor called on her finally.

Adele's house, he pointed out, was no longer situated out in the country, as it had been in the days of her father, but was in the very heart of the "little metropolis," and for words like these to remain undeleted brought everybody and the town itself into disrepute.

Adele listened to the mayor, and drank quite copiously from her "medicine" as the old gentleman simpered and sniffled and begged her pardon for intruding upon her privacy. He was where he was today, he pointed out, owing to her father's having groomed him for the position he now held, and by bestowing on him in that far-off epoch one political favor after another. He therefore ignored her illegal drinking and, what was even more offensive to him, her "smoking," which seemed to confirm the truth of the words written outside on her house.

At first Adele would not hear of the town paying for the whitewashing of the words. She said she could not accept charity for the cost of its being expunged.

"It's necessity, my dear lady, not charity!" he appealed to her.

She was immovable. "Let the words stand!" she insisted.

The mayor then spoke very obliquely of a lawsuit, shaking a sheaf of papers.

Adele fidgeted, the color came and went in her face, and finally boredom overtook her.

She began ever so slowly to see his "side of the matter."

"But what guarantee, my dear Mr. Mayor, have you that the offending words will not reappear in the same place?"

"My dear Adele Bevington." The old man rose now and took her hand. "If in memory of your father, if not for us, you would only tailor your way of life to the standards of the community. I hesitate to speak like this, but the honor of your father's name compels me to. . . . If you would only change your ways, these words could not, would not, appear! We admire your pluck, and your nerve, your talent, and your energy. I especially am one of your greatest devotees, dear Adele. . . . But we are a town of families, families raising children, churchgoing people, a town of businessmen and mothers who want the best for their off-spring. . . . Your many appearances at the window in your pearls and opals . . ."

"Diamonds, Mr. Mayor," she corrected him. "I loathe pearls, and wouldn't be caught in my coffin wearing an opal."

"Very well." He accepted her correction, and loosened his stiff collar. "Your jewels, then, let us say, which, as rumor has it, belong to the period of your . . . first mistake."

Adele fixed him with a stare so ferocious, he let go of her hand, but continued to stand over her. Mayor Grosvenor was very short. Indeed it appeared to her then that he was no taller as he stood urging her to listen to reason than when he was seated. Perhaps he was shorter when standing than sitting, for the chair gave him a certain appearance of being a fairly tall man!

"The spectacle of you in all your jewels at your open window shocks the entire town!"

Adele smiled. But finally, because her head and temples had begun to ache, she agreed to have the words painted out.

"Yes, why not?" she sighed, and signed the papers he had brought with him.

"Wouldn't you be happier, my dear," he ventured as she was ushering him out the door, "if you went perhaps to Chicago, or even Paris and London?"

"Chicago?" She shrugged. "Paris, London?" She looked down at her satin pumps, and briefly out the front window.

"I am afraid I would make no stir there now, Mayor Grosvenor."

"Is it a stir you want to make here, my dear?" he wondered with a kind of sad, commiserative tone.

He had left her thick plush carpet and was treading on the threadbare hall runner which led to the front door.

"My dear Mr. Grosvenor," she called after him. "Stir, no . . . but I do like to be myself. I do like to look out my front window with or without pearls, opals, or diamonds. I feel I have earned my freedom."

"Well, it's best not to worry about it." He turned about as he said this, his hand on the doorknob. "Everything blows over in time. We both know that. Memory is not very substantial with the public, after all. We shall see, my dear, we shall see!"

He blew a kiss to her as he opened the door.

But still he hesitated, and did not go out.

"Adele," he began, and he removed his gray hat with the stained dark blue band around it. "Give up that young man! For your own sake, and for him."

"Which one," she said throatily, then regretted she had said this somehow.

"Keith Gresham," he told her. "The infantryman lieutenant. . . . Forgive me for saying this to you. But I knew your father and your grandfather. . . . You cannot find happiness with that young man! Nor he with you!"

"But what do you expect me to find without him? Have you thought of that?"

"All I can say," he finished, beginning to leave the house now, "you will be better off, both of you, without the other—better if you never see one another again!"

He had put on his hat, and he was gone.

She blew the kiss he had blown to her, but she used both her hands.

"Good night, Mr. Mayor," she said to the empty hall. She heard him laugh as he went down the street. It was his laugh that restored some of her composure. The old man knew a little, after all, she supposed, of human nature, and a little even of the world beyond Fonthill.

"As if whatever I did, right or wrong, happiness would figure in the consequence!" she cried.

She closed the door to her parlor, and locked it tight.

Elaine's long-smoldering resentment, even hatred, of Adele Bevington began to break into open flame. She had pretended to others and even to herself in the "old days" that she was deeply appreciative of Adele's interest in her sons. She even fooled herself into thinking she admired and loved Adele. But at the time she had gone along with the charade, allowing her boys to pay court to the "elderly woman," Adele's reputation had been good, her past was nearly forgotten, and the mother of Alec and Ned assured herself that her boys were being ushered into a higher social stratum than she could provide, she who had to scrub and cook and wash linen and sew, who had never a free moment, while Adele, with her manicured nails and wrinkle-free throat and face, could discourse on the rules of society and the thoughts of great writers.

But the thundercloud, when it came, covered the whole sky, blotted out the sun. And just as any doubt was removed from Elaine's mind that her older boy was to leave her forever, the true "picture" of Adele's life was being broadcast across the town, and into the neighboring counties. The smearing of the words *harlot* and *whore* in pitch across her house set all tongues to wagging, and the stories of Adele's befriending unemployed young men off the street, her standing nearly unclothed except for her jewels in front of her window, and the orgy she had engaged in with Lieutenant Gresham became almost the sole topic of conversation for days on end.

Adele's new moral ruin became almost as much an obsession with Elaine as the crushing realization that her Alec, the very pillar of her house, would soon be gone from her forever. Elaine became presently, overwhelmed with these two tormenting ideas, almost as much a vixen and virago as Widow Hughes, and she ranted and raved about Adele's wickedness and her having poisoned the minds of Alec and poor Ned with ideas and dreams neither would ever be able to fulfill.

There was another reason, however, that made Elaine so

antagonistic to La Bevington (an appellation that Ned had once used affectionately, but the nickname was seized now by the mother and used venomously again and again). It was Adele's growing influence over Keith Gresham, which threatened Elaine's own very possessive relationship with the "infantry-man."

At first Elaine had tried to ignore Keith's almost nightly visits to Adele after he had dined at the boardinghouse. And she had made no comment when Keith had quoted at the table, rather frequently, some remark, idea, or reminiscence of the "old woman."

One evening after supper, when Keith sat in the kitchen smoking and watching Elaine put away the dishes, she had said to him out of the blue: "Keith forgive me, but aren't you wearing a scent?"

He had colored, looked blank.

"I mean"—Elaine smiled in her studied bewitching way—"haven't you put on some kind of perfume by mistake?"

"Oh gosh, Mrs. Cottrell (the formal name had slipped out, and Elaine winced). "I'll tell you what it must be . . . Adele Bevington gave me some white rose cologne, which I told her at the time was not exactly what a man would wear. . . ."

"But you have persuaded yourself to use it anyhow." Elaine tried to control her anger. "I wouldn't put it on, Keith, if I were you," she added in a choking voice.

Keith extinguished his cigarette on the sole of his shoe.

She saw she had made him angry, and she was afraid. She dared not lose Keith also, now that Alec's departure was a fore-gone conclusion.

"Forgive me being so bossy and nosey," Elaine begged him. "I spoke out of turn."

She picked up the heavy ironstone platter now and attempted to place it on top of the kitchen cabinet. But finding it too awkward to manage, she put it down with difficulty again on the white pine table.

"Here, let me, Elaine," he offered, and he took hold of the platter clumsily. As he was lifting it to put it in its place, the ironstone slipped and fell to the floor, and broke into at least a dozen pieces.

Both Elaine and Keith stared unbelieving at the broken china with its design of blue birds and apple blossoms.

Keith stooped down, touching the broken pieces as if he would be able perhaps to put them all together again.

"Elaine!" he called out. "Will you ever forgive me?" Looking up at her, his face burning, he said, "I will buy you a new one, of course."

"I'm afraid there are no new ones like that. . . . That platter has been in my family for over sixty years."

He stood up facing her. "I'll make it up to you somehow." All at once he could smell the white rose cologne on his own person, and its perfume, though faint, was unpleasant, even disgusting, to him at that moment. It was the smell of a sissy.

"You are very angry with me aren't you, Elaine? And for many reasons. You resent Adele, I know. . . . But where else can one go in this godforsaken burg to hear anybody talk and cheer a fellow up."

She had begun to sweep up the pieces of china with a broom and dustpan.

"You sound just like Alec when he was being indoctrinated by her!" Elaine's face, too, was burning with anger and resentment. "You'll go, just as he is about to—and soon! Yes, I can see it coming. You will pack also and go off. . . ."

She emptied the dustpan into a great bin near the door.

"I don't think I could ever leave you, Elaine." Keith spoke in a strange hushed tone. He had crossed the room to where she stood, blocking, it appeared, her motion to the center of the kitchen. She saw to her surprise he was still holding one of the broken pieces of china in his hand. "And unlike your Alec, I have already packed and gone off. . . . I've been . . . *there*. Now I'm here to stay."

They both quailed at the word *there*.

"I've been away," he went on, his eyes widening, his lips compressed, "and I never want to be away again. That's what I mean. . . . Adele means nothing to me compared to . . . here . . . compared to you. . . . But you never seem to have time for me. You are always at work!"

"I see," Elaine said bitterly.

Keith took her in his arms and touched her hair with his left hand, for the other hand held the broken piece of china.

"You may wear any kind of scent you like, Keith," she said, slightly moving away from his embrace. "It is none of my business. I had no right to mention it."

He kissed her again and again.

"Oh, but you did. You do," he reassured her. "Who else has the right if you don't? Who else, I mean, do I have?" he said gloomily.

As much as a woman could, she sensed some of the bottomless misery that was his. She did not want to look into the abyss of his suffering. She did not even want to admit it was there. She felt if she could provide him with the happy "banquets" each evening, the laughter and the cheer, the sorrow, whatever it was, would go away, at least diminish. She felt any man's sorrow could dissolve at her touch, because in the end she believed only in herself.

"Whatever you do, Keith, this is your home and this door is always open to you."

He started at her words. They were almost identical with those that Adele had spoken to him. And though said with such different accentuation, they were both commands that, when translated, meant simply *You belong only to me and to no other*.

But Keith felt he belonged to nothing and nobody but his hell and his anguish. These two beautiful women, Adele and Elaine, and their touch, reached only the outer layers of his being. Inside the fearful fire of his woe could not be approached by anything human, appeased by any kindness, put out by even the most exalted love.

Ever so gradually a remarkable change came over Alec and Ned's mother: a peculiar calm, a resignation, an acceptance of everything. She spent many of her evenings poring over a religious magazine, which had a cover illustration of so many flowers and birds that Ned had first mistaken it for a seed catalogue, to his mother's grudging amusement.

"It is my only consolation, Neddy," she explained to him as he leafed through its cheerful advice on how to bear sorrow and disappointment, and ever to look to the morrow, when all tears will be wiped away.

"Except for you and dear Keith, I would not know where to turn," she said. Ned had taken his mother's hand then. Her calm meant, he knew, that she had given up Alec.

"I will not stand in the way of his success." She paraphrased the religious tract's wording. "I will bless his endeavors, I will let go and let God . . . I will not stand in the sunshine of his success or darken his way with my shadow."

This was an Elaine whom Ned could barely recognize. He preferred the Elaine of old, with her tantrums, bewailing of her widowhood, sharp scolding and ranting and tempests of tears.

Widow Hughes, entering as usual surreptitiously by the kitchen door, took up the religious tracts one afternoon while Elaine was sleeping.

"Heretical, my dear." She gave her judgment when Elaine appeared finally in the kitchen to put on the kettle in preparation for the evening meal. The old woman read offending passages out loud, clicking her tongue, and adjusting a falling hairpin. "Hedonism, not religion." She went on with her criticism of the text. "Promising happiness in *this* life! Entirely contrary to Christian teaching. . . . If only Pastor Hughes were here to set you straight on this! My dear, we *cannot* know happiness in this world. Only resignation, and the strength to carry our cross."

Elaine barely listened to what the old woman was saying, but the mere presence of the widow comforted her, and ignoring her friend's theology, Elaine went on repeating the phraseology of the religious text: "I will let go . . . I will let my son depart. I will not hold him back. God will show me the way, where to human eyes there is no way. Where to mortal effort no path is feasible, with divine guidance all will be clear."

An even greater change had taken place in Alec. Now that every preparation had been made for him to go to Chicago, he was paralyzed with an icy terror.

From his practice of days on end of barely tasting his food, Alec had become gaunt and pale, while his eyes, as if increasing in size, flashed accusatory glances at objects and people.

One night Ned was once more awakened by someone roughly shaking his shoulder.

"Move over, why don't you."

Alec had climbed into bed with him again.

"I am having a chill, I think," the older boy complained.

"Well, your feet are like kegs of ice, that's for sure," Ned scolded. "Shall I go down and get the hot water bottle?"

Alec did not reply for he had not even heard what his brother said.

"I've said this before but it bears repeating. I have not always been a good brother to you, have I, Ned? Don't answer." He put his hand over Ned's mouth. "I tell you, I have not slept for a week . . . just little brief snoozes. But I know I will go now, even if it kills me, which I guess it will."

"We've all made our decision, Alec." Ned spoke in the words of Elaine, almost in the words of the religious tract. He hardly knew how to address this shivering wretched fellow holding on to him so desperately in the dark.

"We won't stand in your way, ever, Alec. . . . You're free!"

"Free," Alec repeated and groaned. "Dead's more like it."

Rising up in bed, he addressed his brother: "You sound glad to get rid of me, Ned. . . . Have I been such a damned bully and tyrant, then?"

"You've been a good brother," Ned replied after a struggle with himself. "But our minds have been made up, Alec. You know that. You're to go. You're free to go. . . . Isn't that what you've wanted all these years? Well, Elaine has made her peace with herself, and her duty."

"Who are you quoting now, Neddy?" Alec almost wailed. He hugged the younger boy almost maniacally. "I believe I am going to die, I swear I do."

"You won't die," Ned spoke roughly, like the Alec of old. "And mind this. Your place is already taken, Alec. The decision has been made on everybody's part now."

One could hear Alec's heavy breathing in the room.

"What do you mean, my place is taken?" he wondered in mild hysteria. "And by who, for Christ's sake. By who?"

"Well," came the tardy reply, "by me, and by Keith Gresham."

"Oh, to blazing hell with Keith Gresham. I'm sick of even hearing his name. . . . So I'm driven out of my own house by that mutilated little pissass."

"But isn't this what you've wanted all these years? To have us *let* you go? Now when it's all sealed and sanctioned and the ink dry on the paper you mean you want to back out?"

Ned was considerably taken aback to hear the short dry sobs coming out of Alec's chest, as if he were trying to bring up some great stone that had choked him there for time out of memory.

"You can bet on one thing, God damn it, I will never back out now, no, by Christ . . . not after what you've just said." He swore and cursed then for a full minute.

"By what I've said?" Ned whispered. He was more and more bewildered at such a show of feeling.

"Yes, by what you've said, you idiot. So my place is taken by you two, is it? By a kid and a ball-less little doughboy with his hero act!"

"Keith's strong, Alec. I can tell you," he whispered.

"You sound like you're in love with him, too, if you ask me!"

Ned stared at his brother in confusion.

"All right, all right, forget I spoke that way. I don't know what I'm talking about, I see," Alec apologized huskily. "Forget I ever was your brother, why don't you."

Having delivered himself of this, Alec jumped out of bed.

"You're still shivering," Ned pointed out.

"Yes, so I am." The older boy bent over as if in pain, and looked down at his feet.

"You'd better sleep with me tonight till you calm down, shouldn't you?"

"I am calmed down . . . I am dead calm . . . I know now what I have to do."

"But you're shivering and shakin', Alec. You're havin' a real chill."

"So my place is taken, is it?" Alec spoke as if he were alone in his own room.

"Look here . . . I am going downstairs to get the hot water bottle for you, Alec," Ned informed him, "and you stay right here under the covers and wait till I get back, hear?"

He threw on a ragged bathrobe, which had belonged to his dad, and which Ned had had to wait to wear until recently, when it still barely fit him. "You get back under the covers."

"So my place is taken, is it?" the older boy went on muttering, but he obeyed and got under the bedclothes.

"Well, I'll show them," he went on ranting while his brother was downstairs heating the water. "I'll go to Chicago and be damned forever before I ask them if I can stay here. I'll go to the city and go to the dogs or I'll make more money than they could ever even count if they all lived to be a hundred and ninety. So they've driven me out, that's it. By God, I'll go and I'll show them."

Just a short time before Alec Cottrell's actual departure from Fonthill, there was an occurrence that occupied public attention to the exclusion of almost all other concerns.

A fiery cross had been erected and burned on the front lawn of Keith Gresham's house. This took place just a day after the "frightful" words had been painted on Adele Bevington's residence.

Alec read and reread the account of the "episode" in *The Courier*. He cut the piece out and took it along with him to his work. It was curious, he felt, for he had planned to go to Keith's house in any event and perhaps "have it out with him" about his taking Alec's place in his home. And though he felt no anger or even sympathy for what the unknown vandals had done to Keith, at the same time he could use the cross-burning as an excuse for his calling on the "hero."

It was a cool November day, a day that combined the best qualities of spring and autumn, a bright but not hot sun, a delicious soft breeze coming from the hills, and a resplendent panoply of maple, oak, and elm leaves flying through the streets and fields.

Alec found Keith seated on the swing on his front porch in easy view of the cross.

Alec removed his hat, and acknowledged Keith's dry "good morning" and his offering him a chair near him.

Alec remained standing, his hat held awkwardly by his side.

"Why don't you take it down, Keith?" Alec finally inquired.

When there was no answer, Alec sat down on the chair the veteran had offered him.

"Keith!" He repeated his question.

"Oh, yes, the cross." Keith spoke absentmindedly. He took out what looked like an imported pipe, and fumbled around trying to light it. Then he put it down and picked up his pack of cigarettes, offering one to Alec, who refused it. "A singer's throat," Keith remarked apologetically.

"Everybody is furious they did this to you, Keith," Alec mumbled, blushing.

"Everybody except you," Keith said. He struck another match for his smoke had gone out.

"That's not quite fair, Keith."

"I know you resent me," the veteran said indifferently.

"No, I don't. . . . I might have at first. I don't now. Believe me. I know you are good . . . for my mother and brother. Thank you."

"Well don't bawl," Keith replied, inhaling deeply on his cigarette. "I can't stand any bawling this early in the morning."

"As a matter of fact, Keith," Alec told him, "I don't exactly know why I came to see you. But I know if I had a grudge against you ever, it's gone after these past days. . . . Fact is, I'm getting cold feet about going away . . . to Chicago, you know."

"I know," Keith said with a little more civility.

"And since you're the one with real . . . guts . . ."

Keith flushed deeply.

"You've been through thick and thin," he finished lamely.

Keith glared at him.

"There's no question in my mind you are . . . someone to look up to."

Alec was dumbfounded at his own words, his own turnabout. He was saying all at once what he had denied up until now, he was conveying to himself, that is, what he really believed about the man who was "to take his place."

"If I've seemed cold and unkind," he stumbled on, "overlook it."

"Oh, for Jesus' sake, will you stop." Keith smiled broadly in spite of himself.

The older man sensed that Alec meant exactly what he was saying. In this young man's mind Keith was a hero in the same incontrovertible sense he was of the male sex. It wasn't praise the way Alec said it, or irony, but mere irrefutable, unchangeable fact. And it was this "fact" Keith would never be able to understand—how people saw him as some larger-than-life savior when he could barely tie his shoelaces without groaning, and each day

seemed to last a thousand years, such was its pain and disappointment.

"See here," Keith began. "If you don't leave now, Alec, you'll
be foaming mad at yourself the rest of your life. . . . And if you
do leave, you'll probably be furious with yourself also, for giving
up your life of peace and contentment. But your days of happy
heaven are over in any case. Don't you understand that? They
don't last, these days. Do you understand? Of course you don't!
But the best is over for you. Nothing will ever be as wonderful as
the days just now drawing to a close. Boyhood, they call it, or
youth. . . . Nothing will ever be that perfect again."

"Well, that's a lot to look forward to it, ain't it?" Alec said
wistfully, twirling fiercely a strand of his yellow hair in his
fingers. At the same time Keith could see Alec was glad he had
spoken so.

"After those cloudless sunshiny days," Keith went on as if to
himself, "what is there but the grindstone and the sweat, and the
dullness and ache and the bad taste in the mouth, and the heavy
load to be taken up again and again? I quit counting the years
after they sent me to the trenches. I'm like the clock in that old
movie theater on the edge of town that burned down a few years
ago, stuck at noon. And that year, if clocks told years . . . I came
clean alive in 1917, and I died twelve noon, June 1, 1918."

Alec shook his head and looked out toward where the river was
moving somewhere behind all the trees and clouds.

"I'll leave in a few days, Keith, but I still don't know where I'll
get the courage."

"When I signed up to go overseas"—Keith went back to the
day and the year and the hour when he had been last "alive"—"I
was so numb with fright if the fellow in front of me hadn't been
there I would have fallen down flat on the floor when the
sergeant told us to raise our right hand and swear, and then I
heard the words 'You are now a member of the army of the
United States of America. . . .' I knew I would never come back
home at that moment, not necessarily because I would be killed,
but I knew I would never be a carefree young boy again. . . .
And that was all I wanted out of life, just to laze and dream on the
river and to while away my life in the woods and the glades and
the little hills hid in the mist. . . ."

The tears began to well up in Alec's eyes, but Keith gave him so fierce a look, it seemed the tears pushed themselves back and were dried.

"If you come with me to the train station, you'll see to it I don't get off and stay, Keith," Alec said desperately.

"You won't get off . . . and you'll never be back. . . . Even if you come for a visit, Alec, you won't be back. Your boyhood days are done."

"Yes," Alec responded. "I know that. And your tellin' it to me maybe gives me the strength to do it. You'll look after Ned and Mama, won't you?"

"You bet your life . . . like they were my own, Alec."

The younger man rose now, dropping his hat as he did so, and then, as he picked it up, he found Keith's hand in his.

"You should pull down that cross, Keith," Alec advised him. "Do you want me to go out and take it down?"

"No. The law is comin' to photograph it this morning." The veteran grinned.

"You're so cool and brave to just let it stand there."

"I've given my country everything but my life." Keith spoke in a low voice. "They can have that too if they want. I don't have no more to give, and they're welcome to what's left if they want it."

"Keith," Alec began, fiercely fingering his hat, "don't you get nothin' out of living?"

The older man sucked in his breath, and stared at the hat.

"Oh, the sunshine and the birds when they sing is nice, Alec. . . . But try as I will, I don't feel like going out and singing with them as I did when I was *me*. . . . If I come back in another form one day, I'll try to choose being a bird, I think, and if you ever hear one a while from now that sings louder than the rest around here, maybe that will be me."

"I will never so much as breathe a sigh, Rita, or shed one tear." Elaine's telephone conversation with the music teacher repeated itself day after day. "He will never know from me that his place is here with me and Ned. . . . No, I will push him on that train myself if need be, full force, but that boy will go to Chicago. I will not hold him back. I will never let on it is the wrong thing he is doing. I held his dad back in many ways."

"I don't believe that," Rita replied to Elaine's outpouring, and she hastily took up one of her gold-tipped Salome cigarettes. "You were your husband's chief source of inspiration." She soothed and consoled, as Elaine had soothed and consoled her when her lover had betrayed and left her.

Something stirred in Elaine's memory, the suspicion she had always had that Marius Cottrell had been "soft" on Rita, had gone there frequently under the pretext of inquiring about Alec's progress in his study of pianoforte.

But actually Elaine no longer cared. When Marius was alive, she was almost maniacally jealous of him. He was a born flirt. He went to the racetrack and was often reported seen with some questionable-looking woman, heavily rouged and in very high heels, what Fonthill called in those days an "adventuress."

But today, her mouth held over the black mouthpiece of the telephone, talking with a woman who had perhaps been her rival, Elaine had the capacity to think of only one thing, the loss of her son, the fall of her house. Yes, the pillars of her home were falling about her, and the only persons she could hope to depend on were two, Ned, and the veteran, Keith Gresham, and the faithfulness of the latter was already suspect, for didn't he continue to go on the sly to see Adele, the Adele who had taken Alec away from her in the first place with her preaching the gospel of self-fulfillment and individual freedom.

Putting down the phone, Elaine considered her best stratagem. She must be very cautious with regard to Keith. She must not say or do anything to "queer" herself with him. She must allow him his infidelities with Adele, must sympathize wholeheartedly with him concerning the cross-burning on his front yard, although she felt in her heart he had deserved it, owing to his shocking relationship with Adele. Yes, she must let Keith know that her door was always open to him, night or day. She must not drive him away with the possessiveness that was the cause of Alec's going to Chicago and before that Marius Cottrell's incessant hunting trips and other unexplained absences.

Alec's imminent departure brought Keith closer to Elaine and Ned. He understood departures, Elaine realized. He had agreed on the "terrible" morning to drive them all to the depot, which was about five miles north of Fonthill. The train had to be flagged at a mournful little breakwater named Tilston Gap. The conductor would alight then from the flagged train, put down the "step" on which the prodigal would ascend and then, helped into the dark gray-green coach by a black porter, would pass into manhood. Yes, Keith murmured to himself as he witnessed the spectacle in his mind, Alec would never be free if he went to the most distant star. He would never be free of Elaine, or Ned, of Adele Bevington, or of him, or of Fonthill. If Alec died and lived in bliss, he would not be free of them, and if he dashed his brain into a thousand aching particles, each particle would speak of who he was and to whom he belonged, and if those particles again were dashed into infinitesimal pieces, they would testify like motes in sunbeams, telling again to whom he belonged and whose he was for all eternity.

Then the true day of wrath came. It was so close to Thanksgiving, Elaine pondered. Perhaps if Alec waited till after the holiday. But she knew that if she did not let him go now, she would never release him, and he would never have the strength to accept release.

Elaine, Ned, and Keith then were waiting in the broken-down but still beautiful old Studebaker four-seater for Alec to come out with his last grip, but the minutes were ticking by, and no Alec.

"I think I know what it is," Elaine said at last. Both Keith and Ned watched her. She looked young and fetching in her sky-blue frock and the pearl necklace inherited from a maiden aunt. She walked back to the house with head a bit too high. Ned shuddered, and Keith took his hand, and the younger Cottrell thought he heard the veteran say, "Steady."

Elaine found Alec in the library, his head pressed against the elaborate bookcase, which he had himself designed and had custom-made.

"Mama, I can't leave all this," Alec told her. He had not needed to look up to know who had entered the room.

"Alec," she replied in a voice not recognizable as hers, "you have set your heart on this, and you shall go."

Alec looked up then, for her voice was as deep at that moment as his dad's.

Elaine drew near and kissed him on the forehead, but if he

lived to be a hundred he would never forget the quality of that kiss. It was like a brand, cold at first, then burning. It was the kiss someone might imprint on a loved one who has died violently.

"If you stay now, Alec, you will be the sorriest boy in the world, and you will make your mother and your brother acutely wretched also."

"You want me to go, then, Mama?" he groaned.

"It isn't what I want or what you want even, Alec. . . . It is what must be."

For a long time later Elaine wondered at herself, wondered how she had got the strength to say these words. It must have come to her from Marius, she mused. She had let *him* go, and now she had let his son go also.

At the depot when the conductor had put down the step, and just as Alec had turned to say goodbye forever, Ned put a single garnet rose, which he had kept hidden until then, into Alec's hand. It was almost a fatal mistake. The flower extended like that nearly brought Alec back to them, but a fierce look from Elaine sent him away from them, into the Pullman. The train's brakes screeched, and the huge engine rolled its wheels, and all the cars departed with incredible velocity, as if they had resented being flagged for this jerkwater stop.

Keith and Ned waved to the vanishing face in the Pullman window, but Elaine's eyes were suddenly blinded, not so much by tears as by a paralyzing pain in her head.

When the three were seated again in the Studebaker, Elaine said, still in her Spartan, dreadful new voice: "Ned, can you reach me the little bottle of heart medicine in my purse?"

"Heart medicine, Mama." Ned spoke querulously, and opened the small bead purse, drew out the tiny bottle, and handed it to her.

The bottle had a little rubber stopper, which Elaine coolly removed, and drank down some of the medicine, then handed it back to Ned, who put it away and held the purse for her.

"Shall we go home?" Keith inquired, and looked at Elaine. Then, bending down slowly he kissed her on the lips, tasting as he did so the bitter drug which had stained her mouth. Then turning to Ned in the back seat he gave the younger Cottrell an impassioned, fraternal wave.

A piece of news was brought to Elaine a day or so after Alec's departure, news that so angered her that she was unburdened of some of her anguish and sorrow over her separation from her son.

The news was brought to her by Widow Hughes, and caused her to turn to Ned and say, "Not even your father's death has so broken my heart as what I've just heard."

According to the old widow, Adele Bevington had managed to have the train flagged once again, this time two stops from Tilston Gap, where she would not be observed by anyone from Fonthill. Adele had entered the Pullman car where Alec sat bemused and deathly pale, and had ostentatiously handed him a bouquet of violets, a new gold watch, and a sealed envelope. Then like a fairy godmother, she had kissed him farewell, and without a word got off the train, assisted down by two porters, who were handsomely tipped.

For some time after this apparition, Alec had stared now at the violets, now at the watch, and finally at the sealed envelope. He was unable to summon enough strength to open it. When he did so he found within a check for two thousand dollars—in those spare and austere days a fortune for a young man. Around the check was a thick piece of stationery with the words:

I can never repay you for the happiness and joy you have bestowed on me. I will hold you in my heart forever.

A. B.

The flowers, the watch, the check only increased his acute misery. His grief was so overwhelming that for a moment he felt he was about to stop breathing, and in order to quiet his own overwhelming suffering he promised himself he would simply buy a return ticket back home as soon as he reached Chicago. Of course, once he got off the train he was to change his mind. But he held the violets and Ned's rose tightly in his right hand for a good hundred miles until one of the porters suggested the flowers be put in water and placed at his seat in the dining room, where the "kind lady" had reserved a table for him.

People thought that Adele's sudden decline in strength and

health in body and mind came because of the departure of Alec Cottrell for Chicago. Elaine was positive this was so, and there was nothing to make Ned think otherwise in turn. Besides, by speaking of Adele's grief over the loss of her protégé, the towns-people were able to give vent to their own sorrow over losing their pride and joy and their model young man.

"But, Ned, have you noticed that Keith is brooding over something?" Elaine asked her younger son one evening after the supper dishes were put away, and the two of them were sitting on the front porch, although the evenings were now a bit too chilly for porch-sitting.

Ned bit his lip. "He does act funny," the boy admitted. "Maybe he's drinking again."

"I think he's sorrowing over Alec leaving, in part . . . But there's more to it than that . . . Do you notice how he jumps whenever Adele's name is mentioned?"

"Perhaps," Ned agreed. "I think he does some private legal business for her, though, at his office," he added very casually.

"Thank God at least Alec is no longer at her beck and call." Elaine sighed luxuriously. "Though God knows under whose influence he will fall in that dreadful metropolis on the lake. He always has to have some old woman or unmarried man around telling him what to think and do wherever he goes."

Ned had barely said a word since supper.

"I want you to do something for me, precious," Elaine whis-pered, though there was no need to whisper tonight. There was nobody around for blocks.

"Listen to me," she went on. "I want you to find out from Keith what is bothering him."

"Oh, Mama, please, no!"

"He needs our help also. . . . We are all he has."

"I thought you just said he had Adele."

"Oh, well. She's for entertainment. That's all anybody goes to her for. She's theater."

Ned snickered in spite of himself.

"Don't make fun of your mother like that. Please try to find out, won't you?"

Yes, Elaine was beginning to stir again. She had wept her river of tears over Alec's leaving her. For several days after he had departed she lay on the Circassian walnut bed with a sick head-ache, not taking any nourishment, but in the evening driving herself to prepare as usual the sumptuous repast for her boarders.

It was, strangely enough—she observed the phenomenon in herself—Keith's deep sorrow, coming from some unknown source, that assuaged in part her own grief. She would worry about the young veteran now.

And she was more right than even she realized about Keith. There was something very pressing on his mind.

And again Elaine was right about Ned's getting it out of the veteran. People did tell Ned their secrets. And Ned and Keith were close, those two. Keith was like a new brother to him now, she had observed, and though she did not dare say it, and hardly dared think it, Keith was a much better brother than Alec could ever be, for Alec, despite his sterling virtues, was jealous and spiteful at times, short-tempered, and hypercritical.

"You won't fail me now, will you, dearest?" Elaine kissed Ned on his cheek that night before he went to bed. "I know by the way he acts he is about ready to tell you something in any case."

Ned would have scolded his mother and remonstrated with her over such a request, but he said nothing, owing to Alec's having left. And he decided it was a little thing, after all, to share confidences with Keith. If Keith's secret was too fearsome, he need not tell it to Elaine. After all, he knew how to lie; living with her and Alec had taught him that. He could lie by the book. He would never betray Keith, for he loved him dearly. He felt both protected and happy when in the veteran's company.

So he would go and find out Keith's secret and then keep his own counsel.

"I can always depend on you coming round, can't I?" Keith remarked, opening the door on Ned. "Maybe you're the original bad penny, kid, who knows? Well, what are you staring at, may I ask?" Keith put his hand to his face with one of those quick self-conscious movements so characteristic of the veteran.

"Your hair is all slicked down tonight, Keith. . . . And you're all dressed up."

Keith flushed.

"I thought I would go to the Valencia Theater across the county line. There's a movie on there I haven't seen."

Ned went on looking at Keith sideways. With his hair slicked down like this, he looked as dark-complexioned as Val Dougherty, while when his hair was without the pomade, especially after he shampooed it, it was a kind of tawny color. Keith's face was also a mass of cuts and traces of styptic pencil, showing he had shaved too close tonight. But the pomade's odor made Ned's nostrils tingle.

"We can't talk at the Valencia Theater," Ned said abruptly.

"Talk?" Keith acted astonished. "What is it you want to talk about?" he snapped. After all, he had just been to Ned's house an hour or so before to take his evening meal.

"Maybe you would like to play a quick game of hearts before you go to the Valencia."

"No, I wouldn't."

"You've got something on your mind, Keith. Don't tell me different."

The veteran loosened his collar a bit. He was wearing a rather wide tie with a flowered pattern that made Ned smile in spite of himself, for it reminded him of the pattern of honeysuckles on one of Elaine's party dresses.

"I'd give a lot sometimes to know what goes through that head of yours," Keith barked. He fingered one of the cuts on his chin. "Oh, well." He shrugged his shoulders. "Let's go to the Valencia. I'll pay your way."

"I can pay my own way."

Ned knew that if he didn't get at him tonight he'd not be able to work himself up again for quite a spell. In the end he was more curious probably than Elaine.

The movie bored them to tears. It had to do with a rancher whose land was being taken from him by a band of thugs, who were in the pay of a powerful mining company that had discovered precious ores of some kind on the rancher's land. The best part of the film, both agreed, as they munched Cracker Jack and Hershey bars, was the horses and a few stray Indians.

"I have to get up early tomorrow," Keith explained after the film, and drove Ned directly to his home. He parked, though, in the rear of the boardinghouse, and that meant he would talk.

"I think you have a secret that is bothering you," Ned brought out.

"*A* secret," the older man snorted.

There was one of Keith's pained silences then, but he did not tell Ned to get out of the car. They were both waiting. Ned heard him take out one of the imported cigars his boss had brought him from Florida, and Keith lit it rather grandly.

"I'll listen good if you want to tell," Ned coaxed him.

"Nosey as all get-out," the veteran grumbled, and then started the car. They drove by turns fast and slow and even nearly stopped once, as if the car was running out of gas. Then Keith headed toward the fairgrounds. He parked in front of the still, tar-black water of the river. Keith jumped out. One would have thought they had committed a robbery or were planning to do so, their movements were so erratic.

"If I tell you, Ned, I suppose you'll go right to headquarters or write your brother in Chicago."

"No, I won't, and you know I won't."

"*No, he won't!*" He spat out a piece of the cigar. "Here, puff on a man's smoke for a while till I make up my mind."

There was no way out but to take the cigar from Keith and pull on it, though it turned his stomach. Ordinarily Keith would have observed his discomfort, but now he was too wrapped up in his thoughts, or perhaps trying to find the right words to begin telling what his "secret" was.

"I know where her son is," he began, and took back his cigar from the boy.

This "secret" was overwhelming somehow. Ned had not been prepared for it.

It seemed that an hour went by in silence before he went on:

"As a matter of fact I was with him in France. . . . Can you believe it? Well, it's so. The truth is always queer. We were in the same outfit over there. He was wounded, though, before I was. . . . I visited him in the hospital. I knew he was from this part of the country by the way he talked, almost the way he looked. He *looked* Fonthill, but it never dawned on me he was her son. Not then, anyhow . . . not till a month ago."

He took hold of Ned's shoulder and pressed until it pained.

Every so often from then on, as he talked, Ned would take the cigar from Keith, puff on it, and hand it back to him. It kept the secret coming out.

Just then they heard a coughing sound, probably that of a fox, and heard the leaves rustle not too far off, but they barely made note of any of this.

"I knew, of course, she had been going to the Soldiers' Home," he went on. "Val Dougherty put her on to that. I think he knows her secret, too. That is, knows it's her son, but he don't care enough to put her wise. Or maybe he cares a lot, who knows. There was one fellow in the Soldier's Home she would look at. That's him. You see, I thought she would recognize him. He looks so much like her! He looks *just like her.* I thought she would see that, since she's so smart. Well, to tell the truth, she looked at him the most when I went there with her. But I guess, as they say in church, God hardened her heart, or blinded her eyes. She seen him but she didn't see him. She never let on it was him, in any case. She could have been playacting, of course. But I know when she playacts, which is most of the time. But she wasn't playacting at the Soldiers' Home. No, God has blinded her."

"How do you know it's her son for sure?"

"I looked up his papers. . . . I asked first at the Soldiers' Home. For some reason they give me no trouble. Then I went to the probate court. And then—remember the time I went to Chicago? I found his birth certificate there. I paid a man a hundred dollars in Chicago, can you imagine a hundred dollars? Yes, he's a bastard. Her son. Yes, he was her son and the son of that stuckup coward of a millionaire who got her in the family way. . . . But after I had found out all the truth, and was stuck with it, I couldn't tell her. . . . I hated the secret, I hated the boy, I hated her. . . . You see, *I wanted her to tell me.* That is the only way it will ever work. I still take her there occasionally. She thinks she's doing the soldiers good with her gifts and candies and little get-well notes. . . . But when she comes to his wheelchair and bed, well, you see, Ned, her boy don't know anything. His mind is dark. He barely sees. His eyes move but they don't report back to his head."

Ned took the cigar this time as if he would not give it back.

Keith took the boy's free hand in his. "Her boy don't know

anything. His eyes, as I say, are clear and all, he can move like anybody his hands and legs. But the light in his mind is gone. I guess the doctors don't even understand it. His mind is all darkness."

The "secret" was more than Ned had bargained for, and the cigar had made him sick. But gradually he controlled his nausea enough to get out: "Shall I keep it from Elaine?"

Keith laughed in spite of himself.

"No, we will share what we know, Neddy. We'll tell her. Maybe she can come up with something."

The revelation tonight made Alec's going away for good seem suddenly of little importance, made Alec himself seem not so life-size and all-pervasive in his life and heart.

There was then a son of Adele's. The reality she had based her whole life on did exist. But if that reality, if that son, knew nothing, perhaps saw nothing, though his eyes were clear, Keith said, wasn't it more terrible than if he had never existed or had died in Chicago as a boy after she had relinquished him from her breast?

So Keith's news was very terrible. It kept Ned awake all night, but he could not wake Elaine to tell her. He would wait in any case until Keith was ready to speak of it to both the mother and her son in unison.

The day, however, that Keith and Ned had set to tell Elaine "everything," Adele herself—as if she had got wind of all the talk and consultations that revolved about her—summoned Keith. She had never looked so grand, or so "ready," as he later confided to the younger Cottrell.

Keith's heart skipped a beat when he heard her say: "For some reason, I feel like visiting the Soldiers' and Sailors' Home again. . . . Can you get off early from work and accompany me?"

When he hemmed and hawed, she broke out: "I won't take no for an answer."

"I did have another engagement, Adele."

"Break it, Keith."

He stared at her. Then he saw that it was not so much her old imperiousness, rudeness, but some new kind of final desperation. He also began to wonder if, or perhaps hope, that she was beginning to have some stirring spark, call it realization, intuition, that "the one with the glassy stare"—as she referred to the young veteran in the home—was her own boy.

Since Keith had promised Elaine he would be at the boarding-house for supper that same evening, he had to go to her and beg off. Elaine accepted his reason for being absent from her table.

"But why," Elaine wondered softly, "must she go to the Soldiers' Home at such quick notice?" She was more mystified than angry.

"Mama." Keith tried to mollify her, addressing her as Ned and Alec did on delicate issues. "I can explain that better when you and Ned and I have our talk together."

Elaine gave him a searching look.

"I'll be looking forward to that," she said frostily, and walked on back into the buttery and closed the door.

Damn these women, Keith said to himself, going down the front steps. They always know everything before you've got it out of your mouth.

When Keith came to fetch Adele late that afternoon, he was, despite his being used to her ways, taken aback by her appearance. She had almost half her jewels on. Her hands looked pinioned against her blue velvet coat with the weight of her many rings. She was also over-rouged and wore a scent that could be smelled for a city block. An immense wide-brimmed hat with a rose large as a peony completed her costume.

"What is it, Keith?" she inquired as she was locking the door to her house. "You look positively bilious. What is troubling you?"

"Have you forgotten we are going to a hospital?" He raised his voice, and he gave her a last look of disapproval.

"I suppose I do look as if I were going to a ballroom," she agreed. "But it's like this. What I have on, and I admit it is quite a bit, well, all this gives me the courage to go there. You wouldn't understand since you're a man. But without what I have on"— and she looked down at herself and then back to him—"without *them*, I don't think I could go at all."

"I understand that all right," he said pacifically, "but why are we going today, Adele? On the spur of the moment, I mean."

"Because, just because," she almost wailed. "Oh, all right, I'll tell you. . . . I've had this same dream for several nights. My sister comes to me in the dream—she was my favorite, you know, of all my family. She comes to me so clear and she says, 'Go to the Soldiers' Home, Adele. Please go.'"

Keith averted his face from her as she stood there as if she saw her dream all over again in reverie.

"You know, Adele," he said, "I believe you miss Alec much more than you are aware."

She started as if she had finally come awake from her dream.

"Maybe that's why you're so keen all at once on seeing your other boys at the Home."

She grasped his chin in her hand, and though they were now in public view, she kissed him slowly on the lips.

"My other boys," she repeated, and smiled.

"I've brought a rather heavy box full of gifts for those boys." She pointed to an enormous box left standing near the curb.

He picked it up without difficulty, and they went toward his car.

It was another of the beautiful sunshiny days that cause people to talk about Indian summer, or whether winter will be late, or if deep snowfall is expected.

While they were signing their names in the registry book at the hospital, the matron remarked: "I didn't know you had a relative here, Miss Bevington."

Adele's mouth forced a smile, but she did not reply.

With Keith holding the heavy box of fruit, candies, cigarettes, cigars, and Irish linen handkerchiefs ("People who are in wheelchairs or in bed all day long need soft, expensive handkerchiefs," she told Keith), they entered the great room of the forgotten soldiers.

At first Keith was certain she was going directly to the boy he was positive was her own flesh and blood, but as she approached the bed next to his, she stopped in her tracks. She complained she was tired. It was a good thing she did not look at Keith's face just then. Its paleness and contortion would have dismayed her still more.

But *he* turned to look at her. His name was Moorbrook. *He* was seated in his wheelchair as usual. He looked, Keith thought, younger each time they came here. Keith had read in some medical book once that those whose minds are asleep often do not age like other human beings. But he had not read that these sleepers grow younger by the day. Yet this young man, this Moorbrook, looked hardly older than a boy. Much younger than when he had been in France. Then, to Keith's growing unease, Adele slowly turned her gaze toward him, toward Moorbrook, and the disabled youth, contrary to his usual expression of sheer vacuousness to all that surrounded him, gave Adele one long and penetrating look; then, chin down, he relapsed into his former empty obliviousness.

Adele stood by his wheelchair. But she looked only at the floor.

"Perhaps we should give him something from the gift box," she told Keith after a long silence.

"If he will accept it, Adele," Keith said, and took out several of the gifts.

"Give him the orange."

"But he is not able to peel or even eat it, Adele," Keith whispered.

"He can hold it, though." She spoke with a prayerful tinge to her voice he had never heard come from her before.

Keith took an orange and went over to the staring young man. He took the soldier's hand and tried to open the fingers. When this did not succeed, he placed the orange very gently in the invalid's lap. The ex-soldier looked down presently at his gift. Then with a very great effort he touched the orange with one trembling index finger. His head fell gently back against the wheelchair's back, as if the effort of touching the gift had tired him.

But when Keith turned his face back to Adele the expression he saw there was such that his words carried loud enough to be heard to the matron's desk: "What on earth is it, Adele?"

"My dream of the past few nights, my dream!" she exclaimed. She turned to hold Keith's arm. "Let us be going. We've given them gifts. Let's leave at once."

"Adele," Keith admonished her.

She picked up the gift box and handed it to him.

"We needn't stand on ceremony with men who are not even aware we have visited them," she explained. "Keith, there is more life in Poplar Grove Cemetery than here."

"But then all the same, every few days, she would have to return. To the Soldiers' and Sailors' Home, that is." Keith told it all later, first to Elaine, then to others, and finally to everybody. "I think she suspected then that *he* was there. But curiously, on her many visits she paid scant attention to him, Moorbrook, the real object of her visit. She looked at all the other soldiers and sailors with more care and attention, sort of omitting *him*. It was the fact she always omitted him that told me volumes. I did not dare guide her to his bed, beside which was a comfortable chair with the back covered with a cloth depicting bluebirds in an apple tree. . . . But I felt Adele knew *I* knew. I felt Adele knew that I had been aware all the time he was here. She knew that I had seen his *papers*, that I had made the investigation, that I was the real detective. And I think she knew why I hadn't blabbed, or told. She knew I would never tell, not even her.

"But after the tenth or twelfth visit—oh, yes, she brought candy and apples and chewing gum for all of the men there, bestowing the presents herself on each one—this last visit she made she finally came to him, and all at once sat down on the chair with the bluebirds, but not looking at him, she took my hand—not his—in her white-gloved one.

" 'Tell me the truth, Keith Gresham.' Her voice sounded like it came from under the boards of the floor. 'Tell me, *is it him?*' "

"I could not have replied even if I had wanted to. My voice was gone.

" 'Just say the word,' she went on, looking round to where I stood but not able to turn her eyes far enough to see me.

" 'Keith, just say the word,' she went on. 'Just say, *"Yes, it's him."* '

" 'Why don't you take a full good look, ma'am?'

"She repeated that last word contemptuously after me.

" 'Go ahead now,' I urged her when she kept her head turned in my direction, like she was frozen in this posture.

" 'Well, if I must, I . . .' She let an endless while go by. Then she moved the heavy chair, and looked only at his chest, very gradually raising her eyes to his face. It seemed too apparent to me he had her luminous blue eyes, her slightly large, eloquent mouth, with the upper lip rather small in proportion to the fleshier, beautifully shaped lower one. And on the chin of both of them was the slight hollow place resembling a dimple.

"There was of course no recognition by him of her, for he recognized almost nothing, nobody. I believe he half-responded to the orderly who took him occasionally to the bath, brushed his fine-spun auburn hair, and kept fastening the frogs on his pajamas, but all others were like air to him.

"She indicated after a long wait that we must leave now.

" 'Look a little longer, please, ma'am.' I used the last word on purpose now.

" 'Ah, I've seen enough for today, haven't I?'

"We drove back then to her house, and I went up the flight of stairs ahead of her, took the keys she was fumbling with, and opened her door.

" 'You'll come in and have something, Keith.'

"I followed her on in.

"Of course she went for the medicine, and I confess I needed some, too, by now.

"We drank for quite a while without speaking.

" 'Evidently,' she said at last, 'you have done some research.'

" 'I knew him in France,' I started in.

" 'So he grew right up here after all, in front of me all the time,' she said, 'when I had pictured him so often in Australia or Timbuctoo.'

" 'Shortly after his adoption by people in Chicago'—I summarized my research—'both his adopted father and mother died in an accident. He went to his adopted parents' grandparents here at home. In Fonthill.'

" 'Why, oh why, didn't I recognize him then the very first time, if what you say is true? I've been there so often. As if the Almighty had wanted me not to see . . .'

" 'I didn't know how to tell you.' I began then on my own chronicle of guilt. 'I thought . . .'

" 'And he knows nothing,' she said, speaking really to the windows or walls. 'Having waited so long. I wonder if there is no end to punishment. It seems to me it has no end. Even murderers are finally forgiven, let out of prison after thirty or forty or fifty years. But for some there is evidently no respite.'

"She rose and went to the window, then came back and seated herself again.

" 'I will go alone from now on, Keith. You've been very kind, but . . .'

" 'No, I'll go with you until you're used to him.'

" 'That would be very kind. I don't want to impose on you. . . . You have your own sorrow to carry.'

" 'Going there makes what I carry easier, maybe. Have you thought of that?' I said in a hollow tone.

" 'To think you knew!' she cried, having missed what I just said. 'To think Keith Gresham knew!' "

For her loss of Alec, Elaine found two principal consolations, enlarging her boardinghouse and accepting more evening supper guests, and giving up her "pentecostal religious tracts," returning with devout regularity to the services at the First Presbyterian Church.

But neither her increased labors in the boardinghouse nor her consolation in religion could abate or put to an end her tirades against Adele Bevington. Her chief audience was Ned and Keith Gresham.

"Adele planned to take him away from me years ago—when he was still in short trousers and even then looked so handsome and manly! Had he never met her—!"

The diatribes continued as she made the pie dough, pared the apples, roasted the veal and the chicken, and cut and sliced innumerable vegetables. Even Widow Hughes in her frequent entrances and exits advised her to "forget the diamond queen."

So incensed had Elaine become against her rival that Keith dared not broach the subject of Adele's "found boy," for he felt it would infuriate Elaine more than ever.

After her tirades, invariably ending in uncontrollable weeping, Elaine would carefully get dressed and go to church, which, under the new minister, kept its doors open night and day, with prayer and meditation services for the afflicted always in operation.

Since she was a young girl, Elaine had always received the

greatest consolation from the communion service. The new minister, Reverend Lilley, young, fresh from Edinburgh, was less dour than the old pastor, and he had also appointed new elders to distribute the bread and wine. Ned did not dare refuse Elaine her request to accompany her to this special sacrament. Heartbroken over Alec's apostasy and dereliction as his mother was, Ned could only put on his hat and walk silently with her to their pew in the church. The service faintly stirred his imagination now, though only a year before he had announced to both Alec and Elaine over dessert that he no longer believed in God, but his brother and mother were so used to his cyclic announcements of wild notions that they probably did not recall from day to day his change of doctrine or his adoption of some new-found heresy. Certainly Elaine did not remember now that her son was a confessed atheist as they sat awaiting communion.

The organist played "Not Worthy, Lord" as the elders brought the bread and wine. The youngest of the elders whispered in Ned's ear that he might have two wafers if he cared to, and Ned reached immediately for the extra helping. While Elaine wept copiously behind her veil, so that Ned had to lend her his blue-dotted bandana handkerchief, he studied the huge stained-glass windows of Christ's ministry, his eye lingering for a while on the Good Shepherd, then on Jesus with the woman at the well. The Christ who hung on the cross was depicted with astonishing bloodthirstiness, Ned thought, but what struck him to the point of open-mouthed astonishment was that the young man nailed to the wood of the cross bore such a strong resemblance to Val Dougherty, while the Christ talking to the woman at the well looked almost exactly like Keith Gresham.

"Keep your eyes lowered, dear," Elaine cautioned him several times. She felt his open-mouthed, wide-eyed scrutiny of the stained-glass windows was disruptive to the sacredness of the occasion. But who knows, perhaps she also recalled he no longer believed in the Christ.

At the most solemn moment in today's service, Adele Bevington appeared. She wore only one of her diamond necklaces, but it shone so brilliantly in the subdued light of the church that she might as well have put on all her jewels.

There was a murmur and stir in the entire congregation, and

the eyes of every member of the choir followed her every movement. The minister was calm and collected. He now knew her entire life story, but in the days when Adele had committed her sin, he was still in the nursery.

Adele greeted the elders almost effusively, and they seated her in the pew that her father had paid for in perpetuity, in the very first row. She could hardly be barred from it, whatever anyone may have thought of her, and all through the years nobody had ever sat in her place. A kind of superstitious dread had kept the seat always unoccupied.

Adele appeared almost penitent, certainly considerably bowed with anguish. Elaine later so described her own impression of the "diamond queen." But Adele made, as usual, one terrible infraction of decorum. She insisted on having *three* of the tiny crucibles of wine, which she drained hurriedly, one after the other. She refused the bread in a loud whisper with the criticism it was too sweet to her palate.

During the long silent prayer that followed the partaking of the bread and wine the entire congregation heard Adele's deep voice intoning: "Let God's own Son tell me if he is *mine*. Let God's own Son give me the truth!"

The grief in that voice broke something also in Elaine's spirit. She wept now unashamedly, to Ned's great discomfiture and embarrassment. Like his father before him, he found women's tears a great trial and humiliation, and his eye went for support in desperation to the various Christs in the stained-glass windows.

Young Reverend Lilley was later both praised and blamed for his welcoming back the "lost soul" of Adele. He was especially criticized for having gone out of his way at the church door, once the service was ended, extending his greeting to her, and after his rather elaborate blessing of her with his right hand, he gave her an open embrace, which his enemies said was quite inconsistent with the theology of the church he was a minister of.

Perhaps even more sensational was the meeting a short distance from the church door between Elaine and Adele. The communion service evidently had dissolved much of Mrs. Cottrell's anger with Adele. The two women embraced. At that moment perhaps they understood one another, at least acknowledged one another's common hurt.

"If you feel," Adele was saying to his mother while Ned dug his toes in the mud surrounding the brick walkway, "if in your heart there is bitterness against me for having sent Alec off on his travels, I hope time will soften your anger against me, that we will all see it was the young man's destiny."

"Adele talks like some character out of *East Lynne*," Elaine confided to Ned when the older woman had got into her limousine and was driven off by a man from the livery.

Ned and Elaine stared after the departing machine.

"She did offer to drop us off, though, Mother," Ned remarked in order to have something to say after such an exhausting morning.

"I wouldn't be caught dead alighting from her car." Elaine began to revert to her more customary view of the world and of Adele. "Imagine her coming to communion late and consuming three cups of wine!"

"And no bread," her son reminded her.

"What on earth did you find so eye-riveting today in the stained-glass windows?"

"Oh, was I looking so hard at the windows?" He coughed and looked away. He could not tell her who Jesus had reminded him of.

Elaine had told Keith and Ned that she would not "last the winter" the day the train pulled out at the depot, taking Alec away from her. But the exact opposite had been the case. After weeping, in Ned's words, a river, faced with the second mortgage on her house, Elaine came out of her reverie with death and extensively remodeled Alec's library into another dining room. She advertised in the local paper that she would be serving evening dinners to "persons of quality." Soon she had more customers than she knew what to do with, and by Christmas her dining establishment was considered voguish—better, the food was superb. Elaine had tireless energy and was, as Alec had once said disparagingly of her to Adele, "only happy when she was sweating and slaving in the kitchen."

But even more meteoric than his mother's success as the

operator of a fashionable boardinghouse was Alec's rise to fame in Chicago. Elaine had confidently expected him home by Christmas. He would have had his experience in the big city; his suffering and disillusionment with the world of music and entertainment would be complete. No one was prepared, therefore, for Alec's picture appearing in all the Chicago newspapers as the "singing sensation" with a popular orchestra of the day, which broadcast on nearly all radio networks.

Instead, therefore, of having the prodigal come home, Elaine, Keith, and Ned had sat quietly mesmerized at nine-thirty in the evening on a Friday, just after the pre-Christmas banquet Elaine had served to "her very own," and had been treated to the phenomenon of hearing their own Alec sing to them on the radio. They had often gathered before the radio in times past, Keith, Elaine, Alec, and Ned, to hear Madame Schumann-Heink sing "Silent Night" and other Christmas songs. But now their ears were treated to the voice of their own "constant companion" coming to them from hundreds and hundreds of miles away, and already barely recognizable as that of Alec Cottrell.

Elaine wept as if she were attending her son's funeral. Yes, of course, they were tears of happiness, she told everyone, but they were also the tears of a mother who knew she would never see her boy again except on short, perfunctory visits. She had lost him forever. Her hope that he would return when he found the world and the theater far beyond his reach had been proved without foundation. He had gone up the ladder of fame at one bound. He had "arrived" almost the same day he had got off the train, stumbling with acute homesickness and despair.

Alec's infrequent letters spoke of a Mr. Tetworth, who had happened to see him in a theater lobby, and was later convinced he was a genuine "talent." It was this same Mr. Tetworth who had introduced him to all the "proper" people, and who had procured for him the audition with the well-known orchestra leader with whose band he was now star vocalist.

There was only one other occupation into which Elaine threw herself with as much energy and enthusiasm as she devoted to her cooking for boarders: her letter-writing. She poured out all her hopes and fears and her love in these epistles to her "lost" son in Chicago. She told of all the events in Fonthill, gave every scrap and bit of news of Adele, with the saga of her own lost son returned, kept him informed on the doings of Widow Hughes, of Keith's devotion, and Ned's acute missing of his only brother, and a minute chronicle of her new commercial endeavors and the resounding success of her fashionable restaurant, which still lacked a name. The letters were so bulky that she had to use sealing-wax to keep their contents from spilling out, and she would command Ned to take them to the main post office at once so that they would go out on the midnight express.

Once Ned had opened one of his mother's letters on the way to the post office. He had waited, however, to read it until he was inside the cavernous federal building itself, built a little after the Civil War, where under the dim green lamp of the writing desk he perused from beginning to end Elaine's outpourings to Alec. Alec was addressed as "her only treasure" and "her dearest soul." She told of her anguish at losing him, of the tears she had shed constantly since his going, and the never-ending hope one day he would return home, and they would build a house worthy of such a fine boy and then at last begin to enjoy life as life was meant to be enjoyed. There was no mention of Ned. Stuffing the myriad pages into his coat pocket, he went to a small stationer's store and bought some library paste and sealed shut the ten-page sheaf of pages as best he could.

An overwhleming, sickening anger came over Ned. So she loved Alec best! Of course he had always known this in his secret heart. He realized he must run off, too, but he must go where no one would know he had gone. But where was this place? He did not want to be on the stage, anyhow, or sing like a bobolink and win perfect strangers over to put him on the stage. He did not want to dress up or make people misty-eyed at meeting him. All, he guessed, he had ever wanted to do was go hunting with his dad, and his dad had run out on him and died instead! He had only Keith, and when he was in his right mind perhaps Val, but he knew they really cared very little about him.

"What took you so long, dear?" Elaine inquired on his returning from the post office.

"Your letter came open," he said glumly. "I had to buy library paste and stick it together again."

"I suppose you read it also while you were at it?"

"A whole book like that, Elaine?" he said airily. "Why, I'd still be there, and you know it. . . . Must you write Alec a whole book? After all, he is a busy man now."

In spite of herself Elaine burst into laughter. Ned chimed in.

"You have something even your brother never had, Neddy. You can say things that sound serious and yet are very funny."

"Even my brother, yeah. I expect you thought he had everything."

"Don't say that, Neddy. You know how dear you are to me. Don't look so black and despondent, sweetheart. Come over to Mother."

But Ned merely looked at the wall, and shook his head.

"When Mother works so hard, why can't you be nice?"

"It was Alec who was nice, remember?" he told her. "One nice boy in the family is enough, ain't it?"

"Oh, Ned, Ned," she wailed, but he had already left the room, and was racing up the back stairs to his room two steps, even three, at a time.

"I knew you at least would come back to me," Adele told Ned after she had opened the door on him, and he stood wiping from his feet the snow that was beginning to fall rather heavily outside. They sat for a while in silence, watching the couples come out from the last showing at the Royal.

"In the end, you are the only one I can trust," Adele began. "I can't tell you how much Alec's departure has afflicted me. I know your mother suffers, of course she does. She is his mother. But, Ned, don't you see that in a way I am *more* than his mother. I do think you understand. I believe you understand everything, though you are still on the threshold of childhood. You know more than Alec did. You are the silent one. But I gave Alec everything I had. You know that. Your mother gave him life, nourishment, herself. She was his all, *is* his all. No one can take the place of Elaine Cottrell. But you see, I gave him his talent. I can say this because I feel I am at the end of my life. No, don't start like that. I believe everything is drawing to a close here. As I say, I gave him his talent. I gave him himself, which no mother can do. She may have been his physical mother. I was his spiritual one. I sent him away. At the time perhaps I did not realize all this. But now, in the almost complete darkness that is descending, I do. More than Elaine, I did not want to lose Alec. . . . She has you, after all, and her ceaseless activity, unremitting. . . . Oh, I have been so unwell of late, dear Ned. So beside myself, so close to the black river. I must tell you something. I believe Keith Gresham is crazy. Don't laugh. Or do you agree with me? He is crazy and he is trying to drive me crazy."

"I think I know, Adele," the second son managed to get out, but perhaps she did not hear him. Like Elaine, she often did not let herself hear anything once she started to speak on a matter that was pressing, and where no solution presented itself.

"He has dragged me countless times to that Soldiers' and Sailors' Home. . . . He says I am drunk when I go there! Look who's talking, for pity's sake! I am never drunk, you know that. Half of that brandy I take as a stimulant has been watered by the apothecary. . . . Ned, Ned, do you think, though, what Keith says is true? Tell me, now, what you may think. Don't hold back, dearest."

"You mean what the truth is, Adele?" Ned blushed, and looked toward the electric red, white, yellow, green, and mauve lights of the movie house.

"Call it the truth if you like," she said slowly. "I ask you now. Is that young man who can't talk or walk, who sits like a statue in the Soldiers' Home, who has known nothing since 1918 . . . Is he mine? Is he my boy?"

The snow was beginning to obstruct their view of the Royal, for it stuck to the high windowpanes.

"Keith," Ned began, "yes, he did explore the idea with me a little. . . . I believe it's all he thinks about! Sometimes he believes, yes, he is your son, that is, the man in the Home, and sometimes, he—Keith—is not sure."

"If you only knew how much money I have spent on detectives, on the police, with anybody who could find the least scrap of proof. And the fortune-tellers and mediums and spiritualists, and the rest!" She rose, and then as if wondering why she had risen, she sat down again. She watched the snow fall for a while. "You will never guess," she said after a while.

"Oh, I know you have shelled out a lot of money searching."

Ned spoke desperately. His eyes, too, were fixed on the snow.

"*Shelled* out!" Adele repeated and laughed. "Oh, that speech, darling. That wonderful speech of yours, for all the books you have read from my library. I used to spend every cent I earned at *The Courier* on finding out. 'Information guys,' the men at the newspaper called them. . . . It all led nowhere. 'Why do you bring him up now when I am at the end of my life?' I asked Keith. 'Because,' he replied, 'it has got under my skin, too. I can't bear not to know, either. I want you and me both to know, Adele.' "

She got up and drew the high long blind down so that the snow was less visible.

"I am more worried about Keith than anybody else just now," she began again. "I told you I think he is crazy. And that his notion that young man is my son is part of his craziness. . . . That veteran is no more my son than he is the Lost Dauphin."

"Oh." Ned laughed and came out from his own reverie. "That story, yes." He raised his voice. "They never found out about him either, did they? Never."

"The truth is," Adele began, and then all at once she motioned for Ned to observe that the lights of the marquee of the Royal were going out, making the snow more white, more present to them. "The whole truth is he is dead. My son is dead."

"You have . . . a certificate?" Ned stumbled the words out.

"A certificate?" She seemed insulted by the word. "If my son were alive"—she spoke as if to the blurred glass of the windowpane—"he would have searched for me! He would have left no stone unturned, if he had to go on foot through every inch of the nation."

"But Keith said this young man's toe was injured just like you said your son's was." Ned's desperation was growing, and he winced at his own words.

She waited a while. "Do you know how many soldiers must have injured toes!" she said huskily. "Or injured hands or eyes or brains? Why just his toe? Have you seen this young veteran? Well, then, why don't you go and take a look at him. For my sake! For Keith's sake! He is no more my boy than . . ." She began to cry, but hard dry tears, unlike the tempest Elaine was capable of shedding. Tears like rock.

"I don't know why he had to bring it up now," she finished.

"He thought it was all you wanted after Alec left you."

"Alec is not dead. The fool! I mean Keith, you know. Such an idiot . . . but I've grown so dependent on him, Ned. Isn't it shameful to need people when they're not even right for one? Alec treated me so shabbily toward the last. He was in another world, of course, by then."

She walked over to a little stand and picked up a Chicago newspaper, and brought it back to him.

Ned barely glanced at it, explaining he had seen it. It was quite a "piece," with Alec's picture (he had had his eyebrows plucked and his hair was longer). The clipping told of the "sensational singing star" and his overnight rise to acclaim.

Ned was a bit taken aback when he saw Adele kiss the clippings as she put them away in a little box. She looked very much like Elaine as she pressed her lips to the newsprint.

"So, to return to this puzzle"—she faced him—"this riddle he has brought to me from France. From the ocean, or from wherever. . . . He is not my boy, that boy in the Home. Yet see what has happened to me. I can't say he is not! Do you understand? I cannot say Moorbrook—God what a name!—is not my own flesh and blood. That is the gift Keith Gresham has bestowed on me."

"He told me he has papers proving he is your son."

"I've looked at those so-called papers, Ned. They say so little. I even had a lawyer look them over. He understood nothing from them. Another blatherskite for you! Lawyers, detectives, preachers! At least Judge Hitchmough had the decency to try to kill himself. But you say Val Dougherty rescued him. The more fool he. . . . Men! I would like to corral them all in a stable somewhere and set fire to it then with my own hands. I would laugh when I heard them scream."

"I bet you would." Ned spoke in a strange accent.

"Laugh and congratulate God. Who would miss them all? Who?"

She walked up to the window, blurred with the snowstorm, then over to where Ned sat, then around the room and back to the second son.

"And where, will you tell me," she commenced again, "where are these alleged foster parents of Moorbrook? Will you tell me that? Dead, they say. Well, isn't that convenient! There is nobody at all to prove who he is. And he can barely speak! These papers"—she whipped the air with her hands—"proving he was adopted from some person or persons whose names could not be mentioned. . . . So, you see, my very good friend George Etheredge paid a fortune to hide it all. . . . And if he were here tonight, I would strangle him with my own hands! He has hidden what I want to know, so that if the earth gulped the whole nation, it could not be better hidden."

Going straight up to Ned, she cried: "I hope George Etheredge occupies the hottest seat in hell. At last I know what he did to me. I spit on our love now. Val Dougherty at his slimiest I hold dearer!"

"George Etheredge was the father then?"

Adele stopped and touched her breast. She had no jewels on tonight, not even a ring or brooch. But she was so used to touching the necklace, the great necklace. Her hand remained on her breast.

"That's right, Ned. I never told you outright did I? I went around Robin Hood's barn with you. Let me tell you straight. Yes, George Etheredge is the father. He took all that was promise away from me. He took my life. He took my boy. In return he gave me stones. They have weighed me down and have got heavier year by year. . . ."

Ned had put his palm over his eyes. She took it away and threw back his head against the back of the chair.

"Some day, even you will be leaving me. You are getting to be a man, too. You will probably only remember the worst parts of me. You will remember how you learned about life from the fount of corruption itself, as that old preacher used to say of me."

He realized then how much she prized her downfall. After all, it was her whole life.

"Go home, dearest. Your eyes are heavy with sleep. And forgive me." She pushed him toward the door. "One last thing, though." She kissed him feverishly across the face, the lips. "The next time you see crazy Keith will you just tell him straight out: He hasn't proved a thing. The papers he shows could be testifying to anybody's boy. Doesn't he see that? Doesn't he know cold print can prove nothing?"

She left her lips on his for a long time; then she opened the door and closed it on him.

Keith and Elaine had their most serious quarrel over his "discovery," and the veteran saw for the first time what opposing her in her own domain could mean.

"Moorbrook!" She spat out the word. And mimicking his own words just pronounced, she went at him: " 'You speak as if you didn't want her to have her son back, Mrs. Cottrell!' "

This time she smashed a dish and sent its fragments flying through the kitchen.

" 'Mrs. Cottrell!' " she vociferated. "If I hear that again from your lips! And don't dare to pick up the pieces of that dish! Do you hear me?"

Nonetheless, bending low, he picked up every piece and laid them on the white pine table. Then they fell into one another's arms.

Keith arranged all the broken pieces of the china plate till it was a whole.

"I can mend this for you."

Thinking back to his talk with Dr. Radwell, Keith said, turning away from the broken plate, "Once, when she was in her cups, Adele said a terrible thing about Dr. Radwell, you know."

Elaine had taken her position before her ironing board. She was "going over" for a last time one of Ned's dress shirts, though the only place the boy had to wear it was church. She sprinkled some drops of rosewater from a glass bottle onto the fabric. Still angry, she showed no interest in what Keith was saying, but by her deep silence Keith knew she wanted him to tell her.

"Dr. Radwell loves his chauffeur," he said at last.

Elaine gave him a look of contemptuous reproof. He had forgotten that Charles Radwell was her own physician.

The same afternoon of the broken plate and the words about Dr. Radwell's chauffeur, Elaine accompanied Keith to the Soldiers' Home.

"You will know if anybody does," he had said to Elaine just before they went in to visit Moorbrook.

Elaine stood patiently by the silent former soldier. Keith was unprepared for the absorption on her face as she stood before the mute, damaged wreck of a man. He turned away finally and said he would wait for her in the car.

"It is true," Elaine told him as Keith drove her back a few minutes later to the boardinghouse, "he has her wonderful eyes and her strong chin. But, Keith, what farm boy around here does not have blue eyes and a strong chin. And his hair is not like hers. It is coarse as a pony's tail. And he doesn't want anything."

"Doesn't want anything?"

"While Adele wants the whole world with strings tied to it."

So one stormy scene after another was enacted in various houses in Fonthill apropos of Keith's revelation about Moorbrook. And the whole "discovery" that Keith Gresham thought he had made was slowly turned to naught. Nobody believed that the young man with the improbable name in the Soldiers' and Sailors' Home was Adele's son. Dr. Charles Radwell was, of course, summoned to offer an opinion on it. He went to the Home and made a thorough examination of the veteran. His verdict: It could not be Adele Bevington's boy.

Going to Keith's home, Radwell had warned him: "You must not torment that woman any longer. She is not at all well."

"What do you mean 'not at all well'?" Keith wondered languidly, sitting with his back to the doctor.

"Exactly what I say," Dr. Radwell replied with a kind of indifferent admiration of the veteran's rudeness.

Many people said later on that it was Keith Gresham's harping on Moorbrook's being her son that drove Adele Bevington to her final "chapters of disgrace." She turned her front parlor into a kind of dance hall, which had a bar in the rear and served illicit drinks. The authorities evidently decided to turn their back on the whole affair. She was on the whole discreet—for her. But almost the only persons who attended these "soirées" after the Royal had closed its doors were young unemployed men—some so poor the shoes were falling off their feet. They were often hungry, so she served them cuts of beef and egg salad with their near-beer and their "medicine." Then they would dance with her.

Adele had always been fond of dancing, and she insisted on dancing with each of the young men from the streets and the courthouse benches. But most of the time they all merely listened to her Victrola and her talk.

The evenings never gained popularity, despite the generous fare and the music. Sometimes, however, the front parlor was as crowded as a train station, then again only one or two of the unemployed men would turn up. Very often she pressed a five-dollar bill into their hands as they left.

"I lost a son, you know." She would invariably bring up this topic as the evening wore on. "But the rumor he is Moorbrook is without foundation or fact. I have called in specialists from all over the world," she lied, "to examine him. And before the specialists there were many detectives from Chicago. . . . I believe my son is dead. You, you"—she would turn to the blank faces of the men who had never held a job—"you are my sons! All of you."

But the very name Moorbrook seemed to haunt her. They said it was on her lips when she died.

Keith went on believing the mute soldier was her son. It became a kind of "fetish" (a popular term of the day) with him. Dr. Radwell described it as an "obsession." And there were even times as Keith's own illness progressed that he wondered if *he* were not Adele's son.

Then gradually the scandal of Adele's dance parlor finally died down. People almost accepted the fact that there was such an establishment. After all, on the northwest side of town there had always been one or two houses of malodorous fame, and the Carlyle House flourished only a few blocks from the post office and the newspaper office.

At last people merely ignored her evenings, and opinion grew that Moorbrook was not her son. Nobody believed he was. Except Keith. He persisted, but he gave up speaking of his belief, and kept it against his heart like a hair shirt.

"If my boy were there," Adele would tell the young unemployed visitors to her front parlor, "do you think I would be having open house? Do you think we would be drinking and laughing if my boy had recognized me, and told me I was his own flesh and blood! Were I his own mother, he would have stood up and embraced me though he had no power at all in his arms and legs! He would have known me."

"But, Dr. Radwell," Keith had pleaded when he visited the physician for the fourth and last time, "don't you realize Moorbrook was born on the very day when Adele's son was born? The records themselves prove it was the same day."

The doctor merely looked blank.

"I am moved by your wanting him to be her son so very much, Keith," the doctor said. "It is rare to find anybody in this day and age who cares about anything. . . . Your caring so much that Adele find her son . . . is a phenomenon."

Keith's lips moved as if repeating the last word. After that he gave up. He no longer went to the Soldiers' Home, and he quit visiting Adele. He was with Ned almost constantly. He was teaching the second son how to shoot. The lessons took all day, even went into the night, when the target was illuminated by flares. Elaine's protests fell on deaf ears.

"It's in the boy's blood," Elaine said to Rita. "His dad, you know, and before him his dad's father, and his father before him—they were all soldiers and hunters. Weren't at peace unless they held a rifle in their hands."

The "evenings" at Adele's came to a halt. Perhaps that is why she died, some said. She had nobody toward the end but the unknown drifters. Once she opened the window so that the snowflakes would touch her. She always said they were souls, trying to comfort the living. Ned felt he was not wanted any longer in her parlor because she had so many other young men waiting attendance on her. All the unemployed chaps of the Depression, as she called them. They began to sleep at her house some of them, wandering in and out as she slept in her chair by the front window. And she had not made a mistake in her judgment. Not one turned out to be a scamp or a thief, none took her diamonds or made unfair advantage of her generosity. They slept with her instead, sometimes four in a bed. They slept with an old woman, and loved her. She loved all of them.

"Moorbrook is not my son," she told each and every one of them.

The physician, who was also the coroner, said she died from a rare kind of pneumonia. She was said to have slept before the open window wearing only her diamonds and a slip. She was burning with fever, she told one of the young men, and asked him to let in more fresh air. The flakes of snow fell thick and fast within the room.

She was conscious to the very last, two of the young derelicts who were present when she died told the coroner.

"I have no son," she told the two and kept looking out the window.

It was some months after Adele's death and the opening of her will that Dr. Radwell confided in Keith Gresham that there was still something the lieutenant did not know about his "great and beautiful friend."

"I'm afraid there was a lot none of us knew about her," Keith answered back.

"But this missing piece in a puzzle of puzzles," the doctor went on in the monotone he used in his consulting room, "explains for me, as a medical man, her death."

Keith's eyes opened to a kind of stare. "Go on, sir," the veteran said.

"Adele went to the Soldiers' and Sailors' Home," the old man went on, "early one morning, the day of her death. Before daybreak. They rise early, you know, in the Home. . . . Curiously enough, she referred to the young man as 'my Moorbrook.' "

Keith grasped the doctor's hand; then perhaps ashamed at this betrayal of his feelings, he let go of his grasp and closed his eyes, repeating the two words the doctor had said.

"She was in all her finery at five o'clock in the morning! Her diamonds, pearls, whatever you call her jewels, she had them all on."

Keith nodded, and kept his eyes closed now.

" 'Charles,' she began, 'I am in deep trouble, Charles. . . . He has spoken to me. Yes, don't look that way at me. Be serious for once in your life. . . . My Moorbrook has said something, but oh, Charles, I am so frightened.' "

" 'You are positive he said something?' I inquired.

" 'Oh, my, yes. You can ask the other soldiers there and the matron. They will bear me out.'

"I gave Adele a tablet then, and she asked for two. After they began to calm her a little, she asked me to hold her in my arms while she spoke."

Dr. Radwell broke off as if he, too, needed tablets.

"Adele told me"—the old man bent closer to Keith—"that Moorbrook said in clear tones, 'Meet me by the river tonight, Mother.' "

Keith lay back against the faded velvet of the chair, his mouth open. From his mouth a black substance came out. As if he had expected this, the doctor wiped his mouth dry with a large cloth.

"Go on," Keith said, as the doctor staunched the flow with another cloth.

" 'You must stay at my house for a few days,' I told Adele," Charles Radwell continued, but it was clear now his more complete attention was with Keith Gresham, for he saw how very ill the lieutenant was. That is, he had suspected how ill he was before, but the hemorrhaging from the mouth just then made him perfectly certain.

"She would not obey me!" Charles Radwell intoned.

"She could only obey herself," Keith said. "That was why she was Adele."

The doctor held the two cloths in his hand.

"So you see, she went home to die," he finished.

The funeral given for Adele Bevington was planned and executed and every detail looked after meticulously by Keith Gresham in person. The service was patterned after those he had seen in France as a soldier. There were plumed horses and carriages and, to the scandal of Fonthill, Keith had even arranged for there to be "paid mourners" so that the funeral would at least have more persons in attendance than Elaine, Ned, and himself to follow the corpse to the cemetery. The entire ceremony was without any church affiliation. A few of the young men who had so often been Adele's "guests" followed the cortege on foot to the cemetery. But the town itself turned out to see the procession go by, even though a fine sleet was falling, and the roads and streets were treacherous.

The funeral was, all the townspeople agreed, in the worst possible taste, like her life. Yet it sank into public consciousness, this funeral, as Adele's life had done. She would be talked about in Fonthill forever. In the end, more than Alec Cottrell, for he was, after all, only a popular singer, and eventually a movie star of early rise and fall. But Adele was something, somebody, no one could explain, but whom her friends and enemies could not forget, or even forgive. And none of the details of her life were ever quite clear.

Another peculiar happening was that Moorbrook died at almost the exact hour, minute, and second at which Adele departed Fonthill forever.

The Royal Theater is closed now, but the marquee is still standing, and the display cases that held the faces of the matinee and silver-screen idols. Nobody knows who owns the theater. That is, nobody knows why it is not torn down and turned into a parking lot or a filling station. Like a blind man it stares across at the high window from which Adele used to look down on the young men and women leaving the theater, with the make-believe still in their eyes.

That was what made her go on, she once confided to Ned, the look of make-believe in the eyes of the young.

The bulk of her fortune she left to Ned and Keith. She left nothing to Alec, and in her will she had insisted that the lawyers put in black large type the sentence: ALEC COTTRELL DESERT-ED ME WHEN HE SHOULD HAVE BEEN MY MAINSTAY THROUGHOUT.

Her will had been drawn up nearly a month before she began going again to the Soldiers' Home, so that talk will never die down as to what she might have done with regard to Moorbrook had she had time to make another will.

"Only a child and he's a millionaire!" Elaine often repeated to Rita on the telephone, and to Ned himself as he sat with her after the evening supper. Actually Adele's estate had come to very little, what with taxes, lawyers' fees, and debts, and her own reckless spending. Keith received twenty thousand dollars, and Ned forty, but in those far-off bare-cupboard days such bequests were a fortune.

A few months after Adele's death Ned Cottrell quit school and went to Canada. He told his mother he wanted to visit the places where his father had so often gone hunting.

"Of course, I could have put my foot down," Elaine told everybody. "After all, he is a minor, and not as mature even as many boys his age. And his school work! How will he make that up? But he behaved like a wild man. Very much like his older brother. When *he* made up his mind to do something, hell and high water could not stop him. And Ned accused me of not wanting him to honor his father's memory! That did it. . . . I had to let him go."

At the same time Elaine bitterly refused to accept any of the money coming to Ned from Adele's bequest.

"I will not touch a cent of it," she said again and again to Widow Hughes. She expected the old woman to agree with her, but she saw that Rosa was thinking about something other than accepting or refusing bequests.

"What is it you have to say?" Elaine finally asked the widow.

"I don't want to speak ill of the dead." Rosa made an effort to choose her words.

"I'm afraid the dead don't care very much what the living say."

"That's where you are badly mistaken, my dear girl." Widow Hughes studied the younger woman as she went about preparing the sumptuous evening meal for her boarders, for her boarding-house now was such a success that she had to advertise for help. But the kind of help she hired was not up to her standards, so she labored even longer hours.

"I'm afraid, Rosa, I am badly mistaken about everything."

"Your chief mistake, dear Elaine, was letting your boys go to Adele's in the first place. They would both be with you today had you kept a shorter tether on them."

Elaine sighed deeply.

"What is wrong now, my angel?" The old woman studied her friend sharply.

"I have the sad realization, Rosa, that with the success of my boardinghouse, the quality of my cooking has declined. No, don't contradict me! It is not up to my standards. And the sad thing is, nobody notices it but me. Once my suppers became fashionable, everybody took it for granted the cooking would remain superb. But oh, how it has declined."

"You should not change the subject, dear heart," Widow Hughes remarked severely. "You should have kept your young men under lock and key, and you would be a happy mother today."

The strangest result of Adele's death, or perhaps her life, was its influence on Keith Gresham. He spent his evenings now compiling his "notes" about her, from her diary. One could hardly call what he put down writing. Nobody knew he could write at all, and his colleagues in the lawyers' office complained about his wretched command of the language. And Melissa, who had been in school with him, recalled how poorly he had done in English, while he had excelled in physics and mathematics. It was she, in the end, however, who was his source of encouragement and assistance, though she invariably would say after reading what he had put down: "But where did you get all these . . . details, Keith?"

"But didn't everybody know all . . . the details?" he wondered.

She looked at him closely, then back to the bulk of the pages. She sensed there was something in all of it she could not understand, and as the volume of what he had written increased, his own health declined, the feverish look in his eyes and cheeks grew more pronounced, and almost each day he looked several pounds lighter. His extreme thinness made him look much more the way she remembered him in high school.

Finally one evening at the supper table, Elaine looked over at Keith. She stopped what she was saying in the middle of a sentence, actually in the middle of a word.

She waited until the hired help had cleared the table of the dishes, and all the guests had departed from the boardinghouse. Then she put on an old coat and a worn hat and walked all the way to the telegraph office.

Once there, she hardly knew what to write. The clerk stared at her. She sat a long time, spoiling one telegram blank after another. Finally, in desperation, she sent the following message to Canada, to Ned:

UNCLE KEITH IS DESPERATELY ILL. YOU MUST COME AT ONCE IF YOU HOPE TO BE ABLE TO SEE HIM FOR THE LAST TIME.

LOVE, MOTHER

But as Elaine later told Rita countless times, the weather conspired against Ned's getting back in time. Keith died even before the telegram was on its way to Canada.

"I will never forgive Ned for being gone so long," she told everybody. "His dad didn't need him up there for him to pay reverence. But Keith and I did."

With Keith Gresham's death and Alec's absence, all the meaning of the boardinghouse seemed to have disappeared for her. Elaine delegated more and more of her duties to the paid help. And the "standards" she had always maintained declined still further. But the success of the establishment increased out of all proportion to the lowering of its quality.

After Ned's return from Canada, he spent almost all his time looking over the papers that Keith had left behind.

"Can you believe such a thing?" Elaine would cry as she saw him poring over the immense stack of tiny, handwritten pages. "All about a woman he barely knew, when all the time he was a larger-than-life infantryman and a decorated hero. . . . I imagine it was the TB maybe which affected his reason. But still I can't understand why such a fine young man would spend all his last days writing about a woman like Adele."

Then the day came when Ned went to the local printer. He was there all morning and afternoon and most of the evening, skipping supper at the boardinghouse.

When he came in finally that night he was all smiles. His "sunshiny" face reminded Elaine of the "good old days" when Alec and he and Keith had all been together.

"What is your good news, Neddy?"

"They have agreed to print three copies of it, the printers."

"Three copies of what?" She looked so astonished he laughed.

"Why, of Keith's book."

"Keith's book? What on earth are you talking about?"

"And it will cost only five hundred dollars."

The sum dumbfounded her.

"You don't mean you would spend perfectly good money printing what that poor sick boy wrote down when he was not himself. You wouldn't do a thing like that, Ned."

His happiness in keeping safe and permanent what his friend had written made him almost oblivious of what Elaine thought or said.

"What will people say if they should read what he has written! Think of the scandal if he has put down her whole life, as I understand he has."

"But it won't be for . . . people," Ned spoke up. "It will be for just the few who knew who Adele was, and what she stood for."

"Neddy, Neddy." But she lasped into silence. Something in what he said made her thoughtful, perhaps reverent.

"*We'll* see, too, what her life was like, Mother."

"I hope you're right," Elaine said softly. "Of course, it is your own money. It's her money also. Yes, Neddy, I can see you are right. And Keith loved you so," she added in a very low voice.

"I think Alec will like what Keith wrote about Adele. When he gets tired of the stage and comes home, he can read it."

"But I wonder really and truly what Adele would think if she knew someone had put down everything she thought and did. Do you think she expected such a thing?"

"All I know," he said, putting away the bill for the printing costs in his hip pocket, "is that if Keith Gresham felt he had to write it all down, sick as he was, and struggled as he must have to do so, then the least I could do was see it was printed."